CW00523413

BOOK ONE

Index of Characters and Places

Lugaid mac Róich *(Lu-gay mac Ro-eck)*

Lorcan mac Róich *(Lor-can mac Ro-eck)* editor of Ulidian Shield

Aoife mac Dara *(Ee-fa mac Dar-ra)*

Conall mac Dara *(Ko-nal mac Dar-ra)* Brother of Aoife mac Dara, Ulidian Commander

Caoimhín Breathnach *(Qui-veen Breath-nack)* Member of Conall's Triad

Oisín mag Uidhir *(Aw-sheen Ma-gw-ire)* Member of Conall's Triad

Finn mac Dara (son of Aoife mac Dara)

Ferdia Ó Ceallaigh *(Fair-dee-a O Kell-eh)* Member of Finn's Triad

Donall *(Dough-nall)* Member of Finn's Triad

Ó'Móráin *(O Mo-ran)* Connachta Commander

Ó Gallachóir *(O Gal-la-ker)* Member of Ó'Móráin's triad

Ó Floinn *(O Flinn)* Member of Ó'Móráin's triad

President Darragh mac Nessa of Ulidia *(Dar-a mac Ness-a)*

President Aillil O Flaithearta of Connachta *(All-yill O Flaith-heart-a)*

King Cuilennáin of Mhumhain *(Cul-li-nan)*

Chancellor Áed Ó Cosrach of Laighean *(Ade O*

1

Cos-rach)

Vice-president Ó Braonáin of Connachta *(O Brenan)*

Bradán mac Neill *(Bra-dan mac Neel)* spokesman for President Darragh mac Nessa

Aodhán mac Murchadha *(Eh-din mac Mur-chada)* Ulidian senator

Mac an Bhreithiún, Brehon law-giver *(Mac an Bre-han)*

Arch Druid Mac Nuadat of the Druidic Order *(Mac New-a-da)*

Uí Eochada *(E-O-Chad-da)* Chair of Ulidian Senate

Calgach *(Kal-gack)*

Adair *(A-Dare)*

Ulidia (Ulster)
Laighean *(Lay-gin* Leinster)
Connachta (Connacht)
Mhumhain *(Mum-han* -Munster)
Mhí Protectorate *(Meev-*Meath Protectorate)

Emain Mhaca *(Ow-win Ma-ca-* Twins of goddess Mhaca)

Béal Feirste *(Bell Fair-ste-* Belfast)

Átha Cliath *(Aw-ha-Clia* -Dublin, capital of Laighean)

Cruachan Aí *(Croo-a-kan I* -Rathcrogan, capital of Connachta)

Corcaigh *(Cor-kay* -Cork, capital of Mhumhain)

Uisneach *(Ush-nack* -capital of Mhí Protectorate)

La Tène *(La Ten* -capital of FCTS Federation of Celtic and Teutonic States

An tSionnain *(An* -*Sha-non* -River Shannon)

Alba-Scotland

Figure 1 Eireann 1994

For my mother

TALES OF ULIDIA :

THE TRINITY KNOT

PART ONE

1

It all started with the misplaced objects. Or at least objects I thought had been misplaced. Small insignificant items, of no interest to any potential housebreaker, of no intrinsic value, but things I had recently used, or would need to use the following day. In effect, property of mine I would soon notice had gone astray. That was what was so strange about it, and also, of course, what first drew my attention. Even stranger was the fact that the missing possessions would soon return to the original places they had occupied, after several days of fruitless searching on my part, without even the remotest disturbance of dust. A magazine I had been reading, the sleeve of a record to which I had been listening, a biro I had been using - a collective bric-a-brac of lost and found that would disappear and reappear as if behind the moving veil of some street magician. It mattered not if they were big or small, metal or plastic, heavy or light. Nor was it only living room artefacts that fell foul to this frustrating piece of vaudeville: a tin opener from the kitchen, a toothbrush from the bathroom and a pair of slippers from my bedroom, among many others, joined the litany of articles playing hide and seek with my emotions during those first few weeks.

Most of us in my position would no doubt have considered all this a minor aggravation at best. Who hasn't lost their car keys when rushing out the door only to discover them later in the most ridiculous of locations? Rose once lost hers on the morning of her first job interview only to locate them soon afterwards in her make-up pouch, having put them there while hurriedly applying her cosmetic regime for the day. However, with the passing of time, and no end in sight to the geographic mischief I was having to endure, I started to have thoughts the ordinary person only rarely has. What was happening wasn't *normal* I remembered thinking. And then, very quickly it seemed, that thought became 'why was this happening?' And since we all like to drown in our own sorrows, that snowballed soon to 'why was this happening *to me*?'

At what point in the story does the ordinary become extraordinary I suppose is what I am trying to remember. A person lives their life going from nine to five, from A to B, only to be displaced to a new unknown time zone or section of the alphabet. Soon, they discover they cannot tell the time or even read the signs.

I lived alone back then and thought I was

happy. Who knows, maybe I was. Things like happiness can only truly be evaluated if one life is laid alongside another and compared in the same way as this orange in the supermarket shelf is compared with that orange. You need to have both in your hands at the same time, and even then, you need to squeeze them both simultaneously to achieve a fair reckoning. Nothing can be left to chance. Looking back in retrospect never works. In fact, it's counterproductive. How can a life now be compared to one lived before? You are looking through a lens, the exact opposite of a crystal ball, and you can't help but give the past an oiled brushstroke the monochrome canvas doesn't deserve. So, let me say I thought I was happy, or at least happier than I was the decade before.

It was 1994, I was forty-four years old and 'the troubles' were just coming to an end. The troubles? I had never understood that phrase. The rest of the world suffers wars or regional conflicts between wars, but we, in Northern Ireland had our 'troubles', a euphemistic leftover from the 1920s, passed on like a Chinese whisper to my own generation, like an Olympic torch, without ceremony, fanfare or even much notice. But this is not a story about that. That history is here as simply a backdrop to the main events, like the ocean waves which batter a rocky outcrop and only sometimes cast in spray the lighthouse beyond.

Peter Surridge was one of my two best friends at that time. The other was Pritchard, my erstwhile employer in the Department of Celtic an Irish Studies at Queen's University, Belfast where I had worked for twenty years. For some reason, it was Surridge with whom I had decided to share the strange account of my nomadic odds and ends. Would things have been different if I had chosen Pritchard? For him, of course; but not really for me.

We were seated at a table in a city centre bar, quite close to where Surridge worked.

It was the night that peace had been declared which was why, no doubt, I had accepted Surridge's invitation to join him for a celebratory drink. After all, the best thing about a war is the street party after it ends.

'My dear Lewis,' he informed me, swinging his wine glass around in a wide arc in such a way that some of its contents almost cascaded over a thirty something woman with purple hair in the table behind, 'you can put the entire cultural elite of this city in the back seat of a taxi! And I'm the fool who has to drive the miserable lot around!'

'Mind your merlot, Peter.'

It was just after six in the evening and the bar was filling up quite nicely with, for the most part, bankers, journalists and off-duty members of the RUC who shifted uneasily in their seats every time a blast of cold, winter air swept shut the main door of the saloon.

'Why don't they ruddy well fix that door?' Surridge continued. 'It's colder than an Arctic expedition in here and those young chaps, Ulster's finest, are having kittens each time that door does a fine impression of a bomb going off!'

He laughed heartily at this, his cheeks turning a shade of Vesuvian red. It was during moments like this, when I saw the innocence in Surridge's face which laughter so often betrays, that I realised why I liked him so much. That and the fact that he was a chain-smoking, jazz-loving wine fanatic who lived in the flat above mine. When drunk, Surridge would boast of his Irish credentials, some maternal grandfather or other who had fought in the 16th Irish division in World War One. Like most of his boasts, they were the stuff of dreams; dreams that padded his pillows at night while he slept. He was originally from Buckinghamshire and, upon arrival in war-torn Belfast in the mid-1970s, was as about as far out of his comfort zone as Bertie Wooster would have been if he suddenly found himself, Jeeves-less, in a field full of pigs. He eked out a modest living as a writer then, publishing infrequent poems in *The Honest Ulsterman*. Now, he contented himself with vitriolic articles on arts and culture for the *Belfast Telegraph*.

'Keep your voice down, Peter,' I answered, noticing what I presumed was the purple-haired girl's boyfriend looking up from his Guinness, the black of his drink contrasting with the red curls of his hair, like a piece of coal sitting in a bed of fire as the glass rose to his lips. He looked familiar and I wondered if I had seen him before.

'Haven't you heard, old bean? The war is over. The good guys won.'

'And who exactly are the good guys?'

'Everyone's the good guy, Lewis. Everyone. No one can lose face, you know that.'

Surridge poured himself another glass of merlot. He tipped the bottle over my glass before realising it was empty. 'Ooops, sorry old bean. I'll get us another bottle.'

He removed a thin cigar from a silver case and lit up while we waited on the wine. Once our glasses were refilled, I tried again.

'But what do you think, Peter? About what I said before?'

'What? Raffles visiting in the dead of night and repositioning the pieces on the old chessboard? You're off your rocker, Lewis.'

'How else can you explain it?'

'There's nothing to explain. You're losing your marbles, dear boy. The loss of which is severely impacting upon the old noodle. I mean, really! Someone breaks into your flat without either one of us hearing...'

'...Well, you're either in a drunken haze or playing Ornette Coleman at full racket.'

"The Shape of Jazz to Come', Lewis,' he announced, imperiously, 'no other way it can be played.' There was a pause while the saloon door crashed loudly upon its hinges again. The RUC once more froze, a weird version of musical statues. 'Look,' he sighed, 'you are saying someone gets through the main street door, then the door to your flat, hangs about for a while playing silly buggers, doesn't pilfer a pea and then sods off into the night. He then repeats the performance the next night, but not every night, and when he does, he plays 'pass the parcel' with your bits and bobs.'

'That's about the size of it.'

'Bonkers!'

On the television screen behind the bar I caught a brief sighting of the nightly news. Loyalist paramilitaries had announced a ceasefire thus bringing their campaign of violence in Northern Ireland to an end. By doing so, they were joining their republican counterparts who had already ended their hostilities weeks before. I scanned the room. No one was paying attention. A young couple to my right were raising their voices, an argument about a previous argument, it seemed. A man in a pin-stripe suit was swaying against the jukebox, performing a spontaneous rendition of *Zombie* by the Cranberries, to the encouragement of two female colleagues. An old regular at the bar, who looked as though he were about to catch fish off the coast of Donegal, was complaining about the head on his pint of ale. I caught the eye of the curly-haired boyfriend again. He shrugged, as if following my thoughts. A private acknowledgement between two strangers, sharing the irony of a moment soon to be lost in the annals of history. He smiled. I smiled back. Maybe his girlfriend wasn't his girlfriend, after all, I wondered.

'Are you listening to me, Lewis?' Surridge was saying.

'Hmm?'

'You were away with the fairies there for a minute, my friend.'

'Sorry Peter. I have trouble paying attention to you sometimes.'

'Anywaaay,' he shot me a warning look, 'as I was saying. Maybe you walk in your sleep? Potter about your gaff at night, shuffle things about? Remind me never to give you the key to my flat.'

'Don't be ridiculous, Peter.'

'No, no, I mean it. I did a feature on somnambulism a few years back. The catalyst for the piece was the story of some Canadian chap... what was his name? Fields? No, that wasn't it. Meadows...? No. Not that.'

'Parks?' I volunteered, playfully.

'The very name.'

I groaned.

'Seems this Parks gets out of bed one night, drives ten miles or so through a blizzard to his in-law's house, in a complete trance the whole time, and quietly strangles his father-in-law as he lies in bed. He goes to the mother-in-law next, she hasn't heard a thing, and bludgeons her with an iron! And then... then he stabs them both, just to put the icing on the old blancmange! After this, he leaves, casually turns up at the local cop shop sometime later and offers himself up for arrest! You see, old bean, anything's possible.'

'Have another glass, Peter,' I replied, shaking my head.

'Typical,' he announced after a long pause.

'What is?'

'Canadians! I mean what exactly is the point of them. Throw them out of the Commonwealth I say.'

It turned out to be a good night, the sort of evening when you seem fortified against the world. It didn't matter how much wine, and later whiskey, we consumed, both Peter and I located the precise vocabulary, the perfect turns of phrases, exactly when we needed them. We never got too drunk but stayed, trapped in amber, under a magical influence, maintaining the same threshold of insobriety until closing time. The stories segued into one another seamlessly, a patchwork quilt of anecdotes and jokes, each of us doing our part, speaking and listening in turns, a Socratic dialogue I will never forget.

Even the local constabulary had allowed themselves to breathe in the atmosphere. They had taken off their helmets and sampled the air, even joining us a few rounds later. I must have overindulged as I vividly remember walking a tightrope to the toilet at the end of the night. I passed the smiling boyfriend who was sitting at the bar reading a book. This time I was the first to smile, but he looked away. His girlfriend had long since cast him adrift.

I knew how he felt, I remembered thinking later, as I lurched homewards with Surridge, back to our flats on Eglantine Avenue, stopping off on the way for a joyless kebab, loitering with the crowds spilling out from bars, a last-ditched pretext for my friend to try out his charms on whatever passing female might fall for his snake oil routine. I had always admired Surridge for his tenacity in that regard. For me, it was different. Rose, my wife, had been dead well over thirteen years by then and my life, I knew, had already begun to let out a soft sigh, a gradual deflation of air after the relentless charge that was the 1980s. Not that I was particularly successful with women or would designate my evenings in their pursuit. Since

Rose I had had a series of relationships, mostly minor, and a few casual one-night stands. I had only been unfaithful to her once during our long years together, and that was with Eva. As it turned out, perhaps, in retrospect, it was Eva to whom I had been unfaithful.

A little later I was wishing Surridge a good night's sleep on the stairs leading up to his flat. I didn't realise then, as I watched him struggle to negotiate the banister with one hand and a cold, uneaten kebab with the other, the simplistic, underrated beauty of such things when compared with what was about to happen to me just a few hours later.

It began with the telephone. It was ringing somewhere in the dark. How many times it had rung I couldn't be sure? What was certain was that the ringing had started at the denouement of a dream, a dream of a world where telephones did not ring. Perhaps they did not even exist in that world. The ringing continued, a persistent, mechanised vibrato that perforated the silence. With my head still beneath the eiderdown, I turned and stretched out my right hand. It fumbled for the handset, normally snug in its base, as content as a roo in its mother's pouch, but feeling nothing on the bedside cabinet, I reluctantly rolled my body over the edge of the bed. My fingers scurried over the carpet, an unnerving spidery crawl, plucking at the darkness.

The phone hadn't fallen to the floor. It simply wasn't there. It had been disconnected from the wall socket and was ringing somewhere else. I caught sight of my alarm clock. Its rosy numerals read 05.21. It was too early, too early even for a hangover.

'Bloody hell, not this again!' I exclaimed.

Turning on my bedside lamp, I navigated towards the hallway. The plum rotary dial that usually monopolised the console table there had been replaced by a more modern cordless phone, the same phone that should have been in my bedroom. It was anyone's guess to where the former had absconded.

I picked up.

'I need to speak to you,' a voice said.

'Who the bloody hell is this?' I answered, exasperated. I was standing in the hallway in my underwear, the soles of my feet cold against the porcelain tiles of the floor. I had forgotten my dressing gown and was not in a friendly mood.

'It's important that we meet.'

'If this is you Surridge...!'

'...Surridge? Ah yes, Surridge,' the voice repeated, after a slight pause. 'The man in the dwelling above yours. Yes, Surridge. He too is part of the story.'

I instinctively monitored the ceiling above for sounds of activity. It was nearly half-past five in the morning, but Surridge's solo drinking marathons had sometimes been known to push on until daybreak. But not this morning. This morning I knew exactly what he had consumed the night before. This morning, all was quiet, right down to the absence of sound from the wall clock in my kitchen at the end of the hall. Its ticking too seemed to have stopped. It was too early even for the dawn chorus. Outside a streetlight discharged its humble rays through the obscured glass of my front door, patches of sodium animating the mosaic like a window at church. I began to shiver. I carried the phone back to my bedroom and thought about ending the call and getting back into bed.

'If you are cold, Mr Summer, why don't you put on your dressing gown?'

I dropped the phone as if it were a hand grenade, as if the voice on the phone had just removed the pin. I took cover in the eiderdown. Giving myself a moment, I inhaled deeply and put on my dressing gown. In doing so, I realised I had just done what the mystery caller had instructed me to do. I shivered again and tried to recall my dream. Perhaps, I was still asleep?

The phone lay dormant on the floor. I inched towards it, then recoiled as it trilled into life once more. I let it ring, realising after a while, the caller was not going to give up. This particular bell was going to toll until the end of time. I gathered the phone to my ear and listened.

'My apologies, Mr Summer. I sometimes forget where I am. I didn't mean to frighten you.'

'Listen you, whoever you are. If you don't stop calling, I am going to phone the police!'

'Really, Mr Summer? Really? Your police? I don't think so. No, I really don't. And besides, what would you tell them, this police force of yours? Would you tell them, for example, that you received a phone call in the middle of the night, admittedly at a very unseemly hour, and spoke to a peculiar voice on the other end of the line? And what is so criminal about that, Mr Summer? Your police are quite busy at the moment, are they not? And how would they respond? Would they arrest me for the simple act of making a telephone call? Would they free up a space in jail just for me? And what would they do with the criminal whose place I would have just taken? Soon, in fact, the police will not be the police. Things are changing, Mr Summer. Things always change. I know this to be true. What was, is. What is now will no longer be. And the future, from one's perspective, can also be the past from the viewpoint of another.'

'Look, what the hell are you droning on about?!' I exclaimed. 'You're not the full shilling!'

"The full shilling'. Such a curious expression. Irish, of course. And what if I were to say to you, Mr Summer, you, yourself, are not 'the full shilling'. In fact, you are only half the shilling and the other half is somewhere else. But that is for later. We must not rush these things. I must wait for the others to catch up. Everyone must keep in step with everyone else. Everyone must hold the line and move together. Everything must be held in place. This is the way it has always been. And yet I too can become impatient. Ridiculous, I know. There is only this moment, and then the next, and then the next after that...Mr Summer, can I call you Lewis?'

'How do you know my name?'

'I am sure you don't mind. It's a good name. Lewis. An old name and not without significance. You know this, Lewis. There's nothing about you that I do not know and there's nothing about you that you do not know. I am not telling you anything new. You also know me but pretend that you don't. You know yourself, but you have forgotten. That is fine. That is understandable. I need to be patient. I must allow you to play the game a little bit longer. I too like playing games...at least for a while. Your furniture, for example...'

'...What about my furniture?! Wait, are you telling me you are the one breaking into my flat and moving my belongings around? I'm calling the police.'

'The police? Again? Oh stop, Lewis!' For the first time, I noted a tone of irritation in the voice. It heaved a sigh and then continued. 'As I said, Lewis, I enjoy games. You also enjoy games. You have played a game with yourself most of your life, but now, old friend, it's time for the game to stop. The police?' The voice giggled. 'Have any of your 'belongings' been stolen, Lewis? Are there any signs of forced entry? We two are beyond the world of the police, beyond the world of the criminal, or the terrorist, or the freedom fighter. They are all in stasis, Lewis, and we are the only ones able to manoeuvre. The plastic bullet is trapped in its orbit, held in suspension by an invisible thread. If I wanted to, I could pinch it from the air and put it in my pocket. The Molotov cocktail is an eternal flame, caught in mid-flight, a missile never reaching its target. I could snuff it out and place the bottle on a doorstep, prepared for the milkman's collection.'

'Look, whoever you are, what the hell do you want?'

'I want what you want Lewis. Ultimately, I am here to help you. I have always been here to help you.'

'Help me? You break into my flat! You move my things around...!'

'...If it makes you feel better, I will tell you the truth. Those that entered your flat will never do so again,'

'Those?'

'I make you a sacred promise and I never break promises. You can trust me, Lewis. Besides, they only did that to show you...'

'...Show me what?'

'That magic is possible, of course.'

2

Finn braced himself for the familiar impact of the instructor's sword. It was a few days before the sacred festival of Beltane. The new cadets of RBK Youth, Setanta class, were standing in a shield wall, thirty cadets long and three cadets deep. In a foetal position to his left lay his best friend Ferdia, groaning at the pain just administered to his ribs. To his right, another cadet, whose name he had long since forgotten, had just vomited out the remains of his breakfast onto the grey gravel of the training ground. The cascade of bile reminded Finn of the shape of water he had seen, arcing from fountains, in history books of ancient Carthage.

Not that he himself was much older than a child. He was thirteen summers old and in another eighteen months would finally complete his three years of military service in the youth wing of the Red Branch Knights. If the rumours were true, and war with Connachta was finally coming to an end, perhaps he would never have to pick up a sword again, wooden or otherwise.

'Why the hell do we have to use these bloody wooden swords anyhow?' Ferdia had moaned to him upon rising in their bunks that morning. 'That idiot Crunniac has a great big titanium blade! I'd like to see how he'd fare with this crappy bit of elder.'

'You have a point there,' yawned Donall, the third member of their triad, stretching out with his left arm while simultaneously scratching his balls with his right.

'I wish I had a bloody point to my sword! That's the bloody point!'

'You know the rules, Ferdia,' Finn intervened. 'No real swords until Beltane. It's a security issue.'

'Balls to their security! Who in the hell is going to attempt an assassination of mac Nessa? He's not even in Ulidia?! Especially,' he continued, beside himself, 'given where the peace talks are now!' He picked up Donall's hurl and whacked it against the thin mattress of the latter's bed.

'Hey, watch out! You nearly had my leg that time!'

Finn observed Ferdia with a mixture of pride and misgiving. Although only five foot six, he was built like the legendary Brown Bull of Cooley itself. In close combat, you couldn't rely on anyone better. And yet, that temper of his could make trouble for him one day.

'Anyway,' Ferdia continued, 'Beltane is days away yet! Besides, even that bugger's titanium sword looks ridiculous these days! When are we going to get our hands on those new CT Federation rifles?'

'Come on mate,' replied Finn, getting bored now with his friend's complaints, especially since he hadn't had breakfast himself yet. 'It's traditional, ceremonial, you know that.'

'Balls to tradition!'

And now his friend was lying in a heap at his feet, the metal boss of his shield balanced against the side of his head, like a coin showing neither heads nor tails.

'Right then, soldier,' Crunniac yelled. 'Let's see if you are any better than that piece of cowardly, Dún na nGall trash!' He pointed at Ferdia with the tip of his sword, before thumping its hilt against the intricate knot pattern that meandered a course around the great oval of his shield, its bright colours suddenly shimmering in the early morning sun. Finn tried to remember his training. He adopted a defensive posture, bent his knees slightly and pivoted himself on the balls of his feet. He leant his left shoulder into his shield and readied his sorry excuse of a weapon. His larger opponent smiled, enjoying the unfairness of the contest.

Ferdia was right. Crunniac was an idiot. And yet he was the perfect, unthinking drone that the RBK favoured these days. Patriotic to his very core, Crunniac preferred to spike his hair blonde, bleached with a mixture of lime-wash and urine. Now, as it was approaching Beltane, he had also smeared spirals of blue woad across his face in tribute to the millennia-old guise favoured by legendary Celtic warriors.

A smile passed across Finn's lips. As though guessing the thread of the young cadet's thoughts, Crunniac's face darkened. He raised his two-handed sword with the obvious intent of conveying Finn into the next world.

'Finn!'

Both teacher and student looked across to their right. There, with a bolt action rifle slung over his left shoulder, stood Conall mac Dara, Finn's uncle, commander of the Red Branch Knights' 1st Ulidian Division. Standing next to him were two of his trusted subordinates, Oisín and Caoimhín, the other members of his officer triad.

'A word in your ear, boy,' he called out again. 'If that's alright with your tutor, of course?'

'Yes, sir!' parroted Crunniac, his sword still poised in mid-air. Remove the sword, Finn thought, it would have looked like a gesture of surrender.

'Thanks uncle,' Finn whispered when they were a suitable distance from the training ground.

'Thought you might need a little help there,' the commander replied.

'The situation was under control, sir,' Ferdia sniffed.

'Hmm.'

They were ambling in the direction of Loughnashade. Along with the King's Stables which gave home to the Ulidian Senate; and the Palatial District, a small municipality where the president kept private residence; the suburb of Loughnashade marked out what citizens called, quite simply, 'the third'. Together, the three vertices linked up to form a triangle, mirroring at night the strange, geometrical constellation that Ulidia's ancient stargazers had used as the architectural blueprint of the first settlement. All three areas made up the sacred old town of Emain Mhaca, out of which the modern city had flourished over the centuries, the centre point of which were the Presidential Gardens.

'You need to be more careful, lad. These are interesting times.'

As if, by reflex, Conall tapped the stock of his Federation rifle. That and his pattern service dress uniform was something an RBK Youth cadet could only dream of wearing at the end of their final round of training.

'What? Crunniac? That big oaf? I can han⸝ him.'

'In a few years maybe. It's today we h⸝

worry about.'

Finn thought about this. His uncle was right, of course. He was still young. By modern standards, not yet a man. And yet, like every Ulidian child, he had been raised on a steady diet of Cú Chulainn, nightly ladlings of blood and sacrifice, served from the brimming cauldron of the past. Unlike every other child, however, his guardian, none other than Lorcan mac Róich, had been one of the finest storytellers in the land. This was, no doubt, the reason why he worked for the Bardic Press now. Finn had heard it said that Lorcan had once even been considered for a seat on the Druidic Council.

Conall halted, puffed out his cheeks, and turned towards his nephew.

'There are things you don't know, Finn. A lot, nephew, that you still need to learn.'

'You mean about my mother?!' Finn snapped.

Conall sighed and surveyed the scene around him. 'Lugh knows I hate this time of year!'

The cobbled streets of Loughnashade were beginning to hive with the excitement of the approaching festival. Street hawkers vied with each other from competing stalls, drawing attention to their cheap jewellery, face-paint and hair-lime. A butcher caught Finn's eye, honing his knives next to what looked like the ˄arcass of a small wild boar. Brats, checked and embroidered with gold, were being peddled to the odd wealthy Punic tourist who had somehow managed to acquire travel permits into the FCTS during the holiday season. Young children, free from lessons for weeks, were chasing each other in and out of shop fronts, tooting cow horns or launching bits of sour dough at any lucky magpie that seemed to be passing. Their parents, glad off the distraction, watched idly from tavern doors, toasting the god Bel and argued politics.

'Your mother, my sister, is a vate,' Conall continued, raising his voice slightly. 'With that comes great responsibility. You have heard of the clearing stations, but you have no idea what they are like. What Aoife and others like her have done at the front to aid the maimed and injured is not something the Bardic Press wants us to be made aware of. That would be inconvenient, a blow to general morale. No, what we need, apparently, are endless headlines of triumphalist propaganda reporting on yet another victory over a weak and defeated enemy. The reverse is true, of course. The Ulidian spirit isn't maintained by such an obvious and infantile recourse to myth and legend. It's 1994. What ennobles us, would ennoble us, is a collective reaction to the very same adversity people like your guardian is hiding from us.'

'Lorcan is a patriotic servant of Ulidia! Finn

exclaimed, passionately. 'The Bardic Press are just as important as the brehon lawgivers and the vates. *Three Orders into One! One Ulidia.*'

'You're not going to burst into song, are you, boy?' Conall snorted. 'Is that the kind of clap-trap the RBK Youth are spewing out now?'

Finn blushed. Inside, he could feel his anger mount, the nape of his neck beginning to prickle, as a sensation of heat slowly inched its way like an unrolled sheet of scroll across his back. He loved Lorcan, the old man who had stepped into the role of parent in his mother's absence, his own father having died soon after he was born. And yet, he resented the Bardic Press. Everyone did. He despised himself for defending it, but he also adored Conall.

He tried to speak, but his mouth was a hot, bitter brew. There were too many ingredients, all rising to his lips at once, and he did not have the palate to set them all apart. Instead, he stammered something incomprehensible before haring off mindlessly into the labyrinth of streets, accidentally upturning a stall of sweetmeats to the raucous delight of a coterie of geese that had been lying in wait for an early lunch.

Finn ran without direction, ignoring his uncle's cries. When he could run no more, he stopped; his chest heaving great lungfuls of air, his fringe of blonde curls matted with sweat. He looked around and found himself at a junction.

To his left, around a further turning, lay the Sráide Mhaca, the main boulevard that linked the old city to the modern urban centre, and which also led to the Presidential Palace. Finn observed a cortege of horse-drawn carts, bottle-necked at the corner, each one carrying its fill of willow and hazel, no doubt for the burning of festival sacrifices there.

To his immediate right veered a narrower avenue which led into the heart of Loughnashade and, if pursued to its end, led out of the city and into open countryside. Finn opted for this course, crossed into the thoroughfare and, in the process, nearly ended up under the wheels of one of the new, ethanol-powered chariots that had started making an appearance in Ulidia in the last few years and whose production was spurred on by President mac Nessa's latest war economy drive.

Finn took out his pocket timepiece and glanced at the time. 12.30. He had half an hour before he had to be back at the training grounds. At the gates of Loughnashade Park, he bought an overpriced, pigeon pie from a middle-aged street vendor, dressed in a traditional, Celtic tunic, the side of his face striped in blue.

'Here,' Finn suggested sarcastically, flipping him a shilling, 'buy yourself another two pies.'

'Bloody RBK cadets!' the man shouted after

him, 'Mind you don't trip on your sword!'

In a city that thrived on politics, and where politics thrived on the past, the lake of Loughnashade was one of the most significant political locations in all of Emain Mhaca. On the north corner of the lake stood the famous Museum of Loughnashade. At the bottom of the thirty-three steps that children counted on their way to its booming entrance doors, four huge, sculpted bronze horns had been elevated onto limestone plinths, two on each side. The horns curved skywards as if admonishing the heavens with a deafening blare.

The museum had been built at the time of the Celtic Renaissance centuries before. It housed the national collection of artifacts and antiques, with relics and curios dating as far back as the Bronze Age, and, certain academics argued, from the mythological past beyond even that.

What historians could agree on was the majestic beauty of the four horns of Loughnashade, locked away deep inside the vaults of the museum. Semi-circular in shape and two metres long, each metal horn featured long, curving tendrils, hammered in high relief at each end. The ten-foot versions that sat on stone outside the museum's walls could barely do them justice. Finn remembered seeing them on display as a child during one of their rare public outings. It was, he remembered, during the last series of peace talks between Ulidia and Connachta several years before. Some rumours had it that arguments over the exact provenance of the trumpets were one of the reasons behind the ancient enmity between the two nations.

Finn found an empty bench in view of the museum and took a mouthful of his pie. As he expected, it didn't taste of pigeon or indeed any other kind of fowl. More likely it was dried mushroom, pulped and stewed with the extract of some meat or other. The war might be coming to an end, Finn thought, but there seemed no end in sight to the rationing policy the senate had enforced on the citizens of Ulidia since well before he was born. He broke off a piece of pastry and tossed it towards a pair of coots that had sashayed across the surface of the lake in the hope of a free morsel. One good thing about the RBK, it seemed to him, was the guaranteed supply of tinned food, tea, coffee and even chocolate, every month from the central storehouses.

It had always been like that in the military. Since earliest times, when Celts had congregated into clans of sixty to eighty people, each clan would have their *curadmir*, a designated champion whose job it was to become proficient in the use of all weapons and upon whom the clan could depend on if they suffered attack from beyond their palisades. Their great defender maintained his strength by receiving the honour of the 'champion's portion', a first tranche of pork, sliced only for him, but for the good of all. Had things really changed since then, Finn wondered.

He looked down at his pie. His two dining partners, sensing something in the air, raised their beaks in expectation. He stared for a while at the composite of crust and filling in his hand before flinging the whole mixture into the lake. This in turn led to an outbreak of hostilities between the two erstwhile feathered friends. Finn watched them peck more at each other than at the food, their temporary alimentary alliance completely shattered. He smiled wryly.

In 1969, twelve summers before Finn's birth, Ulidia had declared war on Connachta. According to the latter, it was they who had declared war on Ulidia. Even on this they couldn't reach agreement. This was, officially at least, the third war this century between the two nations. Finn had read the others had been shorter affairs, minor skirmishes which, on reflection, were merely rehearsals for the main event. On the island of Éireann, they had stopped counting their wars centuries before.

The border campaigns of 1914 and 1939, according to Conall, were a mutual testing of resolve, a matching of current and rapidly developing technologies, a practice ground which sampled the endurance, not only of the soldier on the field, but also of the citizen on the street. The thirty-year truce since had been the longest period of peace on the island in hundreds of years. Perhaps the incentive of membership to the Federation of Celtic and Teutonic States, and the financial benefits to be accrued via trade with the super state, had been the allure which had brought both sides to the negotiating table. A cynical political analyst would suggest, however, that upon membership of the Federation in 1967, there was no longer any excuse for the two most bellicose of Éireann's lands to maintain the charade of friendship. This time, the reason for war was the disputed hinterlands to the west of the Mhí Protectorate, the central region of the island, which had once been a country in its own right millennia before, but whose lands had been subjugated by the Druidic Order. These traditional druidic schools were the spiritual cornerstone of the land. Their protectorate was inviolate and their territory sacrosanct.

Laighean and Mhumhain, the other two nations on the island, were used to the spectator sport that passed for war between their geographical neighbours.

Traditionally, Laighean, the land to the south of Ulidia's borders, was a heartland of commerce and free enterprise. Their capital city, Átha Cliath, was one of the richest cities in the whole Federation, having over the millennia maximised on the success of its trade links with other continental ports. Its tentacles in the last hundred years were now sprawling southwards, exploiting markets beyond the Federation, into the remnants of what was once the Holy Carthaginian Empire. The Laighean were a forward-looking people, the first to break bread with the Norse a thousand years before, and the first, naturally, to commit their future to the new alliance across Northern Europe. More often than not, Conall had quipped that when a Laighean man rolled his eyes northwards, it was more at the antiquated behaviour of their Ulidian cousins than at the behaviour of anyone in his immediate vicinity.

The Mhumhain, on the southwest of the island, were known, on the other hand, for their artistic and cultural pursuits. Historically, the best bards, painters, actors, singers and musicians hailed from this fiercely proud land who looked up and across at their fellow cohabitants with quizzical headshakes and pinched noses. Its capital, Corcaigh, boasted one of the largest natural harbours in the world but it mattered very little to a people who prized the sublimity of the muse above everything else.

And then there was the Connachta.

Finn rose from his seat and, with his right hand, gently swept the folds of his tunic. A mini avalanche of crumbs sloped off in the direction of the ground, only to be parachuted away by a sudden breeze. On the bench opposite, two shabby-looking bearded types with matching herringbone flat caps were feeding the ducks. They both gave Finn a brief sideways glance, perfectly synchronised. Finn responded with a conciliatory nod. The flat caps looked away, returning to the task at hand, seemingly absorbed by the gaping beaks they both targeted with the crusts of their hard-earned bread.

When Finn got up to leave the two flat caps waited a minute or so before following.

3

It was one of those crisp autumnal days when the good folk of Belfast could look directly into the heart of the sun, its pale corona perfectly exposing a blue backdrop of sky. The curvilinear glass panes of the Palm House did their very best to squint whatever rays they could into the eyes of the readers I passed, lingering on benches, stretching out a few extra minutes of their lunch break before the inevitable return to work. I was in the Botanic Gardens, only the throw of a well-aimed stone away from the manicured lawns of Queen's University where I worked. The gardens, if I remembered correctly, had been opened a decade before Queen Victoria had first perched on her throne; the new monarch would have to wait a decade or so more before the university welcomed its inaugural intake of young, eager minds.

I glanced at my watch, sipped some coffee from my thermos and gathered a weary-looking sandwich from my lunchbox. I inspected it closely and considered instead a bread offering to the birds that were scavenging off bins all around the park. He was late, I thought. But then I noticed him, case in hand, his long chalk-scratched gown like a black sail billowing behind him, a long crow of a man with an aquiline nose. I warned myself, once again, to say nothing to him about my mysterious caller from a few nights before.

'Sorry, I'm late, Summer. Cold, isn't it? Ha! Hear that, Summer? Cold! Summer cold!'

Professor Emeritus Jeremy Pritchard had been my Head of Department when I had first coupled my somewhat insignificant carriage to the academic powerhouse that was the Faculty of Celtic and Irish Studies back in 1974. Now approaching seventy, and although officially retired, he still tutored part-time. He continued to consider himself the de-facto Head of Department even though he had reluctantly ceded the role a few years before.

'It is a bit,' I lied, automatically reaching for the zip of my jacket in a bid to assure the much older man that he wasn't feeling his age.

'What have you got for your Head today? Cheddar?'

'Would you care for an earl of ham, prof?'

'Will do the job very nicely, Summer.'

I handed over the sandwich which he deposited into his mouth as rapidly as a card late for the Christmas post. He chewed with great satisfaction, a spot of mayonnaise escaping to the corner of his lips. I knew better to alert him to this infraction. Professor Jeremy Pritchard might have had the appearance of a jovial, aging Dickensian caricature but, beneath the veneer of jollity, he had the kind of brutal, mathematical calculation which would put a slide rule to shame. Over the years he had nipped in the bud quite a few departmental coups, the ringleaders of which, more often than not, soon found themselves 'between positions'.

'What do you think of that harridan, Clarke?' the professor enquired, darting me a look. 'Did you hear our new chief of staff this morning? 'Perceptions of Femininity in Early Irish Clans'. Ha! That's her latest one. Tell that to the ancient Celtic feminist who's busy burying her butter in a bog! Madness! And I've heard she's looking to extend her office once O'Malley goes. Over my dead body.'

'It is cold, isn't it?' I replied, searching my pockets for a scarf.

'And' he continued, undeterred, 'I bet she'll want to arrange the yuletide party this year. I heard her whispering with Fitzpatrick yesterday afternoon on the landing of the stairs and I distinctly heard her say the word 'yule'.'

'Are you sure it was 'yule?'' I wanted to say but didn't. Instead I asked him if he fancied a quick promenade. We both had lectures at two and time was pressing on.

As we walked, I thought about how I had first cornered myself into these prandial encounters. It was April 1980 when I really got to know Professor Jeremy Pritchard, by which I mean, beyond the hallowed halls of academia. I am certain of the date because Rose had just turned twenty-nine. Her birthday was April 9th, just five days before my own.

That year, I recollect, we filled our miniscule, one-bedroom maisonette with so many gifts that it was virtually impossible to conceal them from one another. That was also the birthday when Rose, upon cramming our washing machine with laundry, brushed her hand, she later told me, against the sharp corners of a cardboard box. I must have put it there after one too many Jamesons I confessed afterwards. When she removed the present for closer examination, she couldn't help but have a look inside. We laughed about the incident in the weeks that followed, the way lovers laugh at something trivial, yet shared.

The gift, it transpired, was a tiny wooden Indian elephant I had bought at a charity shop weeks before. It had a saddle, I remember, painted in gold relief, and over its head what I later learned was called a *nettipattam*, its sharp primary colours indicating some kind of crown perhaps. Rose loved elephants and she had always wanted to travel to India. Sadly, she never got the chance. Little did we know those were the last birthdays we would ever share together. However, what happened to Rose was ten months away.

The sky over Botanic Gardens, that fateful afternoon when we both encountered Pritchard, was different to the one we were enjoying today. There was an ominous sense of burden being upheld by the great slate dome that hovered above our heads then; a Damoclean sword on the point of striking from the clouds like a guillotine, finally and forever segregating our two communities. The IRA hunger strike was all over the national newspapers. Only a few weeks later Bobby Sands would die; a refusal to eat on one side of the political divide counterbalanced by a refusal to recognize the political status of prisoners by the other.

But that hadn't happened yet, and I was in love, still in love after six years of marriage, and nothing was ever going to get in the way of that. And yet, there was a sense of anticipation in the air, a prevailing malevolence that we all did our best to ignore that spring, like tourists at an aquarium, peering through thick walls of glass at a great white shark and convincing ourselves that this killing machine, which knew nothing but death, meant us no harm. I had read somewhere of the curtain of despair that had descended over Hitler's Berchtesgaden in the summer of 1939, engulfing his lair and darkening even the dictator's thoughts. And though it wasn't to that global degree, I admit, I had the feeling we all knew, and chose to ignore, that the 'troubles' were about to transition to a new level of horror.

Rose and I had just made our usual circuit of the grounds, loitering a while outside the Physical Education Centre, when we first heard Pritchard call out.

'Summer!' he cried out. 'Over here!'

And there he was, the man who had been my employer for over six years, looking like I had never seen him before. Gone was the black cape, the traditional garb of the pedagogue since time immemorial, and in its place a weekend livery that had all the coordination of a monkey playing 'chopsticks' on a grand piano. From ground level, I was able to scan a sunny set of clogs leading to trouser legs of purple corduroy. Above the waist, he sported a green, sleeveless cardigan over a lumberjack shirt. The whole ensemble was topped off by a ridiculous, black ushanka hat. He looked as though he worked part-time in a circus.

'Sir?' I stuttered, taken aback.

'Ha! Surprised to see me, eh? At the weekend? But tell me, Summer, who is this simply divine young lady? Is she your wife? Well, now I know why you never let her come to any of our little departmental shindigs! I wouldn't if I were you either! Certainly not! You're a dark horse, Summer! A dark horse. Come, take a pew. Sorry, let me clear some space, get rid of some of these newspaper supplements. Lord knows why they have to produce so much paper these days. It looks like rain, doesn't it?'

It was an opening gambit, I would soon learn, a meaningless, breathless monologue designed to ensnare its victim. From that moment I instinctively knew our plans for the day were over. The first pawn had been moved and already we had been checkmated. He bade us both to sit down on the bench beside him. Naturally, it did rain that afternoon. It not only rained; the heavens released their fill. I remember first a golf umbrella being popped open to form a shield around us and then, eventually, a quick dash to a nearby cafe for an Ulster fry, washed down with gallons of black coffee. Pritchard took off his socks as soon as he had ordered and was toasting them on the radiator next to our table with scant regard for hygiene or anyone else for that matter. Later, we adjourned to a bar, boxed in at a corner snug, no hope of parole, as he bombarded us with a never-ending supply of Guinness and recounted for us the story of his life.

I had quite a lot to drink that night and so I can't be certain of all the details. Over the years since, I have shared many evenings with Pritchard and each time I have had the nagging suspicion afterwards that everything he told me at any later time contradicted everything he had told me before. It was if a new reel of film was being projected on each occasion, a new twist and turn in the biography. It might be better to describe it as a jumbled series of non-sequential slides that could be equally appraised regardless of whether the viewer was sitting upright or standing on their head. Taken as a whole, his entire story didn't add up but who was I to question Pritchard on that first night?

Jeremy Pritchard wasn't born Jeremy Pritchard. He was born Gerald Richards in 1924 in Bangor, Wales. His father David was a constable with North Wales Police and moved to Northern Ireland after the death of his first wife, Margaret. She was murdered a few days before Christmas that year, just three months after having given birth to Pritchard. Margaret had met her fate one night while visiting her sister, Aggie, in Cardiff. The sisters had just been to the Theatre Royal to see a pantomime version of *Little Red Riding Hood*. Between the theatre and Aggie's home, however, the women were attacked by unknown assailants. According to Aggie, her older sister did her utmost to fight off the posse of young thieves while she, to her eternal ignominy, cowered in the darkness, too frozen in fear to assist her sister. The average age of the attackers, a witness reported, was just sixteen years old. They were never apprehended. The coroner's verdict? A fatal knife wound to the heart. There had only been a couple of shillings in her purse. Funnily enough, Pritchard informed me that night, the manager of the Theatre Royal at the time was none other than a certain Robert Redford.

'Not the real one, of course.' he added, needlessly. 'But 'Little Red Riding Hood', Summer. Can you imagine? I suppose you could say dear old mummy was eaten by the Big Bad Wolf!'

He was drunk but it still wasn't funny. If this man could speak about his own mother like that, in what regard exactly could he ever hope to hold others? Was the rest of humanity all just grist to his mill?

It was probably the alcohol, but I was sympathetic, inordinately so. In my mind, I was there, fully engaged, on the streets of the Welsh capital, screaming: 'Stop! Police!' or words to that effect. And then the moment was lost, vaporised by the irresistible necessity for Pritchard to crack a joke, a rotten egg of a joke that stank the room out, a fart released in a lift stuck between floors, its occupants fumbling for the emergency buttons.

But what did I do? I laughed. I chuckled. I guffawed. An immense, vulgar O lent itself to the shape of my mouth as we patted each other on the shoulders, creased our sides, spluttered

our drinks, coughed out the dregs of our nico-
tine-stained lungs, congratulated one another
for bearing witness to this never-forgotten
juncture in the history of comedy.

The only saving grace was the fact that
Rose, predicting how things were panning out,
had grabbed the first opportunity to disem-
bark the sinking wreck of the evening and had
phoned for a taxi hours earlier.

She missed, therefore, the continuing fable
of Pritchard's past. I, for my part, was meant
to believe that Pritchard's father, David, had
pursued the murderers of his wife with such a
wrathful revenge that, failing to find justice on
the streets of Bangor, he had stalked the steel-
works and coalpits of south Wales in a mad,
hopeless, personal crusade that quite soon
cost the young policeman his job. School leaving age at that time was fourteen, and although
the witnesses swore the boys were older, David
Pritchard had scoured the school playgrounds
of his hometown without success. His superiors had warned him that there would be complaints, that it was no use, that the boys had no
doubt high-tailed it to London or even joined
the Royal Navy. The murder weapon had never
been found. They had worn scarves over their
faces. They hadn't uttered one solitary word
during the attack. But no amount of logic
could penetrate the thickness of his skull and,
when he sought solace in that first bottle of

whisky, the outcome was obvious.

On the very day, an eviction notice was served on his humble terraced lodgings, Pritchard said, his father came across an advertisement in the *North Wales Chronicle.* In Northern Ireland, a few years before, the Royal Ulster Constabulary had been formed out of the ashes of the old Royal Irish Constabulary. The RUC was a new police force serving a new political entity and it was looking for recruits to secure its fledgling status. David Pritchard knew nothing about Northern Ireland beyond the commonly known fact that the folk there didn't get on. His curiosity piqued, he marched down to Bangor Public Library that very afternoon. With the help of a bookish young lady at reception, he navigated his way to the *Times Atlas of the World.* Inside its pages, he located the map of the British Isles. Imagine his surprise when he discovered, on the north-east coast of the island, just outside Belfast, a little town. It too was called Bangor.

'He borrowed money from Margaret's mother,' Pritchard informed me. 'She had a soft spot for him, my father said, but I believe she just wanted to get rid of him. He must have become a bit of an embarrassment by then. What astonishes me is that the old man took me with him. But then again why would a cat release a mouse from beneath its paw?'

'Suffice to say, in Ulster, the man was a brute,

48

not only to me but to every poor bastard he came across on the streets of west Belfast. He didn't have a religious axe to grind, Summer. You must believe that. He hated everyone, Catholics and Protestants alike. Professionally, by day, dressed in his new uniform, he punched and kicked any Catholic that got in his way. Socially, at night, he would pick fights with any Protestant fool enough to sit on the bar stool beside him.'

'We had a typical two up, two down on the Newtownards Road. It was a miserably, cold doss house with decrepit furniture and damp that could have scaled the snows of Kilimanjaro. Most of the time we had no electricity, so we would have to light candles, tapered into empty bottles of Bushmills. Walking into that house in winter, Lewis, was like attending a satanic mass, what with all those candles lit up, shifting grotesque shadows across the ceiling and walls. And over the altar of the hearth, a single extravagance; a picture frame of my parents, he smiling at her and she staring sharp-eyed, straight ahead, as if her future were contained behind the shutters of the camera's lens. I have never seen my birth certificate, so I often wonder if there were, in fact, not three in that photograph, the beginnings of my new life nestling within her. There had to be some reason why she married him, after all. Most of the women he brought back to the house after closing time, I recall, were either as drunk as he was, paid for or seeking some kind of work-related indulgence from him.'

There was more, of course. I just couldn't keep track. There were the physical beatings, the emotional bullying, the hours spent numb in the outhouse defecating into a solid ice bowl, the seething arguments with neighbours, the shattering of milk bottles like pins in a bowling alley every night, the undercooked food, the burnt food and ultimately the lack of food, the ambulance sirens, his pet rat Sammy, the night his school books were used as fuel for the fire... Pritchard spoke in tongues, a mad Moses, delivering his testimony on beer mats which he raised over his head to pummel my unprepared senses.

To sum up, it was a childhood from hell that had branded Pritchard, stamped a seal upon his soul. Pritchard's father eventually ended up in hospital with a punctured lung, the result no doubt of a retaliatory attack by a gang of roughs bent on revenge for grievances that could no longer be endured. The damage to his lung, along with the gradual deterioration of his liver, culminated a few months later in a tag team onslaught on the rest of his organs. He died on November 22nd, 1932, on the very day the new parliament buildings at Stormont were officially opened. Pritchard was eight years old.

What happened in the few years after that must have been so horrific that no level of intoxication could ever have closed down Pritchard's inhibitions long enough for him to divulge. He didn't have many friends, but even if he had, I guessed that not one of them knew the content of those missing three years, the years between his father's death and winning a scholarship to the *Royal Belfast Academical Institution*. That first night, he mentioned a primary school teacher, Mr Hollywood who, impressed by Pritchard's obvious academic merit, put him forth for a scholarship to a grammar school, extremely rare for a boy from Pritchard's background. It might have been then that I discovered that he had been later adopted by the Hollywoods and had gone to live in their charming three-bedroom detached house off the Lisburn Road. As Mrs Hollywood couldn't have children, Pritchard remained their only child. His adolescence was extremely happy, and he thrived at RBAI, passed every exam he took, and at eighteen ensconced himself as an undergraduate at Trinity College Dublin.

'I had to get away,' he explained. 'Spread my wings and all that. And of course, I could hardly keep the name Hollywood and study Classics? You understand, don't you?'

I didn't then, but later I did. Pritchard's career had been meticulously conceived at a young age, I suspected, with each step in its progress a methodical *kinhin*, a slow arching of heel and toe along the path to its journey's end. This is probably why he never married and also why a name like Hollywood did not sit well with the image of the dusty, elbow-patched academic he aspired to be.

Overshadowing all of this were the missing three years of which he never spoke. I imagined abuse, physical or even sexual, but whatever it was Pritchard had suffered in that period, and I did believe he had suffered something truly remarkable; he snuffed those years out of all accounts of his constantly changing life story. In another version, for instance, he told me his mother had died in a traffic accident. In yet another, his adoptive parents were called simply Woods, not Hollywood and so on. However, one thing that never changed was his insistent refusal to surrender any information about those years.

If only he had. But then again, would it have changed anything? Pritchard had told me everything except what he needed to tell me. Perhaps the glaring omission of those three years was his cry for help, the gaping hole he knew I would have to fill in with myself. In retrospect, he was right. And so was I. I was right not to allow the voice into his life then. Pritchard had too many words. They kept him afloat. He didn't need a voice on the other end of a telephone to give him anymore.

It was only a week later that Rose and I encountered him again, by chance, in Botanic Gardens and from then an arrangement was made to meet up for a walk every last Friday of the month, a chance to review the month just gone and talk shop. Outside of holidays or illness, I thought it best to keep the appointments if I wished to further my own career. On other special occasions we would get together for drinks, or even dinner. Rose made her excuses each time. Pritchard made her skin crawl, she used to say. Quite soon, she had the ultimate excuse never to see him ever again.

'It'll soon be Samhain,' Pritchard was saying now, rubbing his hands together, even though he was wearing gloves.

'Yes, sir. It'll soon be time to put on your mask to ward off evil spirits.'

He flashed me a look, raising his eyebrows, weighing up the import of my words.

'You're a curious fellow, Summer, but I've always been a big fan.'

'Thank you, sir.'

'How old are you, by the way?'

'Forty-four.'

'Bide your time, Summer. Things can change very quickly, you know.'

'Sir,' I protested. 'Professor Clarke is only in her early fifties. And then there's Fitzpatrick.

I really don't have any aspirations in that re-gard.'

'And who said I was referring to that, Sum-mer?'

I felt my cheeks warm slightly. 'No, of course not, sir. It's just that...'

'...I'm only teasing you, Summer, relax.' He paused and looked at me strangely. 'You al-ways were a serious fellow. No, dear boy, I am simply saying, things can change very quickly.'

'It will take a lot to get used to, sir, but we'll get there.'

'Sorry?'

'The new peace, Professor. It will take us all time to familiarise ourselves with the normal-isation of our society. Of course, there needs to be reconciliation...'

'What are you fannying on about, Summer?' he interrupted again. 'You sound like one of those dim-witted, political hacks on the UTV news. I couldn't give a fig about their so-called 'peace process'!

'Err...'

'...Never mind, Summer. Sometimes I can't work out whether you have one of the shrewd-est minds I know, or one of the simplest! No offence intended.'

'None taken, Professor.'

He tilted his large bald cranium to one side, his remaining grey hairs in alignment just below his ears, like the brim of an egg cup prop-ping up his massive intellect. He was analysing me, I thought, as if I were a frustrating piece of cipher, a troublesome lock that needed to be unpicked. As far as I was concerned, I had no idea what he was getting at.

'Anyway, moving on, I wanted to ask you a favour.'

'Yes?'

'I've been invited to Armagh. You know Bonnie Prince Charlie was over there in the summer confirming its city status? One thousand, five hundred and fifty years since St. Patrick laid his first foundation and all that.'

'Yes, I had heard our next in line had deigned to visit our shores.'

'Well, there's some kind of symposium at the Navan Centre there. Only...the thing is... it's three weeks away, at half-term, and I have already booked the time off. Field trip to Carnac if you must know.'

'Very nice.'

'So, I was wondering if you can cover for me. You know the drill. Local historical group seeks enlightenment from nationally recognised expert.'

'You said you couldn't make it.'

'Ha! That's more like it, Summer. Flattery will get you anywhere! You don't have any plans for Halloween, do you?'

I didn't, but I wasn't going to tell Pritchard that, I thought. Carnac? The wily, old fox! More likely, his 'field trip' was a quick jaunt across the Manche to stock up on cabernet at some Breton hypermarché.

'What's the group?' I asked.

"Friends of Emain Mhaca'. Ever heard of them?'

'Can't say I have.'

4

Conall had promised his wife, Breanne, he would try to do better. He had commanded armies, been wounded twice, watched on as others had got wounded, shot and blown apart by enemy shells. A few times he had helped the Vatic Medical Corp sweep no man's land for body parts. He had discarded limbs onto barrows, wheeled them off to makeshift stone circles for last rites, wrapped them up in funeral linen, seasoned with rowan and yew and, at night, followed the dense smoke from funeral pyres rise up into the night sky and create a mask for the moon. Why was it then that he found it so difficult to communicate to people, even to his own wife? If it wasn't a directive from military headquarters, embossed on headed paper, and delivered to the war-weary subordinates of the 1st Ulidian, he found himself floundering, inadequate, unable to correspond with the very people he should care about the most. Why was this the case?

Conall thought of his estranged daughter, Caitlin, at present employed as a bookkeeper in Béal Feirste. As a result of the war, he had missed large portions of her childhood. Rare bouts of weekend and holiday leave had merely served to re-emphasise his sense of disconnection. Naturally, it hadn't been his fault, but he had been absent at too many meaningful family milestones, had managed to arrive late at the end of too many ceremonies. And even when he had acquired some leave from the frontlines, he would spend the whole time at home brooding, anxious about the comrades he had left behind. Seated alone in his study, he would sullenly nurse yet another beaker of cider, incapable of stepping out of his skin long enough to enjoy the occasion.

Perhaps his inability to reach out to others was why his sister, Aoife, when she signed up for the VMC, had chosen to let his nephew Finn remain at the home of Lorcan mac Róich, editor of the Ulidian Shield. It was bad enough the boy not having had a father growing up, but to leave Finn with mac Róich had impacted Conall deeply. Her decision afterwards to formalise the arrangement, by making mac Róich Finn's official guardian, had added insult to injury. But then again, he had never truly understood his sister. She had her own secrets. The most important one being the identity of Finn's father about which she had never told anyone.

On the other hand, the boy spent most of his time in barracks away from the old man's influence. Mac Róich, he had learned, had also taken on a young Punic journalist, Maggo, as a tenant. Conall had learned from neighbours that Finn and the Carthaginian were good friends. Perhaps, his nephew would be fine. And yet, Aoife had favoured the old man over her own brother. If he believed mac Róich a fool, what exactly did that make him?

Conall shook his head. In the mirror behind the bar, he examined his new growth of beard and barely recognised himself. How long had it been since he had shaved? Five days? Seven? His whole division had been recalled from the front a week earlier, part of the month's long gradual demilitarisation that had diminished the once impregnable Ulidian lines. Connachta too had abandoned its trenches while politicians, in Uisneach, attempted to hammer out a lasting peace. He had seen it all before, Conall thought. Perhaps, this time it would be different.

He looked around the tavern, hoping to see if he could pick out Oisín or Caoimhín from his command triad. Oisín was there, playing cards with some faces from his own unit, the collars of their uniforms as loose as their thickening tongues. He nodded at a few. They saluted back, too casually, he noted, before continuing with their fraudulent tales of heroic service to any women willing enough to exchange the boredom of a couple of hours for the likelihood of a few free drinks.

As far as his unit was concerned, the war was already over.

'Commander mac Dara, an urgent message from RBK Command!'

Conall swivelled on his stool. A young soldier, second rank, had just bolted into the tavern, and was now standing stiffly, his arms pinned to his sides, his fists clenched, a tiny button of sweat gathered under his nose.

'You forgot to salute, soldier!'

Embarrassed, the young man saluted, before returning to his original pose, like a wind-up toy that had just been wound up and then, for no reason, had grounded to a halt.

'Yes?' Conall encouraged.

'A message from RBK Command, sir,' announced the soldier, offering Conall a tightly squared piece of paper. The bar went quiet.

'Thank you. Dismissed.'

Conall looked around. He gave a practiced stare, cold enough to give the individual occupants of the tavern the permission they needed to mind their own business. Then, he read the note.

'Bugger!' he muttered, under his breath.

'Another?' the barkeeper enquired.

'What?'

'Another cider?'

'I think I'll need one!'

'Glass or traditional cow horn?'

'Bugger off!'

'Bloody well shift over, Donall! Move your fat arse! I want to read the news sheet!'

'Hey! I was here first! Besides, you can't read, can you?!'

'And stop stuffing your greasy face with spuds, will you?!'

Ferdia flopped onto the two cushioned sofa, deliberately catching the side of his fellow triad's thigh, his muscular frame invading the heavier cadet's side of the couch, forcing him into a rigid side-posture that the latter tried to offset by quickly crossing his legs and stretching out his arms in a bid to protect his dinner plate.

'Shit, Ferdia, I can't eat like this,' Donall moaned.

'Well then, I'm doing you a favour mate.' Ferdia replied, fanning out the pages of the news sheet. 'You need to shed a few pounds. You'll never get through the next eighteen months the way you pack it in.'

'Know what you are, Ferdia?'

'No, tell me.'

'Just a piece of cowardly Dún na nGall trash!' Donall answered, repeating Crunniac's insult from earlier that morning.

Finn sat back on his armchair and tried to maintain a straight face, poised for the fireworks which would soon ensue. Instead, there was a strained moment of stunned silence, followed by an outburst of uncontrollable laughter. The two cadets began cackling together like a pair of mother hens, jostling and nudging each other while bits of half-digested potato started to make their way out of Donall's mouth.

Finn joined in, his eyes streaming with tears, but laughing more because he was in the company of his friends than anything else. As a child, Finn had sometimes wondered why laughter, like yawning, was addictive in this way. Once he had even asked his mother that if the presidents of Ulidia and Connachta both started laughing in front of their people, then everyone in their countries would laugh too and, if they kept laughing, perhaps the war would end one day? Whoever heard of a soldier giggling as he fired a gun, after all? It was a childish thing to say, but he had never forgotten his mother's reaction. She turned from the kitchen sink in which she had been washing some plates and stared at him a moment, before saying: 'You're a clever boy, Finn. Just like your father.' And then she drew him towards her and kissed his hair; her wet, soapy hands dampening the back of his shirt. It was a wonderful moment and the only time the word 'father' had ever been uttered between them.

'Here! Lovebirds. Why don't you both have an early night, eh?' Finn said, finally, launching a cushion in their direction.

Theirs was a three-room domicile, no bigger or smaller than the thirty domiciles that made up the nócha, or unit of ninety cadets, that comprised the RBK Youth, Setanta Class. Each domicile had one bunkroom, with a double and single bunk, one small living area and a kitchenette. There were thirty cadets to a barrack and three barracks in all. Each barrack had three floors and on each floor three triads, or units of three. On the bottom floor, however, there was also a larger annexe in which was housed the barrack commander and, normally, two fawning flunkeys who ran errands for him off-camp. This command triad, along with the two from the other barracks, formed the naoi, or 'council of nine', an unelected and unofficial officer cadet class made up of those wealthier cadets whose parents had passed bribes to the top brass in the RBK Youth in return for preferential treatment. For instance, the command triad had their own washroom and toilet and didn't have to stand in line for the communal facilities each morning and evening that invariably spilled over into squabbles and fist fights. They also got the odd weekend pass into town, a source of constant irritation to the other cadets. This was under the guise, the cadets knew, of supposed Central Command meetings between RBK Youth Setanta Class and the other two classes, Macha and Conchobar. Altogether only two hundred and seventy candidates were accepted into the youth wing of the RBK every year and competition in schools for a place was fierce.

It was 20.00 and Ferdia was about to do his party piece, his nightly rendition of the Béal Feirste Banner news, a carefully selected article of current news affairs read out in the insipid monotones of President Darragh mac Nessa. Finn might have considered himself a patriot, but even he had no time for the gnarled, goateed face of the aging mac Nessa. The nation's leader had already served two six-year presidential terms and was actively seeking a third. There was nothing in the constitution that barred him from doing this, of course, but to do so, Finn thought, on the backs of the current peace negotiations seemed a bit opportune, even for a skilled, lifetime politician like mac Nessa. His opponents in the Ulidian Senate were constantly accusing him of using the war to bolster his flagging popularity. Now it seemed he was using the prospects of peace to do the same.

As usual Donall prefaced the upcoming monologue with a cacophony of hums, whistles and toots in mock imitation of the Ulidian national anthem. Ferdia coughed, sniggered and began.

'Today, good citizens of Ulidia, I speak to you

from the steps of the sacred Temple of Uis-
neach, the spiritual heartland of Éireann, home
of the Druidic Orders, burial place of Lugh and
the Dagda. From this temple, built upon the most
revered Hill of Uisneach, if I cast my eyes far
enough, I can gaze at our four great nations
stretching out before me, north, south, east and
west, each one representative of our shared legacy
as fellow men and women of Éireann, each one
with its own separate and valid contribution to
the whole. And so, I speak to you now, not as an
Ulidian, but a proud son of this island that we all
call home...'

'...Bloody hellfire, lads, he's good! He nearly
has me believing this horse shit!' Ferdia declared, interrupting himself. 'Written by that
mouthpiece of his, mac Neill, I bet...'
'...Carry on, Ferdia.' Finn said, genuinely
interested.

'It would not be untrue to say that I have felt the
yoke of the past weighing down on my all too fra-
gile shoulders in the short time I have been here. It
is an honour, as always, to have the opportunity
to put forward the wishes of the Ulidian Senate
and, by extension, those of the Ulidian people. I
gage this moment, above all other moments in re-
cent history, as the single most significant time,
in not only our political, but also our social and
economic lives. The consequences of what we can

achieve this week at Uisneach will send reverberations into our future, a future I know that will be as glorious as our past.'

'That is not to say that negotiations have been easy. President Ailill Ó'Flaithearta of Connachta has his own people to serve, as I do mine, and yet here, under the auspices of the Druidic Orders and with the support of the supreme Arch Druid Mogh Roith mac Nuadat, we both feel that now is the time to put old enmities aside and find common cause for the sake of all our provinces.'

'This, as you know, is only the first in a series of talks. Beltane will soon be upon us, but as a sign of this new time of peace and reconciliation, all delegates from Ulidia and Connachta will remain here in Uisneach to celebrate one of the most important festivals in our Celtic calendar.'

'Yesterday, I met with not only President Ó'Flaithearta but also delegates from King Cuilennáin of Mhumhain and Chancellor Áed Ó'Cosrach of Laighean. Those talks were also very beneficial. It is much too early to make any kind of formal announcement about the content of the conversations I had with those delegates, suffice to say, that I personally welcomed the contributions made by our friends from Mhumhain and Laighean.'

'What I can say, however, is this: Ulidia has had an uneasy truce with Connachta since the festival of Imbolc. Sadly, a few units, on each side, have taken it upon themselves to ignore that truce *and lives have been lost. Today, I would like to announce officially a complete cessation of hostilities between Ulidia and Connachta. All units of the Red Branch Knights, and the Ulidian army as a whole, are to return to base. The status of those parts of an tSionainn, presently under dispute between our two nations, will naturally be the subject of our upcoming negotiations. Until a resolution has been reached, the Mhí Protectorate, has agreed, temporarily, to extend its borders to include those territories around the river region. As we all know, the Protectorate is a non-partisan and apolitical entity interested in only the spiritual welfare of our great island.'*

'Finally, I would like to thank the Arch Druid for his generosity, support and hospitality during our time here. Without this, no agreement today would have been possible.'

'Mhaca's tit!' Ferdia blurted out when he had finished reading. 'Who would've thought those arseholes could actually work something out?' He shook his head. 'Now I'm never going to get my paws on one of those CT rifles.'

'Never mind, Ferd. They're bound to balls it up somewhere along the line! Besides, you need to be sixteen to join the full RBK. You still need to graduate here, finish school...'

'...Ach, piss off, will you?! There's always a hole in your bloody cow horn, isn't there?'

'I'm just saying, that's all,' Donall replied,

meekly.

'Listen, you trout-faced Fir Manach cretin, if you know so much about it, why don't you piss off to the holy land and have a chit-chat with old goat-face himself and that bull-head pal of his, Ailill?! Sort it all out, eh?'

'I was just saying...'

'...Ach shut your mouth and eat your spuds, will you?!'

It was impossible for Donall to do both, but then again, Donall wasn't going to say so. Sometimes even Donall knew where to draw the line. What remained of the evening was suffered in a pervasive, brooding silence as each of the cadets pondered the new future that seemed to have opened up for them.

Donall, of course, would be fine, Finn knew. He had been coerced by his parents into signing up for the RBK Youth and had absolutely no intention of enlisting into the full RBK on his fourteenth birthday. Normally, membership of the RBK Youth automatically led to admission into the officer class of the RBK. There the enlisted would serve five years with the option afterwards of acquiring a permanent billet, with a good chance of promotion, if you kept your nose clean and did what you were told. On the one hand, having this initial time in the RBK under your belt looked very well on any future job application. On the other hand, the Bardic Press had whipped their readership into such a collective, patriotic frenzy in recent years that it was almost unheard of for any full-time RBK to desert his post after the allotted five years, even though by law he could. In effect, once you joined the RBK you were there to stay. At the very least you served twenty years.

There was, traditionally, more room for manoeuvre in the years between the RBK Youth and RBK, but here the state relied heavily on the education system to ramp up the natural competitive instincts of all Ulidians. A scholarship into the RBK Youth was the gold standard. Competition for places was high. A family risked disgrace if their son, having graduated into its ranks, snubbed his nose at the opportunity to stand shoulder to shoulder with his brothers in arms, no longer as boys, but now as men. Bonds made in the RBK Youth lasted a lifetime. To sever the bond at such an early age was an incredibly difficult thing for a gung-ho cadet to do, especially given the military climate in which he was raised. In the interim between the youth wing and the full RBK, graduates of the former spent a long summer camp with instructors of the latter, to freshen up their military training after completing their final exams at school.

In later life, active and retired members of the RBK had their own exclusive clubs, their own seats on transports, their own private hospitality at sporting events. They also received a handsome pension if they needed it. The RBK officer network in mainstream society was a well-connected spider's web and its strands reached out across most areas of business and leisure.

Against this, the ordinary working-class recruit was conscripted for five years upon leaving school. National conscription was the norm in both Ulidia and Connachta. Five years, in both countries, was believed to be the maximum stint a soldier could serve without adversely affecting his mental health on the frontlines and the local economy back home. Both nations had commenced the present conflict by initiating necessary fiscal measures to cope with the stress imposed upon their agricultural and industrial sectors. This 'war economy' drive over the years had simply become 'the economy' as citizens got accustomed to dealing with food and other shortages.

If the recruit showed promise, upon completion of this service, he could be 'provisionally' invited for another five years into the lower ranks of the RBK. After another five years, the new RBK recruit could enjoy all the fruits of a full-time enlistee. Finn's uncle, Conall, even though he was from a well-known clan, the mac Daras, had somehow ended up taking this route to his current command. Finn had never had the nerve to ask him why.

That night, Finn couldn't sleep. He lay on his back, his hands clasped behind his head, looking upwards at the wooden slats which held in place the mattress of Ferdia's bunk. To his right, on the single bed, Donall was snoring loudly, a comic strip folded across his chest. At Beltane, lights out was at 20.30 and it wasn't until much later that Finn, still awake, noticed a chink of moonbeam had angled its way through a gap in the shutters, emblazoning the same line of carved graffiti, as it did every night, on a slat just above his head: *If Lugh shines, then shine on me! 1982.*

Finn closed his eyes and tried to remember his mother's face. It had been so long since he had last seen her. Now that the war was nearing its end, they would finally be reunited. Could it really be true? He thought again of the words of the article Ferdia had earlier read out.

It was the standard political fare, of course, a little bit more nostalgic perhaps than normal, but nothing too unusual. That the Mhí Protectorate would host the talks had come as no surprise either. It was the only neutral territory left on the island, after all. All sides could trust the Druidic Order. The nine members of the Druidic Council, led by the Arch Druid, were responsible, among other things, for the daily upkeep of the temples, cairns, dolmens and stone circles dotted within its borders and, of course, the training of new novitiates into the druidic priesthoods. In addition, they only had a small standing army, the Druidic Guard, whose sole purpose was to protect the sacred sites and provide a personal bodyguard to the Council. How then, Finn wondered, could the Protectorate hope to police the contested region around an tSionainn?

And then, there was the question of the Mhumhain and Laighean delegates. What was their role in all this? Why had they been issued invitations to the peace process? What could they possibly have to contribute? Conall was right. These were 'interesting times' indeed.

5

It had been good seeing Pritchard, I thought, and a trip to Armagh might be just what I needed to forget the voice on the telephone. It had been a week since it had called. A week, in fact, since the telephone had rung. I began to wonder if my phone wasn't out of order. Once, I even picked up the receiver to check. But no, everything seemed fine. Down the line, I could hear the same familiar, ominous tone, continuing for eternity like a fatality on a life support machine.

The caller was obviously a mad man, I told myself. I tried to think back to what he had said. He knew I was cold. So what, I thought. Everyone who rises in the middle of the night in Belfast, in mid-October, is bound to be cold.

The voice knew my name. So, it belonged to someone in my circle; one of my students, probably, embarked on a well-orchestrated campaign of revenge, irate upon receipt of lower than expected grades. Anything was possible.

But it couldn't have been a student, I reasoned. It was the voice of an older man, with all the assurance only experience can give. I hadn't recognised it, at first, but he accent was Irish, though not one I had ever heard before. That was a bit unsettling, I had to admit, but more than likely the voice had affected a lilt. But why affect your accent if you had nothing to hide?

I passed my time like this, back and forth, a tidal flow of questions and answers, answers and questions, as though interrogating a suspect who wasn't there. The voice claimed to know me, claimed that I knew it. It spoke of patience. It accused me of playing games with myself. It implied a context in which other people were involved. I must not allow myself to be drawn into the voice's fantasy, I told myself.

No. The best thing to do was simply to improve my security, change my number and forget about the whole thing.

The last of these proved difficult. The next week was spent like a suitcase on an airport carousel, going around and around; an empty suitcase without purpose, whose owner had long since disappeared.

I attended my seminars at work, corrected my papers, did my laundry, tidied my flat a couple of times, and took out the rubbish. I shopped and cooked myself some nice meals which I did not have the appetite to finish. Once, I met Surridge descending the stairs of our building, his arm around a new girlfriend, or at least she was new to me. He introduced me. She was a typical Surridge prototype: all cleavage and legs, red hair on top, wearing a shimmering, silver evening dress. I wondered if she was a high-class prostitute. Sturridge was decked out in a tuxedo, his bow tie already askew. 'A night at the theatre', he informed me, 'at least, to start with.' He gave me a surreptitious wink. To her surprise, Surridge invited me along for the evening. I declined, made my apologies and wished them well.

Outside of that, I didn't meet a single other soul during that time. I stayed in and wondered if the voice would ring back.

It was Saturday night when I took the second call. I had just poured myself another measure of Jamesons, probably my third or fourth. A Bach cello concerto was emanating from the living room hi-fi. It was around 8.00 o'clock. We were still a week away from Halloween but, in the distance, I could faintly make out the muffled pop of fireworks. Or at least I prayed they were fireworks.

'Hello?'

'...Magic is possible. Yes, Lewis. And not just for children. For grown-ups too. Ha! As if people in your world actually grow up...'

I had expected it. I had sensed it before I picked up the receiver. And now the voice had returned, finishing off where it had left off from before, as if no time at all had passed. As far as the voice was concerned, there had been no interlude, no pause for commercial break.

'...Some do, more than others, but even they are still children,' the voice continued. 'Regardless of what world you choose to live in, or what world was chosen for you. In any case, this is your world now, and the time has come for the game to end. You must wake up, Lewis. This is not a dream. Not that dreams aren't real, of course. They are as real as that phone you are holding in your hand. What I mean, what I want to say, is you must wake up from the dream you are having in your actual waking life. Do you understand, Lewis?'

'It is exactly like Surridge's story about the...the... 'somnambulist'...is that the right word? How language evolves, Lewis! How vocabulary expands! So very many new words to remember. And so very few words that make sense. Ha! The natives in the jungle communicated better, semaphoring with sticks! Anyway, Lewis, Surridge was partially correct. You are a sleepwalker. It's not your fault. Everyone walks in their sleep. But watch out! You might walk off the end of a cliff! So, you need to wake up and pay attention.'

'Very soon I will be paying you a visit. When I do, you have to believe in magic. I am speaking to you as a child. It's not magic. Forgive me. But you need to wake up. You need to grow up. Very quickly. There will not be much time. I will speak and you must listen. After you listen, you must act. Do not waste time. Time, for you, is a problem. Time is a problem for the others too, but without you there are no others. You must be the first to check his watch. The train is about to leave and there's only one train. Only one station. The train will take you where you need to go, and you will pick up passengers along the way. Do you not see?'

'Yes, I am 'droning on'. Ha! I like that. But I have to be a 'busy bee', Lewis. I could speak more clearly. I could reveal it all to you, mathematically, scientifically, philosophically, but that would just frighten you. That would be too close to your reality. The metaphor of magic is best. The more fantastic it is, the better. It creates a distance, from where you are to where you must go. It gives you time, not a lot of time, but enough precious time for you to believe me, believe what you already know to be true about your world. Do dragons exist? Yes and no. Do unicorns exist? Yes and no. You must simply allow for the possibility and then we can move forward.'

'You are a professor, no? A professor of the past? Is it the past you study, Professor Summer? From your perspective, perhaps. Stone Age, Bronze Age and Iron Age, all in a little row, one following the other, one exits and the other enters. Do you think it really is like that, Professor? Can you not find bronze before stone, iron before bronze? Can you not find them all at the same time? You categorise by what you find under the ground. You never think of looking up. The stars have the right idea. They are timeless, from your perspective, gaping upwards, your flat feet on the ground. The further you look, the further back in time. But that is space, Professor. The space between stars. It is an illusion. The stars do not move. They are always there, and time is always there too. Your mind is outside of time and so you don't understand. You try to give it meaning. You call it an 'international date line' and divide the day into night and the night into day. There are Celts, Professor, and at the same time, there are astronauts. They can both exist now. There is only now.'

And then there was nothing. Not even a tone to suggest something. There was no sound at the other end of the line. There wasn't even a line. If I had been holding one end of a skipping rope, then the other end was a limp coil. I was dragging a dog lead without the dog. I had just been engulfed, mesmerised by a quantity of data that would be, I knew, impossible to process. It was a bit disconcerting. As a tutor, I was someone used to imparting information to others. Now, I myself had become the object of a random, ethereal diatribe, the kind of maniacal, white-coat absurdity I had always learned to despise. I realised that this was no longer a question of furniture removal and a change of locks. The material had become immaterial. I had the feeling that if the voice had reproduced its words onto a page, then upon reading, the words would have dissolved, my eyes chasing the ink into oblivion.

And then the phone rang.

'...So, I have news, Lewis,' the voice said. 'Things have become more serious. Time is slow here and fast elsewhere. Slow in the waiting room of a dentist, fast when you are late for work. And so, I shall say this. The man Pritchard. He is a strange man, a good man. He likes to fabricate. He likes to fantasise. He likes to lie. Pritchard lies, yes, but only about small things. You can no longer delay. You must go to Armagh. There. A fact. You must go to Armagh.'

I don't recall much more of that evening. In the morning, when I finally emerged from bed, I set about the task of clearing up the detritus of the previous evening. I noticed the bottle of Jamesons, now emptied of its contents, lying despondently on its side. I nudged it and it spun a little to the right. I nudged it again and it spun back to the left, like a needle on a compass, directionless. If my head was hungover, it was hung over a guillotine. I yearned for the stocks to close in around my neck, the blade to drop and my torment to come to an end.

Vinyls and CDs lay strewn across the living room floor; a potpourri of blue note jazz, baroque classical and Britpop. Nestled in the CD tray, I discovered a copy of *Parklife* by *Blur* which I didn't own. A further inspection by the sofa revealed two empty bottles of Chablis, wine glasses and a half bottle of Bacardi. A saucer on the coffee table had been used in lieu of an ashtray, its numerous cigar ends encroaching over the sides. The whole place reeked of expensive aftershave and cheap perfume. In short, the full recipe of an evening passed with Surridge and his latest bit on the side.

I had a hazy flashback of the two of them, slow dancing to some 80s pop classic in the semi-darkness, and I, with an angle poise lamp, directing a makeshift spotlight onto them, whooping like a mad monkey, in hysteric convulsions at my own ingenuity.

That I had exchanged my usual restful Saturday evening for a boozy disco of wistful nostalgia and pseudo-academic claptrap was abundantly clear to me. Surridge might have invited himself. Or I, in need of company, might have invited Surridge. Did it really matter? I knew from experience it had been an absurd Surridge special of bacchanalian mayhem and tomfoolery. Unlike our previous night together, we had both crossed the line, he and I. Can a person really enjoy themselves if they can't remember they have enjoyed themselves?

For me at least, after the phone call, I had wanted to escape. To put it simply, I couldn't cope with the voice, not merely the import of its words, but the very fact that the voice existed at all. The voice had suddenly become the soundtrack to my existence, had wrung out the rag of my old life, and left it hanging high and dry. In its place was something new, a newness which I couldn't, and dared not, accept. I had been extracted against my will out of the colourlessness of what I had previously accepted as my life and casually discarded into a netherworld which had all the reality of a Hollywood set.

I spent Sunday as if at the bottom of a dry well, staring up at the odd cloud as it passed. I still had a headache as I made my way to work the next day; a dull vagueness had taken up residence at the back of my skull and, from its core, a pebble of pain resonated outwards like a blip on a radar screen. If I had intended to silence the voice with alcohol, then my intention had failed. The voice was still reverberating in my mind, its insane chatter operating on a different frequency, an unbroken, schizophrenic static that couldn't be attuned to the real world.

A couple of my female students, hugging garish, pink lever arch files, smiled at me from the steps of the Student's Union as I walked by, their boyfriends casting me enquiring, knowing looks. I felt a sudden dampness under my arms, a wet breeze on my forehead.

Outside the main door of my department building in University Square I closed my eyes and exhaled deeply. Ahead of me were three flights of stairs, finishing at the door of Pritchard's office. I knocked twice.

'Enter!' Pritchard's voice resounded from within.

There were more books in Pritchard's office than I had ever seen in one enclosed space before. There were books on his shelves, books on his desk, books in open boxes, books in boxes that had not been opened, books on his armchair and sofa, books on the window ledge and tottering tower blocks of knee-height books on his floor. If there had been a safe in his office, it would have been filled with his most expensive books. There might even have been cavities, dug into the walls behind his pictures, for the books he didn't want you to know about.

It had been years since I had last stepped foot into this office. Pritchard called it 'the belfry', the nook to which he had been 'exiled' after the coup that had finally ousted him from power. It was colder here than anywhere else in the building. He kept the radiator on all day and supplemented with a blow heater that parched the air as he worked. I spotted a bowl of water on the floor acting as a humidifier. It was either that, he said, or he would have to start burning books for heat, and he wasn't prepared to do that.

The books, of course, were a prop, as much an accessory to Pritchard as a lighter was to a pyromaniac. They were meant to create an otherworldly mystique for the young undergrads, a sort of temple to his intellect. He only had twelve token hours of tutorials a week, but Pritchard stayed in his office all day, to spite his new female boss, it was said, although it had more to do with the thought of going home to an empty house.

'My goodness, Summer. You look as though your season has finally come to an end and the leaves are about to fall off the trees. What the hell have you been up to? Here, move those books off that chair, take a pew and tell your Uncle Pritchard all about it.' I hadn't fully entered the room. I had just popped my head across the jamb of the door and Pritchard had already completed an appraisal, had worked out some kind of mishap had befallen me. 'Let me guess. That neighbour of yours. Porridge?'

'Surridge.' I corrected.

'Oops! Ha! Yes. Surridge. Had a bit of a late one, eh? I've got some Perrier somewhere.' He started fishing into his desk drawers for the errant bottle.

'No, it's ok, Professor. Really. It was Saturday and...'

'...Saturday! Well, well, well. You must have had a skinful! Party, was it?'

'Something like that, yes.'

He glanced at a sheet of paper on his desk.

'Hmm, says here you don't have a tutorial until 12.00. Now, what has you here at 9.00 o'clock on a Monday morning, I wonder?'

Now that I was sitting there in front of him, I didn't know where to begin. I looked around, searching for an answer to leap out at me from one of his historical tomes. On one level, I had come to inform Pritchard that I had decided to agree to his request to take his place on the trip to Armagh. On another level, I wanted his reassurance that I was not having a nervous breakdown. The bottom line was that I didn't know if I could trust Pritchard. To put it another way, I was scared. Scared of being laughed at. Scared of being mocked. The voice had mentioned Pritchard by name, and I had no idea why.

And then there were those three years in Pritchard's life, his private island of despair. 'No man is an island', it is true. But when the man, or boy, is shipwrecked, is he really prepared to open up that island as a tourist destination for others? It is *his* island, after all. Since Rose's death I had retreated to my own haven on the high seas. Every lonely night afterwards

I had forwarded my address to the rest of the world, a personal SOS scrawled out on the sand. Every morning, I would allow the tide to wash the letters away.

'It's about Armagh. I just thought I'd let you know that I can make the trip.' I heard myself reply.

Pritchard narrowed his eyes and smiled.

'You've come here at nine o'clock on a Monday morning to tell me that?'

'Err...'

'...You have something against phones, Summer?' he enquired, nodding in the direction of his own.

'What's that?'

'I said, why didn't you just call me with this earth-shattering news?'

'I... I was....'

'...You're not really going to sit there and tell me you were 'in the neighbourhood', are you, Summer?! You look like at least two of the four horsemen of the apocalypse! Death or pestilence! Take your pick!'

'No, no, really, I was on my way...'

'...Nothing's happened, has it? Something to set you off?'

'No, well, Surridge...'

'...Yes, that English buffoon. You know, I have two reasons to dislike that fellow. I'm Welsh *and* Irish!' He laughed. I was glad he laughed. I didn't like the conversation when he wasn't laughing. 'You know he gate-crashed a School of Byzantine Studies affair a few weeks back?! He claimed it was for a cultural piece he was putting together on Turkey's first female PM. Anyway, they had to throw him out, I heard. Spent all night drinking and singing *Istanbul, Not Constantinople*. Bloody fool!' He stopped suddenly, then smiled and wagged a finger at me. 'Yes, you're a clever fellow, Summer! But remember. I know you. I know how you operate, my friend. Being a good listener is a fine thing to be. You learn more that way. But you also don't need to divulge anything about yourself either. And you know I will prattle on until the proverbials come home. So, I will, for once, button up and give you the floor. Why are you really here?'

I scanned the room again. I had to give Pritchard credit. He really had transformed his office into a kind of mausoleum, a sort of living tomb where he had been interred to while away his remaining years. It wasn't difficult, I suppose. The room, like the building it occupied, dated from the mid-19th century. The walls supported posters and framed paintings: Turner and Constable replicas, a print of the 1851 Great Exhibition, Gilbert Stuart's Medallion portrait of Thomas Jefferson (Pritchard was a fan of Jefferson's less-known archaeological pursuits) with the former president's famous profile reminding me of a young

Roman senator, perhaps Caesar himself, looking westwards to his future military campaigns in Gaul. Everything had been carefully curated to enrapture you, preserve you in the moment, and by extension, provide a pre-eminence to the room's occupant. Not one item, the phone aside, belonged to the twentieth century. Right down to the clanging pipes of an old steam radiator which chose that moment to issue an earnest, metallic salvo, its musical efforts quickly disappointed by a subsequent, hissy fart.

Pritchard was right. He had been banished there; sequestered, cloistered and forgotten. Deep down though, I knew Pritchard didn't give a damn. He was enjoying himself too much.

'You know I was unfaithful once to Rose,' I suddenly stammered.

6

Maggo put down his bible and thought about what he would make for lunch. It had been nearly six months since he had been back home, and his supply of couscous was running dangerously low. He should have risked an extra bag through customs, he knew. Perhaps one bag less of rice. But there were so many other things to think about back then. There was a weight limit to what he could bring through, and besides, how was he to know that his new employer would have developed an insatiable craving for couscous. That was one of the rare things his eminent patron could not procure, either legally or illegally.

His mother had warned him that Celts had even less taste buds than Teutons. He shouldn't worry about packing any food at all, she had said. Maggo had chosen to defy her. Just once. This was his first spell beyond the borders of the Carthaginian Union, his first time away from his family home in Melita, and he wanted to do everything he could to make a successful transition to his new life in Ulidia.

His mother's two utmost concerns were for

his safety and his faith. In fact, in her mind, the two were interlinked. She had heard that Federation custom officials routinely confiscated any religious material, literature, music, art or scientific journal that contravened their ideological canon. She feared that her son, upon disembarking at the port of Átha Cliath, would be arrested on some trumped-up charge of religious misconduct and thrown into one of the Federation's infamous labour camps. These camps served to punish foreigners for serious offences against the state or re-educate those in the local population that dared speak out against their ongoing oppression.

Maggo had assured his mother that most of what she had learned about the Federation in general, and Éireann in particular, was merely the product of the daily CU propaganda sheets. The labour camps were a myth. He had tried to convince her that possession of the holy book was not prohibited anywhere in the Federation. As long as he did not go out of his way to convert anyone to Christianity, he shouldn't find himself in any kind of trouble.

He reminded her that there were positive signs the regional war between Ulidia and Connachta, the accounts of which sparked daily headlines in the CU press, was coming to an end. Besides, he had assured her, Emain Mhaca, where he would soon be based, was nowhere near the militarised zones.

None of what he said had any effect on her. She worried next about how her only son was going to maintain his faith in a land full of heathens. And so, he made promises, anything to reassure her. He would read the holy book every day. He would not proselytise. He would not go out late at night. He would get eight hours sleep every night. He would remember to eat. He would not attend the pagan festivals. In any case, he assured her, his visa was only for six months. He would soon be home to continue his studies at the University of Valletta and, in the summer holidays, could once again help his uncle in the Bidni olive groves that littered the southern part of the archipelago where they lived.

What he didn't tell her, however, was that he had an option to extend his visa for another six months if he met the approval of his employer and also of, what they called in Éireann, the Brehon Laws.

Maggo returned his bible to the top shelf of the kitchen bookcase that had been specially reserved for all his books and papers and removed a recipe book from the shelf beneath. Lorcan would be back from the offices of the Bardic Press at 13.00 and so he needed to be prepared.

The exchange programme between his university and the University of Emain Mhaca was one of dozens of different types of educational and cultural liaisons that operated along the open lines of communication between the various institutions of learning in the Federation and the Carthaginian Union. The two rival geographical blocs that dominated the landmass of Europe, North Africa, the Middle East and the western parts of Asia had signed a treaty of non-aggression in the early 1900s after the end of the Third Continental Crusades. That final crusade, like the two previous in the late 1700s and mid-1800s, had been the adverse result of fundamentalist hegemony on both sides, druidic and Christian, and had cost tens of thousands of lives. Reckless leadership from Carthage, hand in glove with a disparate and uncoordinated reaction from the druidic schools in the main Celtic and Teutonic nations, had led to a series of invasions and counter-invasions along the frontier of the River Danube. The subsequent Treaty of Danube in 1905 had issued in nearly a century of peace between the two land-locked neighbours. It had also led to the creation of the Federation of Celtic and Teutonic States in 1909, a determined effort on one side, it seemed, to quell the dangerous, individualist spirit of the Celtic heart and keep it in lockstep with the more practical Teutonic mind. Since the Carthaginian Union had risen from the ashes of the old Holy Carthaginian Empire, the former did not have the same concerns about rogue states not towing the line.

Maggo whistled a tune, an old Christian hymn, the words of which he couldn't quite remember. He chopped a few vegetables and contemplated his future. Would he apply for a new visa? Had his time in Ulidia opened up the wide portfolio of opportunities he had hitherto expected?

He had ended up staying in the household of Lorcan mac Róich quite by chance. Looking back, he wondered if he still actually believed that there was anything really left to chance in this odd little nation. He had learned that behind the jovial masks of the average Ulidian citizen there lurked a steely militancy that could be triggered at will by the authorities above them. It was how these authorities were able to maintain the discipline of its citizenry, via its media outlets, that had first ignited his curiosity in the Federation. Not that patriotic fervour in the media was unknown in his own country, or in the CU as a whole. However, Ulidia was at war. Its war machine needed its press. And Maggo wanted to witness the dynamics of that relationship first-hand.

And so, he had come to Ulidia to take up a junior position with the Bardic Press, the overreaching communications organisation that controlled the output of all the daily and weekly news sheets in Ulidia. The particular news sheet of which Lorcan mac Róich was editor, The Ulidian Shield, had provided the young undergraduate with the gilt-edged opportunity to work with one of the most renowned publications. With this experience, and a degree in Punic Studies behind him, he would have the necessary ammunition to blaze a trail in his chosen field of journalism, maybe even acquire a position in one of the major CU cities: Syracuse, Alexandria, Massalia or even Carthage itself.

The role he undertook did not quite match his lofty expectations, however. He worked only one day a week at the headquarters of the BP, with the rest of his week, initially at least, being spent editing articles at his free rooms nearby. His rent, fortunately at first, was paid jointly by both his university and the University of Emain Mhaca. For example, he was able to eat for free on campus and he had an allowance to purchase any books his course required. For the rest of it, he would have to rely on his savings and a modest monthly stipend from his employer. After a few weeks though Maggo had been informed that, due to a clerical error in Valletta, the rooms were no longer available. As luck would have it the editor of the news sheet himself, Maggo was notified, was in the position to offer him a room at his roundhouse just a few streets away from the offices where he worked. This was a great honour; he had been told. Lorcan mac Róich was a very influential citizen and had spent some time in his youth in North Africa. As a result, the editor was a keen scholar of Punic culture. He had even learned some of the Punic language and was eager to revive his studies. If Maggo would agree to offer his employer a few 'advanced' language lessons, would he be willing to accept a new tenancy agreement?

One week after moving in, Maggo cooked Lorcan mac Róich, his mother's favourite dish, *Soppa tal-arma*, the only thing he could think of that used local Ulidian ingredients. When his patron tasted the dish for the first time, he was completely overwhelmed with the unusual flavours that Maggo had somehow been able to extract from the common garden vegetables which grew in the old man's garden. War time rationing had not really impacted upon the diet of Maggo's new landlord. Like other leading lights in society, he could afford shady, after-dark visits from Laighean black market smugglers and bootleggers that provided wine and cheese from Gaul, fruit from Iberia and chocolate from la Tène. Nevertheless, Maggo's broth was very well appreciated by Lorcan mac Róich's ever expanding palate.

After the success of that first dinner, it was inevitable that meals between the two became more frequent as the weeks passed until, Maggo feared, his role in the household had become more of a live-in cook than that of a student journalist.

'Tell me young Maggo. What do your parents think of you moving to Ulidia? They must be worried, no?' Lorcan had asked him during the meal.

'My mother is, sir.'

'And your father?'

'This soup,' Maggo had replied, 'is my mother's recipe. Do you know how it translates in your language?'

'No, I'm afraid your lessons will have to commence immediately, my young friend.'

'The soup of widows.'

At 13.00 Lorcan mac Róich limped through the front door of his impressive roundhouse in the Loughnashade district of the city. He stabbed a blackthorn cane as he carefully traversed the parquet floor of the hallway.

No one lived in traditional roundhouses anymore, of course. There had been, however, an architectural fad half a century before for exclusive Ulidian citizens to shell out huge fortunes to exuberant stonemasons for the construction of massive dome-shaped dwellings of wattle and daub, girdled in oak, in faux homage to their ancestral past.

Lorcan mac Róich lived alone in his vast residence. Maggo had heard from Lorcan's ward, Finn, that there had been a wife in the far distant past, but this wife, if she had existed, was no longer alive. If he ever had a wife, Maggo conjectured, it must have been many decades ago. Lorcan had the insouciant disregard for housekeeping that was the embodiment of the perennial bachelor or widower. For the upkeep of his home, he had hired the services of a housekeeper who visited for a few hours each morning. Maggo was grateful to discover that his cooking chores had not overlapped into dusting and cleaning as well.

Maggo had calculated that his boss was in his late sixties. At work, he conveyed a slightly cantankerous disposition that reminded Maggo a little of his uncle back home. Not that Lorcan mac Róich was rude to his new subordinate. It was just that he possessed an unpredictable temperament that could not be lifted by the calming efforts of others. It wasn't a question of status. Mac Róich treated everyone in exactly the same way. Once you entered his sphere, you had to endure the climate of his mood. At home, he was a different person altogether.

'Well, my Punic friend. How are you?' he smiled the question, his thin lips curling slightly upwards.

'Fine, sir. Lunch is almost ready.'

'Hmm...I can smell it. Curried rice?'

'You have a fine nose, sir.'

'With my taste in wine, I should have, Maggo.' He glanced out the window and sighed. 'I envy your weather. Looks like rain outside.'

He pulled up a chair and sat down, content to survey his employee busy himself with plates and utensils. He was a large man who had been handsome in his youth. He still had enough of his long, silver hair to tie back; it revealed a high forehead, heavy brow and sharp eyes beneath. On the table beside him sat an inoffensive, short-brimmed hat, the current Ulidian trend, which he had removed upon entering the house. He took off his eyeglasses, took out his pipe and yawned.

'I have heard that cretin mac Nessa has actually tried to harvest grapes in that conservatory of his at the palace. I mean what kind of fool is he?'

Maggo noticed a dark cloud descend over the old man's face, as it always did when mac Nessa's name was uttered.

'You look tired, sir? Did you not sleep well?' Maggo asked, trying to change the subject.

'Me? Tired? That'll be the day! They build them to last here in Ulidia, you know, Maggo! Lorcan clapped his hands together. 'No, no, my friend. Lorcan mac Róich is never tired. Never believe what the others say. These modern clans. A few decades old. Bloated up with industrial money. They're nothing to a clan like mac Róich. We have been around for thousands of years. We have staying power. We will be here long after that pitiful entourage that backs up mac Nessa has disappeared from the history books.'

Mac Nessa was also an ancient name, too, Maggo had read. He wouldn't dare say this to Lorcan mac Róich, of course. Nearly six months had been more than enough time to gain an appreciation of the internal clan strife within Ulidian politics. It was obvious from the start that the mac Róichs and the mac Nessas did not see eye to eye, and perhaps, had never had. The Ulidian Shield, like all news sheets of the Bardic Press, had to censor any articles that could be in any way inter-preted as unpatriotic or anti-war. The population would not have it any other way, they knew. Now that peace was in sight, Lorcan mac Róich, and most other editors of the BP, could hardly wait to launch a full-scale verbal onslaught on the mac Nessa regime. For years, they had had to content themselves with the odd scrap of family scandal and political in-trigue, domestic matters, drip fed to them via normal presidential channels. A senatorial di-vorce here. Evidence of bribery there. Paltry pickings. Mac Nessa had been able to divert any major storm and downgrade it to a pass-ing breeze. If the weather failed to change for the better, he rapidly pushed the agenda on to foreign policy using expressions such as 'the greater good' and 'the national interest'.

'And how is Finn, sir? Conall mac Dara tells me he's making great progress in the RBK?'

'Mac Dara? He wasn't here, was he?'

'No, no, sir. I met him in the old town. He seemed to be in a hurry.'

'Probably coming out of some tavern or other! It's a disgrace how the army has been allowed to become so dilapidated over recent months...Well, what did our gallant hero have to say for himself?'

'Just that he had seen Finn and that the boy was doing well.'

'He has been told to stay away from the lad!' Lorcan exclaimed. 'His sister has granted me full guardian rights! I'll go to the law courts if I have to!'

There is something playing on the old man's mind, Maggo told himself, as he served Lorcan his lunch, a steaming dish of rice, mushroom and potato sprinkled with paprika and turmeric and held together by tomato paste. After they had eaten, Lorcan lit up his favourite pipe.

'Tobacco is another thing I'm running low on,' Lorcan moaned, as he puffed generous, thin curlicues of smoke that rose up into the air and dissipated before reaching the ceiling. 'I suppose you have read mac Nessa's latest?' he asked, between puffs.

'Yes, I saw a copy of it this morning. Very well written, I thought.'

'That would be Bradán, his secretary. He was named well, that one!'

'Sir?'

'It means 'salmon' as in a slippery, pink fish,' Lorcan explained. 'He's one of the upstarts, the pit of snakes that slither around their master's heels in the palace. Bradán is the first of the mac Neills though to get close to a sitting president. He's got a bloody cousin in the senate, too! Corraidhín. That means 'little spear', Maggo. His wife knows why.'

He laughed heartily at his own joke until his laughter was suddenly overtaken by a serious bout of coughing. Lorcan, crimson-faced, unable to breathe, waved one hand in the direction of the sink. Maggo, understanding, rose from his chair and fetched him a glass of water.

'But this Protectorate. They have no weapons, your Druidic Order. How are they going to police the disputed territories?' Maggo asked, once Lorcan had recovered.

'Well, Maggo, we might make a politician out of you yet. That's a very good question. One of many I have. There's a story there, of course, but it's not one anyone can write. The whole palace is locked up tighter than a bodhrán. I have sent my best people there. They can't even get through the door. Same with most of the other news sheets. Except the Béal Feirste Banner, of course. That puppet rag gets all the exclusives. Do you know I sent my best writer to the peace talks and he hasn't been granted a single interview with his lordship, mac Nessa? Meanwhile the 'Banner' has complete access to the DO, the Laighean and Mhumhain delegations and a personal audience with our exalted leader. There's something afoot...'

'Something on a foot?' I asked.

'No, something afoot, something happening behind the scenes. The greatest story of the century if I can get my hands on it! But, naturally, I am the last person mac Nessa would want to see with my face in the trough!'

'Truff?'

Lorcan sighed and took a long draw on his pipe.

'Ignore me, my young friend. I shouldn't be bothering you with such distasteful matters. I bet it's the same in Valletta, eh? Politicians are the same everywhere! Worse in Carthage, I'd expect, eh? What's your new Patriarch called again?'

'Patriarch John the Tenth.'

'John? Yes, that's right,' he mused. 'It was John the Ninth, last time I was in the Union.'

He tapped his pipe on the table and set about cleaning out the bowl. He had a special scoop for this which he always kept in the inside pocket of his jacket. Maggo watched on, enjoying the expectation of hearing the old man reminisce.

'Yes, yes. Alexandria. I was only a young man, not much older that you are now. I had to...well...let's just say, it was in my best interests for me to spend some time away from Éireann at that time. Three years I spent there. Eratosthenes, Euclid, Archimedes and then little old me, Lorcan mac Róich. Hard to believe, eh? You think you are civilised, and then, dear Maggo, you see Alexandria for the first time! Ever been?'

'Not yet, sir.'

'You will go, of course. Easier for you than most of us. Well, to say that my young provincial mind was dumbstruck by the sights, sounds and smells of that wonderful old city would not do it justice. I travelled later to Carthage, too. Of course, I have been to Karnag, Vienne and Avebury, but nothing, nothing, compares to Alexandria, Maggo. I remember queuing for the first time to gain entrance to the Library of Alexandria. No amount of advance reading material could have prepared me for such a place. I couldn't believe the scale of it. The vaulted, ornate roofs and towering, Ionic columns. The never-ending walkway, Maggo, into the *Philosophers' Gardens*, the hushed silence of dimly lit reading rooms there, the closed intimacy of smaller cubicles where private meetings might have been conducted. And everywhere, my friend, enormous marble statuettes of the celebrated tutors and students from antiquity, a pantheon of chiselled stone lining every walkway and corridor. And then, for a few extra sovereigns,' he winked, 'access to *The Anthologia*, where I spent one long afternoon, gazing upon the stacks and stacks of papyrus scrolls. Tens of thousands of documents, bundled up and sealed away, behind row upon row of thick glass cabinets, a dizzy panopticon that took my breath away.'

He stopped, stared a moment, removed his eyeglasses again and wiped his eyes. He got like this sometimes, Maggo knew. When his anger subsided, it gave way to a good heart. Maggo was patient, a good listener, his mother had said. But this man, Lorcan mac Róich, Maggo thought, held a deep sadness within and it had nothing to do with the missing headline of a news sheet.

'Dust,' he announced, finally. 'I don't know what that cleaner gets up to here every morning. She's certainly not cleaning, that's for sure.'

7

I had very rarely ever caught Pritchard off-guard. That was the point of the environment in which he had surrounded himself. He caught *you* off-guard, backed you up against the ropes and pummelled away until you were forced to take a knee. Yet for once I detected genuine shock on Pritchard's face, ironing out the usual lines of cynicism. He had no idea where I was going with this. Unfortunately, neither did I.

'Oh...?' He managed to muster after a long pause.

'Yes...yes...it was just before Rose died in '81. New Year's Eve...well, technically, New Year's Day, I suppose.'

Was I imagining it, or had I just seen Pritchard blush? Another first. I ignored it, however, and pressed ahead, sprinting head-long into the dark, running in bare feet over a field full of glass.

'We had been out, Rose and I, with a mixture of her friends from the bank where she worked and some of my old school friends from home. You know, the usual haunts. We made it to midnight and then some of Rose's friends started to cry off. One of them was quite drunk, in fact. Rose offered to make coffee for everyone back at ours, but my friends, not used to the bright lights of Belfast, persuaded me to stay out for just one more cocktail. We made our farewells and then Louis...you remember Louis, don't you? Writer from Newry? No? Well, he had managed to get hold of these VIP passes for the Europa Hotel. He had heard about it on the news, the IRA's favourite place to bomb, and about the dolly-bird night club they had on the 12th floor. 'The Penthouse Poppets'. You remember them? No, of course, you wouldn't. Sorry. Well, neither had I...at the time...I thought it was just a few, quiet drinks in luxuriant surroundings, a bit of a dance, and then back to Rose.'

'Anyway, you know me. As soon as we made it through their security and exited the lift into the club, I knew straight away I was out of my depth. The place was full: a sea of bling, bubbly and bunny tails; bodies swaying as if drunk on the deck of a sinking ship, its cannon booming an ear-splitting disco beat.'

'I deliberately got myself lost in the crowd and made my way back down to the foyer. The effects of the evening had already begun to wear off at this stage. I can't even use insobriety as an excuse for what happened next.'

'It must have been getting near 2.00 am and I had just reached the ground floor when I heard a bit of mellow jazz coming out of the public bar to my left. I followed the sound and before I knew it, I was having a Jamesons and ice on a stool in front of a disgruntled-looking barman who had all the appearance of someone who just wanted to get home and crack open a few ales himself.'

'A few residents were still milling around amongst the wreckage of party hats, pop streamers and an overturned Christmas tree. A gaggle of night clubbers were downing tequila shots in the corner. I couldn't tell if these were nightcaps before bed, or pre-drinks for the musical mayhem still going on above.'

'I didn't see her approach or sit down in the stool beside me. I didn't hear her order a glass of red wine. I didn't smell her perfume. She seemed to have materialised out of thin air. One minute the stool beside me was empty, and the next minute it was occupied. If I had been lost in thought, it hadn't been a very interesting one. Perhaps I had nodded off. I don't know. All I know is when I came round to myself, I felt like the inhabitant of a new body, in a new world.'

'Lewis, I don't think this is the time...'

'...I'm sorry, Professor. For some reason, this morning, I feel compelled to talk about this. And if I don't tell you, who could I possibly tell?'

Pritchard hesitated a moment. 'Yes, of

course,' he said finally.

On immediate reflection, I wasn't sure what he meant by that. Yes, of course, it was best for me to unburden myself. Or, yes, of course, who else could I talk to but Pritchard? I was too overwrought to weigh up the two possibilities. It was as if I was in a trance. I could hear words being uttered. They appeared to be coming from my mouth, but I had become someone else's ventriloquist's dummy, a medium for a spirit who couldn't keep his mouth shut, a vassal for an entity outside of myself, using my body like an astronaut uses a space-suit on the moon.

'I don't wish, Professor, to wax lyrical about any of this,' I continued. 'What happened that night with Eva...that was her name, by the way... has happened to all men since Adam first got his marching orders from the Garden of Eden. A man falls in love with a woman, or the other way around and, if they nose-dive off the cliff at approximately the same time, this love has a chance to survive. Some relationships begin with the ping of a microwave and end up a TV dinner after a couple of years. And some begin as an offering of an apple on a silver platter, too good to turn down.'

'Yes, as far as the world was concerned, I had a one-night stand with Eva. The opportunity was there, and I seized it. That is not to say that I had not had similar opportunities in the past. I could have been unfaithful to Rose previously, but I had never even had the remote beginnings of an inclination to jeopardise my life with her.'

'As soon as I turned to face the woman in the stool beside me, however, I knew that my life was never going to be the same again. Yes, she was beautiful. Yes, she was intelligent, captivating, radiant. Her most abiding quality, however, was her insubstantiality, not in character or deed, but by the sheer fact that she didn't seem real, as though I were looking at her through a thin veil of gauze. She was a projection almost, a trick of light, her structural integrity held together by a force field of invisible beams. In short, if a pumpkin carriage had been parked on double yellow lines outside the entrance of the Europa Hotel that night, it would not have surprised me. I'm sorry, Professor, I promised that I would avoid hyperbole.'

'I think I can appreciate what you are trying to say. Carry on.' Pritchard encouraged.

'Well, there's not much more I can say. The rest of it followed a natural course, at least on the surface of things. One of the tequila girls had just munched into a lemon and reacted with a loud, shivering screech. We both chanced to look around at the same time, and then at each other. I'm not sure who smiled first.'

'She was in her late twenties and wore very little make-up, professor. Her flaming red hair was worn up in a type of loose Edwardian pompadour with the odd strand falling loose over her pale, green eyes. She wore a quite simple floral-patterned dress around which she hugged a plain woollen cardigan. Apart from the way she had chosen to wear her hair, she had all the appearance of a traditional, fresh-faced, Connemara cow-maid, all the way down to the freckles on her nose.'

'I couldn't believe it when she told me that she was a foreign language student from Brittany. She had been learning English for just over a year in Belfast, she said, and worked part-time as a waitress. Once her English was good enough, she hoped to do one of the pre-sessional language courses at Queen's and then study, of all things, History. Her English was that of the new learner, but she spoke, surprisingly, with no trace of an accent. In short, Professor, Eva seemed perfectly content in her own style, at home with the version of herself she had become."

'And then?'

'And then...well we talked for an hour or so, never running out of topics of conversation. She had a great thirst for knowledge, history mostly, war in general, but also my opinion on 'the troubles'. And yes, when I told her what I did, she was fascinated. I think she even had me tell her one of the old tales from the Ulster Cycle. I can still see her now, sitting there, her head tilted to one side, absorbed, while I regaled her with a dramatised version of *Bricríu's Feast*. As I say, English wasn't her native tongue. I suppose I did most of the talking, but I got the impression that she understood the gist of everything I was saying, or pretended to, at least. As for her, when she spoke, it was with a charming, grammatical precision. I guess she couldn't waste words she didn't have. She told me the bare facts about her life in Brittany. She had a brother she was fond of; I remember. Her father worked on a fishing trawler in Brest; her mother in a factory which processed seafood. Apart from that, nothing much.'

'And then?' Pritchard persisted

'Well,' I hesitated, 'I felt it was the gentlemanly thing to do was to walk her home... Listen, Professor, can I just say that even then I had no intentions of sleeping with her. I mean that. I was in awe, not just of her, but of us, the couple we had so easily become. I wasn't ready to debase that with some crude and obvious fumblings under a duvet. Believe me, I know it sounds ridiculous. I feel ridiculous saying it. So yes, I suggested I walk her home. Yes, maybe I was curious about where she lived. Maybe I harboured some faint prospect of seeing her again? I don't know. I just thought I'd walk her home, that's all. I didn't expect things to work out how they did. She told me where she lived. It wasn't too far out of my way, after all...'

There was nothing more to say. I had reached the end. The rest required little imagination. What happened next is a no-go area in polite society, a prohibited zone where even the emergency services cannot enter. If only I had been rescued, I thought. If only I had made my excuses on that walk back to Eva's, returned to the sanctuary of my life with Rose. If only someone could have pulled me out of debris of what I was about to do to my life. Soon it was Rose herself under that debris. Soon she would pay the ultimate price for my weakness, my vulgar, primordial impulse to have sex with someone I had just met.

In a few hours I had been prepared to lay my life, and that of others, to waste. The prospect of children with Rose. Her promotion. A new house. A new-born child. Middle of the night feeding patterns. A first day at school. Teaching my child how to ride a bike. Birthdays. A first boyfriend or girlfriend. Graduation. A life review of a life that had not been lived -this was often the movie I played out, on the ceiling above my bed, on sleepless nights after Rose. But with all that, I still could not bring myself to sacrifice those memories of Eva.

Surely that had to mean something. If it did not balance the scales, at least there was something on the other side to act as a weight against the magnitude of what I had done to Rose. Or was this just another lie? Something to tell myself. That I wasn't just like everyone else. Had I just propped Eva onto a pedestal and forced the recollection of her to be worthy of the sacrifice I had made?

In any case, I wasn't going to tell Pritchard any of this. That at least was none of his business. I couldn't believe I had just arrived in his office, sat down and blurted out my brief memoir of Eva. It was either that or tell him about the voice on the telephone. And I hadn't been prepared to let Pritchard know about that. He sat there, expectedly, waiting for more. But I wasn't going to play ball. The levee had broken, and the waters had subsided into the sea.

'Did you see her again? After that night?' he asked, suddenly.

'No. I walked past her house a few times in the two weeks or so following the New Year. I kept to the opposite side of the street, just watching, but I never had the courage to knock on the door. She lived with students, she had said, and I was afraid that one of them might have been my own. Actually, I don't think I would have had the courage to have paid her a visit. Something about not wanting to dispel the illusion. I thought that if I could see her, just once more, exiting onto the street from her house, it would have confirmed to me that this person had actually existed and that I hadn't dreamed the whole episode up...and then Rose died...'

'Of course. Of course. And you never saw her again, did you?'

I shook my head. There was a long period of silence. The steam radiator seemed to be between its irregular outbreaks of military tattoo. I could hear Pritchard's laboured breathing and I wondered if he wasn't well himself. In any case, he was deep in thought, the knuckles of his withered hands shoring up his chin.

Pritchard had never been married. He had been a bachelor his whole life and so, more than anyone else I knew, most acclimated to the life of the single man. He hadn't really known Rose, but he understood loss, even if it was the loss of something he had never had. He was the bachelor, and I was the widower, a desolate double act when it came to commitment, one who had never been interested and one who was no longer interested. He taught me what it was like not to need women. Desire was another thing entirely. Perhaps it was the sharing of that desire which had rendered him so off balanced.

'Well, well, Summer, you *are* an interesting fellow! He said, finally.

'Thanks. I think.'

'It gets me off the hook, you know.'

'Sorry?'

'Friends of Mhaca!'

'Oh! Anything I can do to oblige.'

'Soooo...' he said, bringing his hands together, bringing the conversation to an end.

'Yes,' I said, standing up.

'If there's nothing else...?'

'Sorry?'

'...On your mind?'

'No. no. All is well.'

Pritchard walked me to the door and examined my face.

'You do look tired, Summer. Why don't you take some time before your trip? Have a holiday. Your family are from that neck of the woods?'

'Near enough.'

'Well, pop in and see them. They'd love to see you again. Get a few hot meals inside you.'

'I might just do that,' I replied

It was a strange end to the meeting, as if paper had been wrapped around a Pandora's box and tied with a neat bow. I couldn't help shake the feeling, once again, that Pritchard had more secrets than I could ever have. He wanted me to go to Armagh. The voice on the phone had wanted the same thing. I hadn't had the courage to speak to Pritchard about the voice. It had all seemed too surreal. What seemed even more surreal was the fact that I, an adult, had decided to go to Armagh, as if following some magical trail of breadcrumbs. I was a child again. The voice had said 'Once upon a time' and I had said 'happily ever after', needing to know the fairy tale in between. I might have called it synchronicity, coincidence, contingency but, in the end, I had time to spare. And I wanted to know what would happen next.

8

The King's Stables district of Emain Mhaca was one of the most significant landmarks in all of Ulidia. Thousands of years before, ancient kings had watered their horses in the ancient pool there, while slaves rinsed down the mud-caked wheels of chariots, finally brought to rest after long campaigns in Connachta or Mhumhain. The king's horses, after a lifetime of service, would retire to pastures specially set aside nearby, their bones buried in the hills beyond. It was recorded that Cú Chulainn's favourite chariot-horses, Liath Macha and Dub Sainglend, had imbibed its famous waters, even preferring them to the pool of Linn Liaith in the mountains of Sliab Fuait.

The sacred pool was now a tourist attraction, carefully monitored by the Ulidian branch of the Druidic Order. Like all religious sites, the land around was owned by the DO. Pilgrims from all over were charged admission to gain access; in the past, they had been permitted to scoop up the holy water into small, clay jars to bring home as votive offerings. However, fear of contaminating the waters had led to an end to that practice. Now, pilgrims contented themselves with tossing their hard-earned shillings into the pool and stretching out their arms skywards in earnest supplication to the gods. The same fears of defilement meant that the coins were collected daily by druidic priests and redistributed to the poor. Or so it was believed.

The DO also held the deeds to the land upon which the nearby Ulidian Senate had been constructed at the time of the Celtic Renaissance. The senate was circular; its external walls were constructed of red sandstone upon which squatted a domed roof made up of a mixture of glass and wrought iron. At noon, when Lugh, the sun god, was at his highest point in the sky, his rays shone through the dome and lit up the limestone head of Macha, the sovereign goddess of Ulidia, whose statue stood at the centre of the senate and whose watchful gaze frowned down upon all the political shenanigans that went on around her.

'If she could, she would bloody well shake her head,' Conall thought, as he entered through the main doors of the empty building. He looked around and, in spite of himself, was visibly impressed by the majesty that surrounded him. It was very rare for members of the military to walk upon the sacrosanct floor of the senate, its limestone floor warm now beneath the soles of Conall's feet. The senatorial class liked to make decisions affecting the military when the military wasn't around. Maybe that was a good thing. If generals actually witnessed how these pompous old fools arrived at some of their absurd decisions, would they ever agree to go to war?

And yet, Conall couldn't help but allow his eyes to survey the walls upon which were adorned huge twenty feet paintings that travelled, clockwise, on a pictorial journey of Ulidian history, beginning with the birth of Tuatha Dé Danann and the origins of Éireann itself and coming all the way around to a present day portrait of President Darragh mac Nessa that held pride of place over the Senatorial Chair.

'Bastard!' muttered Conall, under his breath. He wanted to spit but thought better of it. Senatorial eyes everywhere, probably, even at this time of day, he thought. He cast a quick glance around the oak pews of the Senatorial Chamber, three rows of velvet-cushioned benches organised in a horse-shoe around the Chair; a homage, no doubt, to the hoof-sodden bog upon which the entire talking shop had been built.

'You say something there, mac Dara?' came a voice from a doorway to his left.

Conall swung around and in one deft movement un-holstered his pistol.

'You know, you're not supposed to bring any weapons into the Senatorial Chamber,' sounded the voice again, rising in volume as it approached, along with the sound of heels clicking on the limestone floor.

Conall couldn't make out the identity of the figure that was drawing near to him. A last ray of evening sunlight from the glass panes above had made a bright smudge of the man's face.

'There was no one at the gate to say otherwise,' challenged Conall. He despised these sneaking senatorial types whose innate talents, if they ever had any, had been bred out of them by a political system that esteemed a clan's wealth more than anything else. The same dozen or so clans had been running Ulidia for generations and he hated the lot of them.

'Ah, yes, mac Dara. It's the holiday season. The senate's in recess. Besides, all the important folk are in Uisneach.'

Conall finally made out the face, its features hardening into focus. He recognised it immediately.

'Mac Murchadha,' the face said. 'Senator for southern Tír Eoghain.' He extended an arm which Conall felt obliged to clasp, not before swapping his pistol into his left hand.

'What's it all about? Was it you sent me the message?'

'Ha! I heard that you liked to get straight to the point, Commander mac Dara. Probably that's what makes you so efficient.'

"Efficient'? I suppose,' Conall replied.

'Err...you know you can put your illegal fire-arm away you know,' mac Murchadha said, waving a nonchalant finger at Conall's weapon. 'I am a man of Ulidia, born and bred, just like you. Not an ounce of Connachta blood in my family tree. You and I are not at war, you know!'

'You are from Tír Eoghain, though.'

At this the senator laughed, probably too much, Conall felt. All that fawning around the upper echelons of the senate had obviously left their mark on the younger man. Perhaps he had lost the capacity to distinguish what was funny and what was not and so laughed just in case. Tír Eoghain, the senator's county, bordered Ard Mhaca where Conall had been born and raised. The latter was the region which encompassed Emain Mhaca. The two counties had long established clan rivalries, raiding cattle off each other in the far distant past.

The commander returned his pistol to his holster and waited for the young man to recover himself. He was young, probably in his mid-thirties. His clan had made their fortune in quarrying: stone, copper, lead, zinc, copper, silver and gold. It was probably their sandstone that built this bloody place, Conall conjectured. Later on, the mac Murchadhna business interests had diversified. For more than a century they had been heavily involved in the manufacture and distribution of weapons. Nice people, Conall thought. This one, Aodhan mac Murchadha, he had read, had recently joined the ranks of the noble assembly upon the death of his father. He had qualified from the House of Brehon Law as a Brehon law-giver but had left to pursue a political career. An older brother was looking after the family business, it seemed. Politics for you in Ulidia! Conall shrugged and tried again.

'So, you *did* send me a message to come directly here? The note said 'RBK Command'.

'The Ulidian Senate *is* RBK Command', commander. I am simply a conduit, mac Dara. A go-between. A random piece on the fidchell board.'

'Who sent you?'

'We'll come to that,' he answered, looking around. 'Shall we adjourn to the Chair's private office? You're right to be cautious here, mac Dara.'

Conall followed him to the room from which mac Murchadna had just appeared. In the enclosed space within, his eyes strained to make out a bureau crammed with scrolls bound with string, two bookcases, a desk, two chairs and a leather sofa. The room was carpeted but had no natural light. It was obvious that the office was not meant to be seen by the world beyond its walls. A reading lamp on the desk provided a spotlight on a large stack of papers, a pen and a pair of eyeglasses.

'You have heard of electricity, senator, or has our president finally managed to turn all our lights out?'

'You're no fan of President mac Nessa?' Mac Murchadna asked, narrowing his gaze.

'I didn't say that.'

'Sometimes, mac Dara especially in this place, it's what you don't say that gets you into trouble.'

'I'll bear that in mind, senator. In the meantime, can you flick the light switch?'

Mac Murchadna obliged, and the office was filled with light. Now that he could see everything clearly, mac Dara's other senses came to the fore. The lack of a window lent the air a mildewed stuffiness over which a blanket of silence weighed heavily.

'Quiet in here,' Conall said.

'Yes, it is. It was constructed that way. That, of course, is a false wall,' the senator explained, pointing at a part of a rectangular section of wallpaper. The gap behind that and the exterior wall cushions the sound. Also, you noticed the double doors as you came in? That also prevents eavesdropping from the senate floor. A decade or so, the Chair's secretary was caught listening into a private meeting. He was discovered and allowed to spend the next twenty-four hours imprisoned in the space between the doors as punishment. He lost his position, of course.'

'Of course.'

'But I am forgetting my manners. Have a seat, commander.' Conall sat down on the offered chair while mac Murchadha lounged on the larger armchair opposite. He was feeling quite at home in someone else's shoes, Conall thought. He would have to be careful with this one. 'You weren't seen coming into the senate?'

'Is that a question or a statement of fact?'

'We have to take precautions.'

'We?'

The young senator picked up a pen and weaved it through his fingers. He was wearing the senatorial robe worn by all who held office. As he was from Tír Eoghan, his robe was red, fringed with white, its county colours. A spiral pin over the area just above his heart denoted his clan. Senate, county, clan, but not in that order, Conall knew. Once a senator, you were one for life. And even though you were supposed to have the interests of your county at heart, the location of the clan pin told a different story. Under the robe, mac Murchadha wore a fashionable suit and tie.

'As I have said, commander, you are not here at my behest.'

'But Chair Úi Eochada knows about it.'

'Obviously, or we wouldn't be sitting in his office.'

For the first time, Conall detected a note of annoyance in the senator's voice, a momentary lack of self-control. He had been enjoying his role too much up until then, plucked from the senatorial backbenches to undertake some politically significant task. Conall wished he would just bloody well get on with it.

'The Chair has kindly consented to allow us to use his office,' mac Murchadna paraphrased, recovering himself. 'But the request I have to make of you comes from the presidential palace itself.'

'Oh?'

'You read yesterday's news sheet?'

'Yes, I couldn't miss it. It was all over the Bardic Press.'

'Ah, you see, that's a sign of the times we are living in, commander. The first presidential address ever delivered from beyond the borders of Ulidia! Your thoughts?'

'I'm not paid to think, senator.'

'Oh, come now, commander. I can assure you; my lips are sealed.'

'If you want me to tell you if I am happy the war is over, then that depends on the peace. And that's a political matter.'

'Answered like a true politician. Well, it looks like the Mhí Protectorate and the regional delegations will have their hands full.'

'Especially if they want to have this whole mess cleared up by the elections later in the year?'

'Ha! I really think we need a mac Dara back in the Senate! It has been too long since your clan has honoured us with their presence! Anyway, there is no way of saying how long the process will take. And yet…'

'…And yet?'

'And yet, is peace what everyone wants, commander?

'Mhumhain and Laighean?'

'Mhumhain and Laighean?' he repeated. 'Oh, I see, you think that it's in their interests to see Ulidia and Connachta continuously at each other's throats? No, that would be too…too simplistic, commander. Laighean are, as usual, interested in the commercial opportunities that will arise with the new peace.'

'The rumours are they have funnelled armaments through to both sides, from the Federation and beyond…'

'…Unsubstantiated rumours, commander! Never proven!' the senator snapped, impatiently. 'Laighean are looking at trade deals. Post-peace. When our war economy finally comes to an end.'

'And Mhumhain?'

'Let's just say they have their reasons. That's all I can tell you for now.'

'So why am I here?'

'Our security service has heard rumours of a possible assassination attempt on mac Nessa?'

Conall whistled. 'Source?'

'Undisclosed.'

'Not our side, surely.'

'We don't know. That's the problem.'

'Not a rival clan! No way!'

'The elections, as you say, will soon be upon us. There are a few out there who do not *appreciate* everything our president has done for us over the last dozen years. They fear that the success of these talks will almost certainly culminate in another six-year term.'

'So, you think someone from our own side will try to take mac Nessa out?'

'I... sorry, *we* don't know. I have been asked by the Chair, who himself has been asked by the president himself, to ask you...'

'That's a lot of asking...'

'...off the record, to put together the president's security team. You can choose a couple of your best men, your own triad if you like.'

'Wait, you are not suggesting that this assassination will take place in Uisneach?'

'What better place? If the attempt takes place there, the blame for this can be shared around. The smokescreen would be impenetrable. There are greater ramifications, of course. If blame is attributed to Connachta, the war will recommence, and it will be another twenty-five years before we get to this stage again!'

Conall looked at mac Murchadhna and

examined the featureless topography of the man's face. There was more to this, but the senator, young though he was, had learned enough to suppress any random tick or twitch that might have suggested otherwise. It was of no consequence, in any case. An order was an order, Conall knew. There was no possibility of refusal. He and mac Murchadhna had simply performed a jig around the formalities.

'Why me?'

'Sorry?'

'Why me? Why not some other commander?'

'I have no idea. An indication, perhaps, of the great esteem in which the president holds you.'

Or an opportunity to rid himself of a thorn in his side, Conall thought. He knew his opinion of the current regime was common knowledge around the taverns of Emain Mhaca.

'That doesn't give me a lot of time. The truce is being signed in two days.'

'You leave today. And remember, commander,' mac Murchadna added, with renewed gravity, 'this is a clandestine operation. Between you and the men you choose to go with you.'

Conall stood up and saluted. The senator, caught off-guard, his face reddening, attempted to acknowledge the gesture and planted a right fist over his heart. In his confusion, he found himself doing so between a sitting and standing position.

Always in the act of shitting itself, Conall thought. That's a Tír Eoghan arsehole for you.

Finn liked Maggo. He didn't know why he did, but he did. Possibly it was the sense of peace that seemed to permeate from him every time he spoke. He never seemed to lose his temper. He had remarkable reserves of patience. He didn't judge. He was kind and generous; two qualities which were not valued currency in Ulidia. He would have liked to have thought that his father would have had these qualities if he had lived.

Ulidians, however, were traditionally very competitive, a genetic after-effect of the old clan networks that pervaded the land before the creation of the Ulidian state. Now, the ancient system of clans existed as a mere tokenism, a relic of a bygone era. Outside of festivals, when clans assembled under their heraldic banners; and politics, where senators paid lip service to it as a vehicle for advancement, no one claimed to care to what clan a fellow Ulidian belonged. Clans had amalgamated into counties which had then unified into a state. The idea was that Ulidians would compete not as one clan against another, but as one individual against another. Healthy, honourable competition would drive Ulidia forward, in business, sport, work and politics. A competitive edge was required for a state that spent a lot of its time at war with its neighbours.

Finn had never left Éireann's shores but Lorcan, his guardian, had told him that this meritocracy was the same all across the FCTS, a personal championship each citizen had with themselves to extract their fullest potential. In reality, of course, a family's wealth remained the key to success in life and the old clan network still existed.

Maggo had been raised beyond the pale of the Federation. The Druidic Order permitted Punic tourists, and those on long-term visas, their private modes of worship, but it forbade outright any *child of Éireann* to participate publicly, or privately, in a Christian service. No Ulidian had ever been known to convert to a faith that had spread, in two millennia, to cover a large proportion of the globe.

It was the Sixth Day, and so a day of rest. Every third week, Finn and his fellow cadets were permitted to spend the day with their families. The next day, the Seventh, meant the typical few hours spent burning incense and making offerings at the druidic temples. It was forbidden by law to miss more than three Seventh Days in a row.

'You should come along tomorrow, Maggo. We don't have a proper temple at the base, but we do have a ceremony of sorts. Crunniac offers a rabbit to Lugh, but my friend reckons he has a stash of them somewhere. He sacrifices more of them to his stomach than to the gods, Ferdia says. Bastard, eh? Oh sorry!'

'Why are you sorry?'

'Swearing and that. I swear my swearing's got worse over the last year and a half!' He laughed.

'No need to apologise, Finn. You know, we use language like that in the Union too, you know. And besides…'

'Yes?'

'An expletive is not the same when it's not in your native tongue.'

'I suppose not. So, will you come?'

'What makes you think I haven't already been?'

The two were having supper at an expensive eating house in the Palatial District of the old town. Steak, creamed potatoes and weak beer for Finn and a glass of apple juice for Maggo. It was Lorcan's treat and a way of apologising for being called back unexpectedly to the office.

'So, what else did Lorcan say?' Finn asked.

'Just that he would not be able to come to-night. He will see you later, probably around 22.00. He wants to sit up late and play a game…*Clans and Crowns*?'

'Clans and crowns? How old does he think I am?! Six summers!' Noticing Maggo's confusion, he added: 'It's a board game… I used…we used to play it together.'

'Your mother?'

Finn nodded. 'She's at the clearing stations. She's a vate.'

'Ah yes, like a nurse?'

'Yes. She looks after the wounded.'

'And you miss her, your mother...?

'...What else did Lorcan say?' Finn said, avoiding the question.

'Nothing more. All I know that is the entire Bardic Press has been extremely busy since the release of your president's speech.'

'Hmm...I wonder what's going on.'

'And your uncle called around this afternoon.'

'Oh, what did *he* want?' Finn grunted.

'Lorcan and the commander had a long talk in the study. Maybe twenty minutes or more. Then the commander left in one of those armoured chariots. Soon after, Lorcan gave me a few shillings and told me to meet you at the base and take you here for dinner.'

'You got a light, friend?

The request came from a bearded man in a flat cap, seated at the table next to them. His partner, who also had a scruffy beard, was holding a cigarette between two fingers bedecked with gold rings. They looked like brothers, possibly twins.

'I'm sorry, sir. I don't smoke,' Maggo replied.

'I wasn't asking you, Pune. I was asking the

boy.'

'He's not a Pune. He's from the Carthaginian Union. From Valletta,' Finn intervened, sharply.

'Valletta?' questioned the other beard. 'What's that? Some kind of ice-cream?'

Finn could feel his anger beginning to mount. He looked across at Maggo. His friend was smiling serenely.

'So, you have a light then, boy?' The first beard asked again. 'Or are you cadets not allowed to smoke?'

Finn made to stand but Maggo held him back. He was still in his cadet fatigues. This had sometimes led to Finn suffering abuse from drunks when on leave. There were always a few deadbeats, too scared to take on a full RBK, but quite happy to chance their arm with a second-year cadet. This time, though, Finn wasn't with Ferdia, Donall or others from his barrack. He was with a Christian pacifist who had never even raised his voice in anger, never mind a fist.

The two strangers looked like mercenaries, the type of hired muscle that collected on debts, shillings loaned out at exorbitant interest to desperate housewives who had run out of rations to feed their hungry children. Dark welts on both their faces were an indication that they didn't mind how they supplied their income. Or for whom.

But flat caps? Finn mused. Now where had he

seen flat caps recently?

'How about, Sencha', the first beard said, 'the Pune runs out and buys some matches for us? I mean, that'd be kind of him, wouldn't it?'

His partner began to laugh. A coarse, well-practiced, suggestive laugh designed to antagonise.

'How about I smash your bloody head in?!' Finn shouted, struggling to break himself free from Maggo's grip.

'How about you calm down, young mac Dara?' replied the first beard, looking around. The sound of Finn's raised voice had caused a few heads to turn. If the first flat cap wanted something, it wasn't attention. That was certain.

'How do you know my name?'

'Everyone knows the nephew of the great Conall mac Dara. You're a brave lad to talk to me like that, young Finn. Maybe one day you might make a brave soldier. His mother was right, eh, Bren?'

'What do you know about my mother?' Finn asked, taken aback, finally returning to his seat.

'Oh, Bren and me are very well acquainted with your mother. Isn't that so, Bren?'

'True enough, Senc.'

'How do you know her?'

'Well, we...sort of know her...in a professional capacity, you might say. We'll tell you all about it. But first, get rid of the pious Pune.'

'I told you not to call him that!'

'Fair enough,' said Sencha, pulling a box of matches out of his pocket and lighting his partner's cigarette. 'You don't wanna hear about your old ma...then...well...there's nothing else for it. Shames she's in trouble, though. Eh, Bren?'

'Absolutely, brother. Ah well. Time to go.' They both stood up.

'Wait, who are you? What trouble is she in?'

'Just a couple of old soldiers, your mother had the kindness to look after...at the clearing stations,' Bren said

'You were wounded?'

'Maybe.' Bren replied, sitting down. He leaned towards Finn. 'Your Ulidian bullets nip a bit. I got mine in the old leg.'

'What? You're Connachta?!' Finn whispered, in disbelief.

'Not another word. Get rid of the prayer mat.' Finn glanced at Maggo. 'No?... Fine.'

The two brothers made for the door. Finn looked anxiously at Maggo. Maggo, in return, nodded politely.

'Wait... my friend has agreed...to wait outside. Just for five minutes. That's ok, Maggo, isn't it?'

'Of course, Finn. I'll be at the window of the bookshop across the street.'

Maggo got up to leave. He had just reached

the door when he heard one of the men call after him: 'Happy reading!' He looked back and noticed Finn had joined them at their table.

Outside it was raining. It was still light, but the streets were quiet. Maggo put up what the Celts called a *skyshield* and crossed the road to the bookshop. Even a simple thing as an umbrella had the menace of the battlefield, as if you had to defend yourself from something as innocent as rain. He looked at some of the books in the shop window, mostly sensationalist paperbacks with some colossal, burly male hero grinning out from the covers, weapon in hand, explosions detonating behind him. Just then, at that moment, Maggo missed his homeland. He missed his mother and uncle. He yearned for the simple reciprocation of a watering can and an olive tree, the smell of salt in the breeze, the friendly wave of a passer-by.

A little while later he looked at his timepiece. A quarter of an hour had passed and still his young friend was nowhere to be seen. He crossed the road and re-entered the restaurant.

His table and that of the Connachta were empty. Their dishes had been removed. The smouldering embers of a cigarette in an ashtray was the only thing to suggest that the Connachta and Finn had ever been there.

9

Pritchard was correct. My family did live nearby. I spent some time with them, catching up with gossip. My mother fussed and read out obituaries of people I either couldn't remember, or more likely, had never known. My dad shook my hand upon arrival, a handshake, I had noticed, that had lost a little bit more of its once intense vitality. They were both getting old. My mother was finding it more and more difficult to attend to her hydrangea; my father's back was giving him issues. Years of teaching, of standing upright in front of a class of schoolchildren had placed a strain there.

They had both been loving parents, however. I had no complaints there. As usual, after a few glasses of wine, the old, black and white photographs were once more exhibited. The oldest one of me was as a two-year-old, a few days after my adoption.

I was too young to have any memory of my first day in my new home. The picture showed me, snivelling on the doorstep, reluctantly holding the hand of my new mother, dressed in a hooded raincoat. I am told it was red.

It was 1952. Lucky for me, two years after I was born, the *Adoption of Children Act* had been amended in Northern Ireland to provide the basic foundations of an adoption service here. This was at a time when Britain, as a whole, had witnessed huge social and attitudinal changes regarding the notion of the nuclear family unit. My stepparents, who couldn't have their own children, had got on board from the very start. When the time came to tell me I was adopted I was seven years old.

I remembered the day well. My father had suddenly produced a book that he had borrowed, he said, from the public library. It was heavy, leather-bound and smelled like the shoeboxes in which I kept my little museum of hidden artifacts I used to gather from our garden while pretending to be an archaeologist.

He asked me to sit on the sofa opposite, opened the book at a predetermined page and began reading me a story.

My father had known of my bizarre, childish preoccupation with Celtic mythology.

Back then, I might have played cowboys and Indians with the local children but, unbeknownst to them, I was rewriting those engagements in my mind, exchanging them for long-forgotten battles: Ulster versus Connacht, Connacht versus Leinster, Munster versus Meath. For example, if I were Setanta or Conall Cernach, my seven-year-old playmates shared the unenviable task of being their sworn enemies, Ferdia or Cet Mac Magach. My companions knew nothing of this, of course. To them, I was either a cop or a robber, one football team or the other, the one who had to hide or the one who had to seek. It was of no importance. I would insinuate my own narrative into whatever pastime we had, layering a new, silent commentary over the games we played.

And now, when I should have been doing my homework, I was staring across at the flushed face of my father.

Ferdia and Cú Chulainn had been great friends, the story went. They had trained together as warriors under the fierce warrior, Queen Scathach of Alba. Ferdia was from Connacht and Cú Chulainn from Ulster. In spite of this, they had a close, unbreakable bond, unusual in those times for men from rival provinces.

Later, Connacht and Ulster went to war. Queen Maeve of Connacht demanded that Ferdia bring the conflict to an end by defeating the legendary Cú Chulainn in single combat. When Ferdia refused, the queen offered him tremendous riches and the hand of her beautiful daughter, Finnabair. Still, Ferdia refused. It was a question of honour, pride and, most of all, friendship, Ferdia said.

The queen, therefore, changed tact. She bade the warriors in her court to spread the false rumour that Cú Chulainn had been insulting his former ally. When Ferdia heard this, he was incensed and finally agreed to fight his comrade.

When they at last met in battle, it is said they fought with spears, darts and shields for several days. However, each night, exhausted, they would renew their friendship around a shared fire, healing each other's wounds with balms and ointments. It was only after the third day when Cú Chulainn gained the upper hand. He used his secret weapon, a *gae bolga*, a specially barbed spear, against his old friend.

With Ferdia dying in his arms, Cú Chulainn wept bitterly at what he had been forced to do.

'You see, son,' my father added. 'They were foster brothers as well as close friends.'

Who knows what words my dad actually employed as he narrated this story? He was telling it, simply, nervously no doubt, to a seven-year-old, unaware of the significance of the revelation that his father was about to make.

Little did my father know that I already knew the story or that he had also forgotten to follow the words on the page as he read. Aware of my fervour for these ancient tales, he had memorised the story, in preparation for the day, that day, when he would finally break the news to me that I was adopted. My mother, I imagine, must have been listening from behind the kitchen door. She had stopped singing, the way she always did, when she washed the dishes.

The large leather book, as it transpired, was one of the bibles we always kept at home. My father had been careful to hide its pages from view as he read. I remembered the cover and discovered it on a bookshelf a few days later.

But the story had mattered to me. It helped me deal with the anguish of the next few months. At first, it was my puerile identification with my hero Cú Chulainn. It made me feel heroic to compare myself to him. Years later, it was the gentle, faltering voice of my father, trying to remember the words of a story that he had learned by heart, as if his own heart had depended on it.

After the visit to my parents I left for Armagh and booked myself into a local hotel. It had been Rose's favourite, the same lodgings where we had stayed a few times in our early years of marriage, when work necessitated that I go on field trips to take soil samples around Navan Fort, or waste valuable summer light, poring over huge volumes of research in the Robinson Library.

One afternoon, I decided to go for a walk around an area known locally as *The Mall*, just east of the town centre. It was an expanse of grass, an oval for cricket in summer, but that had once been used, in pre-Georgian times, for horse-racing, bullbaiting and cockfighting. Later, it was transformed, by Armagh's great benefactor, Archbishop Richard Robinson, into an elegant, promenading circuit, flanked on either side by the remnants of Armagh's old gaol and its still active courthouse. Crime and punishment neatly laid out, I thought, on either side of an centuries old, architectural draft.

I was rehearsing a speech I had to deliver to the *Friends of Macha*, shivering in my winter coat, observing the lilting patterns the dead leaves made, buoyed up momentarily by the wind across mid-wicket, before being scattered ignominiously to square leg. I had only another day to get the speech right and I preferred to move as I did so, hoping that the motion of my feet would add to the cadence of my words.

It was too cold, however, and so I took shelter, at least for a while, in a nearby cafe. I ordered a cappuccino, took out a newspaper and attempted the daily cryptic crossword. I was feeling tired as I hadn't slept well the previous night.

I had had a nightmare about the voice. In my dream I was at home. The telephone had rung, and I had picked up as before. The words of the voice had begun, as they always did, but then suddenly, they had morphed, changing accent and tone, into the voice of my dead wife. It was an irritable, exasperated, nagging voice, the meaning of which was lost, scattered to the four winds

It had been months since I had last dreamt of Rose. In the years after her death, she had, more or less, taken up a permanent residency in my head. And now, here she was, reduced to a senseless gibberish on a telephone. All I knew was she had joined forces with the voice, had united her cause with its own. Rose and the voice were now one and the same. Soon the letters of the puzzle I was doing became scrambled, individualised, unrelated to the words they were meant to serve, as incoherent as the speech I had been trying to prepare. I gave up, closed my eyes, and surrendered to my thoughts.

I lost Rose on Valentine's Day, 1981. Fate, at least, has a sense of humour. Millions of women received roses from the men in their lives that day and I lost the only one that had ever meant anything to me. It was six weeks after my night with Eva; five weeks after I had confessed to her what I had done.

Had I been a fool to ruin my last weeks with Rose by letting her know of my New Year's indiscretion? Of course, I couldn't have predicted what would soon transpire, but ever since I have sought an answer to that question. Undoubtedly, the long-term lothario would categorically state. Probably, the part-time philanderer would sheepishly add. But the one-time transgressor? The once in a lifetime, guilt-ridden, self-loathing, morning-after coward who wallows in his own misery and tittle-tattles all, not for the benefit of his loved one, but simply because he cannot bear his own torment?

I was the coward, of course. I was more afraid of myself than Rose. I wept, begged forgiveness, bartered my apology with a dowry of never-to-be-broken pledges, flagellated myself, pulled my hair out, kissed her feet, everything I could to prevent her from leaving. In the back of my mind, although I was genuinely remorseful, terribly so, I couldn't shake the feeling that I was approaching the scene with the arithmetic precision of the catchall confessional. I wanted my slate wiped clean, a finger-snap forgiveness. Yes, I knew it would take time. I wasn't that naive. And yet, I wanted the momentum of that first domino to lean backwards into the second and for it to topple the third in its turn and set in motion an inevitable momentum that would reset both our lives at some stage in the not-too-distant future.

Valentine's Day 1981 was that not-too-distant future. The preceding weeks had been a living hell. Rose had walked out and gone back to her parents. They welcomed her, as I expected, with open arms and told her the things that she had actually wanted to hear. I was a pig, a monster, a fraud, a charlatan and a liar. They would have used other words, but nothing vulgar or uncouth. In all the years I had known them, I had never heard them swear, this loving church-going couple who I knew would have forgiven me long before their daughter ever would. They had simply spoken the words that they knew their daughter wanted to hear.

They even shook my hand at Rose's funeral. Pritchard patted me on the shoulder after her coffin had been laid to rest. Surridge gave me a bear hug. My students had bought me a bouquet of flowers. My father and mother later invited me to spend some time with them at home. It compounded my misery, these acts of unmerited sympathy, left me to flail wildly at a strawman in the weeks that followed, punch at the air, howl at the moon. I had no one to blame but myself. Surrounded by this much kindness there was nowhere left for my pain to go but within.

Her death itself, for those who didn't know her, was just another statistic of those times, an anonymous glyph on a cenotaph wall, just another name in the roll call of the dead. And yet, it wasn't that either.

It was Sunday and she had been to church with her parents and her younger brother, Steven. He, at least, had the good sense to shun me at the funeral, my offered hand frozen in the air between us, the hand of a leper reaching up from the pit of a well. They had just eaten lunch together, the five of them including Steven's girlfriend, and then Rose had suddenly decided she wanted to take a quick jaunt into Belfast to catch up with one of her girlfriends. Her parents lived in Lisburn, so she wouldn't be long, just there and back, a cup of coffee with Ruth in between and, by the way, could she borrow her dad's car?

I had often wondered what possessed her to make that journey that particular afternoon. I used to study the route so many times on blown-up maps of the city and still I couldn't work out how she ended up where she did. Ruth lived off the lower Lisburn Road; Rose and I off the Donegall Road. A right turn at the roundabout at Kennedy Way onto the Outer Ring would have considerably shortened her route, bringing her directly to Ruth's house. Why on earth had she decided to stay on the M1?

And then it struck me. By continuing on the motorway, she could leave it at a later junction and then double back, approaching the Lisburn Road from the City Centre end. That particular junction would have led her onto Donegall Road and right past our front door if she had wanted.

I am not saying that she was thinking of paying me a visit, that she had noticed the date on the calendar, circled it in red, and pre-planned some sort of Valentine's reconciliation. The accident occurred when she had already passed the turn off for our street. But perhaps she had been overcome by the impulse to drive past our house, had wanted to see the car we had bought together parked outside, and if it hadn't been there, would have wondered where I had gone? And what of me? Had I been indoors watching mindless television or sleeping off the dregs of the night before? If so, had I raised myself from the sofa, pulled across the curtains to peer outside, shielded my weary eyes from the sun, could I have waved at her a final goodbye?

Or had she simply fancied a bit of shopping in town? Quite possibly, I had not even been an afterthought in those last hours? Perhaps she had wished to buy a new party dress? She and Ruth could have conspired to spend Valentine's night together, chinking wine glasses in some upmarket bar, offering each other the solidarity of their gender, bemoaning the existence of all men. Then maybe later, tipsy on chardonnay, they might have changed their minds...A simple phone call to her parents would have arranged everything if that were what she had wanted. Her father was retired and wouldn't have needed his car next morning.

And so, it went on. I switched from one scenario to the other during my waking hours, invented others while I slept, replayed the sequences over and over in my head, haunted not by the ghost of my Rose but by the potentiality of her not having died.

I have said her death was an accident. In a way, it was. And yet, I fundamentally believe that if it hadn't been for the troubles, Rose would still be with me today.

A child of the troubles is a troubled child. Their very childhood troubles them. They impersonate. They emulate. They imitate the adults around them. They have to accommodate what it means to be a child with what it means not to be a child. One moment they are playing with toys, the next moment they are playing with fire. First, they are catapulting stones at greenhouses, next they are lobbing rocks at army patrols. Nightly rioting requires daily practice, however.

The large rock that shattered the windscreen of the *Austin Allegro* Rose was driving was a shot in the dark, a once in a million bullseye, an asteroid landing right on the Whitehouse lawn. There was no intention, I am convinced, to cause death. The target in question was a derelict warehouse directly across the road from where the group of children were standing. Somebody, an older child no doubt, had had the hair-brained idea to launch rocks and bricks over the top of the traffic, a game of dare that had quickly got out of control. The weaker arm of a younger boy or the tired arm of his older friend had been all that was required for the catastrophe to happen.

Rose would have been unfamiliar with the controls of her father's car and momentarily unsighted, her instinct would have been to brake and steer the car blindly into the opposite direction from which the object had been hurled. Before she would have even had time to correct the steering wheel, she would have felt the fatal impact of the ten-tonne articulated lorry coming straight towards her.

She hadn't been wearing a seat belt.

They say that when you crash at thirty miles per hour you possess the weight of a baby elephant. Neither vehicle had been travelling beyond the speed limit. The driver of the lorry, from his higher vantage point, had been spared the horrendous moment when Rose's head smashed through the already damaged windscreen, a detonation of broken glass shattering into smithereens over the crumpled bumper of her car, leaving it a snarling mess with all the consistency of aluminium foil.

It wasn't until two years later, 1983, that

the wearing of front seat belts became compulsory in the UK. By law, they had to be fitted into all motor vehicles from 1967 onwards. A sixteen-year discrepancy, therefore, between the obligation of the motorist and that of the manufacturer. Sixteen years where you could roll the dice and take your chances. Rose unbelievably hadn't been wearing hers. I had never known her not to.

The infidelity six weeks before, the trip to Belfast on that never-to-be-forgotten Sunday, at one exact time and on one specific route; the troubles, the children, the rock, the warehouse, the seat-belt and the lorry. Everything had aligned, a horoscope of interplanetary bodies in perfect synchronicity for one woman, among billions of others on planet Earth, to meet her untimely end.

'It must be tough?

I looked up. A curly-haired waiter, in a green apron and a Red Sox baseball cap, was smiling at me, shaking his head.

'Sorry?'

'Your puzzle? Must be tough.' He leaned over for a closer look. 'Ah, cryptic. Sure now, aren't they the worst? You must be a clever fella?'

'Not so much.' I replied

'And modest too... Would ya like another one?'

He had a cheery, Dublin accent. Its conviviality probably helped him sell more coffee.

'No thanks,' I replied, getting up. 'If I have any more, I'll not sleep tonight.'

'No problem, sir. Coffee's not worth losing sleep over!'

When I got back to the hotel, the receptionist stopped me just as I was about to enter the lift. She was a woman in her thirties, carrying a clipboard. Her badge said 'Orlagh'.

'Oh, Mr Summer? Sorry, sir. A couple of gentlemen were here to see you. You only just missed them.'

'To see me?' I said, genuinely surprised. 'Did they say what they wanted?'

She blushed slightly. 'They were from the police, sir.'

'The police?'

Orlagh lowered her head. 'They wondered if you wouldn't mind calling down to the station. At your earliest convenience, they said.'

'Did they give any names?'

'One of them did,' she glanced at her clipboard. 'A Detective Sergeant Conway.'

An hour later I was staring at the pale green walls of an interview room at Armagh Police Station. There wasn't much else to occupy my senses as I waited for DS Conway. One laminate wooden-effect table, two plastic chairs and a small window. On entering the room, I had been told to sit on the chair to the right, furthest from the door. I had read enough crime fiction to realise why.

DS Conway entered the room, assessed me briefly and sat down to my left. He was in his late thirties or early forties, slightly overweight, had short, salt and pepper hair and gave off an unfortunate mix of Brylcreem and carbolic soap. He had a buff-coloured file in his hand.

'You fancy a cup of tea, Mr Summer?'

'No, I'm fine, thanks.'

'So, Mr Summer. Is this your first time in a police station?'

'Err...yes.'

'Look, there shouldn't be anything to worry about,' he said, opening the file.

'Shouldn't be?'

'You're a professor at Queen's, yes? he asked, ignoring me.

'Yes. Celtic and Irish Studies.'

'And your wife, Rose Summer passed away in...in February 1981,' he continued, reading from a sheet.

'Err...yes,' I replied, wondering where the sergeant was heading with all this.

'Tell me, Mr Summer. Why exactly are you in Armagh?'

'I am giving a lecture at the Navan Centre tomorrow. Halloween night.'

'A lecture?'

'Yes, work-related. A colleague asked me to take his place...'

'...Your colleague's name?

'Dr. Jeremy Pritchard.'

'Dr. Jeremy Pritchard? Dr Pritchard asked you to come here?'

'Yes. Is that relevant?'

'Possibly. You never know,' he removed a spiral-bound notepad from his jacket pocket, extricated a small pen from its top coil and commenced to jot something down.

'But you came early?' he continued.

'Well, I fancied a bit of a break. I know Armagh well. I used to come here quite a bit with...'

'...With?'

'With...Rose, my wife. Sometimes we would meet up with family and friends.'

'Friends?

'Yes.'

'Female acquaintances, by any chance, among these friends?

'Some, yes.'

'Hmm...' He made another note.

'Look Sergeant, I don't wish to be rude, but why exactly am I here?'

'We'll get to that, Mr Summer... Are you sure you don't want a cup of tea? Coffee?'

'No, thank you.'

'A glass of water?'

'No.' I don't know why I had refused his offer.

My mouth was dry, and I felt a sharp pain in my temple.

'You never remarried, Mr Summer?' he began again.

'No.'

'But you've had relationships since...since the death of your wife?'

'Look!' I said, losing my temper. 'What the hell is this?'

'This is an interview, Mr Summer! he exclaimed, leaning towards me. 'I am very sorry if these questions bother you! There is a reason for them, after all!'

There was a vague smell of peppermint on his breath. That in addition to the Brylcreem, the soap and the lack of air was beginning to make me feel quite nauseous. It was like having cabin fever and I needed to get out on deck.

'Do you mind if we open the window?' I asked

DS Conway smirked, before answering. 'Yes, of course.' He rose and unlatched the window. A fresh draught of air invaded the room.

'So, you have had relationships since your wife?

'Yes, of course.'

'And your students?'

'What about them?'

'Ever had relationships with any of them?'

'Absolutely not! No way!'

'Nothing wrong with it, Mr Summer. Not illegal, bit unprofessional, mind."

'No! Never! Not me!'

'Ok, alright…' he gestured defensively with his hands. 'Now then, Mr Summer,' he said, reaching a conclusion. 'You're here today to answer a few informal questions'

'Anything I do to help, officer.'

'Let's hope so. It's a cold case. Missing persons. The lady in question went AWOL around the end of August. You don't happen to know what you were up to around that period back in 1981?'

'No… no.'

'No, I wouldn't think so. She was a foreign national, it seems, a member of the European Economic Community as it was then. French.'

'French?'

'Yes, Mr Summer. French. Brittany, if you must know.

'Err…no… I don't think so.'

'No? That's a shame. I have got a picture of her, though. Would you mind having a look?'

'No, that's fine.'

DS Conway took a photograph from the file and passed it to me.

'Her name's Eva Beaufort. A little bird tells me, Mr Summer, you once rang in the New Year with her?'

10

Conall hadn't been to Uisneach for years. Like most Ulidians he had visited several times as a child. The last time had also been during Beltane, the annual fire festival which marked the first day of the Celtic summer, a mid-point between the spring equinox and the summer solstice. A time of purification, the festival historically ushered in a period when animals moved to new pastures, when hopes were high of successful harvests.

According to tradition, every hearth+ in Éireann was extinguished in eager anticipation of the new flame from Uisneach's fire. A shroud of darkness descended across the island during the celebration. When the sacred fire of Uisneach was lit, it was passed via a relay of torches to every sacred hill on the island, creating a dizzying network of fires all over the land. The best place to view this panoramic display was from the heights of the Hill of Uisneach. Ancient kings, and now modern political elites, stood and proudly surveyed the journey of the Uisneach fire like concentric ripples emanating from a revered source, to every point in the compass.

The advent of electricity in the last decades had led to the newer practice of every home in the four nations switching out their lights in the hope of imitating an effect similar to that of their ancestors. Mac Nessa, not one to miss an opportunity, had promised that one day, not too far distant, one of his successors would be transported in a new flying machine over the island and witness the fiery spectacle in the same way as the gods themselves do, and had done, since time immemorial. These machines, mac Nessa had promised, would soon make their way across the Atlantic from the Western Continental Alliance. Economic links were currently being forged with the new superpower and Ulidia would be the first to reap the benefits. If it were true, Conall did not envy the future generations of RBK who would pilot them. It seemed more natural for him to assume that they would no doubt be utilised in some future war. Most new technology was.

Conall shook his head. In the distance, he could see the Hill. A helix of granite steps, ascending upwards, wrapped itself around its sides and served to elongate the torchlit procession of the Druidic Order which would soon snake its slow path to the summit on the early morning of Beltane. His sister Aoife, and their parents, had had to make do with the bottom of the Hill, of course. And yet, it remained one of his earliest and happiest memories, his first boyhood trip to Uisneach, hoisted upon his father's shoulders, stretching out his little hands toward the huge central fire, up above in the distance. His father had died a few summers later.

'Cat got your tongue, mac Dara?'

This was typical of Bradán mac Neill, Conall thought. His nickname was 'silver tongue' and, by extension, everyone who paused slightly for thought in his company, was 'as dumb as a dolmen' in comparison to the effortless effluence that discharged from his mouth every time he spoke. For someone who enjoyed the sound of his own voice so much, he had the thinnest lips Conall had ever seen. Add to this a pair of non-existent eyebrows and you were left with a face dominated by two wide blue eyes above a drinker's nose. He was also underweight, balding and told terrible jokes.

'I was just wondering why they call it the 'Cat Stone', mac Neill.'

'Well, there's the cat, mac Dara,' he replied, pointing at a portion of the stone, 'and there's the mouse. Plain as the nose on your face!'

Conall looked away, stifling a laugh. 'And which one am I, mac Neill?'

'Depends on whose company you're in.'

'At the moment?'

'Now? Mouse, obviously.'

'Obviously.'

Ail na Míreann, the 'stone of divisions', was the central standing stone in a ring of stones that formed just one of the stone circles that dominated the landscape of not only Uisneach but the entire Mhí Protectorate. This particular circle had a spiritual significance, however. Ail na Muireann was the bedrock upon which all four of Éireann's lands hoped, one day, to herald a new period of peace. Engraved deeply upon the side of the rock was the Trinity Knot, the emblem of the Druidic Order, a single incision that looped around to form a triangular shape and which represented each of its three branches of power.

Conall and mac Neill were both standing on a walkway, a little distance away from the consecrated earth upon which the thirty-tonne boulder had been fixed and under which Ériu, the goddess of the Earth, was also supposed to be buried. It was, therefore, no surprise that it was the location specially designated for the signing of the upcoming armistice between Ulidia and Connachta.

'Funny, isn't it?' mac Neill continued.

'What is?'

'The Cat Stone. They say politics is a game of cat and mouse, after all.'

'I met one of those cats back in Emain Mhaca.'

'Oh?'

'Mac Murchadha.'

'Now that one...' mac Neill said, thought-fully, 'that one will be a tiger one day.'

'If you say so.'

The implication, Conall thought, was that mac Neill was already a tiger. Conall looked across again at the Hill. It took three hundred and thirty-three steps to wind your way to the plateau at the top, a long back-aching ascent that was not for the very young, or very old.

You could scale the same heights in half the time if you took a more direct course. But there was a lesson being taught to all those who chose to scale the steps the long way. It was like life. You had to learn to circumnavigate, tiptoe around the snares and pits left out for you by your rivals. In one sense, mac Neill must have needed the claws of a tiger to scratch and scrape his path to the inner circle of Ulidian power. In another sense, after mac Murchadha, mac Neill was just another layer of bureaucracy that Conall had to cut through to get to where he needed to be just to do his job.

'Where's mac Nessa now?' he asked.

'The President is the guest of Arch Druid mac Nuadat at the Roundhouse.'

'Ó'Flaithearta, Cuilennáin and Ó'Cosrach?'

'The Connachta President and his staff have also taken up residency there...the opposite wing of the House.'

'I bet.'

'Mhumhain and Laighean will arrive tonight.'

'You do realise this is complete madness. All four leaders and the Arch Druid together in one place? It's crazy. Folly. It's never been done before. I know a dozen men in my unit alone with good enough arms. Any one of them could launch a grenade and blow the whole lot of them to the otherworld!'

'No one else is allowed on the summit of the Hill for Beltane. You know that. They'll only be altogether, in range if you like, for five minutes. Right here,' mac Neill gestured towards the boulder in front of them. 'Now, who in their right mind would risk damaging the stone?'

'You read too many novels, mac Neill! It's not the stone I am worried about!'

'You're worried about the DG?'

'For one thing, yes. The Druidic Guard may be the only folk in the entire Protectorate permitted to use arms, but they haven't fired a shot in anger for centuries! Which brings me to another point.'

'Yes?'

'Your speech. How in Lugh's name are the DG going to patrol an tSionainn and the towns and villages either side of the river? Even if Ulidia and Connachta maintain the ceasefire, who's upholding law and order in the area? The population there has been living in a war zone for a quarter of a century. There's no real economy left to speak of; its entire infrastructure has collapsed and there's more shells in the river than fish!'

'Ha! 'Shells'. Very good, mac Dara.'

'I was being serious, mac Neill.'

'Well, then, let's be serious. You're right, commander, the DG, as you know it, cannot administer to the region. That is true.'

'What do you mean? 'As you know it?''

'Do you really think that all of this has not already been considered, thrashed out, analysed at the highest levels? Do you think the president's announcement was just some 'spur of the moment' declaration? Mac Dara, that speech was the culmination of months and months of clandestine negotiations between the two sides. I wrote the speech, of course, but individuals of greater import than I were responsible for ironing out all the details of the agreement, picking apart every single bone of contention, reshaping and making palatable the grey areas where discord was most obvious.'

'And the timing suits mac Nessa, of course.'

'Grow up, commander! The timing suits mac Nessa. It also suits Ó'Flaithearta. Do you really think he's popular either? In his own senate?'

'What about an tSionainn?'

'Control over the disputed territories will eventually be overseen by a governing Assembly of Representatives from both Ulidia and Connachta. The people will vote democratically for these Representatives and they in turn will oversee civil and cultural rights, demilitarisation, justice, the Guards and so on. Eventually, there will be elections that will elect a dual leadership, one from each side, probably based on the old Punic *sufet* model.'

'You're joking?'

'Over the Assembly,' mac Neill continued, ignoring the interruption, 'there will be a 'Council of an tSionainn' that will meet regularly to ensure the peace holds. On that Council, one delegate each from the four lands and the Mhí Protectorate will sit.'

'So that's why Mhumhain and Laighean are involved.'

'Precisely.'

'And the DG?'

'During the transitional phase, the DG will be supplemented by troops from the four lands. Picture it like this. An tSionainn will be divided into five areas of administration: a central area under the Druidic Council and four others under the different regions. A sort of mini-Éireann...'

'...Oh, because that has worked out so well for us in the past!'

'The past will soon be the future, mac Dara. The two areas with greater Ulidian and Connachta population densities, the Iron Mountains and Loch Rí, will be administered by their own regional troops, supported by the DG. The rest will be looked after by a mixture of Mhumhain and Laighean forces, again supplemented by the DG. Only the DG will be militarized.'

'Say again?' Conall asked, incredulously.

'Trust needs to be built up, Commander. That will take time. It's only temporary, after all. At the moment, the peoples of an tSionainn are economically and psychologically exhausted. The only guns they will countenance, if any, will be held by the Druidic Guard.'

'There's no way the DG has enough weaponry to patrol the whole line, from the mountains to the lough.'

'They will have. They already have.'

'What?'

'They have been given them.'

'Given them?'

'Yes. From Ulidia and Connachta, mostly. On loan. From the arms that have already been decommissioned.'

'So, we just trust the Druidic Council in all this?!' Conall exclaimed, his temper rising.

Mac Neill paused briefly, as if to reassess Conall. 'Are you aware of any reason why we shouldn't trust the Council, commander?' Conall didn't reply. 'Anyway, the Federation is in agreement with it all. They even volunteered to send a peace-keeping force of their own...'

'…I bet they bloody did!'

'It's either this way, or not at all, mac Dara? Can you think of anything better?'

Of course, he couldn't. But Conall still didn't like it. A lot was happening, and it was happening very quickly. And behind closed doors. Arbitrarily handing over weapons to another military force, even if it was the DG, didn't sit well with him. It whiffed too much of surrender. He thought suddenly of his sister.

'What about the clearing stations?' he asked

'All being closed down once the last casualties are brought back to their respective regions.'

At least something good was coming out of this. Aoife, his sister, would soon be back home. Finn would have a mother again and he'd be out of the clutches of Lorcan mac Róich.

'So, are you ready?'

'Ready?'

'To meet mac Nessa. He wants an audience. In a few hours if you don't mind. That will give you enough time to piece together a plan of action for tomorrow…And mac Dara?'

'What?'

'He's been looking forward to finally getting to meet you.'

Although it might have been the first time Finn had travelled in a hospital chariot, or chariot of any kind for that matter, the distinct odour of ethanol was not unfamiliar to him. The pungent smell of disinfectant had always been a welcome mnemonic. It was within this cloud of antiseptic that Finn's mother would register her return from the clearing stations, the perfume her young son inhaled off her vate's uniform every time she picked him up and hugged him to her chest. It was a pure, clean smell which could decontaminate a room. It was strange, he thought, how associations can so quickly change.

After leaving the city, the sound of other traffic had gradually abated, leaving only the spluttering rattle of the chariot's engine. The rocky movement of its wheels juddered Finn uncomfortably, as he shifted on the hard, wooden bench at the back of the chariot. He braced his spine against the walls, and jammed his heels against the floor, stiffening his legs to prevent himself from toppling forward as he worked his body against the momentum of the vehicle.

His wrists and feet had been bound with leather strips, his mouth with a bandage. The hessian bag over his head was beginning to cling with perspiration against his forehead while the constant jolting of the chariot was weakening his bladder. He took shallow breaths and tried to remain calm.

He had been a fool, of course. It had taken all

of twenty minutes for the flat-capped brothers to provide him with the sort of tale to which any young cadet would eagerly respond, the kind of blind, high-flown yarn that most boys his age wouldn't have been able to resist.

It had gone something like this. A mother befriended by two enemy combatants; first, their wounded bodies are discovered by accident in no man's land; next, against protocol, the mother overcomes her partiality and heals the two injured soldiers; they, on receipt of this act of charity, reflect on their misdeeds and vow to change their ways; to this end, the Connachta swear an oath to always protect the mother; then, ironically, the heroic vate is assailed by borderland brigands, desperately in need of morphine; on finding nothing, they then kidnap the woman and demand a ransom; the ransom cannot be met, however, and so the flat caps search an tSionnain in vain for the kidnappers; unable to locate them, laden with guilt, the brothers next travel to Ulidia, home of their former enemy, risking their lives, to seek out the nephew of the famous Conall mac Dara, to seek his aid in locating the mother. And so on...

The entire spiel was ludicrous, embarrassingly so. No one in their right mind could be duped by such obvious drivel, spoofed by such apparent subterfuge, and yet Finn had allowed himself to be taken in. What the flat caps had known, and what he had failed to realise, was that his willing submission to the narrative was not completely a result of a son's concern for his mother. It was also to do with a young boy, a young *boy's* desire to prove himself a man, to hare off unthinkingly into an unknown adventure, to prove himself as great a boy as Setanta had once been when he had picked up his famous hurl and rammed a *sliotar* down the throat of Culann's hound, thus gaining the epithet, Cú Chulainn, Hound of Culann.

The flat caps were grown men. They were from Connachta. Yet they too had been thirteen summers old. They knew the exact pressure points over which to exert the subtlest of prods and trigger the reaction they wanted. They had also been, he had remembered too late, the same two flat caps that had joined him in feeding the ducks on Loughnashade Lake a few days before.

But what did they want and why had they kidnapped him?

It was also when they had reached open country that Finn realised that he was not alone. It had taken a while for his own train of thought to stop at the various stations of fear, self-pity, self-loathing and anger and to refocus then on the environment around him. There was definitely someone else in the chariot, a presence lying a few feet away from him, possibly in worse shape than he was.

He had heard its muffled groans and the anguish of its fruitless attempts to free itself. The body, Finn instinctively knew, was that of a badly beaten man, or an older man, or possibly both. It couldn't maintain the struggle against its makeshift manacles for very long and the futile attempt to liberate itself was always ensued by a period of strained and heavy breathing. Finn wondered how this other victim was connected to his own plight. Perhaps the brothers had contrived a sort of kidnapping service from the back of their hospital chariot, extracting healthy bodies from the streets of major towns and cities, and then rendering them injured and immobile; a mock, medical practice that operated exactly in reverse, under the guise of the Triple Spiral, the logo of the Vatic Medical Order. The logo had been the last thing Finn had seen on the side of the chariot before he had been blindfolded and bundled inside.

From the brothers, up front, he had heard nothing. He couldn't even be sure it was they who were driving. All he could say for certain was that he, and his companion, were in an emergency hospital chariot and, as a result, would not be stopped by border patrol units, if indeed they were heading for the Ulidian clearing stations near an tSionainn where Finn prayed his mother was waiting for him.

By the time Maggo arrived back home, it had already gone past 23.30. It wasn't really that safe for someone like himself to be out on the streets of the capital any longer than that, especially on a Sixth Day. His enquiries of the staff at the eating house had yielded nothing. It wasn't until he had offered the surly proprietor his work credentials, signed off by the Bardic Press, that he had been able to ascertain the obvious fact that Finn and the two bearded gentlemen had departed the premises a quarter of an hour or so after he himself had done so. He, and none of his staff, had ever seen the men before and no one had noticed where they had gone. Maggo had wandered the old town aimlessly after that, every corner of the Third and the Presidential Gardens had been investigated. He had kept to the shadows, avoiding the ethanol street lamps for fear of encountering, at best, a city guard, or at worst, a party of rabble-rousing locals, drunk on cider, looking for someone to fight now that peace had finally arrived.

The hallway of Lorcan mac Róich's residence echoed to the sound of Maggo's sandals as he entered. Maggo searched every room in the house, at least every unlocked room, but knew in his heart it was a fruitless task. Lorcan had not returned from the Bardic Press, in spite of his promise to Finn. Unwashed dishes in the kitchen basin had proven his patron, at least, had eaten.

But where had Finn gone? And why had he not left a message with him, his supposed friend, about where he was going? Perhaps the answer was simple, a voice inside whispered. Finn wasn't his friend. He was just a curious boy who one day wanted to travel the world and who had used him merely to glean stories of fanciful, foreign shores. He had been nothing more than a tour guide for the lad, filling his head with sunny anecdotes from beyond the Federation. He had noted the look the boy had given him in the tavern, torn, it seemed, between loyalty to him, a temporary migrant, and to the mother he adored. They might have been from Connachta, the two strangers, but at least they were from Éireann, the voice continued. How could a man of peace possibly have anything in common with a boy brought up in war?

Maggo remembered his meditative practice and pushed these doubts to the side. They weren't going to help him now. He had to be rational, think critically. Lorcan was still at the BP. He had rushed off there after having spoken at length to Conall mac Dara. Had Conall passed on some important information to him? Not likely. The two didn't seem to like one another. And yet, why had Conall visited?

Perhaps, if Lorcan did not return, he could

go to the BP first thing in the morning and seek out his employer. But why hadn't he gone there straight away? The answer was simple. He hadn't thought of it! No, that wasn't true either. Maggo had thought of it, but he had wished to resolve the problem himself, a problem that he had helped to create, after all. If he could find Finn himself, perhaps Lorcan would never have needed to discover that the boy had gone missing.

Could he go to the Bardic Press now? No, it was far too late. There was a curfew of 23.00 on all foreign nationals and he had already been at risk of breaking it once tonight. Could he send a message? No again. Outside of Finn, Conall, Lorcan's housekeeper and the staff of the Ulidian Shield, he had failed to make a single other acquaintance in his six months in Ulidia. There was no one to pass on such a message. The best thing he could do was wait for Lorcan to return. He would sit up all night and be prepared. Perhaps the two of them could then make plans? But plans to do what?

The brothers had mentioned Aoife, the boy's mother. Lorcan had spoken fondly of her in the past. She worked at the medical camps, aiding the sick and wounded in the disputed zone around the River Shannon. Had the boy gone there to find his mother? Without a father in his life, Finn clearly idolised her. The brothers must have persuaded Finn somehow that his mother was in trouble. How else could they have so easily persuaded him to go off without a word to anyone?

Or perhaps an intoxicated Finn would walk through the door right now, fumbling with a beaker of cider, crooning some patriotic shanty at the top of his voice, having come across some of his cadet friends in a late-night bar? Perhaps he was overreacting? And yet, this was the first time Lorcan had deemed it fit for him, a 'Pune', to look after his ward for a few hours. And just look at the mess he had made of things.

Maggo set down at the kitchen table and rested his head in his hands. He thought of his mother and said a prayer to his God.

11

It was just a routine enquiry DS Conway had said. Nothing to get myself worried about. He had offered me his hand at the end of the interview, but the perspiration on it, married with that on my own, had caused our hands to slide apart as soon as they had touched. There had been nothing firm about the handshake. There had been nothing firm about the interview. There had been nothing firm about Conway.

It had started to rain by the time I had left the police station, a bitterly, cold rain that came down in lines as if under the dark cloud of a comic strip. The cloud followed me all the way to the nearest bar, my boots making a slalom of the deep puddles that reflected the amber of street lights as I skipped quickly past, my head bowed, and my shoulders hunched against the wind.

The bar was warm inside. An open fire glowed on one side and around it sat a company of young drinkers, dressed up in Halloween costumes: a diverse selection of skeleton T-shirts, pointed hats and witches' shawls. Someone had seen fit to drape orange and black decorations everywhere. In place of electric light, candles burned on tables. An open coffin had been propped up in one corner and inside a grinning Dracula stared outwards, his fangs dripping blood. I approached the bar and ordered a whiskey. A girl with purple hair and a blanched face served me.

'Still raining out there, I see,' she enquired, as she turned to fill my glass with an optic full of Jameson's. 'Sure, you don't want this hot?'

'No thanks,' I replied.

'You need to look after yourself. You'll catch your death out in that weather without an umbrella.'

'I know. I left my brolly back at the hotel.'

'Hotel? You from the Big Smoke?'

'From Belfast, yes.'

'Belfast? Me too! Halloween, eh?' she said, with a nod to the crowd. 'So commercial these days!'

I wondered what she meant by 'these days'. I smiled politely, took my drink and found myself a quiet snug. I needed desperately to gather my thoughts. The tapestry of my whole world was beginning to unravel and none of it was being helped by the ghosts and ghouls that were wandering back and forth for makeshift goblets of Guinness at the bar.

The photograph of Eva had shaken me more than any unearthly apparition could. I had visualised her face many times over the years, of course, had assembled a photo-fit of hair, eyes, nose and mouth in my mind's eye. Over time, her image had gradually begun to lose its form. It had become blurred at the edges, lacking definition, like the face on a stamp partially hidden by a postmark from a long time ago.

And yet, as soon as I had seen the photo, it had all come rushing back to me, the smell of her hair and skin, the lilt of her voice, the very texture of our one evening together yielded itself to my fingertips. She was smiling radiantly from the bright throw of a sofa, a cushion beneath her elbow, her knees slightly parted in black leggings under a floral-patterned dress. The shock and joy of seeing her again was so much that it took me a second or so to realise that she was pregnant.

Eva Beaufort had become pregnant sometime at the beginning of 1981. The picture, Conway had told me, had been snapped by her flatmate around early July that year, just before the Twelfth holiday. Her flatmate, Martha, had remembered it, as both girls had been the only ones not to return to their family homes that summer. Martha had been interviewed, at the time of Eva's disappearance. She had stated that Eva didn't return home one night at the end of July. It was a Friday, the last day of the month as it happened. She knew this as it was also payday and she had just received her wages from the owner of a cafe where she worked. Eva, Martha said, had got a new job as an usherette in a cinema and would frequently come back late on Fridays and Saturday after the midnight screenings. When Martha awoke on Saturday morning, she assumed Eva had met some boyfriend or other and had gone back to his flat. When she still didn't return after a couple of days, she took the liberty of checking her flatmate's room. Nothing had seemed amiss. Her hairbrush was still on her dressing table. Some old clothes were strewn across an unmade bed and the remainder were still hanging up in her wardrobe. An empty suitcase was still lying, untouched, beneath the bed. It was the clothes which compelled Martha to phone the police. Without them, she thought it unlikely Eva would have gone back to France, especially without informing her beforehand.

The RUC at the time performed the usual preliminary checks. There was no record, however, that Eva had ever worked at a cinema or cafe in the Belfast area. There was no evidence of her ever having attended a language school to improve her English. In fact, the only person who could verify her actual existence was Martha herself. If it hadn't been for the photograph, the police would have suspected that the girl had made the whole thing up.

The French police, meanwhile, could find

no trace of an 'Eva Beaufort' matching the description of the girl in the photo. Interpol too drew a blank. They assumed that the girl, if she was French, had provided a false identity, probably based on the name of an eleventh century chateau in Saint-Malo, Brittany, they believed. Neither the French or British transport police had any record of her having ever exited or entered their respective countries.

In short, Eva had been a phantom, a spectre that had appeared at one end of a maternal cycle and vanished at the other. Belfast had been her chosen place of confinement and I had been, without my knowledge, an unwitting participant in the drama from the beginning.

Not that DS Conway had ever accused me directly of being the child's father. That accusation was left unsaid. It hung, however, in the air between us, like an elephant in the room, raising its trunk and letting out a deafening exclamation mark over and over again. There was the possibility, of course, that conception had not occurred between us. After all, there was no way of knowing the exact date of the child's birth. Eva could have had a boyfriend. Perhaps, I was merely a random passion, a sexual release precipitated by the fireworks of New Year, a casual flirtation that had gone too far, enjoyable yes, but regrettable, nonetheless. And if Eva had not been in a serious relationship at the time, she was still a remarkably beautiful woman who could easily have commanded the admiration of many.

I had gone through the story of that night with Conway, all the while his little blue pen scratching the gist of the encounter in his notepad. I had kept to the details, had attempted to maintain a neutral tone throughout, neither painting myself nor Eva in the best or worst of lights. We were consenting adults who had agreed to sleep together. It had been an impulse on both our parts, an over-reaction to the very pheromones that make the world go around. No money had changed hands. It had been a non-verbal contract, requiring no signature, nothing except the ability to read between the lines.

As matter-of-fact as I had attempted to be, I knew Conway hadn't believed a word of what I had said. He had wanted the facts. How I dressed up the facts was a matter of complete indifference to him. Except to lead us both to the inevitable conclusion that, try as I might to be aloof and stand-offish, Conway knew that Eva did not seem the kind of woman to have regular one-night stands. The reason being? He could tell I was not the kind of man to do likewise, in spite of his earlier jibes. He was too experienced an officer not to be able to assess a person within the first five seconds of meeting them. And I just wasn't the type. By extension, I was also not the type to sleep with a woman who was accustomed to passing her evenings with a variety of sexual partners. If I were going to err from the marital path, the decision would be momentous and with someone significant. The upshot of all this was that Conway and I both knew that the chances were high I had just become a father.

If he had made a note of that conclusion in his investigator's pad, he wasn't going to tell me. He drilled me instead on the approximate time of our departure from the hotel, the time of our arrival at Eva's flat, the time I eventually walked home. Did I meet any of her friends that night? Anyone on the way to her home? Had I seen her again? To all these questions I had provided an unequivocal 'no'.

And what of the questions I now asked myself? I had too many of them, too many question marks that flashed before me like fishing hooks, empty of bait, cast one by one into an empty ocean. Who was Eva? Why had we met? What had happened to her? Was she still alive? Was I the father of our child? If so, where was that boy or girl now? To these questions, there were no answers, not even the possibility of answers. If two national police forces had not solved the case, then it was highly unlikely that I would. But there were newer questions: who had given my name to the Armagh police and why now?

I finished my drink, got another and thought about all the people who had learned the truth about that night. Rose, naturally. And later her entire network of family and friends. Surridge, of course - if he could be bothered to remember the details. I was certain, however, that I had not shared Eva's identity with any of them.

Possibly, Martha, Eva's flatmate? Conway, though, had let slip that she had emigrated to New Zealand in the late eighties. Besides, Martha had never been entrusted with the identity of Eva's child's father. If I was the father, then Martha wouldn't have knowledge of my name, let alone of my exact whereabouts in Northern Ireland, especially not from a base of operations in Auckland or Wellington or wherever she lived now. No, that didn't make sense either. It was someone who both knew Eva's name and also that I was in Armagh.

There was only one person it could have been. There could be no doubt. I had known it all along, denied it to myself, sifted scientifically through the alternatives, yet as soon as Conway had voiced the name 'Eva', I knew it had to be Pritchard. I didn't know how he had discovered that Eva had gone missing, but my friend and colleague of twenty years had somehow thought me involved in her disappearance. Possibly also capable of murder.

'Pritchard lies', the voice had said. 'But only

about small things.' I hadn't had the courage to ask him about those lies and this is where I had ended up. If it weren't for the fact that the professor was still in Carnac, I would have gone back to Belfast there and then and confronted him.

There was a new girl on reception by the time I got back to the hotel. She barely looked up from her paperback as I entered the lobby. At least there had been no further messages from the police, I thought. It had been a long day and the only thing I wanted to do now was to take a long, hot shower and climb into bed.

When I opened the door to my room, and stepped inside, I realised instinctively that something was amiss, that something was not quite right. Little did I know I was about to cross a threshold from what I thought I knew about life to what I had always felt I had known. My childhood fascination with myths and legends, my meetings with Pritchard, my work, my feelings for Eva, my preference for my own company, even the death of my wife had been opaque screens which now, for the first time, were about to permit the first rays of light to pass through.

I didn't realise it all at first, of course. There would be further supporting information, an additional cast, evidence I would witness that my eyes would not be able to deny, a smorgasbord of later detail that would fill in the cracks of my disbelief. I would have to undergo a process through which my assumptions and suppositions about what constituted a normal life would be gradually turned on their head.

There were three individuals in the room - I later discovered that there always had to be three -two I recognised by sight and the other I would soon recognise by voice. The two individuals whose faces were familiar to me stood either side of my wardrobe: one male and the other female. The other figure was a lot taller and it had chosen to occupy the armchair beside my bed. It, or its partners, had turned on the bedside lamp, the shade of which gave the room a soft, violet radiance.

The male was dressed in ripped denim jeans, trainers and a casual, brown leather jacket. He was in his thirties, had deep red curly hair and a smooth, pale complexion. It was the waiter I had met in the cafe earlier and also, it suddenly dawned on me, the boyfriend who had sat at the table behind Surridge and I during our last night out together in Belfast. It was the same man as before, but his skin was more luminous somehow, as though he either extracted light from without himself, or exuded light from within.

His girlfriend that night was also smiling back at me now. She had just played the role of the purple-haired barmaid I had last seen not fifteen minutes beforehand. It was impossible, I knew, for her to be standing there in front of me. She had suddenly materialised, in a weird, purple ensemble of jacket, tutu and leggings; all to match her hair, I supposed. I could tell by the way she looked at me that it was the same girl from the bar. Her eyes were greener than before, as green and cold as two chips of malachite.

If I thought this couple were slightly out of place with what was generally considered the norm, then it was only because I hadn't yet fully appreciated the strangeness of the odd-looking creature sitting in the armchair by my bed.

It was very thin and tall, with an unnatural, angular face. Two lines of cheekbones met at a pronged chin out of which sprouted a small tuft of short, white hair. A long, aquiline nose, on which pivoted a pince-nez, added to the geometric longitude of its overall appearance. Perched atop a mass of wavy, white hair, the being wore a Victorian teacher's mortar board that matched an old-fashioned, pin-striped suit beneath. It would have almost looked human if it hadn't been for the fact that it was slightly too tall -just under eight feet. It wore a black robe over its shoulders that matched its length, and its legs were crossed, uncomfortably, as if unfamiliar with the space in which it had suddenly found itself. A bamboo cane weighed slightly in its hands.

Most of the description of the scene that awaited me in the hotel room that first night my mind pieced together later. In truth, I didn't take in too much apart from the elongated form of the ancient school master. Its appearance shook me to the core, and I am still not sure to this day if I passed out for a moment or so.

I can't remember much after entering the room, and my first recollection afterwards was sitting on the edge of my bed, my head between my legs, inhaling rapid breaths, my heart beating fast, praying that I had not just witnessed what I had thought I had witnessed. When I finally recovered myself, assisted by the red-haired boyfriend who helped straighten me up, I was still too frozen in fear to look at the teacher directly. I needed time to attune myself to the frequency under which this new world was operating, to measure the wavelength that separated me from it.

'I know, I know. All a bit of a surprise, Professor Summer. And yes, time is so precious now.'

It was the same voice as before, the same intonation and pitch, delivered at exactly the same pace. It helped me, at first, to hear its familiar tones. My eyes were still closed and, if I could pretend that I was holding a telephone to my ear, perhaps I could also believe that none of this was really happening and I could be back, back in the safety of my flat with Surridge's jazz only the thickness of a ceiling away.

'It has to be this way, I am afraid, Professor Summer. May I call you Lewis? We can be more...formal now, no? These are my friends, Angus and Brigid.'

'You can call me, Bridge,' the woman interjected.

'Yes, Lewis, best to call her that. These younger...types...like to use more modern diminutives. And I am Cathbad. Like the druid, ha! You see, Lewis? Angus, Bridge and Cathbad. ABC. Very geometrical. Bridge is the bridge between our names. A bridge in more ways than one...They are my eyes and ears in this world, and I am their voice, so to speak...'

'This is not real...it's not happening.'

'That is right, Lewis. Keep your eyes closed for just a little bit longer. But not too long. Not too long.'

'Who are you?! What are you?'

'Who am I? What am I? It would take too long to explain, Lewis. I will tell you, but sometimes words are not enough. That is why I have had you brought here.'

'Had me brought here?'

'We will come to that, Lewis. Everything must have an order. Who am I? I have told you. I am Cathbad. What am I? Well, let us say I am a sentinel, custodian or guardian?'

'What are you guarding?'

185

'I am guarding the bridge. Or the gateway? The portal? I am the voice. I control words, Lewis. I could present you with a whole thesaurus of terminology, a semantic symposium of ideas, the whys and the hows, but again, it is best that you just see. And you will see.'

I opened my eyes and forced myself to look at the sentinel. He was waving its cane in the air, like a baton conducting an orchestra.

'Are you human?'

'I am as human as you are.'

'What does that mean?'

'This form, you see, is not my true form. It is more difficult for me...I am... more distant from this *world*...my imprint is not as easy to define. For obvious reasons, unlike my friends here, I cannot appear before people. Ha! Maybe tonight though? In that bar you were in? I might have just got away with it.'

Angus chuckled at this. Bridge simply rolled her eyes.

'We don't have time for this, Cathbad! she said. 'Just tell him. He's ready.'

Cathbad closed his eyes and sighed. 'There is still enough time. Do not worry, Brigid.'

'But why me?! Why are you here?!' I exclaimed. 'Why did you move my furniture around?! What the hell is going on?!'

'Good. Good. You are coming around to yourself at last. Anger at least indicates an acknowledgement...' he brandished his cane, 'of all this. Your furniture? That was my two friends here. My eyes, ears and... sense of touch. They can appear and disappear at will, render themselves invisible, change form.'

'I don't believe it!'

'No? Turn around, Lewis, and face the wardrobe! I can promise you it is not large enough for both of them inside!'

I turned around quickly. The pair were no longer there. They had simply disappeared. I began to feel nauseous. A metallic dryness filled my mouth. I wondered suddenly if I could make it to the wash basin in time. 'Have a glass of water, Lewis,' Cathbad said gently. 'You will be fine. I promise.'

I staggered to my feet, stumbled to the basin and doused my face in water. I filled a glass and sipped, slowly at first, before emptying the contents and filling a second.

'Better?'

'Where...where...are they?'

'Come closer, Lewis. That is right. Now, look at me. Keep your eyes on me.'

For some reason I did as I had been instructed.

'Now, look again.'

When I did so, I noticed both Angus and Bridge had returned to the very locations they had previously occupied, either side of the wardrobe.

'They cannot do that in front of you,' Cathbad explained. The best they can do is to disappear and reappear out of the corner of your eye. But they can watch you when you cannot watch them. And they can move things around, unnoticed.'

'But why? Why me? Why were they in the bar that night?'

'They have been keeping an eye on you, Lewis. They and others like them. Your whole life.'

'My whole life?'

'Yes, Lewis. They have been preparing you, and your subconscious mind for this moment.'

'I don't...don't...believe you.'

'Yes, you do, Lewis. You already do. It's the only thing left that makes sense. I can read your thoughts. That's my...you would call it a 'gift'. It's nothing, really. A means of communication where I come from. I can also relay thoughts to people as well, mostly to children. Their minds are more open to such things.'

'What are you talking about?'

'Have you ever wondered why you have been so fascinated by folklore, myths and legends? Celtic heroes? That was why you became a professor, no? That voice in your head was my voice, narrating your childish play...'

'No!'

'I was telling you stories that all the children of that age are supposed to know...at least children, not of this world.'

'What do you mean? Not of this world?'

'Professor Summer. The truth is you are not from this world. And we, my friends and I, are here to help get you home.'

12

'So, who did you say you were looking for?'

'His name is Finn mac Dara. His uncle is...'

'...I know who his uncle is!' the guard interrupted, examining Maggo's papers again. 'So, tell me, Maggo... Calleja, is it?'

'Yes, sir.'

'What business do you have with Cadet mac Dara?'

'It's personal.'

'Oh? Personal?'

'His guardian is...'

'...Lorcan mac Róich. I know that too...And you say you stay at his residence?'

'Yes, sir.'

The cadet couldn't be much older than thirteen years old. Back home, a boy his age would be discovering girls. This boy, however, had sacrificed his childhood for a tightly buttoned uniform, hobnail boots and a bolt-action rifle. His fellow cadet, on the other side of the entrance gate to the RBK Youth training grounds, looked like his clone and shared the same stern expression as his colleague under his peaked cap. The second cadet looked straight ahead, determined not to glance in his direction, but Maggo could tell he was curious. It wasn't every day a foreigner paid a visit to the head-quarters of the Red Branch Knights. Maggo felt sorry for the first boy too. Beneath his guise of rigorous efficiency, Maggo thought, he was desperately trying to resist the temptation to ask a grown-up for help.

'There's little chance the cadet is here,' he continued, passing the papers back to Maggo. 'I don't suppose you know it's the Seventh Day?'

'Oh yes. We have them where I come from too.'

'The point is,' said the cadet, reddening, 'that mac Dara is a local. All the local lads...I mean...cadets are off camp. The only cadets here are those from other parts of Ulidia.'

'Would it be possible to see commander mac Dara?'

'Commander mac Dara? You want to see him, do you?' the cadet enquired, with new interest.

'Yes. If he is here?'

No, the commander is not on base.'

'Do you know his current whereabouts?'

'No. He is not in Emain Mhaca.'

On hearing this, Maggo's disappointment was obvious, even to the cadet. Behind his implacable eyes, Maggo could detect the first flicker of empathy.

'Cadet mac Dara spoke of a friend of Finn's.

From Dún...sorry... Dún...?'

'...na nGal. Dún na nGal,' the cadet repeated slowly.

'Would he be available to speak? Just for a few minutes?'

'You will have to wait until the end of the ceremony. I can have someone relay a message to the cadet in question.'

'Ferdia's his name, isn't it?'

'Cadet Ó Ceallaigh will be informed,' corrected the young man.

'That would be most helpful, thank you.'

Beyond the fence, Maggo could just about distinguish a thin thread of grey smoke rising up above the military barracks. From there, a faint, indecipherable chant was being carried on the wind towards him and was greeted, intermittently, with a low, choral response that sounded like a deep wail. First the voice, then the wail, over and over again. It reminded Maggo of the funeral laments he had heard as a boy in church.

He thanked the cadet again and sat down on a nearby wall, keeping himself in sight of the two young guards. He looked at his timepiece. It was almost 11.00, almost fifteen hours since he had last seen Finn.

A few hours earlier, he had decided it might be worthwhile to check the premises of Finn's mother, Aoife. Perhaps the boy still had a key for his family home? As expected, however, the house was empty. The curtains of every window had been pulled across and weeds had started to proliferate on the once neat lawn at the front. After that, he had visited the offices of the Bardic Press.

Although it was the Seventh Day, the BP was a hive of activity, none more so than the floor occupied by the Béal Feirste Banner which, unlike the Ulidian Shield and the other more local news sheets, had somehow acquired a monopoly on all the news reports coming out of Uisneach. Maggo had always thought it strange that the media of an entire nation, albeit a small one, was run out of a single, central nine storey building. It had something to do with bardic tradition, Lorcan had once told him. Maggo had checked every floor for his employer, had enquired of his whereabouts from colleagues from his own and rival news sheets. He was met with the same response everywhere; no one had seen Lorcan mac Róich since the previous evening. Not only that, Lorcan had already missed one important meeting that morning and, as a result, another one had been hastily rearranged for after lunch. For want of anything better to do, Maggo had returned to his own desk and considered what to do next. Something was not right, he knew. It seemed both Lorcan and Finn had simply disappeared, and the timing of their disappearances indicated that they had to be connected somehow. Had Lorcan learned of his ward's absence and had initiated his own search for the boy? If that were the case, would he not have informed his colleagues at his news sheet? He thought briefly of contacting the local police but dismissed the idea quickly. Like most foreigners in Ulidia, Maggo tried to keep contact with the Ulidian guards to a bare minimum.

The only other person who could help now was the boy's uncle. Maggo knew that the commander had called to see Lorcan the day before. He knew that the two did not normally see eye to eye and avoided each other if possible. So, something important must have compelled Conall to visit. What had they talked about, he wondered? If Maggo could learn the nature of their conversation then it might help him find Lorcan, and, in turn, locate the boy. At the very least the commander could use all the resources at his disposal to instigate a major search for his nephew.

It took a while before the cadets on guard went off-duty. They were immediately replaced by another couple of hard-nosed toughs. If he hadn't seen the physical exchange of the first pair for the second, Maggo would never have guessed the substitution had occurred. A quarter of an hour later, a short, stocky youth could be seen stomping towards the gate. Finn had described his friend as a bull. It was an accurate description. The thickness of the boy's neck and the roundness of his shoulders could not suggest otherwise. They seemed to lean into the air as he walked as if even the air was somehow an impediment that had to be waded through and left in his wake. He was wearing the pale, ceremonial tunic worn by all Ulidians who attended sacrifices on the Seventh Day. The new cadets saluted him as he passed through the gate.

'Couldn't this have waited?!' Ferdia barked immediately.

'I'm sorry.'

'At least until I could get out of this little girl's dress! Bloody lunch has started! It's roast beef on the third weekend!'

'It'll not take long. It's Ferdia, isn't it?'

'Yeah,' Ferdia replied, eyeing the stranger, suspiciously.

'My name is Maggo. Has Finn mentioned me to you?'

'Yeah, you're the Pune...err... I mean the Punic journalist. You work up at the BP?'

'Yes, that's right. I live with Lorcan mac Róich.'

'Very cosy.'

'Sorry?'

'Nothing. Don't worry about it.' Ferdia shivered suddenly, looked skywards. The sun was nowhere to be seen. 'Look, it's bloody freezing! Can we just crack on? What's this all about?'

'It's Finn. He has gone missing,' Maggo answered.

'What do you mean? Missing?'

Maggo quickly went over the events of the previous evening and his abortive attempts to locate Lorcan that morning.

'So, you're telling me that a couple of Connachta might have kidnapped Finn and brought him where? The clearing stations?'

'Yes. No. I don't know. They might have just used his mother as a ploy to entice him away.'

'So, he could be bloody anywhere!' Ferdia shouted. 'Mhaca's left and right tit! And where were you when this was all happening?'

Maggo noticed one of the cadets on duty cock an ear slightly in their direction.

'They wanted to talk to Finn in *private...*' Maggo replied, stressing the word while nodding in the direction of the guards.

'So, you bloody well left them to it.' Ferdia forced a whisper.

'Yes,' Maggo said, lowering his head slightly.

Ferdia shook his head and scoffed. 'Unbelievable? Are they all like you in the Union? I don't know why the Federation hasn't already invaded you lot!'

'The point is, Ferdia, commander mac Dara is also not in Emain Mhaca, it seems.'

'Yeah, I heard the rumours. Something big.'

'Big?'

'Yeah. If he's not here, he must be in Uisneach. Heard he took a couple of his unit with him as well.'

'So,' Maggo said, trying to organise his thoughts, 'we don't know the whereabouts of Finn, Lorcan mac Róich or commander mac Dara?'

'Yeah, seems that way. A proper little lost triad...Triad,' he added, thoughtfully.

'Sorry.'

'It seems you need a bit of help, friend. And I know just the lad to lend a hand.'

Conall mac Dara had come a long way in his life. At nearly fifty summers old, he had been in command of the RBK 1st Ulidian Division for over a decade. In that time, he had managed to build up a strong bond between himself and the thousands of soldiers under his command. It had not been easy. He had achieved his lofty position the hard way. Although his family name was enough to qualify him for a position in the RBK Youth, he had lasted only one full year in the organisation. Not that he wasn't tough enough to cope with the physical and mental challenges all new RBK cadets face. He was tougher than anyone his age. It was simply that he had hated taking orders. 'A problem with authority figures' was how his instructor had described it. And he was right. Conall had been wilfully disobedient with all his officers, downright rude on some occasions, and no amount of punishment made any salutary impact on him, even at the age of twelve. Finally, he had managed to engineer a way for himself to be discharged before the end of his first year. Conall had intentionally struck another cadet on the head with the boss of a shield, rendering him unconscious. It hadn't even been their turn to practise.

His parents were devastated at the news of his dismissal. His father refused to speak to him for almost a year. During that time, the latter had a stroke; and then, soon after, it was too late for words. At the time of his father's death, Conall was sixteen summers old. His mother had been aware of the gulf that had developed between father and son, a chasm of emptiness that neither had chosen to fill. But there could be no common ground between them in spite of her best efforts. His little sister, Aoife, had also known of the estrangement that had existed between her father and brother but was powerless to do anything about it.

A few years later, Conall decided to re-join the Ulidian army for a contracted period of five years. A second five-year tour of duty followed upon its completion, this time as a provisional member of the RBK. After another five years, Conall signed up as a full RBK recruit.

Whether he had enlisted as an act of contrition or self-punishment on his part, no one knew, but it wasn't long before the young mac Dara rose steadily through the ranks. His time spent in both the regular army and RBK had helped Conall to realise that it was the ordinary working-class soldiers who were the heart and soul of the Ulidian army. The officer class from the youth wing of the RBK were, in his opinion, rich, arrogant upstarts who preferred the nib of a pen to the barrel of a gun. Perhaps this was why he had been so against his sister's decision to have his nephew recruited to its ranks. For this he blamed mac Róich.

But now, for the second time in a matter of days, Conall mac Dara, from such humble military beginnings, was on the verge of entering another one of Éireann's most famous landmarks. This time: The Roundhouse, home of the Arch Druid of the Druidic Order. His father would have been proud.

Depending on your point of perspective, the Roundhouse was more than one house. Three interlacing arcs formed the perimeter of three adjoining structures belonging to the respective Houses of the Druidic Order: The House of Vates, the House of Bards and the House of Brehon Law. It was from these Houses that degrees and diplomas in Medicine, Journalism and Law had been issued in the past to students from all across the four lands. In modern times, the Houses merely ratified the rolled-up scrolls of parchment administered to students upon graduation. No formal education took place there. Instead, they offered grants for medical research, censored any articles by the four institutions of the Bardic Press that were deemed to have contravened slander and libel laws and affirmed legislation passed by the governing bodies of all the nations of Éireann. The Houses were seen by all as performing purely cosmetic functions. Up until now, it was unheard of for the Druidic Order to move beyond their original remit.

The Roundhouse also contained a small hospital, the largest archived collection of books in all of Éireann and was the seat of the Druidic Council headed by Arch Druid Mogh Roith mac Nuadat. It was the formal residence of the Arch Druid and visiting dignitaries from other druidic organisations across the Federation. For the first time in its history it was hosting simultaneous visits from leaders of all four Éireann nations including President Darragh mac Nessa of Ulidia and his Connachta counterpart, President Ailill Ó'Flaithearta.

Conall was walking down a long corridor leading to mac Nessa's living quarters. He had been ordered by a commander in the Druidic Guard to leave behind Oisín and Caoimhín, the two soldiers of his triad that he had chosen to join him in Uisneach. In their place, he had been provided with an attachment of four DG, all with Federation rifles. Rifles or not, Conall didn't fancy these men's chances against his own. Still, 'when in Carthage' he thought to himself, smiling at the memory of the Punic saying he had recently learned from Maggo, mac Róich's foreign tenant, when he had last seen him in Emain Mhaca. He had asked the young man how he had been adapting to life in Ulidia and had been surprised at the novelty of the Carthaginian's reply.

Conall liked Maggo and he knew Finn did as well. For some reason this was some measure of comfort for him.

At the door of the President's chamber, the four DG were in turn replaced by members of the President's own security detail: two spade-faced, muscle-bound types with spiral tattoos all down their arms. After knocking, the door was opened by another similar looking guard inside.

'Ah, commander mac Dara. How are you? It's been a while. Now let me think. Last Imbolc?

'Samhain, sir,' Conall replied.

'Samhain,' he repeated, reflectively. 'A lovely celebration. Cold! But lovely.' He jolted his head once and within a few seconds the detail departed, leaving them both alone.

'Have a seat, commander.'

'I am used to standing, sir,' Conall replied, hesitantly, 'if you don't mind.'

'Well, the exigencies of age, I'm afraid, compel me to sit.'

He sat back, resting his elbows either side of a green leather armchair, made a bridge of his fingers and balanced his goateed chin on his thumbs. Conall waited for the president to begin. There was a long silence during which he wondered whether or not it was customary for him to speak first. Or perhaps, the old man had forgotten what he was going to say, Conall thought.

The president was at least seventy summers old. He was thin, grey-haired and wore a stylish, dark, three-piece suit. There was nothing altogether remarkable about him if you excluded his famous goatee beard. He had allowed it to grow beyond his chin so that it resembled a short, silver dagger. There was a rumour that the president trimmed it daily, using the appendage as a suggestion of threat intended to unnerve his opponents. This, and the caprine narrowness of his face, had earned him the pseudonym, 'Púca', amongst political circles. This was in reference to the creature from folklore, whose ability to shape-shift into different animal forms, symbolised mac Nessa's well-known capacity to sail in the direction of whatever prevailing wind necessary to maintain his grip on power. The rest of the population just called him 'goat-face'.

'You spoke to mac Neill?' he asked, finally.

'Yes, sir.'

'Your thoughts?'

'Politics is not my place, sir.'

'I meant your opinion of mac Neill?'

'Err...I... I'm sure he is a competent...'

'He is mac Dara. And I can trust him. That has to be enough for now. You want to know a secret, mac Dara?'

'Yes, sir.'

'The mac Neills are like most of the old families in the senate. Their preference, if they only knew it, is to be in opposition. They wouldn't know what to do with real power.'

The President stared at Conall momentarily, slapped his hands suddenly on the arms of the chair and stood up. He looked around the room until his eyes finally settled on a portrait hanging over his bed. It was a picture of an old, wizened druid, dressed all in white, standing on a hilltop, his staff stretched out towards a full moon. It looked expensive, probably half a millennia old.

'Do you recognise the druid in the picture, commander?'

'No, sir. Art is also not something I am familiar with.'

'But surely you recognise those famous features, mac Dara?'

Conall paid the painting more attention. 'Cathbad?'

'The very druid, yes. The famous druid

who served my most celebrated ancestor, King Conor mac Nessa. The Arch Druid had it removed from his personal collection and positioned there...just for me.'

'That was thoughtful of him.'

'Thoughtful?' The president offered a wry smile. 'Perhaps. You know, of course, the old legend of 'Deirdre of the Sorrows'?'

'Who doesn't?'

'Yes, indeed. One of the first tales you learn at school. According to legend, she was one of the most beautiful women ever to have graced our sacred land. Cathbad, of course, divined that her beauty would lead to war. King Conor decided to sequester the child with an old poetess with the full intention of marrying her himself when she came of age. But Deirdre grows up, falls in love with the handsome, young Naoise...well...you know the rest.'

'Yes.'

'Not my ancestor's most edifying moment. Would you agree?'

'I have never really given it much thought, sir. It's just a story...'

'...I had a sister, mac Dara,' he interrupted, suddenly. 'It's common knowledge. She died. Years ago, now. You know what her name was?'

'No, sir.'

'Deirdre.'

'I'm sure the Arch Druid didn't...'

'...Of course not, commander. He's the most

famous druid from the Ulidian Cycle. It makes sense the Arch Druid would honour our country with his portrait.' The president returned to his seat. 'So, mac Neill has filled you in about how things are shaping up politically. Good. That's good. I can't stress enough, commander, how essential it is the signing of the peace treaty goes off without a hitch. The eyes of Éireann and the entire Federation are on Ulidia at this time. Have you received the itinerary for tomorrow?'

'Yes, sir. Seems straightforward enough. The three other leaders, yourself, the Arch Druid and the Druidic Council leave the Roundhouse at 05.00. That's one chariot with you, Ó'Flaithearta and Arch Druid mac Nuadat. A second with mac Neill acting as a consort for the Mhumhain and Laighean leaders. A further three chariots carrying the individual members of the Council. That's five chariots. Another couple of chariots for the Bardic Press. That's seven in total. I will take the first chariot along with two DG, directly in front of the presidential chariot...'

'And the head of the Connachta security unit...'

'...What?'

'You know how it is, commander. Once Connachta found out about you, they had to have their own people.'

'Do we know them?'

'You should. Ó Móráin. Their best man, apparently.'

'And the others?'

Ó Gallachóir and Ó Floinn. Two hard men, by all accounts. They will ride with your men.'

'So much for trust.'

'Trust needs to be earned, mac Dara. Hopefully, this is when the earning begins.' Conall didn't agree but remained silent. Ó Móráin had the reputation of being firm but fair. Conall could live with that. He didn't know the other two.

'But to continue...?'

'Yes, well, my two men will follow behind you and the Connachta president...with Ó Gallachóir and Ó Floinn. The DG chariots will be interspersed between the other chariots in the cortege. We arrive at the base of the Hill at 05.10. There will be no crowd permitted into the area on the other side of the Hill until 05.30 so no issues there. Ascent at 05.15. Arrival at summit at 05.30. Speeches and lighting of the Uisneach fire just before dawn at 05.45. Descent of the Hill and arrival at the Cat Stone at 06.30. Same cortege as before. End of ceremony just before 07.00.'

'What about security at the Cat Stone?'

'A separate detail of DG will have already taken up position there. In fact, they will go straight to the Cat Stone immediately after our departure from the Roundhouse,'

'Perfect, commander. I hope you don't mind me asking you to go through all that. I prefer the personal touch.'

And he's shitting himself, Conall thought. The only danger to mac Nessa, as he saw it, was at the signing of the treaty at the Cat Stone. He had warned mac Neill already of that, but his concerns had fallen on deaf ears. Even the DG hadn't wanted to know.

'And my men will be permitted weapons?'

'Of course, commander. A special dispensation has been granted by the Arch Druid...for the duration of the event only, of course.'

'Of course.'

The president smiled again. 'You don't like the idea of peace, mac Dara? Not having a weapon?'

'On the contrary, sir. I could do with putting my feet up for a bit. As long as everyone else is,' he added.

'Ha! Yes. There will be a lot of feet toasting themselves upon many a good hearth come winter.'

'Yes, sir. If that will be all?'

'Yes, I will see you on the morning of Beltane.' Conall turned to leave. 'Oh, commander?'

'Yes, sir?'

'How's that old codger, mac Róich, faring these days? He's looking after your sister's boy, isn't he? Finn?'

'Yes. Finn. To be honest, sir, I don't see much of mac Róich.'

'On purpose?' Mac Nessa enquired.

'Well, he's not my most favourite person in the world, sir.'

'Nor mine, Conall. Nor mine. But that's a story for another day, eh?'

As he walked to his chariot parked outside, Conall wondered about what lay behind the president's closing remarks. There was a lot more to this Lorcan mac Róich than he had ever thought possible. As soon as this business was over and Aoife was back home, he was determined that mac Róich would be out of all their lives for good.

13

'Right! I've had enough! I'm going to call the police!'

I realised I was shouting. Or was I screaming? Inside my head, the words did not seem my own. I couldn't remember the last time I had ever truly raised my voice. Even with Rose, our worst arguments were quietly intellectualised, simmering and brooding debates that would lead to long periods of sulking and pouting on her part and a stubborn unwillingness to accept blame on mine. Yet this was a voice from the inner depths of my being. It was as if a pass key had been inserted and something inside me had been triggered. The voice was not mine because, if what I was being told was true, I was not me. Or at least not the person I thought I was. I was from another world.

'The police?' Cathbad asked. 'But we have already discussed this police force of yours. Or, I should say, of theirs.' Cathbad closed his eyes, concentrated a moment, and then looked at me again. 'Your Detective Conway is no longer at his work, Lewis. He is at home, getting ready for bed. He has already forgotten your case and is thinking of another.' He gestured with a finger at Angus. 'Perhaps a glass of your favourite whiskey? Jamesons?'

From the corner of my eye, I detected a subtle inflection in the air, a tampering with light and shade and then a hand extended towards me. In it, lay a crystal tumbler of whiskey.

'Not just a pretty face, Angus, is he?' Cathbad said. 'Take a sip, Lewis. Try to relax. One thing I can assure you is that we will soon depart, and you will not be harmed in any way. Is that agreed?

I took the glass, forced myself to sip its contents. I took a breath and nodded my head.

'So, we shall begin. Now, you already know that this is all actually happening to you? You realise that you are fully awake?'

I nodded again.

'My friends have already demonstrated what, in this world, would be considered 'magic'. Or would you like further proof…?'

'…No…no…' I replied.

'Good. Now. Be still and I will explain. You are not from this world. This implies, of course, you are from another. I, and my friends, belong to neither but can operate in both. I am a sentinel. Or a gatekeeper if you like. I guard the gates between this world and your other world. Other sentinels, like me, guard other gates, between other worlds. I cannot stray too far from these gates as I... how should I explain it...? Your scientists, Lewis... when they are experimenting with other diverse forms of life in their laboratories, say a bacterium or a virus, they are worried about their safety, no? They wear special, protective clothes. They maintain the organism in a sort of vacuum and analyse it from without. Sometimes they can reach into the space it occupies using a pair of gloves or glove box. That way they, or at least their hands, can in some way exist in that different 'atmosphere' and manipulate what passes for actuality there. My 'gloves', or ability to manipulate on a physical level, can only extend so far. There is a gate in Armagh which is why I needed you to come here so that I could speak to you. I cannot be too far from that gate as this form, which you can see is not perfect, will begin to dissipate further. In short, I am connected to the gate by a kind of invisible, umbilical cord. I can project my thoughts some distance, but for everything else I need the help of my friends here. So far, so good?'

I sipped some more whiskey and nodded.

'Now, my only role is to maintain the integrity of the gates between this world and... well...your world.'

'What is *my* world? If I am from another world, how did I get here? My parents. My biological parents, I mean, are they from this world too?'

'All in good time, Lewis. All in good time,' the sentinel repeated. 'Now,' he continued, 'for the most part, my job is quite boring. Tedious, in fact. Gates between worlds are normally very stable, and when they are, they release one form of energy. Several cultures, in your distant past...let us say, certain native peoples, more attuned to the natural frequencies of this planet than your present technological generation, were able to sense this energy. They thrived off it, honoured it, even worshipped it with stone circles and the like.'

'You're talking about ley lines?'

'Yes, in a way. Ley lines. Good. Now, I, and other sentinels like me, control the opening and closing of these gates, or portals, at certain times of the planet's annual cycle. It is of interest to us...shall we say...to *monitor* the universal impulse towards this energy in its positive form.'

'You mean you have appeared to these natives? Allowed them to worship you?!'

'No, never! We sense a disturbance on the 'other' side of the gate and we simply pop through to have a look. No one sees us. The natives 'feel' the good energy, like it and work out, in their own limited way, that it is good for their crops and so on. If they decide to make offerings and sacrifices to a gate or portal that is their own affair. Now, you have heard of the archaeological excavations on the site of the old mound at Navan? Emain Mhaca, as it was called in your past? That, by the way, is the portal to which I am currently linked.'

'Yes, a team carried out a survey decades ago.'

'1950 to be exact.'

'1950. Yes. The year I was born.'

'That's correct,' he said, thoughtfully. 'If a site survives from a time when these energetic points were integrated into a people's cultural or religious practice, they are sometimes the subject of archaeological curiosity in later centuries. Mostly, it is actually seismic shifts, tectonic interference which breaks down the code...'

'...The code?'

'What the sentinel uses to open and close the gates. In any case, Lewis, an excavation, like the one on the mound at Navan, can cause a shift to occur, due to unforeseen pressure exerted onto the energetic vortex of the gate at one end. After a little time, perhaps a couple of years, the portal or gate on both sides may simply snap open. The survey, unintentionally I might add, initially created a fracture in one of the gates on the site at Navan that opened up eventually to form a corridor...to the other side. That was how you were able to cross over to this world at an undesignated time in the calendar when the energy is normally not sufficient to warrant such a crossing.'

'You are talking about a wormhole, aren't you?'

'Yes. Good. A wormhole.'

'But don't you patch up the wormhole as soon as it opens?' I asked.

At this, Bridge snickered. 'I'm beginning to like this guy. 'Patch'! That's hilarious!'

Cathbad ignored this and continued. 'So, normally we can resolve the issue. Especially with wormholes just between one world and the other.'

'Just?' I asked, shaking my head, in disbelief.

Cathbad sighed. 'There are different types of gates and sentinels. So, there are 'local' inter-dimensional gateways between one world and its particular 'other world'. And there are similar gates, more complex, between one world and an infinite list of parallel worlds. And there are gates between one world and another world, in another location, in the same spatial grid. In the same universe if you like. No sentinels are required for those.'

'So, you're a local sentinel?'

'That's right, friend,' intervened Angus. 'We're right at the bottom of the pecking order!'

'Sorry to hear that.' I said, sarcastically.

'But, let me explain more. Each world has its own particular 'other world'. They are locked together in a sort of psychic partnership. At various times of the year...'

'...You mean, the designated times? I said.

'Yes, at those times, depending on the motion of the worlds, or rather their two physical spheres, the gap between these worlds narrows. This is at what you call solstices or equinoxes and what the ancients here called Samhain, Lughnasa and so on. The walls thin a little. This happens everywhere between all locked worlds and establishes a connection between the two. When that happens, there are crossovers. As time passes, and a society 'develops', it loses touch with the truth of what it once knew. What was once a belief system becomes a folklore. You understand?'

'Yes, I think so,' I replied.

'Now, when a rift occurs by accident, it is easily rectified, especially in modern times when such beliefs in vortices and ley lines are surpassed by technological advancement.'

'He means,' Angus added, 'that normally the area around the gates are forgotten by the culture that used to venerate them, as is the case with this world. There are mounds, cairns, stone circles, dolmens; but all of them are easily dismissed as relics of a less 'evolved' time. It is simple for the sentinel to undo the damage done without any...mishap.'

'So?'

'In the case of this world, your world, it has, like so many others sadly, progressed beyond an understanding or appreciation of the energetic imprint the universe leaves on your world. If you really understood it, you could reshape your whole technology...'

'What happened?' I asked impatiently.

'Your other world happened. Or one part of it, at least -the mirrored representation of what you call the British Isles and Northern Europe. The world, with which this world is partnered, has developed an entire religion around their concept of the energy field surrounding these portals. This religion has survived there right up until the twentieth century. In your world, it died out centuries ago.'

'You mean, paganism?

'Yes.'

'So, they believe in some false gods. So what? There are atheists and agnostics in my world. I am not seeing the problem.'

'They created a pantheon of gods based on this religion. Not a problem in and of itself. They're free to develop spiritually how they choose. The problem for me was that the area that is a simple archaeological dig on this side of the wormhole is part of a huge edification on the other side. That makes it more difficult for us to organise 'departures' from that world to yours. Anyway, as I said, it worked out for the best. We were able to get you across, under cover of darkness, during a time the portal there was less...supervised. You came with another but only you stayed. Afterwards I was able to repair the gates.'

'Who was the other person?'

'Your father.'

'My father,' I stammered. 'You mean, my father is from this other world as well.'

'Yes, of course.'

'Is he...is he still...alive?'

'Yes.'

'But why would my father leave me in this world? Alone. Without family. I don't understand.'

'That will be explained to you, Lewis. But not by me.'

'Who then?'

'That too will be revealed to you. Patience, Lewis. I know it is difficult. You are doing well. It is a lot to accept.'

'You think? So why now? If any of this is true, why tell me now?'

'Events are happening on the other side. Events that have a direct connection to you.'

'To me?' I asked. 'How is that possible? You say my father is still alive. He hasn't died... wait, is it my mother...?'

'No, I am afraid your mother is...'

'...Stop. Don't say it. I don't want to know.'

'I am sorry.'

I breathed deeply. 'Well, what the hell is it then? Brothers? Sisters? Uncles? Aunts?'

'I think you already know.'

I turned to Angus and Bridge for support. I didn't know why. I was desperate. I didn't know what they were, but I didn't care. I just needed help. They looked human, or at least more human than Cathbad. Perhaps they had human empathy, too? But I couldn't read their faces. If they had emotions, they knew how to hide them well. I wrung my fingers through my hair.

'I can't...can't think.'

'Yes, you can,' Cathbad responded. 'It is important that you make the connection. It will help you make the transition.'

'Eva,' I said, finally.

'Yes, Eva,' Cathbad repeated slowly. 'You have a child by Eva. You already know that, of course. Think Lewis. Think. The furniture. My voice on the telephone. Detective Conway. Eva. A child you have never met. And then us. Tonight. In this room. All of it for a reason. To shatter the existing paradigm of your world, in order to create a new one, the real one from its ashes. You had to be broken down in order to be built again. Unlike your Humpty Dumpty.'

'Eva,' I repeated.

'Eva is from the other world too. You know what I am saying is true.'

'But my child?'

'Also, in the other world. Tomorrow night is Samhain. By the winter solstice it will be too late. That's when you will return. From the mound of Emain Mhaca.'

'I am not going anywhere unless I know more about Eva, this child and this other bloody world you're talking about!'

'Yes, of course. Tomorrow afternoon. On the mound. At midday. You will have all the evidence you require. But for now, try to get some sleep.'

And with that, they were gone. I sensed the absence of Angus and Bridge, less by their absence, but more by the imposing, seemingly newer presence of the wardrobe behind me. The sentinel, on the other hand, had vanished, between blinks, or in the interval it took my eyes to notice.

I was too exhausted for thought. I am not sure how, but I slept soundly that night. My mind had been inundated with information that it couldn't or didn't wish to process. No doubt I collapsed onto the bed and fell asleep instantly, for in the morning when I awoke, I was fully clothed, my head face down on the pillow. I looked around for the glass of whiskey that Angus had provided. It too had vanished.

The next day, after a late breakfast, I took a walk out of town, heading in the direction of the village of Killylea, just outside the city of Armagh. After twenty minutes or so, I turned right, and soon found myself on the Navan Fort Road. It had stopped raining overnight and the temperature had risen slightly.

It was a familiar route that I had taken many times with Rose, a winding country lane, strewn with cowpats in the summer, but now laden with the puddles of the previous night's downpour. My feet seemed to know where they were going even if I didn't. I, for my part, was still absorbing the events of the night before, trying to extrapolate meaning from them, compartmentalising the fact from the fiction. But it was all fiction. In the cold light of day, it had to be.

I thought also of the speech I would have to give to the *Friends of Macha* that evening and then remembered with an almost dizzy relief that I could be in another world by then. The whole thing was absurd, but I knew I was in no shape to deliver a talk. Perhaps it would be better to phone the department and have someone take my place. Fitzpatrick? Or even Clarke herself? It felt good to think of fundamentals like this. It kept me in touch with a world that was gradually slipping away.

After a while, my feet halted at their accustomed place. The meadows around were still, a patchwork quilt of fields, dotted with sheep, their sporadic bleating infringing only slightly upon the silence.

I had found myself at the pool of Loughnashade, a small body of water, where once, in 1794, a bronze horn had been discovered, polished and immediately secreted away to the National Museum of Ireland by triumphant archaeologists. The lough the horn had left behind looked forlorn now, almost melancholy. A token plaque provided passing tourists with the briefest of explanations. The sentinel had used terms like 'psychically advanced' and 'evolved'. That might be true, in this other world, I thought. But then again, time passes on. He said that too.

On the way back I noticed the hill fort of Emain Mhaca; two grassy mounds, rising up in the distance, were all that remained of a settlement which had once served as the meeting point of all the clans of Ulster. In 95 BC, historians believed, a sacred temple had been erected there, and then, strangely it seemed, had been razed to the ground as an offering to the gods. Festivals, ceremonies, hand-fastings had all been celebrated between its walls. Legendary figures had fought and died to protect Emain Mhaca, Ulster's ancient capital including, of course, Cú Chulainn and the Red Branch Knights.

I looked at my watch. It was still only half past ten. Ninety minutes before I was to climb the main mound and receive the evidence that the sentinel had spoken about. From a distance, it looked empty, just a few random tourists, bracing the cold to reach its summit and be rewarded with a view of the skyline of Armagh.

I filled the time by ordering a quick lunch at the Navan Centre, the site that had been recently opened to serve as a tourist attraction for those interested in Celtic traditions and provided walking tours to the hill of Emain Mhaca. At a quarter to two, I made my solitary way along the path which led to the base of the mound. As soon as I passed through the kissing gate that patrolled the numbers gaining access to the sharp incline beyond, I detected a figure I thought I recognised, absorbed in thought at one of the signs that lined the route to the brow of the hill.

To my utter astonishment, it looked like the familiar stance of Dr. Jeremy Pritchard.

14

He had been looking forward to this year's Beltane. The usual, celebratory atmosphere that lasted for weeks beforehand was something every Ulidian child adored. After the burning of the national and county fires in the National Arena, each extended family would then return home to gather around, and leap over, the smouldering embers of their own family fires. Once extinguished, the ashes were collected and preserved because of their inherent, protective powers. Finn's favourite part of the day was the family feast afterwards and the offering of food and drink to the aos sí, the spirits who were believed to inhabit the world between worlds.

The RBK Youth, however, prided itself in only permitting one day's holiday to its cadets in spite of the significance of the event. Last year, his first year as a recruit, it had been difficult to spend time away from his mother during the holiday period. This year, Beltane was following just after the third weekend. Finn had been looking forward to spending the extra day of freedom with his mother, Lorcan,

Conall, Breanne and yes, even with the Carthaginian Maggo, for whom he had developed a fondness since his arrival in the winter. A letter from his mother a few weeks earlier had scuppered his hopes. As a leading vate at the clearing stations, she had been enlisted to help oversee the evacuation of all medical personnel from an tSionainn. She would not be able to make it back to Emain Mhaca for the holiday, the letter had said, but she looked forward to spending more time with Finn now that the war was almost over. There was talk of her assuming a post in Ard Mhaca and so, very soon, the two would be reunited.

The news had been a blow to Finn, of course. However, his first feelings of disappointment soon evolved into anger and then, finally, a cold armour of indifference. Why should he care? He was used to coping on his own. He didn't need anyone.

But now this self-defence mechanism was badly in need of an overhaul. It was beginning to rust, falter against the continuing motion of the chariot that was propelling him, and his unknown passenger, to an uncertain future, a future that couldn't care less for his hopes and dreams, his reminiscences and regrets. How he would have dearly loved to be just another face in the crowd back home, staring up in wonder at the fires of the new summer. Finn bit his lip, fought back his tears and prayed to the gods for the first time since a young child.

He had lost track of the hours. For all he knew it could be Beltane already, or still the day before. The flat caps had taken a serpentine route across the island, eschewing major border crossings, roadblocks and war zones. A little while late, the chariot came to a halt. In the subsequent silence he could make out once more the faint, erratic breathing coming from the floor beneath his feet. He heard the doors at the front crank open and the sounds of boots stepping out and making their way around both sides of the vehicle. A handle right behind him clicked and then jerked open a set of double doors, allowing a rush of night air to embrace the inside of the chariot. At least, it smelled of night, Finn thought. Somewhere in a field beyond a cow lowed mournfully.

'Right then. Out you come. You first, mac Dara.' Finn recognised the voice of Sencha. He had the feeling this was the older brother of the two who had kidnapped him. 'Bren, you drag the other one over here,' the voice continued. 'Looks as though he's still out. How hard did you bloody hit him anyway?'

'Just a wee tap, Senc. That's all,' the other brother complained.

'Aye, I know all about your 'wee taps'. Right lad. I'm going to untie your legs. You try kicking me and Bren here will knock you out cold! Nod your head if you understand.'

Finn nodded. 'Right. Nice and easy.'

He heard a knife scrape and then a quiet snap. His legs were free at least.

'Now, easy does it. Onto your feet. Bren!' he said to his brother. 'You're gonna have to carry the old man out.'

'Some chance! You seen the weight of him?'

'Drag him out then!

In a minute or so, Finn and his fellow victim were sitting on a grassy, dew-laden verge on the side of what felt like a quiet, country road. He tried to think. Even with avoiding main routes, the Protectorate and the war zone, they could already be on the outskirts of Cruachan Aí itself, the capital city of Connachta. They must have crossed the border sometime during the night while he had slept, Finn thought. If they were Connachta spies, they could easily have negotiated safe passage back to their homeland.

'How's the old man?' Sencha asked.

'Alive. If that's what you mean.'

'He better be brother. For both our sakes!'

'Shall I wake him?' Bren asked.

'Aye, throw some water over his face.'

Finn could hear steps to his side, the sound of a leather being cut, and the rasp of tape being removed. Water was being splashed over the man's face. Whoever the man was, he was starting to revive, his mouth wheezing and coughing into life.

'Don't drown the poor bastard!' Sencha remonstrated. 'Right then, lad. Your turn. You're in for a wee surprise.'

Finn felt a hand clutch his shoulder and another on the bag at the top of his head. With a wrench, the bag was roughly removed. It took a moment for Finn's eyes to accustom themselves to his surroundings. He had been right. It was still night. The headlights of the chariot had been left on, however, and their glow provided enough light for Finn to see the scarred face of Sencha grinning back at him. He blinked a few times and then struck out with his leg.

'Whoa...easy lad! Easy. Not in front of the in-laws!' Sencha said, laughing, recoiling a little. Over his shoulder, lying on his side, Finn could make out the bloodied face of his guardian, Lorcan mac Róich.

Conall had not slept very well. The quarters that had been allotted to him and to Oisín and Caoimhín, the two experienced officers that comprised his command triad, had been comfortable: too comfortable and too quiet. His mattress had been unduly thick, and his pillows overly padded for a soldier used to bivouacking in the marshy fens of a war zone where trench foot or frostbite were commonplace and where shells whistled overhead, sometimes all night long.

They had been put up for the last number of

days in the main camp of the Druidic Guard. Conall wondered how the DG made their early morning roll call given the quality of their sheets. It was a small army, he thought, that had never seen action: a military force whose boots and buckles were too polished, whose peaked caps and tunics too starched for the awful realities of modern warfare.

At 04.00, still two hours away from dawn, he had shared breakfast with his triad. Oisín, typically so cold and unresponsive at that time of morning, had seemed oddly over-excited and garrulous. No doubt, the prospect of being in the presence of all four leaders of Éireann and the Arch Druid had stirred up some sense of the magnitude of the occasion in him. Caoimhín, on the other hand, had appeared surly and uncommunicative. Not unusual for him either, Conall thought. He had spent breakfast polishing the woodwork of his CT rifle with a flannel and some linseed oil, cleaning the barrel inside with a length of cord that had a nail attached to one end.

'You expecting trouble?' Conall had asked.

'You never know, sir,' Caoimhín had responded.

Around 04.30, Conall had gathered the contingent of DG together and had given them his final instructions. In spite of the presence of the Connachta unit, he had still demanded overall command. The Connachta, Ó Móráin and his men, looked on indifferently.

The chariots had been parked in a line the night before after the late arrival of King Cuilennáin of Mhumhain and Chancellor Áed Ó'Cosrach of Laighean and their respective delegations. The two leaders had elected to arrive at different entrances to the Roundhouse which had been fortunate as they had turned up unexpectedly at the same time causing a flurry of frenzied activity. This had provided Conall with no end of amusement as he looked on from the woods beyond. He and his men had been checking the grounds for snipers even though he knew that it would be impossible to breach the defensive shield that had been put in place. In all his time in the RBK Conall had never witnessed such security measures.

'But you never know,' he whispered to himself, echoing Caoimhín's sentiments.

It was now 04.40. The electric lamps of the Roundhouse had been kept on all night and they blazed from every window, casting great beacons of light onto the cobbled courtyard outside, just one of the three courtyards over which the high walls of the Roundhouse loomed. Every year, the Arch Druid used a different House from which to make his departure for the Hill of Uisneach at Beltane. This time round, it was the turn of the House of Vates to pay host to the frantic hustling and bustling that went on inside.

Outside, the drivers of the chariots in the motorcade had turned over their engines and were now smoking final, satisfying cigarettes, leisurely chatting to each other, cracking jokes and slapping one another on the backs. In stark contrast, Conall, his triad, the Connachta and the DG stood in separate groups beside their respective chariots, each one locked into the task in hand, their minds ticking over the agenda of the next few hours.

To Conall's surprise a dozen or so soldiers from Laighean and Mhumhain had arrived, a few minutes before, and were now standing on the steps of the main door, preening in contrasting dress uniforms. Conall had approached them immediately and been assured, by their commanding officers, that they were part of the Transport Guard that had ferried their contingents to and from their respective lands. They would play no part in the itinerary to the Hill or the Cat Stone but had simply been asked by the Bardic Press to provide personnel for the photographs that would ensue as soon as the leaders finally made their appearance. The BP, represented in Ulidia by the Béal Feirste Banner, had looked on with interest from the rear of the convoy, enjoying Conall's remonstrations with the soldiers. One of them waved sarcastically at Conall to which the latter had replied with a middle-fingered salute.

Vermin! Conall thought. Still, it had irked him. As with the Connachta unit, Conall hadn't been informed of this minute alteration to the morning proceedings. It wasn't a good omen for the rest of the ceremony.

At 05.00 precisely, to the blare of a cow horn and the solemn beat of a bodhrán, the entrance door to the House of Vates was opened and out stepped Arch Druid Mogh Roth mac Nuadat, clothed immaculately in a silver robe, wrapped at the waist by red sash. The cowl of a hood concealed the top part of his face, and, in his hand, he conveyed a long, oak staff, the twisted handle of which fitting neatly between the old man's knotted fingers.

An Arch Druid, once elected, was an Arch Druid for life, Conall knew. To be an Arch Druid, you had to have money behind you and work your way up through the druidic priesthood. No one had ever become Arch Druid without first having had tenure on the Druidic Council. The Council essentially selected one of its own to be Arch Druid upon the death of a predecessor. The current occupant had been in post for over a decade. News sheets aside, Conall, like most, had only ever seen mac Nuadat from a distance at festivals, a small, silvery dot at the top of a hill. The first thing that surprised him was that the old man did not appear to be that old in the flesh. He might have been nearly sixty summers old, but he didn't look a day over fifty. Rumours in the Ulidian Senate suggested this particular Arch Druid was highly favoured in the Federation Druidic Order. Some even believed that he had the chance to become Éireann's first Supreme Druid.

Behind him, shoulder to shoulder, followed Presidents mac Nessa of Ulidia and Ailill Ó'Flaithearta of Connachta. Ó'Flaithearta's familiar, perfectly round face and short, waxy hair was a source of constant amusement to all Ulidians. In a bid to lampoon and denigrate their enemy's leader, tens of thousands of postcards of the Connachta president had done the rounds of the Ulidian trenches during the war. Some soldiers, Conall noticed, simply doodled a simple twirl of moustache in keeping with his slick, brilliantine hair; others made his face into a time piece, adding numbers all around and even a pocket chain. The joke was that if anyone in Connachta wanted to know the time, all they had to do was stare at their president's clock face.

After them, came the tall, bearded figure of King Cuilennáin of Mhumhain, of whom it was said, was a great exponent of the harp and Chancellor Áed Ó' Cosrach of Laighean who, of all the four leaders, had shied away from traditional Celtic garb and wore instead a three piece suit indicative of the commercial credentials for which his nation was famous.

All the time, Conall was scanning the surrounding environment for any sign of unnatural activity; a movement in the tree line, the glint of a barrel from a window above or a face he didn't recognise in the contingent from the Bardic Press. It was them he had been worried about the most. A trained marksman could easily have infiltrated their ranks he thought. This was why he had Caoimhín and Oisín vet and memorise each journalist's file and study every detail of the photographs contained within. Conall gave Caoimhín a quick look and was met by a slight shake of the head. Oisín did likewise. Nothing seemed out of place. He shared a look with Ó Móráin. Nothing in the man's cold, rugged features gave anything away.

It took another five or ten minutes, during which the four leaders, the Arch Druid, mac Neill and the soldiers from Laighean and Mhumhain adopted various individual and collective poses and stances for the flash cameras of the BP, before the dignitaries finally entered their assigned chariots and Conall could gently release his finger from the trigger of his rifle. In the seat opposite sat Ó Móráin. The Connachta soldier avoided eye contact, staring out of the window of the chariot, content to feign interest in the darkness of the fields that swept quickly by.

At the appointed time, the cavalcade

reached the base of the Hill of Uisneach. In keeping with their location, an eerie silence had descended upon the party. Conall noticed the Arch Druid mutter a few words to mac Nessa who offered a smile in exchange. Even the BP were maintaining a disciplined sense of the occasion. Conall looked up at the Hill in the distance, making out nothing but a constellation of stars that hung like nails in a wall in the blackness of space. There, a gibbous moon still shone.

As predicted, the usual crowd of spectators for Beltane had been kept aside and were out of view on the other side of the Hill. They had been sequestered into a holding area, had paid the Druidic Order quite handsomely for the privilege, and knew better than to make any noise. The lack of cloud cover overhead leant the air an icy chill.

After the torches of the Arch Druid, leaders and Council were lit, the solemn group began their slow climb to the summit of Uisneach. Conall led the way, insisting on the same formation as before, with Ó Móráin, the AD, mac Nessa and Ó'Flaithearta directly behind him. The granite steps were steep and several times Conall had to glance down to verify his footing. Given the average age of the congregation, he was amazed that no one tripped, falling back into the ranks of those behind. Mac Nessa and Ó'Flaithearta were keeping in step with each other, neither one wanting to display any signs of fatigue, although both, no doubt, secretly longed to be back home, overseeing a more modest Beltane ceremony, on more even terrain.

Upon reaching the summit, the four leaders assumed their pre-designated spots either side of the huge, bronze basin which would soon welcome the sacred fire. The famous *babhla tine* or 'bowl of fire' stood on a tripod and was embossed with symbols that marked the four sacred elements of earth, water, air and fire. The Arch Druid stood behind it, the Presidents of Ulidia and Connachta to his immediate left and right, and the other leaders just behind them. The nine members of the Druidic Council formed a circle of fire all around them. Conall, the Connachta and the DG corralled the Bardic Press into a closed group, out of sight, to the extreme right of the main protagonists. He and everyone else who had weapons, formed a shadowy outer circle which encompassed the smaller circle of torches within. Mac Neill joined them, Conall noticed, for once eschewing the limelight.

Sunrise was still a quarter of an hour away. From his position, Conall could testify to the solemn severity of every face he saw. Each participant's torch was lofted high above their heads, igniting the features of those beneath, furnishing them with a flittering dance of light and shadow.

Arch Druid mac Nuadat took a few steps closer to the bowl, paused, looked around and received his cue from one of the members of the Council directly in front of him to begin. It was customary for mac Nuadat to deliver a few lines before lighting the fire. Conall detected a wave of hushed expectation from the crowd below. Looking down the incline, he could make out its individual torches flicker like fireflies in the gloom. If he didn't get on with it, Conall thought, glancing towards the horizon, the sun would be up, and the lid would be blown on the whole affair.

Mac Nuadat stretched out his arms. The microphone in front of him whistled suddenly, an ear-splitting, spine-tingling, electric whiplash that caught everyone off-guard. He tapped the mic twice, as if bringing this new, deviant bit of technology to heel. In the darkness, someone else coughed.

It happened fast. First, the muffled pop of a flare, a blasphemous precursor of dawn, lit up the sky with an orange glow. Next, the sound of gunshots cracked through the silence. After that, pandemonium.

15

'You?!'

'Shall we walk?' Pritchard asked.

'I don't...don't... understand, Professor.'

'I know. Come on. Let's take a stroll. For old time's sake.' He was wearing an ushanka, his winter hat of preference, but for the rest, it was the same, customary riot of colour: fading blue chinos, red anorak and olive-green, wellington boots. He held up his brolly with a gloved hand and poked it in the direction of the mound. 'There's a storm crossing the Atlantic, Lewis, and I want to see the old hill fort before it gets here.'

I looked up. Dark, swollen clouds were already beginning to hang heavy overhead. Pritchard was right. I felt spores of wispy rain tingle on my face, carried on a brief shuttle of wind.

'I am not going anywhere, Professor, until you tell me exactly what's going on.'

'Let's get to the top first, Lewis. Then I will tell you everything you need to know.'

I had no choice but to follow him: a small number of stone steps, an expanse of grass, another few steps, a deep breath at the outer bank and then a more severe, last push of legs to the main hill. I knew every foothold, every minor facilitation and encumbrance of the five-minute route. Pritchard did too. And so, we made our way in silence.

At the top, we surveyed the outline of Armagh in the distance. Its two proud cathedrals squatted like asymmetrical goalposts either side of the town, high above the streets below. The twin spires of one countenanced the crenelated towers of the other.

"You say Armagh, and I see the hill. With the two tall spires or the square low tower', Pritchard quoted suddenly.

'Heaney?'

'Hewitt,' Pritchard smiled.

'Two cathedrals, Summer. Both called St. Patrick's. It's a wonder both sides agreed on the name.'

'I think our patron saint predates the Reformation, Professor.'

'An historical fact, Lewis?'

'Of course.'

'And what difference do historical facts ever make? To the people on this island? That's why I... we...study mythology. It's as real as any misinterpreted fact that any biased saint or scholar ever reads. Even if the words in a history book speak an unassailable truth, they are edited, paraphrased and regurgitated via an innate filtering system that is sometimes not even aware of itself. Who can say if fifty thousand years from now, all this,' he made a sweeping gesture with his hand, 'won't be some future generation's mythology?'

'It probably will be.'

'Oh?'

'Of course. History can always be perverted. All we can do is our very best in the here and now, in the few years we have on this Earth ...but it's not just here, Professor. It's there too, isn't it?

'Yes, there too,' he replied, softly.

'This other world?'

Pritchard nodded. I don't know if it was because I held slightly higher ground, or that he had lowered his head at the particular moment, but Pritchard suddenly appeared very small, almost shrunken, as if the secret, or whatever it was that had sustained him all those years, had suddenly deflated the impressive largesse of his ego. I thought of him as a mad professor in a hot air balloon that had been forced to land, emptying volumes upon volumes of old books in a vain effort to stay airborne. He had aged dramatically since the last time I had seen him. If I hadn't had so many questions to ask, I would have put my arms around him and wept on his shoulder. I think it was at that moment that I actually realised what Pritchard had meant for me. He was a colleague, a friend, a confidant, but he was also a father-figure; someone who understood me better that my own father ever could. He raised his head and held my gaze. 'Yes,' he replied, finally.

'Tell me, Professor. If anyone can tell a story, it's you.'

He smiled at this and spun around once more to face the layout of the town that lay a couple of miles away.

'We spend our lives wondering, don't we, Lewis? What was it like back then? I mean if you think about it, what really is history? Even if what we know is true, what do we really know? We know, for example, the Emperor Augustus followed Julius Caesar and was followed in his turn by Tiberius and so on. We know the names of leaders, battles but so very little about the life of the daily citizen there. And what of Rome, Lewis, at the time the greatest empire the world had ever seen? Everyone knows about Rome. Or ancient Egypt. And the Greeks. We know so much less, sadly, about our own past. If your own history has been lost, what do you do? You have to create a mythology and hope for the best. But what do we have? A Parthenon? A Colosseum? No, Lewis. All we have are a few significant sites, stone circles, archaeological excavations of bronze age beakers, iron age brooches and... mounds like this.'

'And this parallel world?'

Pritchard sighed. 'You know, Lewis, ours is the most honourable and perfect science. Archaeology and mythology. We, you and I, squeeze out every last bit of data available to us. You cannot argue with a broken bit of pottery or a myth that has been passed on for millennia. And even if you could, why would you want to? Some historians, on the other hand, ignore what doesn't sit well with them. You speak of 'parallel worlds'? Quantum physicists, since Max Planck at the turn of the century, have been marginalised, trivialised and fictionalised into B movies. The mainstream doesn't want to know about parallel worlds or counter-Earths. The universe is a very large mechanical clock with tiny cogs that have been rotating since the days of Newton.'

'But these worlds exist?'

'You know they do, Lewis. In this world, we are standing on an isolated hill on the outskirts of an ecclesiastical capital whose religion brought an end to an entire culture. In the other world, at least the one locked in with ours, Rome, for example, never existed.'

It took me a moment for his words to fully penetrate.

'But if Rome never existed...How...? Why...?'

'Quite simple, really. 'Hannibal antes portas'!'

I tried to bring back my schoolboy Latin.

'Hannibal is at the gates?'

'Yes, but what if he and his elephant herd had marched through those gates, defeated the might of Rome at a time when it was at its most vulnerable?'

'The Punic Wars?'

'The Second Punic War to be exact. If Rome loses that war, there is no Roman Empire. Carthage dominates the Mediterranean. They are a seafaring, mercantile people, less interested in military expansion. The barbaric tribes north of the Rhine and Danube are left to their own devices. Later on, our Holy Roman Empire is their Holy Carthaginian Empire and so on...'

'...I don't believe it! It's incredible!'

'Any more incredible than the existence of another world in lockstep with our own, connected by a gateway atop an agglomeration of ley lines; a mound of earth in one leading to a modern Celtic temple to another?'

'So, the crucifixion...'

'...Ah! Well, let's just say, all of that took place as it had to.'

'Celtic culture never died?'

'Yes, Lewis. It never died. Where we are standing now is one of the major sites of a capital city Ulidians call Emain Mhaca.'

'Ulidians? You mean...'

'Yes, the old stories still flourish there. Christianity has never reached their shores.

There's no St. Patrick, Lewis, and Ireland is still full of snakes.'

'But what system of government do they have? Economy? Industry?'

'You will discover all that soon enough, Lewis.'

'You mean when I go there?'

'Yes.'

'But what's your part in all this? How do you know about this 'Ulidia'? How do you know the portal? About...?'

'...About Eva?'

'Yes,' I stammered.

Pritchard released a long breath. 'I will tell you everything, Lewis. Do you mind if we head back to the Centre? Grab a coffee?'

'Sure. Ok, I think.'

'We can talk on the way.'

We began the return leg of our journey. I had to grab the old Professor's arm once or twice to prevent him cartwheeling down the greasy, rain-slicked slope. Once we had got to even ground, he continued his explanation.

'I don't know everything, Lewis. I don't have all the details. Only information that is volunteered.'

'You mean by the sentinel?

'Sentinel? Ah, Cathbad. Strange fellow that, eh?' Pritchard laughed.

'Just a bit.' I replied.

'So where shall I start?'

'Eva.'

'Ah yes, Eva. Such a beauty she was. Probably still is.'

'You knew her?

'Yes. She came across in 1980, I think. Cathbad, the voice on the other end of the phone, had opened the gate for her. He said a young woman was going to need my help. I was to give her money, help her find a place to live et cetera.'

'But why you?! Why ask you?'

'First things first, Lewis. Let me explain it in my own way.' I nodded, apologetically, and gave him a moment to collect his thoughts. 'She turned up at the department one evening when I was working late. She told me her name and that she needed help. She was looking for a man on this side, on behalf of another man from the other side.'

'She was looking for me?!' I exclaimed, astonished. 'You knew, Pritchard! You bloody knew about us!'

'I only knew that she needed to meet you. Her English was so bad back then.'

'Wait a minute. Easter 1980? That was around the time we started our walks together. That meeting in Botanic Gardens. That wasn't by chance, was it? You were interested in me, probing me for information! Because of her!' I exclaimed

'No, I knew *about* you long before. But I

needed to know why Eva wanted to meet you.'

'Fine, Professor. We will put that one to the side for now. Continue.'

'She wanted to meet you but not straight away. She wanted to learn about this side of the portal, study, educate herself, learn the language. I had no idea what she had in mind. I would meet her every so often, give her books, help her with her English, pay for her flat, travel costs around the country...Newgrange and so on. And then, just after Rose...well... sometime after the funeral, she came to my office unexpectedly and informed me she was pregnant.'

'I assumed you were the father but dismissed it immediately. You had given me no indication of any kind of infidelity or modification of behaviour up until the time of Rose's death. I had begun to think I had got the whole thing wrong. She wanted more money. That summer, I met her for the last time in Botanic Gardens. She was obviously visible with child by then. She told me she was going back to her world and thanked me for everything I had done. It wasn't until you told me about your evening with her that I really ever knew for sure.'

'And the police. It was you who told them that I was in Armagh. It was you who told them about that night.'

'Cathbad needed you to be in Armagh. He

needed you prepared, reawakened. You really don't know what he's like, Lewis. You don't hear from him for years and then the phone never stops ringing and then you hear him in your head...'

I thought about this and gave Pritchard a conciliatory look. 'So, I have a child in the other world. And now I am meant just to go there for a... a reconciliation? Why me? Why now?'

'I don't know. I don't think the child was part of the plan. I think Eva, when she realised what had happened to her, made the decision to return and raise the child with her own people.'

'Cathbad told me that I was from that world too. That I had been brought here as an infant.'

'Yes,' he replied.

'Isn't that a bit of a coincidence?'

'What do you mean?'

'You and I just happened to work in the same department, in the same university, in the same city?'

'No, not really. The same impulse that drove you to mythology also drove me. That impulse was ingrained in you at a genetic level. I'm no expert, but for you I don't think you had a choice. We are a small, insular people in some regards, Lewis. The chances were you were going to end up at Queen's or Trinity College Dublin or somewhere else on these islands.'

'That doesn't explain what impulse drove you. Or why Cathbad connected with you. You're not telling me you too are from the other side.'

'No, no. not in the way, you mean.'

'I don't understand.'

'I have spent time over there. In Ulidia. I was only a child. I didn't even realise at first where I was.'

'The three years. The years you never talked about. You were over there?!'

We made it back to the Navan Centre just in time, awkwardly running the remainder of the way, shoulder to shoulder, huddled under Pritchard's umbrella. The grass roof above the round walls of the centre were an architectural homage to our Celtic past, but in stark contrast to the automatic doors that whirred inwards as we crossed into the building's foyer. A cafe close by was separated off by willow frames with little gaps that allowed you to appraise the comings and goings of tourists.

Sitting down, I ordered two mugs of strong, sugared tea. Pritchard removed his hat, gloves and coat and drank half a cup before continuing.

'I told you about my father, didn't I?

'Yes, I remember. From Wales, originally?'

'Yes. Well, he died in 1932. I was only eight years old at the time. I ended up going into care for a few weeks and then, one day a young couple must have turned up at the children's home. I was told that they were my new foster parents.'

'Their names?'

'Corcoran. Aidan and Brenda.'

'Go on.'

'So, I remember hugs and farewells, a car journey out of Belfast during which I think I fell asleep, or they had put me to sleep somehow, arrival at a car park and then being helped up a steep hill in the snow. I must have passed out because when I woke up it was daylight and no longer winter.'

'Winter solstice?'

'Yes. Probably.'

'This couple?'

'I saw them only occasionally after that. But you have met them already. One of them likes to wear purple.'

'Angus and Brigid!'

'Very good. And you know how 'Corcoran' translates into English?'

'No.'

'Purple.'

I shook my head. 'Aidan and Brenda Corcoran. ABC.'

'Yes, they have a sense of humour, those two.'

'So, they brought you over?'

'Yes.'

'Then what happened.'

'Three of the happiest years of my life. It was difficult at first. Everyone spoke a different language, very similar to modern Irish. I didn't realise that until much later. The Corcorans would drop in now and again at the beginning. They spoke English and reassured me, told me that I was very important and that I would be going back home soon. You know, the kind of things a child wants to hear, Lewis. I was young. I simply thought I was in a foreign country.'

'A foreign country called Ulidia?'

'Why not? How many countries does an eight-year-old know? As far as I was concerned, I was abroad. And besides...'

'Besides?'

'Besides, I was with new parents that actually...'loved' me. You know what my father was like, Lewis!'

'Who were these new parents?'

'The mac Róichs. I can't really remember their first names. I really just called them *máthair* and *athair*, mother and father, or whatever the equivalent was. They were in their early forties. The woman was beautiful, I remember. Green eyes. The man had a nice smile. He taught me how to throw a spear.'

'Throw a spear?'

'Yes. It's different over there. You'll see.'

'I'm not too sure about that. So, what else?'

'A teacher, well I suppose she was a teacher, would come and visit us.'

'Us?'

'Yes,' Pritchard's face lit up at the memory. 'The couple had a son, and we were schooled together.'

'You remember his name.'

'Yes, of course. His name was Lorcan. He was roughly the same age as me and it was Lorcan who helped me with the language barrier at the start. The Corcorans had left some books and dictionaries with the teacher. I think her name was Mrs Ó' Cuinn. She was friendly too.'

'What else do you remember?'

'Just meals together at night, festivals, lots of festivals. Horses and carts...'

'...Horses and carts?

'Yes, I don't think I saw a single car the whole time. They are not as technologically advanced over there as we are. Thinking about it later, I would say about seventy or eighty years behind us. So, for me in 1932, it was like being right in the middle of the Victorian Age, without Victoria, if you see what I mean.'

'Anything else?' Pritchard looked away. 'Professor?'

'I hated leaving, Lewis. It nearly destroyed me. Lorcan and I... well, let us say we were very close. Real brothers, you know!

'What happened?'

'Around Samhain, 1935, the Corcorans returned. They told me they had found me new parents who wanted to adopt me. I told them I was happy where I was. I begged the mac Róichs to let me stay. I knew they wanted me too, but I sensed they were powerless to prevent my leaving. And so...I was taken back. And I started my new life with the Hollywoods.'

'But why take you there, just to return you? Why you?'

'I have been asking that my entire life. If Angus and Brigid are aos sí, and that's what I think they are, then perhaps they were simply performing a role they have been performing for epochs: the theft of children to the otherworld.'

'Hmm,' I said, 'I think there's more to them than that. But why bring you back?'

'Later, much later, around the time of the archaeological excavations here at the start of the fifties, they showed up again along with the sentinel Cathbad. I was in my mid-twenties then. The adult mind isn't the same as the child's, Lewis. It wasn't a direct intrusion this time around. I don't know how but they, or it, simply infiltrated my sub-consciousness as I slept, drip-feeding me memories of the other world, Lorcan, my other parents, Mrs Ó' Cuinn and so on. This went on for months. Waking up in the middle of the night, my sheets saturated with the perspiration of vivid dreams, I was being reacclimated to the sense of the fantastic, to the pages of the fairy tale that the normal child grows out of. Finally, things started to go missing around the house...and then the phone calls.'

'You too? That's how they communicated...'

'Yes, me too.' He paused briefly, added another spoonful of sugar to his tea and stirred it thoughtfully.

'But why?' I asked.

'I was told that a young boy had crossed over from their side. I assumed, naturally, it was another boy like me. I wanted to meet him, share experiences, revive my own fading memories and so on. No, was all the voice said. The boy was too young. An infant. And then Cathbad told me...'

'...Told you what?'

'Told me that the boy would soon be a man and the man would have an interest in Celtic mythology that surpassed even my own. I wasn't given a name. But when I first met you back in '74, I thought you might be the boy. Again, it wasn't until Eva that I knew for sure.'

The automatic doors opened again. A young, eager woman, toting a box file under her armpit, had just entered the foyer. She leaned over, opening and closing her umbrella to shake off the rain. In doing so she tilted her head to one side and caught sight of us in the cafe. Her hat chose that moment to fall to the floor.

'Oh, Dr. Pritchard! Dr. Pritchard,' she exclaimed. 'You're here!' She put down her umbrella, grabbed her hat and approached. 'I thought you were in France! So, you *can* do the talk, after all! Barbara Riley, chairperson of the *Friends of Macha* group!' She stretched out her hand. Pritchard, standing up, shook her hand happily while surreptitiously passing me a note with the other. 'And you must be, Professor Summer?'

'Yes,' I replied. I pocketed the note, made my excuses and left.

It continued to rain all day. I spent long hours in silence, entertained only by the raindrops falling down my hotel bedroom window, leaving strange, unpredictable trails in their wake. By nightfall, I heard my first fireworks in the distance, and soon afterwards, the early commotion of parents and children in the street below, venturing off to parties and the thrills of trick-or-treat.

I thought about Halloween masks. Had I been wearing one my whole life? I was not Lewis Summer, after all, it seemed. I had not belonged to this world. There was a reason now for all those years of disconnect. And yet, the revelation of who I was, or might be, made me feel like an imposter in my own body, an undercover agent in a world who could no longer recall his mission. I was between worlds, a peripheral outcast too frightened to move forward, not frightened enough to turn back. I wanted to belong somewhere, to someone again, but I couldn't shake the feeling that it was already too late.

I ate a final meal in my room and thought about packing a suitcase. It was absurd. Preposterous. But if I failed to keep my appointment with Cathbad and the aos sí I knew that I would regret it. The rest of my life here would be a post-apocalyptic, dust-filled netherworld, a lunar landscape devoid of life and even a reason to stay alive.

The note Pritchard had passed to me had simply, and somewhat theatrically, said: 'Midnight'. It was typical of Pritchard. I thought of a life navigated in his shoes, how he had been plucked from the gates of hell and placed... where? An intermediary holding area where he learned to love and accept love for the first time in his life, only to be pried away once more and reinstalled back in his own world, a child of Lir, with a lifetime of experience that he had kept locked away in a corner vault, somewhere in the recesses of his mind. Was this why he had never married? Had this world, and everything in it, paled so much in comparison?

I looked at my watch. 10.00pm. Pritchard would be just finishing off his talk now, a tall tale of fairies and fays, and then a procession with the *Friends of Macha* to the mound, a sham ceremonial addendum to an evening made all the worse by the reality of what he knew. Was it wrong of me not to attend? No doubt. But it was too much for me. I needed those hours to think. Pritchard had had a life-time of digging in the earth for a culture that he knew had survived, pristine, in another world. I thought of the mournful tragedy of every trowel of dirt he had scooped from the soil of our world, a desperate bid to find evi-dential proof of the three years he had spent in the other.

As for me, it was far too early. My years of research had become suddenly toxic to me. Every word I had ever written was a life-less, meaningless monogram: every academic thought and pedantic proposal, a source of em-barrassment. I was no different to the child in the Halloween mask, as far from the mean-ing of Samhain, and what it represented, than a child's sparkler in the thunderstorm outside my window.

A couple of hours later I retraced Pritchard's, the eight-year-old boy's, steps once more over the hill of Navan Fort, or Emain Mhaca as it was known. I was better prepared this time for the weather: coat, um-brella, scarf - but no suitcase. The idea of lug-ging one up a hill in a gale in the dead of night was too ridiculous to countenance. There was no light to guide my way and I struggled against the prevailing force of the wind.

When I reached the summit, however, I was suddenly struck by how serenely quiet everything had become, as though an invisible dome had been erected over the top of the mound and I had travelled through an unseen force field to find myself beneath. Looking back, over my shoulder, I could make out the tops of trees swaying wildly, but soundlessly, in the darkness. In front of me, all was eerily still. I detected a light source, emanating underground, it seemed, from the centre of the mound. I looked around. The rain had stopped. Whether it was because I had already transitioned somehow from one reality to another, I didn't know, but as I stood, alone, listening to my own rapid breathing, I was convinced that Cathbad and the others were there, taking note of my every move. For that reason, I remained where I was, stubbornly refusing to move to the pool of light, thirty yards or so from where I was standing.

'I know you are here. You might as well show yourselves!' I shouted. I felt a faint ripple of light and space and, looking left, I noticed Brigid, dressed as before. She was lit up from within somehow, but completely visible in the surrounding blackness. I didn't need to turn right to confirm that Angus too had arrived. Directly ahead, stood Cathbad. This was the first time I had seen him stand; he was as tall as I had imagined, perhaps almost nine feet in height. The sight of him sapped me of my remaining reserves of will.

'Are you ready, Lewis? You just have to approach the central light. I will do the rest.'

'I still have free will then?' I asked.

'But of course, Lewis. You have made your own choices up until now.'

I thought of his badgering phone calls, the childish pranks the other two had played at my home, my friendship with Pritchard. Have I? I wondered. 'You can turn around, Lewis,' Cathbad continued, 'return to the maelstrom of your world. Or you can be true to yourself. See Eva and your son. Be 'happy'.'

'My son?'

Yes, didn't we say? Eva gave birth to a boy.'

'A son?' I repeated. For some reason, the confirmation of gender, made the child suddenly real to me.

'His name's Finn. You would be proud of him. But he's in trouble, Lewis! His life is in danger. His mother, Aoife, doesn't yet know...'

'...Aoife?' I exclaimed.

'Yes, Aoife. That's her real name, Lewis. Eva is a close approximation in your language. These helpers of mine, these aos sí, can only move through their local gate at the major festivals, solstices and equinoxes. They have been here, in this world since your last equinox. Tonight, they will return with you to Emain

Mhaca. Once there, they will find Aoife, and then together, you will find the boy.'

'Emain Mhaca?'

'Yes, the Emain Mhaca on the other side. The one of which Pritchard spoke.'

'Pritchard?! You mean, my friend? The one you discarded!'

'Discarded? The one we saved from the pain of a neglected father? The one who was adored by a good, caring family...'

'...And then discarded, confused and rejected.'

'We don't have time for this!' Brigid exclaimed. The light is beginning to fade!'

'Lewis, Brigid is right. If you don't go now, it will be the next solstice before you can next depart. By that time, it will be too late.'

'Pritchard...! I protested.

'Pritchard has had a good life, better than most in your world. I am a sentinel. Although I cannot interfere directly, I can see the timelines, past, present and future. Without the aos sí, I can safely say to you, Pritchard's life would have been a lot worse. You have my word on that.'

'But why is it so important that I return? Why is my son in danger?'

''You are important, Lewis. Your son is important. And your father is important.'

'My father? Who's my father?

'You will meet him, Lewis. Don't worry! He

will reveal himself to you on the other side. I owe him that.'

'Cathbad, the liminal point has almost been passed.' It was Angus. Somehow, he and Bridge were now in position over the light source which had been decreasing in size the whole time we were talking. 'He has to come! Now!'

I could see Angus. He was holding up his right arm which he then proceeded to insert into what must have been some sort of incision in the air, a slice of vertical darkness, perpendicular to the feeble light that was rapidly disappearing on the ground beneath. His right arm was no longer visible, and he stood there, briefly one-armed, his other hand clutching Bridgit's who was waving Lewis on.

'Come on, you stupid fool! It's closing!' she cried out.

'Go on. Now! Trust me! Remember, it's in your blood, Lewis!' Cathbad roared at me. 'Never forget! It's in your blood!'

And with those words, I took a leap of faith. Cathbad was right. There was nothing for me anymore in my own world. Not even Pritchard. If given the chance, he would not have hesitated. I made the decision to run towards the aos sí. I made the decision to run for my life. Angus had already slid out of view. Bridge too had almost disappeared. I could only make out her hand, its fingers outstretched to reel me in.

PART TWO

16

Conall had not witnessed the president slump forward. His direct line of vision had been obscured by both a member of the Druidic Council and by the Arch Druid himself. Positioned on the outer circle, with the rest of the security detail of Ulidian, Connachta and Druidic Guards, he had made sure he had kept a keen eye on President mac Nessa. How was he to know that it would be Ó'Flaithearta, the Connachta President, who would be targeted for assassination?

He had reacted well, as had his two men, Oisín and Caoimhín. Their warning cries had joined his own as they had scrambled forward in tandem, from different points in the circle, ducking from the potential promise of more sniper fire towards the supine body of mac Nessa. The Ulidian leader was playing dead, his hands gripped behind his head in a futile attempt to defend the narrowness of his skull from the width of a bullet.

To mac Nessa's right, no acting was required. The Connachta president was on his knees; his face, Ó Móráin had claimed later, had, upon impact, buried itself momentarily in the back of the Arch Druid's legs, before sliding sidewards to the ground. By the time Conall had secured mac Nessa and checked on mac Neill, Ó'Flaithearta was already unconscious.

The Connachta unit and rest of the DG had replicated the actions of the Ulidian triad, maintaining a swift, low centre of gravity towards their president. The Arch Druid had not been harmed, nor had any of his Druidic Council. They crouched, knelt and lay in the nascent twilight, their torches creating mini fires beside them, at which some of them could only stare now in shock.

It wasn't until after the initial mayhem, when the light of the flare had burned itself out, that Conall noticed the King of Mhumhain and the Chancellor of Laighean cowering together in the ascending gloom. As bit players to the events of the morning, their security had been prohibited from the Hill. In all the confusion they had simply been forgotten about.

That's going to go down well, Conall thought briefly. 'Truce? We'll all be at war with each other by the end of the day!'

With the first light of dawn, Conall was able to extend the defensive perimeter to the base of the Hill and secure the crowd below. No one would be able to leave the scene until every witness had been thoroughly questioned. He realised, of course, it was pointless, but procedure had to be followed. The chances that anyone down there could have seen anything of note were non-existent. Besides, the gunfire, it turned out, had originated from the opposite direction. To that end, half of the detail had been ordered down that side of the Hill in an attempted pursuit of the assailant while some of the Bardic Press had been used to relay emergency messages back to the Roundhouse via electric telegraph. A special station had been constructed in recent years at the bottom of the Hill especially for that purpose. It wouldn't take long, Conall knew, for the news to disseminate across the island via the pitter-patter of Ogham Code.

The Connachta president still had a pulse. Three of the Druidic Council had been vates in the far distant past and they had naturally done everything they could to assist until the arrival of a hospital chariot from the Roundhouse. A tentative, preliminary examination had indicated one of the bullets had gone straight through his back, exiting from his left hip. The other one was somewhere still inside. The top right side of his back was a bloody, indeterminate mess and the vates knew best not to examine that area more until the arrival of the chariot. Instead they took turns using a ripped section of the president's tunic to compress his wounds.

Within a quarter of an hour of the shots ringing out upon the Hill of Uisneach, a stretcher and four bearers were transporting the president of Connachta down the steps once more.

For the first time in recorded history, the Uisneach fire had not been set alight. It was obvious to all that the signing of the Ulidia-Connachta truce at the Cat Stone would not be taking place.

As they stood and watched the stretcher's slow, ignominious descent, Conall caught sight of Ó'Móráin staring at him coldly, his right hand tightly clutching the stock of his rifle.

It was going to be a long day.

The House of Vates at the Roundhouse had a dedicated staff, primed and ready to deal with any sudden, medical emergency befalling the elite representatives of the Druidic Council. It was here that Ó'Flaithearta's hospital chariot was conveyed, the remainder of the ceremonial assembly following slowly behind. Ó'Móráin had concentrated his men and some of the DGs either side of the chariot, unofficially assuming responsibility for the safety of his president. Conall, looking on, could hardly blame him. If things had gone differently, he would have done exactly the same.

Upon arrival at the Arch Druid's residence, the various leaders retired to their appointed chambers and a cordon of heavily armed Druidic Guard prevented the Bardic Press from getting too close. It hardly mattered. It was the greatest news day ever. One of the journalists from the Beal Féirste Banner had decided to headline the story: 'Mac Nessa Survives!' while another quipped an alternative: 'Has the Connachta Clock Stopped Ticking?!' No one outside of the press found any of it very amusing.

'By Bel's sacred fire! We've got major problems, mac Dara!'

It was Bradán mac Neill. He had demanded that Conall wait outside mac Nessa's presidential suite as he entered to consult briefly with the president. Twenty minutes later, he was still inside. Conall strained to listen but heard nothing from within. There were now half a dozen Druidic Guards outside mac Nessa's chamber. Conall recognised two of them as his temporary subordinates from the morning detail. They grimaced at him now, clearly attributing blame to one foreigner for the attempt on another foreigner's life. It had happened on their sacred soil and they were not amused. Neither was mac Neill's face when he finally reappeared. Even his drinker's nose seemed to have sobered up during his talk with the Ulidian leader. 'Follow me.' he whispered.

They walked down a few corridors and stopped outside a heavy, oak door. Mac Neill produced a key and opened it. 'Inside! Quick!'

It was mac Neill's chamber. The first thing Conall noticed was a half-packed suitcase on his bed; either mac Neill was on the verge of leaving or hadn't fully arrived. Conall couldn't decide which.

'Bad?' Conall enquired.

'Bad? Bad? You have no idea.'

'Any word on Ó'Flaithearta?'

'Him?… Oh, touch and go. The vates will know more by the end of the day.'

'What then?'

'Do I have to spell it out for you, mac Dara?!' He counted on his fingers. 'One: an attempt has been made on the life of a leader of a sovereign nation. Two: this is a nation, Connachta, with which our nation, Ulidia, is currently still at war. Three: the attempt takes place on the Hill of Uisneach which means we have the whole Druidic Council on our back. Four: we have just armed their Druid Guard.' He looked at Conall helplessly. 'I need a drink!' He opened a bureau, decanted a large draught of whiskey into a tumbler, and drank it down. He poured himself a second.

'Wait! Hang on, Mac Neill. Ulidia wasn't responsible for today. You know that.'

'Do I?'

'Now, just wait a minute!'

'Wait a minute?! We'll be lucky to have that long!'

'If you are suggesting I, or any of my men, had anything to do with...'

'...Don't you see, mac Dara. It no longer matters what I, mac Nessa or the Ulidian Senate thinks. We have to wait for the Connachta response.'

'So that's Ó Braonáin. He's their number two. That's lucky. Man's as weak as a fart!'

'And Ó Móráin? And the rest of the Connachta top brass? Ó'Flaithearta's decision to enter peace talks wasn't popular in their senate either, you know.'

'But surely the situation can be controlled?'

'They tell me I can spin a phrase, mac Dara,' he swallowed heavily, 'but even I have limitations! Of course, the entire operation was left in your hands...'

'...Me? Oh, I see! It's my fault, is it?!' Conall exclaimed, his voice rising. 'May I remind you that Connachta had their own men there, too?! You yourself passed on that small tidbit to me.'

'Mac Dara, you had *overall* control over the security...'

'...which I went through with you and mac Nessa! If Ó Móráin had taken the lead, he would have done things no differently. I can guarantee you that. Besides, who vets the Druidic Guard?'

'You're not suggesting...?'

'...Why not? They have weapons! Our bloody weapons, I might add!'

'It couldn't have been them. I was there too, remember. The shots came from distance. A skilled marksman, or men,' mac Neill said.

'At least two,' Conall added, 'given that one had to send up the flare.'

'Maybe. We won't know until after a full, forensic examination of the area and... Ó'Flaithearta.' His voice softened a little. 'But mac Dara, you yourself said that if an attack took place, it would be at the Cat Stone.'

'I know,' the commander replied, thoughtfully.

'Well, however it happened, no one's leaving Uisneach or the Protectorate until the men responsible are found. The Druidic Council has the whole place in lockdown. Security has been beefed up at all border routes.

'You can't seal every gap, mac Neill! They'll have an exit strategy.'

'We can try.' He bit his lip. 'And...'

'What?'

'There's an emergency meeting of the senate today. Mac Nessa obviously will be in attendance. He will be leaving for Ulidia just before lunch. The...the Druidic Guard will be escorting him to the border and a unit of RBK will take over from there.'

'And what about me and my men?

'You, Ó'Móráin's team and the Bardic Press...anyone who's not a bloody druid and was on that Hill at the time of the shooting are requested...'

'...requested?

'...to stay behind and assist the investigation team with their enquiries.'

'And who's leading this investigation?'

'Top man in the House of Brehon Law. Mac an Bhreithiún. Of course, the DG will go through the initial evidence, but it will be mac an Bhreithiún who will be asking the questions once all the information is collated.'

'If there is any,' Conall said.

'Indeed. Anyway, I'll be accompanying the president back home and return in the morning. We'll send on one of our own brehon lawgivers to represent you and your triad in case of complications.'

'Complications?'

'Just a precaution. Can't leave you here with all these bloody foreigners.'

'What about the BP?'

'The Bardic Press? You know the media. They have loyalty to no nation. The House of Bards will look after their interests.'

'Who's the lawgiver?'

'Ah him,' mac Neill said, looking away. 'You already know him. A young senator by the name of Aodhán mac Murchadha.'

It could have been any number of the hundreds of abandoned cottages that littered the Connachta countryside. Stacked stones mortared by clay forming walls of fading white-wash. Above, the eaves of a thatched roof jut-ted unevenly. In front, a broken spinning wheel lay on its side next to an overturned barrow with a punctured wheel. Finn and Lorcan were greeted inside by dark, wattle and daub walls and a hearth that dominated the main living area. Creaking, timber beams did their best to bear the weight of the ceiling above. There was little in the way of furniture; a table and a few scattered chairs. What marginal light there was peaked through four tiny, square win-dows, one of which had been broken from the outside judging by the shards of glass strewn across the cobbled floor. One small bedroom reached out to the right through an open door.

'There you go, lads,' Bren had said, upon ar-rival. 'Bet you're glad you can see now, eh? Not to worry, we'll soon have it nice and cosy! Oh, and Happy Beltane!'

The cottage had not been too far from the location of their pre-dawn reunion. The brothers could not have chosen a more re-mote setting. A panorama of rolling grassland, divided up by a maze of dry, stone walls, en-closed fields long since emptied of livestock. The brothers had left to gather wood for a fire but not before tightening the leather bounds around Finn and his guardian's wrists and ankles.

'You can shout as much as you want, lad.

No one about for miles,' Sencha had reminded him.

'Where are we?' Finn had asked.

'Breathe in that sweet Connachta air, boy! Nothing like it anywhere else on the island!'

When they had gone, Finn noticed that Lorcan was still uncommunicative. He had registered shock, of course, upon seeing his ward, but when Finn had instinctively attempted to embrace his guardian, the latter had recoiled in pain. There was a deep cut on his lower lip and a purple contusion had already formed on the left side of his jaw. Perhaps Lorcan was finding it difficult to speak. Bastards! Finn thought. A man of seventy summers did not deserve such treatment.

'Finn!' he whispered, suddenly.

'Yes, Lorcan. You awake? I thought you were asleep,' Finn answered, relief apparent in his voice.

'No, no. Just building up my reserves. You ok, lad?'

'Yes, I'm fine. Don't worry about me. What happened to you?'

'I was just about to leave for the BP when they turned up at the house. I thought it was Conall or Maggo coming back.'

'Yes, Maggo told me that Conall had paid you a visit.'

'Well, I opened the door when I... well I can't really remember. It happened so quickly. One of them struck me and I suppose I must have fallen backwards. The one with the large rings, I'd say. It must have been that which cut my lip.'

'His name's Bren. He's the younger of the two,' Finn agreed, his blood simmering. 'They're Connachta.'

'Connachta? How did you end up with a couple of Connachta?'

'They approached Maggo and me at dinner.'

'Maggo! I put my faith in that young man!'

'It wasn't his fault, Lorcan. We...I... the Connachta said that they had met my mother at the clearing stations. The one who hit you, Bren, he told me that mother had helped him when he had been shot.'

'Aoife had helped...*him*?'

'Yes, and then they told me that mother was in trouble...and so I agreed to go with them. As soon as I got to the chariot, they bound and gagged me...I'm sorry, Lorcan. I was a fool.'

'Don't trouble yourself, lad. They haven't killed us, so they obviously need us for something.'

'A ransom?'

'Hmm...not sure. Snatch me and they have in their hands an editor of a Bardic Press news sheet. I have...well...I have a few shillings set aside as well. Snatch you and they have the nephew of commander Conall mac Dara. I can appreciate both incentives. Snatch both of us though? That's what I can't figure out.'

'Twice the ransom?'

'Too messy, lad.'

Do you think she's alright, Lorcan? Mother, I mean.'

'Don't worry, lad. Those two up against Aoife? They wouldn't stand a chance!'

Finn smiled.

'Still, they are professionals, no doubt about that. They did their research. They must have been following us for days. They knew exactly how to extract their targets and adapt their accent as well to survive in the city. They were clever enough to blend into the Beltane crowds, just another Ulidian tourist arriving in the capital for the festival. There's something, or someone, big behind this.'

'Maggo!' Finn announced, suddenly.

'Yes, that's the other thing. Seems our Connachta don't put much store in our Punic friend raising that much of an alarm about your disappearance, or about anyone taking him seriously even if he did. Not that it mattered. We were well on our way by the time Maggo would have worked out something was amiss. Still,' Lorcan added thoughtfully, 'there's something about Maggo. He's a fairly, determined young fellow. We in the Federation seriously misjudge the mentality of the average Carthaginian Christian. I have spent time in the Union, remember. 'Turning the other cheek' doesn't mean allowing the other fellow to walk all over you!'

'Turning the other cheek?'

'Ha! Don't worry about it. It's nothing. Just something I read once. Anyway, they'll have noticed my absence at the BP. And I am sure you were planning to spend Beltane with your cadet friends. Donall and...?'

'...Ferdia. I have less confidence in them that I have in Maggo. Bet they haven't even noticed I'm gone!' Finn laughed.

'Probably right. Those two are probably with the other cadets, eyeing up the tourists in the presidential gardens.' Finn blushed. 'Anyway, whatever our friends here have planned, they will soon let us, and others, know.'

'Maggo will tell Conall, Finn declared. 'My uncle will have his men looking for us.'

'I don't think so, lad.'

'Why not?'

'That's what he had come to tell me. He's in Uisneach.'

'Did someone mention Uisneach?' It was Bren, standing at the open door, with an armful of logs, his hair matted with sweat. Lugh knows how long he had been eavesdropping their conversation, Finn thought. 'Seems you're not as hurt as we have been led to believe.'

'Whatever it is you want,' Lorcan said, 'it doesn't have to involve the lad! You know who he is! You'll bring the whole RBK down on top of you!'

'Nothing much they can do, eh? Took them twenty-five years advancing and retreating a line a few inches on a map. I can't see the Red Branch marching way down here. Can you, Senc?' His brother had appeared behind him at the door. Unlike Bren, his hair had been newly combed, and he had changed his shirt. Instead of wood, he held a cigarette in his hand. He offered one to his brother.

'He'll not need the RBK! He can sort you two out all by himself.' Finn snapped, proudly.

'I don't think so, lad,' Sencha replied. 'While Bren here was merrily gathering fuel for a bit of breakfast, I discovered something very interesting. Seems there's been quite a ruckus in the Protectorate! President Ó'Flaithearta's been shot, Bren!'

'Is he...?!'

'...No one knows if he's going to make it through the day. And guess who, brother, was supposed to be looking after our glorious leader.'

'Who?' Bren asked

'None other than our friend, Conall mac Dara.'

17

It was the light, the sheer wholeness of it, its overwhelming, blinding whiteness, engulfing the space into which I had stepped, that had forced my eyes to close. Whether that space was a holding space between worlds, a transitory threshold, or simply a readjustment of my vision to the dramatic shift from the night I had left, to the day I had entered, I didn't know. Whatever the case, I had no sense of time having passed or of distance being travelled.

I felt a soft breeze on my skin, then an awareness of temperature, like opening your window on the first morning of spring. With that came a new, sudden, bouquet of smells, an indecipherable combination of fragrances that the tourist appreciates when leaving behind the stale, recycled air of a foreign airport terminal. There was a gentle relaxation of pressure on my eyelids.

When I dared to open them, I found myself blinking, shielding my eyes from a fierce sun.

It took a few seconds for my eyes to blur my surroundings into focus. And then, only then, did I become aware of a tremendous cacophony of sound, arriving like a sonic wheel, a deafening, spiralling wall of noise enveloping an amphitheatre of din.

It was the unmistakable sound of people, thousands of people.

'Come this way!' came a voice to my right as if underwater. It was Bridge. I realised I was still holding her hand. Angus was beckoning to us from behind a stone monolith.

'Keep your head down!' he was shouting, gesturing with his hands.

I ducked and followed, finding myself in the sheltered cavity of a dolmen. It was just about large enough for the three of us inside and offered some buffering from the clamour on the other side.

'They never build these bloody gates in the right place.' I heard Angus moan.

'Cathbad's timing's off. Again! People are still here.' Bridge replied. 'The ritual isn't over yet.'

'How long?'

'Half an hour or so.'

'Too long.'

'What ritual?' I asked.

'What do you want to do?' Bridge asked, disregarding my question.

'We can't stay here. He'll be spotted.'

'Bloody Cathbad! I told you we needed a new sentinel.'

'Look!' Angus said. 'Over there! What's that?'

'It looks like a sculpture. Must be new.'

'No, it's two sculptures! Twins of Macha if I am not mistaken!'

'Twins of Macha?' I muttered to myself. 'Emain Mhaca! I'm in Emain Mhaca!'

'A genius this one.' Bridge said, shaking her head. 'Small wonder he lectures at a university.'

'Right, Mr Summer,' Angus said, coming to a decision. 'We need you to move, on my mark, as quick as you can to those sculptures. Keep as low to the grass as possible. Don't look up. It's only a few yards.'

'Ten yards, Angus. No way he'll make it. He'll be seen.'

'No. He will be fine. The ceremony's over. The fire has been lit. Just a bit of storytelling and dancing now. They're easily distracted at these events.'

'What about you two?' I asked.

'Don't worry about us. We'll not be seen. Besides, we'll be already there waiting for you.' Bridge winked. In the time it had taken her to answer, Angus had disappeared and reappeared out of the corner of my eye.

'Had a quick look,' he said. 'Most of the action is on the other side of the arena. We should be ok. They'll be blowing the cow horn in a minute. Then it will be the traditional fire dance. So, as soon as you hear the horn, Lewis, scamper over there to old what's her face.'

'This is not happening,' I replied.

'You want to see your son? You want to see his mother? You want to find out what the hell is going on? Yes? Then I suggest you move!'

While Angus spoke, the crowd beyond the dolmen had suddenly fallen silent. I looked up. Through a gap in its capstone roof, I could make out a bold strip of blue sky. Suddenly, a cow horn blasted in the distance. Hidden behind the sculptures beyond, Angus and Bridge were already crouching, encouraging me onwards.

I scrambled across the grass, too frightened to look up. The ground felt soft beneath my feet, the air hot against my face. I could tell, instinctively, that not only was I low to the ground, but I was also at ground level in relation to the vast crowd I sensed in tiered seating all around me. An image of a Christian in the Colosseum in Rome flashed across my mind. Until I remembered. Rome didn't exist in this world. I felt exposed, sweating under my winter clothes, like a large beetle, crawling desperately across a garden patio, too large to be ignored by an approaching heel. Somehow, I managed to get to the sculptures unobserved.

'Good! Well done! You might even make it to the end of the day.' Angus said, encouragingly.

'Thanks,' I panted, breathing heavily. 'What next?'

'Just like lily pads in a pond, Lewis. One

more leap.'

'Where?'

'See that ramp over there?' Angus pointed to a wooden ramp that sloped underground. It was another fifteen or so yards away. 'That ramp leads to stalls underground.'

'Stalls?'

'Yes, stalls! For bloody horses! These idiots like to watch chariot races sometimes!' Angus exclaimed, impatiently.

'And they like their chariots to make a big entrance.' added Bridge.

'Now,' continued Angus, 'we are at the north-east corner of the arena. 'There,' he pointed, 'is a fence...can you see it?'

'Yes,' I answered.

'That will conceal the last few yards for you until you reach the ramp. Get underground as quickly as you can. Then we can find you a change of clothes.'

'And later?'

'Your professor's old friend, Lorcan mac Róich.'

Lorcan?! I was too stunned to say the word aloud. I was going to meet Pritchard's child-hood friend! But why?

'As before, listen out for the horn,' Bridge said, suddenly. I hadn't noticed her reappear, but then again, I hadn't noticed her leave either.

When the horn sounded, I scurried across

the grass, making myself as small a target as possible. The wood groaned under my feet as I made my way down the gradient to the stalls below. Angus and Bridge were waiting for me there.

'Here, grab hold of these.' Bridge tossed me some trousers, a shirt, a jacket and a cap. 'Right, follow us!'

We were in a dark, cobbled stables with stalls to our left and right. I counted twenty-four in all, only two of which were empty. The horses stood quietly, gaping without interest at us as we passed. I loitered momentarily, looking around. I don't know why but the familiar sights, sounds and smells reassured me. Perhaps this world was not so strange after all.

'They're bloody horses, not unicorns! And that's shit, not stardust!' Angus exclaimed, guessing my thoughts from my face. 'Come on! In there!' he ordered, opening up one of the empty enclosures. 'A quick change! Don't leave your other clothes. Put them in this.' He passed me a hessian bag. 'Hurry! The stable lads will be back from the arena any minute!'

I did as I had been instructed. The trousers were too short and the shirt too large. I tucked in the latter, in an attempt, without much success, to ameliorate the overall effect. I pulled down the cap and, feeling somewhat ridiculous, re-joined the others.

We made our way through the stalls into an

area lined on either wall by half a dozen glittering chariots, not the wooden antiquities of the movies I had watched as a child, but with gleaming, metal axles, sparkling spokes and tyred with thick rubber; their harnesses dipped low as if in prayer. After that, a tack room of sorts, a storage place for hay, straw and feed and several water pumps. All the while, we followed a slight incline, moving upwards, passing living quarters, washing facilities and finally, offices. In another direction, I saw other sets of stalls veering upwards, no doubt towards street level. Angus and Brigid took turns, vanishing and reappearing, skipping ahead to check around corners. At intervals, I waited for their signals to stop, wait and then move. Soon, sunlight began to appear through windows all around. Ahead, I thought I could hear birdsong and the sound of children laughing.

Finally, we found ourselves outside a door marked *bainisteoir cobhsaí*. Bridge tested the door. It was unlocked.

'My Gaelic isn't that great,' I complained. What does it say?'

'You know, Lewis, when your girlfriend crossed back in the day, we weren't around to help. She had to do things the hard way,' Bridge said.

'What do you mean?' I asked.

Bridge approached me, smiled and gave my

forehead a tap.

'Try again.'

I looked at the sign on the door. It now read 'Stables Manager'.

'You do realise, Lewis,' said Angus, shaking his head, 'that tap was just for effect.'

'What can I say?' Bridge replied. I'm an artist!'

'The sign has changed,' I faltered. 'I can read it now.'

'The sign hasn't changed,' Angus added. 'Your brain's been changed. You will be able to understand spoken language as well now.'

'Aoife didn't have us to help her,' Bridge continued, opening the door. 'She had to survive all on her own. She's a remarkable woman...for a human being.' Bridge looked at me as if asking herself what this 'remarkable' woman could ever see in me. 'That was why old Cathbad had to ask your friend Pritchard to lend a hand. And that, Lewis, was a bit naughty of him.'

She opened the door, and we went inside. It was an old-fashioned office, bathed in the low light emanating from a partially closed blind. A dust-filled beam picked out a thick ledger on a heavy desk, laden with files and scrolls. A typewriter squatted in its centre, an arm length away from a swivel chair. A filing cabinet, two bookcases and a coat stand made up the rest of the furniture. Another door led to the street beyond. Angus did something to the lock and it finally clicked.

'Now, one of us will be with you, but we would rather not be seen,' Angus said.

'Why not?' I asked.

'The good folk on this side have...let us say...a stronger *faith* in our kind. In short, our images, or at least a close enough approximation of our images, sometimes overwhelm them, especially during the fervour of festivals. They might arouse in them a mytho-cultural and quasi-religious connection, steeped as those images are in the consciousness of their collective mind.'

'He means our mug-shots are well-known hereabouts!' Bridge quipped.

'Exactly,' Angus winked. 'And it simply wouldn't do to have one of their bronze sculptures suddenly burst into life and be seen mooching around the streets of Emain Mhaca during a holiday.'

'Probably not,' I managed to say

'Listen, we are in an area of the city called the Palatial District. Lorcan mac Róich's lives in a large roundhouse. You can't miss it. It's about ten minutes' walk from here, but you can save time by cutting through the Presidential Gardens...'

'...Did you say 'presidential'?'

'He did,' Bridge said.

'So cut through the Gardens, past the statue

of Setanta, turn left at the fountain and exit the gates. Then take another left, carry on for five minutes, then go right. Follow the signs for Loughnashade.'

'Loughnashade?! You mean Loughnashade…!'

'…Bloody hell! Not your Loughnashade!' He pursed his lips and blew. 'Ok? Got that so far?'

'Yes.'

Take a second left and you will see a hill. It's the roundhouse half-way up. If you go wrong, we'll let you know. Ok?'

'Ok' I stammered.

'And don't draw attention to yourself. Keep your head down. Don't walk too slow or run too fast! Got it?'

'Yes.'

He stood behind me and suddenly I was alone. Or at least I thought I was alone. I went to the door, forced myself to breathe and tried to gather my thoughts.

Angus had mentioned a fire dance, a festival and a holiday. The aos sí could only cross through their local gate at festivals, solstices and equinoxes and I had left my world at Samhain. Perhaps my Earth's annual rotation around its sun was on the opposite side of the orbital plane to this Earth. So, when it's winter solstice here, it's summer solstice there. When it's Samhain there, it's…Beltane here! A six-month differential. It made sense. I smiled. For the first time in what seemed like a very long time I had reached a conclusion on my own. It heartened me to know that a lifetime spent in the acquisition of knowledge about the past might help facilitate the process of learning about this new present. I took a final breath and opened the door onto the street.

Twenty-four earlier I had shuffled a lonely, rain-swept path around the hill fort of my Emain Mhaca. Now, here I was, traversing the pavement of a busy thoroughfare, teeming with life: slow-moving horse-drawn carts and the odd vintage automobile were grid-locked at street crossings where dozens of people, some of whom appeared continental, waited impatiently, before dashing to the other side, dragging children with painted faces, blowing on cow horns; an open-air market echoed with the cries of merchants; soldiers in pea-green uniforms mixed with others wearing tunics; a newspaper boy was hawking yesterday's news: 'Peace at Uisneach!' It was incredible.

At the end of the avenue, I picked out some impressive looking wrought iron gates and the tips of trees swaying beyond. I headed in that direction and entered into what Angus had coined the 'presidential gardens'. I passed the bronze statue of Setanta, hands outstretched to a larger figure hovering above him. According to the brass plate beneath, the taller sculpture was Cú Chulainn, his future older self.

As I walked, I averted my eyes from those of the passers-by, all of whom ignored me. As far as they were concerned, I was, no doubt, a poor, down-at-heel farm labourer, newly arrived in the city for the festival. I wondered if Angus or Bridge were ambling alongside, invisibly present, or were they viewing me from a distance? I felt like an actor on a large movie set, searching for a hidden camera, being directed in a scene, surrounded by hundreds of extras who weren't aware they too were on film. I saw a sign for Loughnashade Park and realised I at least had not taken a wrong turning.

'Pigeon pie?!' came a voice from the entrance to the park. A tired, gruff-looking man with paint smeared on his face and a discoloured tunic was staring at me with faint hope in his eyes. 'Only two shillings, friend.'

'No, no, thank you,' I replied.

He gave me an odd look as I passed.

'Bloody bog dwellers!' he sniffed. 'More chance the ducks in the pond have bread on them than you!'

Fortunately, by the time I reached the home of Lorcan mac Róich, the volume of people on the streets had begun to thin out. I was in a quieter, suburban area, close to the city centre. Given the scale of mac Róich's residence, Pritchard's old playmate had no immediate financial worries.

'The house is empty.' It was Angus. He had appeared at the bottom of the steps leading to the main door. 'I have already had a good look around. No one. Try the door. It's open.'

I entered a high-ceilinged vestibule with doors either side, some open, some not, at the end of which I could see Bridge. She was sitting at a table in the kitchen, holding a glass bottle to her lips. She read my face.

'What? You think we don't drink? Best cider in either world this. Besides,' she said, taking another mouthful, 'I'm not too worried about my liver...we sorta live forever.'

'Anything?' Angus asked, entering the room.

'Nothing at his work, library, the Gardens...you know, his usual haunts. Tried the RBK, the senate, mac Daras, all over the old town. Had a quick look around the city as well. Nothing. You?'

'No, just this.' Angus picked up a pipe from the kitchen table.

'He has others,' Bridge said.

'I know. This is his favourite, though. Belonged to his dad.'

'Hmm...probably had to leave in a hurry and I think I know why.'

'Why?'

'Things have escalated.'

'How?'

'Well, news hasn't reached the general public yet but...'

'...What?'

'The Connachta president has been shot!' Bridge announced.

'Wait!' I interjected. 'Did you say 'Connachta'?'

'Give us a second, Lewis, will you? This is important,' Angus said. 'Go on,' he added, addressing his fellow aos sí.

'Shot this morning at Uisneach.'

'Before or after?' he asked.

'Before the signing of the treaty.'

'Shit! Pass me that bottle, Bridge.' Bridge passed over the cider and Angus too took a long draught. 'Right. So, Cathbad? I wonder why he didn't see that eventuality?'

'Different gate there, different sentinel?'

'You think they don't talk? This isn't good.'

'Don't overthink it, Angus. Bound to be a reason why that was allowed to happen. Maybe I could speak to the aos sí down there.'

'No point. Sure, they can only do what they are told to do by their sentinels...but our colleagues do need to know that we will be...you know...'

'I can sort that,' Bridge replied. 'They won't interfere.'

While they continued to speak, I decided to sit down. My inability to keep up with the conversation had somehow made me feel very tired. I could understand the individual words but, strung together, they formed an unrecognisable series of idioms, a moving syntax of expression that defied meaning. I lacked context, and without context, there was no point listening. I thought of my father and the memory of the story he had read to me as a seven-year-old child. What would he have thought of all this? Me, in that world, as geographically close to my biological father as I had ever been and whose name I didn't know? Looking for a son, I had never seen? And a woman, his mother, whom I had met just once?

Pritchard, the man I thought I had known, had more sense of this place than perhaps I would ever have. He had spent three years here. I wondered if it had been in this house where he slept, a bed in one of the floors above where a loving mother had tucked him in. He had run through the streets of this city, Loughnashade and the Presidential Gardens, watched in awe at the fires being lit at Beltane, painted his face blue and munched on pigeon pie. He had been happy; he had told me. Back then, Pritchard had not even been the age as my own son now. His name was Finn, and I didn't know if I was ready to be his father, never mind go on some sort of supernatural safari for him, helped by two inter-dimensional beings that drank cider for breakfast!

'So where does that leave us?' I heard Bridge ask.

'There's the Christian, Maggo. He might

know about mac Róich's whereabouts although he's not here either, it seems.'

'Mac Dara is in Uisneach, by the way. He's in trouble too. I heard a few of their senators whispering on their way to an emergency session at the senate.'

'What's up with him?'

'Being held by the Druidic Guard. Seems he, or forces within Ulidia, might have been behind the attack.'

'Bloody hell! You leave the place for a few weeks and the whole shebang goes up in flames!'

'Not nice to have the pieces move around when you are not looking, is it?' I asked, standing up. They both looked at me coldly. 'Now, without doing your vanishing act, I want to know a few things. Who's this bloody mac Dara?!' I exclaimed. They looked at one another. 'Listen, you two! I am not going anywhere, doing anything, until you both tell me what the hell is going on!' I grabbed the bottle of cider from Angus and finished its contents with one long, gulping swallow. 'Now, any more of this?!'

It took about an hour, and a few more bottles of cider, to hear Angus narrate the events of the last few months and a bit more besides. The war; the peace talks; President mac Nessa and his carbon copy in Connachta, Ó'Flaithearta; the newspaper editor, mac Róich; Finn and the RBK; Aoife's role as some kind of nurse in the war; her brother Conall's position as a commander in the army; his wife and children; the geographical make-up of Éireann and other political entities called the Federation and Carthaginian Union.

'So, why am I here? In this house?'

'Oh that?' Bridge furrowed her brow. 'Didn't we say? Lorcan mac Róich is your lad's legal guardian when his mother isn't around. This is your son's house, Lewis.'

18

Maggo had never witnessed such a spectacle. In the pre-dawn darkness, he had filed into the huge *Réimse Náisiúnta*, the National Arena, a lone Christian in the midst of eighty thousand pagans. He had presented his ticket at one of the score of ticket booths that littered the three-tiered dust bowl and, in return, had received a lighted torch which he had used to help guide himself to a number on part of a stone step. He was in the 'home' section, filled with citizens from Emain Mhaca, most of which had family seats which they had no difficulty locating after attending many years of festivals. Maggo's seat was on the bottom level, close to the arena itself. It was cushioned, as befitting a family of tickets purchased by the mac Róich clan. The plan had been for himself, Lorcan and Finn to enjoy the spectacle together; a special treat for Maggo given that it would, undoubtedly, be his first and last opportunity to observe a Beltane celebration close-up. Now, he sat alone, with two vacant cushions to his left, wondering if he would ever see his two friends again.

He had to admit it was difficult not to get caught up in the atmosphere. In the grandstands all around, he could see thousands of torches mark out the progress of spectators to their pews or stilled in a fiery chorus of expectation by those already seated. The torches were enough to cast light on the grassy arena, illuminating parts of sculptures, statues, large torch bowls and what looked like a massive, shadowy funeral pyre in the centre. The reek of paraffin everywhere was overpowering, however, and he could already sense the beginnings of a migraine.

The pyre was the central, national fire, Ferdia had explained to him the day before. It occupied the centre of the arena and would be lit after the smaller county fires, representing the diverse regions of Ulidia, had also been ignited, no doubt to the wild exhilaration of those clans from outside the city. Ferdia and his friend Donall would have to sit with their own counties until then, in other designated sections of the arena. In the short interim, between then and the burning of the national fire, they would try to make their way across to join him.

At a certain point in the proceedings, his neighbours beside him rose expectantly from their seats. Maggo joined them, straining to see the nine members of the Ulidian Druidic Order, each one with torches ablaze, make their way in a line to a fixed point, before branching off in the direction of the nine county fires. The uproar was deafening. Maggo felt himself being jostled and pushed from all sides and it was only with extreme good fortune that he was able to juggle his torch safely back into his hands.

A roar followed the naming of each county and lighting of their subsequent flame. Maggo listened out for Dún na nGall where Ferdia had said he was from and cheered accordingly, more out of respect than anything else. The largest cry, of course, was reserved for the home county of Ard Mhaca. Maggo looked up and caught a brief glimpse of Venus, the morning star. It wasn't so long ago that these people foretold the future from stars like that he thought. Now their scientists had learned that Venus was a planetary body. Perhaps there was hope for them, after all.

In the ten or so minutes during which preparations were completed for the lighting of the national fire, he picked out two torches moving in his direction.

'Get your arms off my back, will you?!' Ferdia was addressing someone behind him.

'I can't see a bloody thing, Ferd!'

'Aye, but no point us both toppling over, is there?!'

'Excuse me!' another voice said, 'show some respect!'

'Piss off!' exclaimed Ferdia

'You shouldn't even be in this section!' the put-out voice retorted. 'You're not local!'

'You still here? Thought I told you to piss off!'

Ferdia and his friend took a seat beside Maggo.

'Bloody hell! Diplomatic cushions, eh Mags? The bones of my arse are killed in those bricks we have to sit on.'

'They're ok in the Fir Manach section.' his friend said.

'That's only because you have a fat arse! Mags,' Ferdia continued, 'this is Donall, the idiot I was telling you about. Idiot, this is Maggo, but you can call him Mags.'

'Please to meet you,' Maggo said, extending his arm.

Donall stared at it, unsure of what to do.

'Well, bloody well take the man's arm!' Ferdia shouted. 'Am sure you'll not catch anything of it.'

'Err...nice to meet you too...Mags.'

'Right, pleasantries over. Let's make the most of these seats. Can't wait to see the fire dancers this year. Some cracking girls last time!'

They sat in silence as the central fire was lit by the Arch Druid of Ulidia. Its lighting was the collective signal for everyone else to cap their own torches. A large bucket of sand was passed along the individual rows to extinguish and collect the wooden staves. After dawn, there was a whole schedule of entertainment to be enjoyed. Firstly, the arena was cleared for a short game of *poc fada*. Following this, there was fire-dancing, javelin-throwing, some sport, Maggo thought, the objective of which seemed to involve stealing someone else's cattle, tests of strength, chariot racing and a group effort spent cornering a wild boar into a pit. This was ensued by a short interval during which Ferdia and Donall left momentarily to participate in a carefully rehearsed battle sequence with others from the RBK Youth. During this, they showed off their prowess with swords and shields, returning just in time for the final spectacle -a long parade of Ulidian soldiers with rifles: on foot, on horses and in armoured chariots.

It was mid-morning by the time the festival was complete. A massive cow horn signalled the end of the proceedings after which the crowd began to disperse via exits all of which led into various parts of the Presidential Gardens. There they found a picnic table that had just been deserted by a family of four.

'Lucky buggers!' Donall sighed, watching them leave. 'Off home for the traditional feast. My folks are going to kill me! They booked lodgings and all!

'What'd you tell them?' Ferdia asked

'Extra training.'

'Extra training?! You?!'

'Well, it worked, didn't it?' Donall smiled.

Ferdia shook his head. 'Anyway, we did our bit. RBK should be happy enough for the time being. Even Crunniac looked half-pleased with the ceremony.'

'What about tomorrow though? If we don't report back, there'll be trouble.'

'We find Finn, Donall. We will be heroes. Think of that!'

'Why don't we just tell Crunniac? The RBK will find him faster than...'

'...We've been through this. Mags here says that Finn is likely to have been kidnapped by Connachta. Old Lorcan's gone missing too. This could be big!'

'Every reason why we should let Crunniac...'

'...That hairy oaf?! No chance! And let him get all the glory? Most of the RBK are on leave, right? You fancy sauntering down to HQ and dragging them away from their dinners? Same with the Youth. It's just us non-locals, Donall.'

'If we do not find Finn or Lorcan before first light tomorrow, Donall,' Maggo added, 'I promise to have you back for morning roll call.'

'Hear that? Even the Christian's showing a larger set than you!'

Donall puffed his cheeks. 'Why not? One condition though?'

'What's that? Maggo asked.

'I'm starving! Any of you two lend me a few shillings for a bit of pigeon pie?'

On the way to Lorcan's, Ferdia explained the plan to Donall. As far as plans went, it wasn't much of one. Maggo was to borrow Lorcan's chariot and the three of them were to widen their search for Finn beyond the city limits.

Lorcan had spoken of an old vehicle which he had purchased at the time when chariots first started rolling off the conveyor belts in factories throughout the Federation. Like most modern technology, it was built in imitation of WCA design, and, Lorcan freely admitted, had been purchased on a whim, a confirmation of his status as editor of the Ulidian Shield. He had even gone so far to hire a chauffeur, but had felt foolish, he had said, sitting in the back seat of a brand-new chariot, making a five-minute journey to and from work every day. He had soon got rid of the chauffeur, recommenced his daily routine of walking to and from his office, and put the vehicle in mothballs in the garage he had had specially constructed.

It was all Maggo could come up with, given the fact that he was a foreigner and the only other people willing to help were two thirteen-year boys. He had simply wanted information, of course. Perhaps his friend, Ferdia, he had thought, might have been able to tell him the whereabouts of Finn's extended family: uncles, aunts or cousins in other parts of Ulidia, in the slight off-chance the boy wasn't already in Connachta. Ferdia had known of other mac Daras, a female cousin, Caitlin, in Béal Feirste, but would only volunteer further details if he and his friend, Donall, could also contribute to the search. The boy had spoken of a 'secret mission', had enthused about 'triad honour' and other such nonsense. The fact was, Maggo knew, the whole idea was ludicrous, a means to fill time until tomorrow, the day after Beltane, when society returned to something approaching normal, at least normal for this country, and he could make other plans. The Bardic Press and everywhere else was closed for the day. By mid-afternoon, according to Donall, the streets of Emain Mhaca would be empty, as families gathered at home for private rituals and feasting. The idea of returning to Lorcan's vast, empty roundhouse and spending the entire day there, sitting on his hands and staring at Lorcan's old pipe was too much for him to bear. Tomorrow, the cadets would return to their base and he would try the Bardic Press once again. Failing that, he would leave the entire case with the city guards. The police would wonder how a foreigner had somehow misplaced two Ulidian citizens, but he would have to risk that. If he were still at liberty afterwards, he thought, he would take Lorcan's chariot and make the journey to Connachta alone. He didn't have a travel permit for other parts of Éireann, but he would worry about that later. He didn't have a driving permit either. That too would have to be put on hold.

As they approached the front entrance of Lorcan's house, however, Maggo noticed signs of activity inside. He could hear voices, one male and one female. They were coming from the kitchen at the back of the house. He told Ferdia and Donall to wait as he rounded that part of the building which led to the kitchen door.

'You going somewhere, friend?' a strange accent suddenly asked him.

Maggo turned to see a man, in his thirties, with a red mop of curls on his head. His trousers were torn and in need of repair.

I had very nearly slit my own throat while shaving with an open razor.

I had gone upstairs to find a suitable change of clothes. In one of the larger bedrooms, I had come across an armoire with a row of simple cotton shirts. I also located a pair of trousers, not my size, but which I thought I could easily adjust with a belt. Any shoes I found were too large, but I didn't think my own would register too much interest; they were quite similar to the leather brogues favoured by adult males in this world.

It was then that I had found the bathroom and made the decision to clean myself up. I washed under my armpits, combed my hair and had a shave, nearly ending my life with a switchblade and a thin layer of soap. I returned to the bedroom, put on a tie to cover up the congealing gash the razor had made, tried on a jacket and checked my appearance in a standing mirror. I looked like a travelling salesman circa 1920; the only thing missing was an encyclopaedia under my arm.

By the time, I had returned to the others, I noticed we had guests.

Two young boys, dressed in cadets' uniforms, were standing with an older man in his early to mid-twenties. The boys looked about fifteen years old; one was short and stocky with a buzz cut and had the stance of a boxer waiting for the bell, his fists primed for action; the other was only slightly taller, overweight, and was staring, open-mouthed, at Angus and Bridge. The older man looked Italian or Spanish. He had sallow features, was dressed in a pair of loose-fitting slacks, shirt, thin waistcoat and sandals. His hair was black and long enough to be slicked back off his forehead.

I studied the boys briefly, scanning them for genetic markers. I wondered if either of them was my son Finn but thought them too old.

'Sure, isn't this lovely, all the same?' Angus

began. 'Lewis, allow me to introduce you to the less-than-legendary Ferdia, Donall, his slack-jawed compatriot and their Punic pal, Maggo. Gentlemen, this is Lewis.'

'Funny name.' grunted Ferdia.

'You have no idea!' Angus said.

'You're...you look like...you...' Donall stammered, unable to take his eyes of Bridge.

'I know...it's the eyes...bit like Brigid's, right? Well, that obviously can't be the case, can it?' Bridge gave Donall a cold look.

'...No, no...'

'...Well that's that then.'

'Lewis here is from the...Western Continental Alliance,' Angus continued.

'The WCA?' Maggo said. The young man approached me and grabbed my hand, ecstatically. 'Welcome, brother!'

'Hello,' I managed.

'You're the first person I have ever met from there!'

'And you're the first person I have met from...err...'

'Valletta.'

'Yes, Valletta, in the...Carthaginian...Union?'

'Isn't that nice...hands across the ocean and all that?' Angus said, filling in the silence that followed.

'Who are you, and what are you all doing here in Finn's house?' Ferdia demanded, suddenly, snatching a knife from a rack on the wall. He grabbed me, and placed the knife to my throat, just above the spot where I had nicked myself a few minutes before.

'Steady lad! Be careful with the merchandise!' Angus warned, pointing at me.

'Who are you? You're not Ulidians! Are you Connachta?!'

'No, lad. Calm down! We're all from the WCA. We've come to help.' Angus said.

'Help? Help how?' Ferdia exclaimed.

'We're here to help you find Finn.'

'How'd you know about him?' I felt the tip of Ferdia's blade press against my skin. I couldn't believe it. The boy was serious. He would kill me if he didn't get the answers he wanted.

'I'm...I'm his father.' I faltered.

I felt the boy's hand relax. 'Prove it!'

'I... I... wanted to surprise Finn. It's the festival of Beltane, after all. So, I came over especially from the err... WCA to meet him. I have never even seen him before, you see. I... we went to the arena this morning...I heard he was in the RBK and was part of the ceremony...but I soon realised he wasn't there. He was taken away from me as a child, you know, by his mother, Aoife. I'm not blaming her. It was a mistake...complicated...I didn't know I had a son until my friends told me a few months ago.'

'How did they know?'

'We were here on business a while back,' Bridge began. 'Lewis asked me to check up on

Aoife, see how she was. Turns out, his mother was spending quite a bit of time away from the family home and had had a son, Finn, whom she had left with his guardian. We went back to the WCA, told Lewis he had a son, and naturally he wanted to meet him.'

'What father wouldn't want to meet their son!' Bridge added.

'So, who are you?' Ferdia asked.

'Me, I'm Brenda. And this is my brother Aidan. He works in... hospitality.'

'And what do you do?'

'Can't you guess?' Bridge asked, pointing at her tutu. 'I'm in fashion!'

A few minutes later we were sitting around Lorcan mac Róich's kitchen table, a makeshift gathering of last resort, our very own strange, impromptu, family get-together. Maggo was happy to busy himself, slicing and chopping vegetables, in preparation of a Beltane banquet for us all. Very soon, the smells of sizzling pork began to permeate the kitchen. I started to feel hungry. I couldn't remember the last time I had eaten. Meanwhile Donall, the other boy, was consuming as much food as the Carthaginian was preparing.

'So, you came here to find your son?' Ferdia asked again and whistled. 'You're out of luck!'

'We tried the training grounds, his mother's house, his uncle's, the Bardic Press,' Maggo added, stirring a steaming pot of stew. 'He and Lorcan are both gone. Tomorrow, I will report him missing to the city guards. These two need to return to their base.'

'Balls to that!' Ferdia exclaimed. I smiled inside. I could see why a son of mine might befriend someone like Ferdia. The boy was fearless.

'Let's not be hasty,' Bridge said. 'Who knows if we can trust the guards?'

'Why not?' Ferdia enquired, raising an eyebrow.

'Ok, prepare yourself for a shock, boys. The President of Connachta has just been assassinated.'

'Balls!' replied Ferdia.

'Huh!' spluttered Donal, almost choking on a pork chop.

'It's true,' Angus said, 'happened just before dawn. The senate's in session as I speak.'

'We would know about it,' Donall ventured.

'The Press will hold off until they hear from the senate,' Angus said. 'Probably be in the evening editions. Anyway, the point is, the whole place will be in turmoil. The guards will have their hands full. The RBK and the army will have to return to their posts. This might break the truce!'

'How so?'

'Conall mac Dara and his unit may well be under suspicion. It was Conall that provided the security for everyone in Uisneach.'

'No way the commander would do anything against the interests of Ulidia!' Ferdia exclaimed, fiercely.'

'Sure, we all know that lad.' Angus replied, almost apologetically. 'But his nephew is missing. His nephew's guardian's nowhere to be found. His sister hasn't been back home in months. That's enough for the guards here to work with. His wife and family will probably be under house arrest soon enough. It'll not take them too long to end up here.'

'What do you mean?' Donall enquired.

'I mean, you, lad, will have to eat and go. You can't go to the guards or the RBK. Not while there's any doubt about Conall's loyalty.'

'What should we bloody do then?' Finn asked

'I think,' Angus said, 'it's time for you, Ferdia, to widen your horizons.'

19

The news from home had been as expected. Shock, outrage, cries of vengeance on one side of the Connachta Senate wall met by patience, forbearance and restraint on the other. Connachta had the 'moral high ground', the message from acting President Ó Braonáin had said. Commander Ó'Móráin 'must utilise the elevation of this position to survey the battlefield before him'.

Useless, empty words, Ó'Móráin knew; the sort of safe, political hogwash that was hard to pin down, appealing to all, but ultimately serving no one. Ó Braonáin had been one of the most outspoken critics of the war, an anaemic 'lifer' who had spent forty years in the senate making cooing noises to the other doves. His election as vice-president, it was hoped, had served to redress the balance between him and the more hawkish Ó'Flaithearta. Now, Ó Braonáin was co-opting the martial language he thought Ó'Móráin would best understand. But it lacked guidance. There was no indication, direct or otherwise, of what Connachta should do next. If he wasn't careful, Ó'Flaithearta might actually die. Then what would Ó Braonáin do? Panic, probably.

At least with someone like Conall mac Dara you knew where you stood. An enemy, due to the vicissitudes of fate in this world; in another world, a potential friend. He had learned a begrudging appreciation for his Ulidian adversary. War was like fidchell. It was a game; a high stake's game, of course, but the strategies you employed could only be improved by the quality of your opponent. If mac Dara were anything like him off the battlefield, there was no way he would have knowingly participated in the assassination of a political enemy. That would have been an act of subterfuge equal only to that of breaking a shield wall when faced with an enemy's sword. A warrior was a warrior regardless of the technology of the weapon in his hand. The old stories stay long in the soul. And he had the feeling mac Dara was a warrior, just like himself.

And yet, he couldn't be sure. He owed it to the people of Connachta, the soldiers he had fought with, to those he had seen mowed down by Ulidian rifles, blown apart by Ulidian shells, to take a more aggressive approach. Ulidia was still the enemy. Mac Dara and his men were still the most obvious guilty parties. This was why, ignoring the entreaties of the Druidic Council, he had demanded to see the Arch Druid, Mogh Roth mac Nuadat.

'The Arch Druid has only a few moments,' a peevish secretary warned, as he opened the door leading into the Arch Druid's private quarters. 'You can understand, his Divinity has been unduly shocked by the events of this morning.'

'Not as much as I was,' Ó'Móráin replied.

Mac Nuadat was seated at one corner of a massive, triangular desk. He was studying, or pretending to study, some papers that apparently required his urgent attention. His preference was still for a quill, Ó'Móráin noticed, which he scratched at the bottom of one leaf before turning over to another. He knew he had made a life-changing, potentially career-ending choice. To demand to be in the presence of an Arch Druid was unheard of, especially by such a low ranking officer as himself. Still, part of him hoped that the exceptional circumstances surrounding the events of the day would mitigate any sense of provocation on his part. Another part of him was feeling tired, prematurely old, and couldn't care less.

'Ah, child,' the Arch Druid said, looking up. 'You wanted to see me?'

Ó'Móráin performed an awkward movement, somewhere between a nod, bow and a genuflection. The Arch Druid smiled and stood up.

'May I first extend my regrets to you, commander, your men and all the good people of Connachta for what passed this Beltane morning.'

'Thank you, your... Divinity.'

Mac Nuadat smiled again. 'Shall we...?' The Arch Druid waved a hand in the direction of a sofa and an armchair.

Ó'Móráin followed, his hobnail boots, totally out of step on the plush, cream carpet. He had forgotten to clean them, or even change into his dress uniform. He prayed that he would leave no muddy aftermath on the ostentatious fittings and furniture of the Arch Druid's chambers. Mac Nuadat sat on a large, high backed chair emblazoned with an arboreal motif. He had changed into a different robe, but around his neck mac Nuadat wore the infamous golden torc which, according to legend, protracted and contracted, according to the innocence or guilt of the accused that stood in the presence of the ancient lawgivers.

'It's not the real one,' the Arch Druid said, following Ó'Móráin's eyes. 'The real one is locked away in the House of Brehon Law. I know what you are thinking, however. You are thinking, if only it could be that simple. Divine inspiration from the gods. The tightening of the torc to indicate a miscarriage of justice, to separate the innocent from the guilty.'

'Yes.'

'Not that the gods would not respond, of

course. These days, we know better than to...test them.'

The Arch Druid had that soft, almost effeminate dialect shared by all who had rarely been beyond the walls of the city of Uisneach. A millennium of peace behind their protective barricade had ironed out the harsh, phonetic ruggedness shared by all other speakers on the island. The untroubled smoothness of his face testified to it as well. Ó'Móráin detected a faint whiff of moisturiser and perfume.

'So, commander...?' he continued.

'It's about mac Dara and his men. I think...we think it would be best if they were to be questioned before a military tribunal back in Connachta.'

'Oh?'

'Yes, your Divinity. It was, allegedly, an act of aggression committed at a time when our countries were, technically, still at war. As the victim of this act is a non-combatant of the highest standing...'

'...A non-combatant of highest standing?'

'Yes, your Divinity, we believe, respectfully, the suspects should be extradited to Connachta.'

'Hmm, tell me, commander. Are you saying that you, or Connachta, have no confidence brehon lawgiver mac an Bhreithiún?

'No...no... But mac an Bhreithiún...well...the House of Brehon Law is...'

'...is...?

'...well, it's not a military body, Arch Druid. Men like mac Dara are hardened professionals. We will never discover the truth of what happened if we don't extricate it from him and his men.'

'Extricate? You mean torture, commander?'

'No, but we have to use some level of force to extrapolate the truth from them. Let's be honest, Arch Druid, the Ulidians are at the top of our list of suspects.'

'And how is the 'non-combatant'?' mac Nuadat enquired, wryly.

'Still no word.'

Mac Nuadat looked at Ó'Móráin with curiosity. The commander was a man accustomed to following orders, and yet, as Arch Druid, he did not have the actual power to order Ó'Móráin, the Connachta senate or their army to do anything which they did not want to do. Druidic and political power existed side by side in a precarious balance. The latter had the real power, of course, but the people of Éireann prized their religious beliefs over all else. As a result, governments had to keep in lockstep with the Druidic Order, even more so given that the Druidic Order was truly international and had tentacles that swept across the Federation. The Carthaginians, WCA and other global regions all had politicians; the Federation was the only region to have a Druidic Order and that meant a lot to their citizens.

'Tell me, commander,' he said finally, 'have you received support for this...strategy...back home. You have, no doubt, heard from your vice-president and senate.'

'Yes, I have heard from them', Ó'Móráin answered, weakly.

'And?'

'He trusts that I will do the right thing.'

'Does he? Does he indeed?' Mac Nuadat touched his torque briefly. Commander, there is a reason, you know, why the Mhí Protectorate is called a 'protectorate'. Do you know why that is?'

'Yes, of course, your Divinity,' Ó'Móráin bristled. 'The protection of the sacred sites, the rituals, the three orders: religion, medicine and law...'

'...Yes, yes, yes...those things are important, of course, commander,' the Arch Druid replied. 'But there's more to it than that. We are a sovereign nation too. Yes, we don't have a president, chancellor or king but we too have ordinary citizens out there, doing ordinary jobs beyond that of the three orders. We have our own economy that relies on those citizens. So, suffice to say, those citizens also need to be protected. Would you agree?'

'Yes, but...'

'...So we have responsibilities within the Protectorate. However, commander, we also have an obligation to the four nations that, for better or worse, find themselves marooned on this island. We can't take sides. We must treat everyone the same and we do not have an army to protect ourselves.'

'Arch Druid, no army would ever think of invading...'

'...Of course not. That is gratifying to hear. But, with this peace process, we have been coerced, against the diktats of tradition, to insinuate ourselves into politics...for the greater good, you understand. My Druidic Guard are, for the first time, learning en masse how to use a rifle so that they can, temporarily, police the disputed territory of an tSionainn. And why? Because neither Connachta nor Ulidia trust one another to do so. So, commander, since we have entered politics, we in the Protectorate must become more 'political'. Wouldn't you agree? In short, Commander Ó'Móráin, I have seen a copy of the Ogham script relayed to you from acting President Ó Braonáin. In no way, does he suggest the Ulidians should be returned to Connachta for further investigation!' Arch Druid mac Nuadat stood up, suddenly. 'Commander, you may contact your people with a view to having a prosecuting law-giver interview mac Dara and the others. I believe, for their part, they have already done so. However, you and your triad must also make themselves available for questions. Who's to say that there is not some internal Connachta plot against your president?'

'Arch Druid, I must protest...'

'...I am also led to believe that there are individuals within your own senate who were against the treaty. To that end, it would be better if you and your men remain here for the foreseeable future until this entire matter is resolved.'

And with that Arch Druid Mogh Roith mac Nuadat took his leave, leaving Ó'Móráin alone in the Arch Druid's quarters, wondering if he might not soon be joining his counterpart mac Dara and his triad in the cells below.

Conall had heard stories of prisoner of war camps. Ulidia had one, secreted away on Reachlainn, an island just off the northern coast. Connachta, he was sure, had its own, probably Inis Mór or another of the islands of Árann. Trench warfare did not lend itself to the easy apprehension of prisoners, but during the twenty five years of the current conflict, it had not been unknown for the odd military campaign to lead to large numbers of soldiers straying unwittingly behind enemy lines, surrendering, or surviving defeat in battle. What happened to the spies that used Laighean, with whom Connachta and Ulidia shared a border, as a base of operations was less clear. The ordinary rank and file, however, had rights under the terms of the Treaty of Allobroges; whether these rights were respected, no one in the wider public knew.

This cell, Conall thought, was more comfortable than some of the homes in which he had sheltered for the night in the war zone. It was warm, the mattress of the bed was padded, and a small window permitted an acutely aimed angle of sunshine to penetrate from ground level several floors above. Oisín and Caoimhín, the others in his command triad, were in similar cells close by, he reasoned. The druidic guards who had brought him down had been less than apologetic. Still, he couldn't blame them. The Druidic Council were, no doubt, merely attempting to appease the cries of reprisal being heard in Connachta.

He asked himself if his own senate would have treated a Connachta suspect any differently. He thought of the countless numbers of undercover agents who had suffered a bullet to the back of the brain in some Átha Cliath back alley. He considered the shots that had struck down the Connachta president. He worried about the consequences for Ulidia if Ó'Flaithearta died. He worried too about his wife and family, his sister, Aoife and Finn; the most important people in his life. Had word reached them yet of his arrest? Had he, in fact, been arrested? He knew he had to give evidence to the top brehon lawgiver, mac an Bhreithiún. It would be a very short statement.

The door opened suddenly and Conall was led by two druid guards down a dingily lit stone corridor, up a flight of steps and into another room. He hadn't been handcuffed. Conall didn't know if that was an indication of the futility of an attempted escape or an assumption of his innocence. The Guard weren't in the mood for idle chit chat, so he decided against asking for their opinion either way.

After a minute or so, he was greeted by the dulcet tones of Aodhan mac Murchadha.

'Ah mac Dara. Dear friend.'

He was dressed impeccably in a suit of the latest fashion, but this time without his senatorial robes. The latter, Conall knew, were prohibited on foreign soil. He flashed the commander a toothy grin. Conall did his best to manufacture a smile.

'Mac Murchadhna. How are things back home?'

'In Tír Eoghain, where the sun always shines? Wonderful, as always! Or perhaps, you mean Ulidia, generally?'

'I mean the senate. Specifically.'

'Oh, the senate? Chasing their tails. Half of them wanting to rearm, the other half drafting an unreserved denial of any Ulidian involvement. They'll wait to see how Connachta reacts.'

'And you?'

'Me? Oh, I have no 'official' position on the matter.'

'Unofficially?'

'In the lap of the gods, mac Dara. But let's see, eh, if we can't give those gods a helping hand.'

'I didn't see anything, mac Murchadhna. The flare went up. The DC went down. And the guards moved in.'

'How long was the area lit up?'

'Usual time. Just under ten seconds.'

Mac Murchadha wasn't bothering to write anything down, Conall noticed. He knew it all already.

'And afterwards?'

'As I said, we moved in to protect mac Nessa. The Connachta headed towards their man.'

'The DG?'

'Well, there were more of them. Some of them headed straight for mac Nuadat; the others towards the Council.'

'Anything else? Anything out of the ordinary...?

'...Out of the ordinary? You mean, apart from a foreign leader nearly getting his head blown off! No, no, I think that was all, senator!'

The senator ignored the commander's sarcasm. 'Down the Hill, commander? Did you see anyone make for the bottom?'

'No.'

Mac Murchadna sighed, produced a case and offered Conall a cigarette. Conall accepted, put the cigarette in his mouth while the senator struck a match.

'Then, there's the flare.'

'The flare?'

'Indicates two men at least.'

'Of course. To make a shot like that, you would want to be primed and ready, not messing about with a flare gun. What about the rifle?'

'Well, the Druidic Guard found a couple of shells. They appear to be from a standard Bel Bolt Action rifle. No variation there.'

'Two direct hits from range? In poor visibility? Where were they found?'

'A hill nearby, approximately two hundred yards away.'

'Makes sense. Still aiming upwards, of course, but enough to give them a direct line.'

'Anyway the House of Brehon Law don't have the expertise to analyse the shells for markings?' Mac Murchadhna said.

'Markings?'

'Just to be thorough. You know better than me, both Connachta and Ulidia use the same Federation rifles and ammunition so they're not expecting to find much.'

'They?'

'Some experts from Laighean are arriving shortly to have a look. Professors from the continent, conducting research at Átha Cliath. Experts in ballistic fingerprinting and all that.

They're the nearest eggheads available.'

'Wonderful! And the Connachta response?'

'Same as ours? Confused. Divided.'

'What happens next?'

'The brehon lawgiver will want to interview you and your men. For the purposes of balance, Ó'Móráin his triad will be asked to provide a statement too.'

'You know, senator, it is possible that elements within Connachta carried out the assassination, you know. Plenty of folk are making money out of this war. Theirs as well as ours!' He fired mac Murchadhna a look.

He smiled. 'Not impossible, of course. Who knows? Anyway, mac Dara, I appreciate your recognition of the political nuances involved. We are going to have to tiptoe over the coals over the next few days!'

'What do you mean?'

'We have to follow a certain procedure. One thing all 'elements' in Connachta currently agree on is moral indignation. Regardless of who is responsible, us, them, a couple of random disgruntled ex-military types, corporate interests, it is to us that the rest of the island will be pointing their fingers. At least for a little while. Unfortunately, that means you and your men will probably come under fire, metaphorically, of course.'

'Metaphorically? Well, that's something I suppose! So while Ó'Móráin and his crew get a pass, my men and I will be hung out to dry! Bloody wonderful!'

'Just for a bit, mac Dara. Look, we all know you and Ulidia are blameless, but it can't be seen that you are simply released without some type of investigation. If there is no evidence to the contrary, Ulidia will not be found culpable.'

'Err...the entire population of Ulidia are not sharing a cell with me, mac Murchadhna!

'Temporary, my friend. Temporary. Let mac an Bhreithiún have his forty-eight hours in the limelight. Emotions are high. They will temper. Don't worry. Now, if there's nothing else...?'

'I want to see my men!' Conall demanded

'Ah! Not permissible until mac an Bhreithiún talks to them. Sorry, commander. It's the same for Ó'Móráin. Now I am just going to pay a call on...on...?'

'Sub-commanders Oisín Mag Uidhir and Caoimhín Breathnach.'

'Of course.'

Much later, back in his cell, Conall lay back in his bunk and replayed the conversation with mac Murchadhna in his head. He didn't know why but he felt a heavy weight on his chest, a sort of ill-defined, premonitory darkness that threatened to swallow him whole. A nightmare-filled sleep awaited him, he knew. From that too there was no escape.

It was his inability to sleep that first made him aware of a presence outside his cell door. Conall was sitting up, thinking about pouring himself a glass of water when suddenly he noticed a slight shift in his perception. His cell was pitch black and the door was locked, of course, but the gap between the bottom of the door and the floor was enough for a thin filament of light to pass through from the ethanol lamps that lit the corridor outside. It was a momentary adjustment in that light that caught his eye. An impulse told him to make no sound. And then, he heard it. The soft scratch of something being placed beneath the door. He waited a moment and then ventured towards the noise. Bending down he picked up what felt like a neatly squared fold of paper. He glanced at his timepiece, but it was too dark to distinguish the numbers on the dial. He would have to wait until dawn before he could read the contents of the note, if indeed that was what had just been delivered to him. He returned to bed and put the paper under his pillow.

When Conall awoke, hours later, he was amazed to discover that he had actually slept. He checked his pillow and grabbed the note. He hadn't dreamt the whole episode, after all. He unfolded the paper and read. There were just two words, penned in large letters: THEY

KNOW!

20

I spent most of the evening in Lorcan mac Róich's library. My son's guardian had an impressive collection of books, not unlike that of his old childhood friend Pritchard. There were shelves of mostly hardback books, and vintage scrolls on every topic imaginable, some of them in a language I didn't recognise. I delved into the history section while meanwhile sampling some of the wine from the old man's cellar. The wine tasted good, no different from any excellent burgundy back home. Surridge would love it here, I thought, and not just because of his predilection for fine wine. The politics of this island was more intricate, more labyrinthine than anything that even I had ever lived through. It was little wonder the main media outlet, the Bardic Press, churned out daily copies of its news sheets in a mad, delirious pursuit of the latest morsel of information to be embroidered, hyperbolised and amplified across the morning headlines. Surridge could have dined out on these rich pickings, probably schmoozing his way to an editorship of the Ulidian Shield, just like Lorcan mac Róich had done.

I picked up a copy of the evening news sheet and read the headline: 'O'Flaithearta Assassinated! Ulidian Senate Emergency Session!' There was more to my interdimensional field trip, I thought, than simply a family reunion. It wasn't simply a tale of romance: Aoife and myself were not 'star-crossed lovers' and I had not travelled across a trans-warp fold in space, or whatever it was I had gone through, simply to be reunited with her. It wasn't just a chronicle of a father and his teenage son meeting for the first time, the two connected by the circumstances of their own births. If Ferdia and Donall were anything to go by, boys were not the same in this world. Angus had said so earlier. Like children in ancient Sparta, they seemed to bypass childhood and militarised their play with real swords and real guns. They needed very little from their parents. Perhaps because they weren't children for long enough to develop that need.

I took a sip of wine and read on. There was no mention of the disappearance of Lorcan mac Róich or Finn. It had only been a day, I supposed. And that day had been a holiday. The RBK, or Red Branch Knights, I was certain, would have more to say about Finn's absence tomorrow when he failed to report again for duty. And yet, mac Róich was an important public figure. Finn was the nephew of Conall mac Dara, an influential army commander, influential enough, in any case, to warrant his use as head of a security detail to protect the Ulidian president, Darragh mac Nessa. These were not casual bystanders, anonymous onlookers at the breakfast table of life, cracking open an egg and munching muesli as they read about events that happened to other people. Lorcan and Finn had been kidnapped. Mac Dara had probably been arrested. A president had been assassinated.

And I, Lewis Summer, who lived alone on an island of my own choosing, who closed my drapes at night to shut out the turbulent world outside, was right in the middle of something that was beyond my control, with people and entities I didn't know, but would quickly have to learn to trust.

And now those entities, the aos sí had left. The meal earlier had just finished, and at the end of it, I was left with people, just people. I had felt, in the immediate aftermath of their absence, like a child that had lost his favourite balloon. I had been holding onto it, desperately maintaining my discipline, the thickest of fingers around the thinnest of strings. Angus and Bridge had been the nexus of communication with my old world. Now, the thread that was holding me together had snapped and I was in danger of unravelling.

'What do you mean? Widen my horizons?' Ferdia had asked, earlier.

'Surely, you understand, lad? Time for you to find Finn,' Angus replied.

'You mean, go to Connachta?' No chance!' Donall exclaimed.

'Don't worry, handsome,' Bridge intervened. 'You're staying in Emain Mhaca.'

'What about you two?' I asked, hesitantly.

'Well, we have been to Éireann before. On business, remember?' Angus said.

'Yes,' I was forced to answer.

'So, we know the lay of the land.' Angus must have noticed the shock in my face as he added: 'Look, we need to separate, at least for a while. Bridge has some business to attend to, first of all, but afterwards, she and I will both go and find Aoife at the frontlines. We'll cross the Iron Mountains, on the Ulidian side. It's dangerous beyond that so...'

'...Give me a CT rifle and I'll come with you!' Ferdia declared, boldly.

'No, lad. Your place is in Connachta, or wherever Finn is. You need to find him. Lewis and... sorry...who are you again?'

'Maggo.'

'Yes...the Christian.' Angus looked at Bridge who shrugged. 'Well, you, Lewis and Ferdia will borrow Lorcan's chariot and leave Ulidia at first light tomorrow. Lewis can drive. Lorcan's chariot has Bardic Press credentials so that should be good enough to get you across the border. You will have to concoct a good reason why you all need to be in Laighean. I suggest heading there first, giving the impression to any passing patrols that you are on route to Uisneach. They'll assume you are going there to cover the assassination. Then head for Loch Rí, the Connachta side of the war zone. Hopefully by then we will be back to help you cross into Connachta.'

'How are you getting to the war zone?' Ferdia asked.

'Don't worry about us, lad. We have our ways!' Bridge winked.

'What did you mean' 'or wherever Finn is'?'

I noticed Angus smiled. Ferdia was as sharp as one of his titanium swords.

'Maggo said the two men were Connachta. That doesn't automatically mean he's in Connachta, now, does it?'

'Suppose not,' Ferdia muttered.

'Ha! Got you there, Ferd!' Donall laughed.

'Shut up, bog dweller! Least I am doing something!'

I took Angus aside and whispered, 'You are sure it's ok for the lad to come. It will be dangerous.'

Angus gave me a long look. 'You worried for him or yourself?' I didn't reply. 'Don't worry,' he added, 'children over here are built differently.'

Bridge in the meantime was blocking Ferdia's route to Donall.

'I'll bloody well kill you!' Ferdia was shouting.

'Ok, that's enough, you two!' Bridge said. 'Donall, you return to base tomorrow. If anyone asks about Finn or Ferdia, plead ignorance! You haven't seen Finn since before the festival and you haven't seen this big lout since after the ceremony! Understand?!'

'Ok, sure,' Donall replied.

'It's your job to get in touch with Aoife if she makes it back here. We don't want to leave a message as anyone could pick it up. Remember, not a word to anyone! So keep checking back! Maggo here will give you his key. Ok?' Donall nodded. Bridge paused and caught Ferdia's eye. 'And bloody well stop eating! Leave something for the guards at least!

Ferdia roared with laughter.

There was a knock at the library door.

'Yes? Come in! It's not locked.

It was Maggo, the Carthaginian, looking less like Hannibal on an elephant than I looked an interdimensional traveller through time and space.

'I hope I am not disturbing you?'

'No,' I replied, pointing at the newspaper on the desk in front of me, 'just catching up on the latest news.'

'Yes, there always seems to be a lot going here.' He approached slowly, looking around with keen interest. 'Lorcan...I mean Lorcan mac Róich...never allows anyone in here. It's his private sanctuary.'

'Oh?' I said, offering the young man a seat. 'Would you like a glass of wine?'

'No, thank you,' he said, sitting down, and looking with more detail at the books in front of me.

'Do you like history?'

'You could say that.'

'Which part of the Western Continental Alliance are you from?'

The question threw me. I had yet to research the different political components that comprised this 'alliance' which I knew, in my world, as North and Central America.

'Oh, the middle bit...you sure you don't want any wine?'

'No, thank you. I think I would like to go there one day.'

'You don't like it here?' I asked

'I have only been here a short while but...well...the people are a bit...how shall I say...aggressive?'

'You think so?'

'Not that Finn and Lorcan are not nice, of course. Lorcan can be a bit...'

'...bad-tempered?' I ventured.

'Sometimes, but it is just his age and he works hard when he really doesn't have to.'

'And Finn?' I asked. 'Is he like Ferdia and the other boy, Donall?'

Maggo thought for a moment. 'No, there's something less obvious about Finn. Ferdia is bullish and quick-tempered. Finn is more...reserved, contemplative, more like you and me.'

'You and me?'

'Well, we don't belong to their Federation with their pagan beliefs, their sacrifices and wars.'

'Perhaps they just need more time,' I suggested.

'If they don't have peace in their hearts, they will always know war.' I looked at Maggo more closely. There was an innate calmness about the young man that drew you into his orbit, made you feel at home in his presence. He had the kind of faith that I had lost as a child, or which life had stolen from me. It was still childlike and innocent, and I envied him for it. 'Strange though?'

'What is?'

'Finn. He has been very kind to me. You know, Lewis, my Union is merely tolerated by the Federation. We are useful for trade and tourism and so on, but our citizenry could not be more different. I am sure it is the same in your WCA. Our collective core beliefs are diametrically opposed and that filters down to the individual. Finn is different. I can't put my finger on it, but he reminds me of one of our own young boys...not that we don't have our Ferdias and Donalls too...but Finn is like a boy who doesn't quite belong here. It's strange. It's as if he had been born in the Union, for example, but raised here, as though an indelible mark was imprinted on him at birth, changing him...Perhaps, it's not having a male Celtic parent as a role model?' He laughed. 'Sorry, I am being unfair. Just a little. Anyway, he's a fine boy, and will be a great man. I have not met his mother, Aoife, but he misses her terribly. She's been away for quite a long time. She and Lorcan are good friends though, I believe.'

It meant a lot to me, more than Maggo could ever know, to hear him talk of my son in that way. His qualities had nothing to do with me. I had not been around for him. And yet, it was what I needed to hear, at that particular moment, on the eve of our departure towards whatever it was that lay in store for us. It reinforced me, provided me with renewed vigour. For the first time in a long time I felt unafraid.

Where else should I be, in either of my worlds, than in Ulidia, the leader of my own strange triad, looking for my son and ultimately his mother? My Eva.

The news that his uncle might somehow be

held responsible for an attempt on the Connachta president's life had come as a huge shock for Finn. He hadn't known about the security detail, of course. No one had. It couldn't be true, he had argued. Lorcan had disagreed. Not that his guardian believed that Conall could ever be involved in a conspiracy to eliminate Ó'Flaithearta, but that did not imply that the Connachta leader had not been shot. There was an old Éireann expression: 'Neither the raven nor the dove!' meaning, as if Finn needed reminding, that there were no absolutes in life and certainly not in politics.

Secretly though, Lorcan had felt his speculation dissolve under the weight of his own analysis. He didn't want to worry Finn but sometimes what was idiomatic was not always symptomatic. There were more than two birds in the world of politics and most of them were birds of prey.

There had to be a reason why his ward had been kidnapped. A ransom had seemed obvious. But why? Could it possibly be linked to the events rapidly developing in Uisneach? If so, did that mean a different motivation behind his own abduction?

They had been fed - a potage of stewed meat and vegetables, offered a beaker of cider and then their hands had been bound again. It was almost evening by the time the two Connachta returned.

'So!' Bren declared, scratching his thick beard. 'You don't believe us, eh? Well, have a look at this?' It was a Connachta news sheet. Its headline confirmed the earlier information they had provided.

'So, what does that prove?' Finn exclaimed.

'He's right,' Lorcan added, 'there's no way mac Dara would shoot an unarmed man from a distance. He would consider that dishonourable, a cowardly act, unbefitting of the traditions of the Red Branch Knights. Whatever else he is, he's not that kind of man.'

'And if he was ordered?' Sencha asked.

'Even if he was ordered. It's well-known he's a difficult man to control. He's a man who knows his own mind. I may not agree with him on a lot of things but at least I can respect him for that.'

'Hmm. Well, it doesn't really matter. That little triad of yours was in the wrong place at the wrong time. They will be found guilty whether they are guilty or not. Our senate will demand that, at the very least.'

''Our' senate? You're very patriotic all of a sudden?' Lorcan asked. 'Why would a couple of Connachta low-life like you be so interested in senatorial debate?'

'Low life?' Bren moved forwards; his fists clenched. 'Do you want another smack, old man?'

'Leave him alone!' Finn cried out, struggling

with the strips that bound his wrists together. 'I'll kill you both!!'

'Settle down Bren.' Sencha warned. 'He's just trying to get a rise out of you.' Bren shook his head, laughing loudly. 'I can appreciate that. It's a fair question, mac Róich' he added slowly.

'I have a few more,' Lorcan said. 'What exactly do you want from us? Money? I have more than enough. You can have it. How much do you want? I have enough to purchase both of our freedoms. You won't get much out of the mac Daras. A commander in the Ulidian army and a vate?! Besides,' he added, carefully, 'if mac Dara is under arrest, he's hardly in a position to negotiate for the lad. Neither is the boy's mother.' Lorcan stared at Sencha. The older brother of the two nodded. 'But you already know that, don't you?

'You're an old man, mac Róich, old and stubborn. Tired, maybe? Solitary? Doing laps of the great roundhouse of yours, no wife or family of your own, nobody to talk to except a young Pune...I mean you must have been badly in need of company if you needed that turnip around! We couldn't be sure you would put much store on your remaining years, off-load your legacy on a couple of 'low-lifes' like us. Now, Finn, here. That's different. He's your reason for wanting to live.'

'But why take me? Why not just take the lad?'

'Why not? You were an easy target. Isn't that so, Bren?'

'Right, Senc.'

'Add to that the incentive that a simple ransom note cannot provide and the undeniable proof that we had the lad. And, of course, you're an editor of the Bardic Press, mac Róich. Who knows what sources you had at your disposal all across Éireann if you had decided to be difficult?' He threw the news sheet at Lorcan. 'That headline might have been different otherwise, eh?'

'How much?' Lorcan asked, wearily.

'Enough. We're not greedy, mac Róich. You'll still have plenty left over for wine and books! There's a branch of your bank in Cruachan Aí. That's the other reason you are here, old man. Tomorrow, you are going to negotiate a rather substantial withdrawal. 'Banks, bards and bullets', mac Róich...Banks, bards and bullets.'

'What about them?'

'None of them recognise borders.'

They had been untied, at least. A pair of dirty, thin mattresses had been scavenged from somewhere by the Connachta while two coarse blankets and the fire in the hearth contributed to the extent of their comfort. The brothers took turns in keeping guard. They were both armed with pistols, open deterrents to any hope their victims may have had of escape. They had somewhere close by, with supplies, Lorcan knew, an Ogham messaging device, for sure, and the gods knew what else. How else had they learned so quickly about the Connachta leader? And what would a couple of Connachta deadbeats be doing with a communication device like that?

They had organised everything very well, Lorcan thought. Perhaps too well? There was something, however, that didn't sit right with him with regards to his two captors. He couldn't help but wonder that it was all too much of a coincidence that the nephew of Conall mac Dara had somehow ended up captive while his uncle was simultaneously under guard in an Uisneach cell. The symmetry was altogether too neat, the parallels too obvious.

It was cold. Finn had offered him his blanket, but he had refused. Pride, of course. Not wishing a display of weakness in front of the thuggish-looking Bren who watched on, a crooked smile playing on his lips the whole time as he twisted the rings of his fingers around and around.

It must have been late as the fire had gone out. Bren had been too lazy to relight it, choosing instead to wrap another heavy blanket around his shoulders. Lorcan had been awake for a while, pretending to sleep, having positioned himself in such a way that he could sense the other man, hear his breathing. If Bren fell asleep, could he risk disarming him? He tried to remember if there had been anything substantial enough amongst all the debris in the cottage to do damage to the big Connachta. With his one stiff leg, would he even be quick enough?

All of a sudden, from outside, Lorcan heard a voice cry out. And then immediately the sound of a gunshot. Instinctively, he sat up and looked across at his ward. Finn was already on his feet.

'Stay back! The pair of you!' Bren shouted; his snarling face lit up by the ethanol lamp over his head.

'Bren! Bren!' It was his older brother's voice again. Whatever was happening, it was serious. Sencha was in trouble. Bren opened the door, held it ajar and jutted his head out quickly, keeping his pistol trained on his two hostages. Another shot rang out. A different sound, this time. Someone else was out there. Bren hesitated, unsure of what to do. He heard the sound of broken glass and then more shots. He risked another look outside.

'Shit!'

Now the door was partially open, both Finn and Lorcan could detect the faint smell of smoke, drifting towards them, carried by the cold, night air outside.

'Shit!' Bren repeated. 'Right, you two! Not a word! Into the corner.' Lorcan saw him glance briefly at the leather strips lying discarded on the floor. He didn't have time to tie them up again, Lorcan realised. Now, it was his turn to smile. 'Stay there! Don't move! Remember, old man, I have a bullet in this pistol reserved just for you!'

Then he left. Lorcan and Finn could hear him curse as he fumbled with the lock outside. There was another shot.

'Bren!' Sencha screamed again in the distance.

Something had happened. The younger brother had been hit. Finn ran to the door but Lorcan managed to hold him back.

'Stay down lad! Keep away from the window!'

'Bren!' Sencha cried out again.

There were more shots, an exchange of gunfire, and then finally the sound of a chariot engine splutter into life, the cranking of gears and the careering of tyres, skidding in mud.

Lorcan and Finn waited in silence. After a few seconds they heard footsteps coming towards the cottage.

'Stand back!' a voice warned from outside.

They stood back and waited. A sudden rifle blast blew the door back off its hinges.

'You both ok?'

Standing there was a woman in her late thirties, her face smeared with blood, a CT rifle slung over her right shoulder, dressed in full combat fatigues. She smiled at Finn.

'Mother!' He cried out, in disbelief.

21

They know? Conall stared at the paper
again. Who were they and what exactly did
they know? And why were they telling him
they knew? He shivered. If this was a game,
Conall wondered whether or not he should accept the invitation to play. But what choice
did he have?

He considered his options. In a few hours,
he had a meeting with mac an Bhreithiún. The
right thing to do was to reveal to him the
contents of the note. And yet he knew immediately the position that would put him
in. He could implicate himself in some wider
conspiracy, the object of which was the assassination of the president of Connachta. If he
chose to stay silent, it would no doubt look
worse for him in the long run if the note were
discovered. Perhaps his loyalty was being put
to the test. Perhaps his innocence was being
undermined. For all he knew, the lawgiver mac
an Bhreithiún was involved. Was the lawgiver
a Connachta shill, bought, paid for and soon
to be pensioned off as a reward for services
rendered? It wouldn't be the first time the par-

tiality of a brehon lawgiver had been induced by something other than due process. Could mac Murchadhna really be trusted to offer his shield in his defence? Or would Ulidia and Connachta haggle over his life in their respective senates, more likely behind closed doors, and sacrifice it on an altar of convenience, one life for the sake of many more.

Conall took the paper, stuffed it in his mouth and swallowed. If only that would be the end of it, he thought.

After breakfast in his cell he was led by four druidic guards to the upper floors of the House of Brehon Law above which his cell was located. As they advanced down a passageway, he passed the sealed doors of the main Chamber of Justice, the 'supranational' court which conducted trials not only for serious crimes committed in the Protectorate, but also those major criminal cases which bypassed national borders and involved two or more of Éireann's judicial bodies. Afterwards, he was led into the chambers of the brehon lawgivers, and then finally, into the room currently being occupied by mac an Bhreithiún.

'Ah, Commander mac Dara, a pleasure!' mac an Bhreithiún stood up, approached and did mac Dara the honour of gripping the inside of his arm.

He had a convivial, round face and wore a curly, silver wig, the traditional colour of age, and as a consequence, wisdom. It hearkened back to a time when having grey hair was a rare commodity in ancient Celtic society, a time when life expectancy was short. A pair of eyeglasses rested on a little pig-snout of a nose and a linen torque wrapped itself around a chubby, short neck. As for the rest, there wasn't much of him. His body and legs were concealed behind a billowing set of black robes. This was a man, Conall thought, who derived his stature by the position he held and not the physicality of the form he occupied. His accent was from Mhumhain, Ciarraí probably, and like mac Neill and mac Murchadhna before him, he was another one who preferred to operate in the shadows, only occasionally exposing himself to the light. It had been years since mac an Bhreithiún had lost a case, he had heard, and in spite of his porcine appearance, he was more hunter than hunted.

'I trust you slept well, commander?'

'Not bad, lawgiver.'

'Hmm, those cells are better than you have anywhere else on the island but still...Have a seat, commander.' Conall sat down. 'You know, I spent a night in one of them myself?'

'Oh?'

'Not for any misdemeanour, of course,' he chortled. 'No, I simply wished to gain an appreciation of what the accused went through before and during trial. See if it could be used for my advantage.'

'Oh?'

'You think that's wrong?'

Conall shrugged.

'Reaching a proper verdict is important to me, commander. I cannot ever foresee a day when I, myself, will ever be on trial, so knowing the mind-set of the defendant is useful...helps me empathise, strategise.' Conall said nothing. 'You're from Ard Mhaca, aren't you?' the lawgiver continued.

'Yes.'

'Terrible business your war, isn't it? And so very close to peace as well. Repercussions for us all.'

'Repercussions?' Conall enquired.

'Yes. Already. Would you believe it? Internationally, too. Reflects badly on the whole island.' If his intent is to get under my skin, he's succeeding, Conall thought. 'Me? I'm from Ciarraí,' he continued. 'Been living in Laighean most of my life but I still can't shake the accent!'

'Why would you want to shake it?'

Mac an Bhreithiún gave him an appreciative look. 'True, mac Dara.' he said, thoughtfully. 'True. But you know how we Mhumhain are seen in the rest of the island. The land of wine and song.'

'But not you?' Conall asked.

'No, not me. Not that you can always escape

your roots. Take your name, for example. Mac Dara. So much history...Speaking of old names. You know, I think we may have a common acquaintance?'

'Who would that be?'

'Lorcan mac Róich. He's a family friend, isn't he? Your nephew's current guardian, I believe?

Conall tried not to stiffen too visibly. 'Yes.'

'Met him years ago at some joint Bardic-Brehon affair. Can't remember where, or when. We chatted briefly about language, I think. Yes, that was it. You know, commander, without the mac Róichs, there wouldn't be a 'Ciarraí' to speak of!'

'Oh?'

'It was Ciar, son of Fergus mac Róich, that lent his name to the county.... that was what Lorcan told me in any case. How is he by the way?'

'Who? Lorcan? Last time I saw him, he was just the same as the time before,' Conall answered drily.

'Oh? And when was that?'

Conall had no idea where any of this was leading. He had expected a brief interrogation on his version of what happened on the Hill, on the morning of Beltane. At the very worst, some adverse revelation pertaining to the message he had received during the night. But Lorcan mac Róich?

'The evening before festival.'

'And have you been in touch since? By Ogham, perchance?'

'No. I simply visited mac Róich to tell him I wouldn't be around for a few days and that to let the boy...I mean...my nephew Finn know. That was all there was to it. Sorry, mac an Bhreithiún, would you mind letting me know where this is heading?'

'I will. Shortly. The boy, Finn. He's a cadet in the RBK Youth?'

'Yes.'

'And his mother, your sister, Aoife mac Dara, works as a vate in the war zone?'

'So? Neither of these currently are crimes under the constitution.'

'Hmm...no. When was the last time you communicated with them both?'

'Look! What the hell is this?!'

At the sound of Conall's raised voice, there was a knock on the door and a druidic guard poked his head into the room.

'Everything ok, sir?'

'Yes, Guard. Everything is in order. Thank you.'

The door closed. For a moment, mac an Bhreithiún and Conall sat in silence. Conall felt more helpless now than he had ever felt on the battlefield. The ammunition being employed in this particular struggle was information. Words, not bullets. The problem was he didn't have enough words because he didn't have enough facts.

'Commander,' mac an Bhreithiún began again, reaching a decision. 'I have just learned this morning that your nephew and his guardian have not been seen since the day before Beltane. Both the RBK and Bardic Press have reported their absences. Meanwhile, your sister, by all accounts, did not turn up for work this morning. I have just heard she's nowhere to be found at the stations.'

'What? I don't understand?'

'What's not to understand, mac Dara? They're all missing. Your sister was the last piece in the puzzle...'

'Puzzle? What puzzle?'

'That's why I took the decision to check on her location. According to VMC officials, she has not been seen since the evening of Beltane. She has not returned to Ulidia... at least not officially, as her transit back would have been recorded at the border. So, where is she? She's neither in Ulidia nor on the Ulidian side of the war zone.'

'Perhaps she has gone hunting boar in the Iron Mountains? Or swimming in Loch Rí?'

The lawgiver smiled. 'You're right, of course. She'll turn up. Best to err on the side of caution, though. The Vatic Medical Corp have informed the RBK and Ulidian army and they are manning a hunt for her now. We wouldn't want anything to happen to her, would we?' It was a veiled threat, meant to throw him off-balance. Conall gripped the arm of his chair. 'Of course, commander, it is all very peculiar. Would you not agree?'

Conall did not reply. He studied mac an Bhreithiún's face. Gone was the forced jollity of before. His accent now lacked the softer Mhumhain cadence reserved to throw his enemies off-guard. It had been replaced by a pressing nasal imperative, more corporate, more Laighean. Even the curls in his wig seemed to have straightened a bit.

'Of course, your people are doing their best to locate mac Róich and the boy. Seems also a resident of the Carthaginian Union has also disappeared...' He glanced at his notes. '...A 'Maggo Calleja'. A tenant of mac Róich, it appears.'

'Maggo?'

'You know the man?'

'Yes, I have met him a few times. He's harmless, mac an Bhreithiún. He wouldn't be involved...'

'...involved? Involved in what, commander?'

'Involved in whatever this is.'

'And what is 'this'?

'No idea.'

The lawgiver removed his eye-glasses, rubbed them with a piece of linen and resettled them on his piggy nose.

'Oh, come on, commander! mac an Bhreithiún exclaimed, suddenly. 'It would save us all a lot of time if you tell us all you know now rather than later!'

'What the hell are you talking about?! Conall shouted, standing up and leaning over the lawgiver's desk. He had felt something release inside; the movement of a valve being opened. The preliminaries were over, and they were now finally getting to the main event. He may have lacked finesse when it came to words, but Conall had often discovered that he could intimidate his inferiors with an outward display of anger, an imposition of his will on the other man. Sometimes, the phlegmatic spittoon of a raised voice, the ominous threat of a clenched fist was all it took to bring a recalcitrant subordinate to heel. It was an act, for the most part, something all officers learned to do in order to glean the very best out of the men under their command. With mac an Bhreithiún, no deception was required. Unfortunately, the lawgiver was not one of his soldiers. He had, no doubt, seen it all before.

Mac an Bhreithiún's face hesitated, flickered an instant as it struggled to deal with the surprise venom of Conall's outburst, before immediately realigning itself to its normal, prearranged status -a calm, bemused mockery. The guard outside, re-entered the room and, once more, was waved away by mac an Bhreithiún.

''What am I talking about?' he pronounced, slowly. 'I am talking, mac Dara, about the remarkable series of coincidences that have occurred over the last forty eight hours. Your nephew Finn, his guardian and your sister have all vanished. You participate in a security detail whose job it is to protect your own president, but which ends up in the assassination of another.'

'If you are implying, I had something to do with that then just come out and say it, mac an Bhreithiún.'

'Alright then, mac Dara. I think you were involved.'

'Really? And your evidence for this?' Conall asked.

''We'll come to that. Have a seat, commander, and let me tell you how it happened.'

'I'll stand, thanks.'

'Suit yourself.' Mac an Bhreithiún checked his notes and began. 'You're an interesting character. It says here, you dropped out of the RBK Youth and then re-joined the full RBK later. Do you know what that tells me, mac Dara?'

'Enlighten me.'

'It tells me you like to do things your own way. You're an individual. Independent. Stubborn. But not without drive. Hence, you go back to the RBK.'

'You missed your vocation, mac an Bhreithiún. I have heard of these new head-shrinkers the Federation uses now!'

'You show courage in battle, rise through the ranks. You have the adoration of your men, the begrudging respect of your superiors. Above all, you are one of those rare things, mac Dara, especially in a place like this. You know what that is?' Conall did not respond. 'An honourable man. There, I said it. And, commander, I freely admit honour is not something I have in abundance, nor is it a prerequisite across any of the three Orders.'

'Can you just get to the point?'

'So it would have been impossible for you to go against this inherent drive, this prime directive that navigates you in all the decisions you make.'

'In the name of all the gods, what are you getting at?!' Conall exclaimed.

'You would need to be compelled somehow. Even a direct order, I am informed by others who know you better than I, would still not have been enough for you to contravene your personal code in such a way. So, if not you, then those closest around you. Commander, I believe you are being blackmailed.'

'That's bloody ridiculous!!'

'Your nephew and mac Róich have been kidnapped by either an anti-Ó'Flaithearta group in Connachta, a similar group in Ulidia, or a combination of both. They forced your hand.

You were approached in Emain Mhaca, probably because you were given the security detail for mac Nessa and *after* Finn and mac Róich had been taken. The Carthaginian, after all, according to RBK Youth, only appeared asking questions the following morning. You're right. He's not involved. Probably gone looking for the boy. But you, mac Dara, you somehow managed to get word to your sister Aoife. As your only sibling, she would also fall under suspicion...'

'...suspicion of what?! Shooting Ó'Flaithearta?! You're mad, mac an Bhreithiún!! Based on what evidence? When I left mac Róich, he was fine. I was on the Hill the whole time! Who am I supposed to have hired to kill the president?!'

'Sit down, commander. I think you will need to.'

Conall sat. He was beginning to feel lightheaded.

'For you, there was no choice,' he began, almost sadly. 'For the others it was a question of loyalty. Finances.'

'What others?'

'Tell me. Last night. What did you do with the message that was put under your door?'

Conall tried not to look surprised. 'What message?'

'Did you eat it? It doesn't matter in any case. Caoimhín has admitted everything.'

'Caoimhin?! What's he got to do with it?'

'Oh come now, mac Dara. Let's move past this part at least.'

'Listen, mac an Bhreithiún! I am telling you for the last time! I have no idea what you are talking about!'

'Have it your own way, commander. So, let's begin with Caoimhin. Caoimhin Breathnach.' The lawgiver began reading. 'Born Emain Mhaca 1952. Usual path from RBK Youth into the senior ranks. Enters your command triad...hmm...oh... 1987. You've known him a long time, I see?'

'And?'

'Would you say Breathnach is a man like you? Mac an Bhreithiún asked.

'A man like me?'

'A man of honour, mac Dara.'

'Oh! I still have honour then?'

'I'm relying on it, commander.'

'Thanks for that at least!'

What about Caoimhín?'

'Alright, mac an Bhreithiún. I'll play along. Caoimhín Breathnach is a good man. One of the best I have ever worked with. Yes, he's honourable. If such a thing exists after a quarter of a century of war!'

'A man whose word can be trusted?'

'Yes.'

Mac an Bhreithiún sighed. He picked up another sheet of paper.

'I have in my hand, mac Dara, a signed confession. It's a detailed account of Breathnach's part in a conspiracy, the originators of which are still as yet unknown. A conspiracy to bring down the Connachta government and thus destroy the Connachta-Ulidia peace process.'

'I don't believe it!'

'It's all here, mac Dara.'

'Coercion! You forced that confession out of him!'

'No. It was made voluntarily. You have my word on that.'

'Your word!' Conall sneered.

The lawgiver smiled again. 'That's fair, I suppose. My word may not mean much. But if you don't believe mine, perhaps you might believe his word...from his own lips. Guard!' The Guard outside once more opened the door.

'Yes, sir?'

'Bring in Breathnach!'

'Yes, sir.'

In a matter of moments, Caoimhín at the point of a rifle, was led into the room. Conall rose to his feet.

'Caoimhín!'

The sub commander could not look his superior officer in the eye. Instead he kept his gaze on mac an Bhreithiún. He was pale, exhausted, but there were no signs of a physical beating, at least none that were visible to Conall.

'Caoimhín!' Conall repeated, his voice breaking.

'It's no use, commander. They know,' was all the sub commander said, before being led away. Conall stood a moment, frozen like a statue of Lugh at winter solstice, before managing to sink back into his chair.

'You see, mac Dara? There's no point denying it. Breathnach was loyal to you, right to the end. That might be of some comfort to you. But it was his own undoing. He bribed one of the guards to slip that warning note to you last night. It was intercepted, of course, but the DG commander wanted to see how things would play out, so he allowed it to get to you. Anyway, Breathnach was interviewed late last night. He says you were approached by unknown parties in Emain Mhaca and informed of the kidnapping of your nephew and his guardian. He also mentioned the potential endangerment to your wife and family. These 'agents' wanted your help for an important mission. Did you tell Breathnach the details of the mission? Of course not, but he must have guessed all the same. But his loyalty to you was such...Well, in any case, he didn't realise he was facilitating the assassins. The DG are still trying to attain the descriptions of the two in the group that fired the flare...and the shots.'

'Wait a minute! What group?'

Mac an Bhreithiún picked out a photograph

from under a sheet of papers. He handed it to Conall. 'Here, take this. Recognise anyone?'

Conall stared at the print. It was one of the pictures taken by the Bardic Press in front of the Roundhouse, before dawn, on the morning of Beltane. The four leaders, the Arch Druid and members of the Druidic Council were standing on the steps of the building, posing for posterity, their solemn faces momentarily stunned by the flash lamp that lit them up in the surrounding darkness.

'Is this some kind of joke? Of course, I bloody do!'

'Look closer, mac Dara. Just on the edges of the picture.'

Conall looked again, this time, scanning every detail of the photo. Again, he noticed the main dignitaries occupying the centre of the photo. He looked at the shadows around. There were other figures there. On either side of the main group.

'That's the transport detail. From Laighean and Mhumhain,' Conall stated. 'They were asked to add numbers for the official pictures. They were all in dress uniforms and ...'

'....and you had an argument with some of them. And that argument was noticed. You weren't happy that they were there, mac Dara.'

'No, I wasn't. It hadn't been cleared with me!'

'Wrong mac Dara! You knew all about it! In

fact, it was your suggestion!'

'Rubbish! Who says?!'

'Caoimhín.'

'Caoimhín? No way!'

'You asked Caoimhín to arrange it with some of the Bardic Press to have the transport detail participate in the photographs. You needed to provide an excuse for them to be there. I have it here. It's in his statement. Of course, the assassins aren't in the picture, but the others will provide a description. You couldn't do it yourself, mac Dara. It is well-known you are no fan of the BP and, I believe, the feeling is mutual. No doubt, that's one of the reasons you and mac Róich are at odds. The assassins were not part of the contingent protecting the King or Chancellor. They arrived separately. Later. It was your job to ensure they were to have access to the area surrounding the Hill.'

'They weren't near the bloody Hill. None of them were.'

'Are you sure of that, mac Dara? Somebody was! I think they followed on and got through the protective cordon at the bottom of the Hill. They used fake uniforms, but real security passes, the latter which you provided. They made their way around to the opposite side of the Hill and then onto the other hill beyond. You could easily have left the rifle and flares for them there earlier. As I said, the others are all being questioned now. It'll not be long before we find the guilty parties.'

'Mac an Bhreithiún! This is madness! I would never...!

'...All I want from you, commander, is the name and description of whoever approached you in Emain Mhaca. There are mitigating circumstances. You were acting under duress -the kidnapping of your nephew and so on. Tell me that now and I promise it will go easier on you.'

Conall remained silent. For the first time in his life, he couldn't think of anything to say.

'In that case, Conall mac Dara, commander of 1st Ulidian Division of the Red Branch Knights, you are hereby under arrest for the attempted murder of Connachta President Ailill Ó'Flaithearta.'

22

Lorcan's car, or 'chariot' did not inspire confidence. If Henry Ford's Model T was the crossroads at which the industrial revolution embraced the age of consumerism, what passed for an automobile in Ulidia and its Federation was the junction at which technological innovation had staggered to a grinding halt. Even Maggo looked unimpressed.

Ferdia, on the other hand, could barely contain his excitement.

'It's an original Láeg! The first model! Beautiful!'

'Leg?' Maggo asked.

'No, Mags. Láeg! Named after Cú Chulainn's famous charioteer.'

'Oh!' Maggo replied. 'I thought it was because it encourages you to walk.'

Maggo laughed, with the added joy of someone making a joke in a second language. His laugh was infectious, and I found myself joining in.

'What are you two laughing at? I suppose the chariots are so much better in the Union and WCA?'

'No, no, Ferd. Not so much.' Maggo stifled another laugh.

'My name is Ferdia. Not Ferd. Ferdia, after Cú Chulainn's famous brother,' he said, proudly.

'Did he have a leg too?' Maggo teased.

'Very funny, Carthaginian. Faster than a bloody elephant anyway!'

I got in. Maggo took the seat beside me and Ferdia, our navigator, sat sprawled out in the back. The boot was filled with enough provisions to last for a few days. Maggo was the only one of us to have any money.

'Ready, everyone?' The steering wheel was on the wrong side, so I presumed traffic kept to the right in Ulidia. At least that was my fervent hope. I turned the ignition, and, to everyone's astonishment, the engine kicked into life.

'Connachta, here we come!' roared Ferdia from the back.

'Lord preserve us!' Maggo added.

It was just after dawn, but already the streets were overflowing with people. Back home in Belfast, Royal Avenue would have been deserted at this time of day. Most would still be in their beds, living lives dictated by the exigencies of a nine to five job rather than the light of the morning sun. Here, people still followed the path of Lugh, the sun god, across the sky. But it was the twentieth century. 1994. The Federation, for convenience it seemed, had adopted the Christian calendar followed in most other parts of this world. And yet, their life cycles were still regulated by the great ball of fire that hung over their head, one lone star in space, personified as a whimsical deity, indulging or disdaining the natives below. I wondered how many of their clerics and scientists had been put to death, theorizing alternatives to this belief system, smuggled into their pagan citadels from abroad, or dreamt up in domestic laboratories with no hope of ever overthrowing the prevailing doctrine. Too much progress too soon could bring the whole system to its knees, I thought. It was a delicate trapeze that swung between pagan belief and scientific fact, a metronome whose momentum was controlled by the druidic schools. If my research in Lorcan's library had taught me anything it had at least taught me that.

As if in keeping with my thoughts, the car stuttered suddenly, jolting leftwards, almost into the path of a passing cart.

'Bloody hell! Watch out!' Ferdia shouted.

'He is right, Lewis. We cannot have an accident. You and I are both foreigners, without local driving permits. This is not our vehicle and the boy cannot drive.'

'I bloody well can!' Ferdia replied.

'So, we cannot be stopped,' Maggo continued.

'How are we going to get through the border

without getting stopped then?' Ferdia said.

'We will think of something. Won't we, Lewis?'

'Of course, we will,' I replied, confidently. Naturally, I had no idea what that 'something' was. The aos sí had spoken of some reason why we all needed to be in Laighean. I was hoping I could come up with something by the time we reached the Ulidian frontier. Also worrying me was the growing realisation I was newly arrived in this universe and already deemed the leader of this merry troupe of misfits: a volatile teenager, who was sitting in the back seat of Lorcan's decrepit rust bucket, honing a sword on his lap and in danger of committing hari kari at any moment and his monkish, moon-faced mate who grinned at life as if it were constantly giving him a reward for something.

'Your family name, Lewis. May I enquire what it is?' Maggo asked.

'Summer.'

'Ah, Summer. So nice. Perfect for today, no? Like Valletta. Yes, Mr Summer. I have every faith that you will think of something.'

The streets of the old town were narrow and difficult to negotiate. The locals seemed to consider it their prerogative to step out in front of traffic with the same casual indifference regardless of whether they were bringing to a halt a horse, donkey, or even a chariot, with or without a Bardic licence. Some were laden down with crates of fruit, vegetables and other wares. Others were at work, busily taking down all vestiges of Beltane. I noticed flags, bunting and stalls being cleared for the new working day. A few had less appealing jobs, removing the clutter of the annual celebration which littered the cobbled alleys. There were a lot of soldiers on the streets too. They looked stern, I thought, chatting and smoking in small clusters. With Ferdia's help, however, I orientated a way out of the arterial network of lanes and soon found myself heading out of the city.

'Which way?' I asked Ferdia.

'Ring of Gullion. Where else?' he yawned, indifferently.

Of course. That too would make sense. Emain Mhaca to the Ring of Gullion and from there onwards to 'the gap of the North' where Cú Chulainn had single-handedly defended Ulster from Queen Maeve's Connacht armies and where nearby the Brown Bull of Cooley stampeded its hooves in defiance of her. Another city, no doubt, awaited there. It was impressive, I thought, this homage to their past but then, for them, it was not the past.

After around an hour's driving, I was soon able to make out Slieve Gullion up ahead. The valley below the mountain was completely different, of course. As expected, a whole town had been erected at the feet of its slope. My attention was drawn to its familiar mesa which I had hiked so many times with Rose. It was exactly the same as the Slieve Gullion in my world, a carbon copy in every detail, the faint line of its summit finely silhouetted with all the finesse of a water colour painting. I swallowed, suddenly wistful for the memory of a world that I had left only days before. Slieve Gullion was nothing, of course, in comparison to the Alps, the Rocky Mountains, the Great Barrier Reef, the Rock of Gibraltar and the River Nile. And yet they were all here, part of the natural topography of this other Earth. It reassured me to think of them, here, and in my world, timelessly serving their transient populations.

We were still a few miles from the Ulidia-Laighean border when we began to see the first Ulidian patrols. Lines of young men, most of whom were barely adults, were pacing at equal lengths from one another, sweltering in thick, woollen tunics and beneath steel bowler helmets. Each one shouldered a rifle, on the side of which a Red Hand motif was also emblazoned. It was like a scene from the Great War but played out for me in vivid technicolour. They were marching southwards, towards the border. In the distance, I noticed a convoy of military trucks, their progress stalled by the sheer volume of vehicles on the road.

'Is this normal?' I asked.

'No, it's bloody well not!' Ferdia exclaimed, crouching down so not to be seen. 'Something's happened.'

'Where are they all going to?' Maggo asked.

'The Gap of the North, of course. These ones are from the Ulidian 3rd Infantry. By the looks of them, recent enlistees. The SR base is up ahead though!'

'SR?' I enquired.

'Setanta Reivers. The best of the best. The reivers protect the Ulidian borders. These are Setanta Reivers. Their job, historically, is to prevent infringement from Laighean.'

'But Ulidia is not at war with Laighean,' I asked, confused.

'I know that. That's why it's strange, this amount of activity.'

'I'd better get off this road.' I said, 'At least, until we find out what's going on.'

I took a right down a single country lane and prayed that we would meet nothing coming the other way. After a minute or so, I parked outside a farmhouse. A gaggle of geese in the yard in front soon alerted the occupant inside to our arrival. A curtain twitched, half a face peeked out and a few seconds later, we were staring down the barrel of a shotgun.

'What do you want?! Be careful how you answer, mind! This old rifle's liable to go off in my hand!'

'Our apologies, sir...' Maggo began

'...Who the hell are you?' the farmer demanded, aiming the gun directly at Maggo's smiling face.

'He's just a tourist,' I said. 'I'm driving him back to Laighean. He's catching the boat from Átha Cliath later this evening back...back to the continent.'

'Boat, you say? And what's that to me?!'

'Nothing, sir,' I replied, 'I just noticed a lot of soldiers around and was wondering if there was another way to cross...you know...the border?'

''You smugglers?!'

'No, no. My friend simply has to get across the border for his boat. I am worried that if we are delayed by traffic, he will miss it and...'

'Border's closed!'

'What do you mean? Closed?' I asked.

'Closed. As in not open.'

'Why is that?'

'You not see the Ulidian Shield this morning?'

'No, we were on the road from Emain Mhaca. We didn't see a news sheet.'

'Hmm...well the border is closed. All borders with Ulidia.'

'Since when?'

'Since last night. Laighean's doing, not ours! Our senate met afterwards. Already sent an official complaint to the Laighean ambassador here.'

'But why?'

'Seems Ó'Cosrach is not pleased with this assassination.'

'What's it got to do with him?!' came a voice from behind.

'Who've you got in there?' the farmer asked, redirecting his rifle.

'Just a boy. He's a cadet,' I explained, hurriedly. 'I'm giving him a lift to Átha Cliath too. He's visiting his father. He works there on business.'

The farmer looked at us with renewed interest.

'A cadet?' He took a step forward to have a closer look. 'I can see that. What's your name, lad?'

'Cadet Ferdia Ó Ceallaigh, at your service.'

'If you're a cadet, you should know that you'll not be crossing the border today. Truce is over. Word just reached us this morning. Course the bloody army have been on the move since first light!'

'The truce is over?' I asked again.

'That's what I said. So you'd be better turning back where you came from.'

'But what's any of this got to do with Ó'Cosrach?' Ferdia asked, with frustration.

'Seems him and the Mhumhain king don't like being shot at. Anyway, truce with Connachta is over. Their leaders voted to end it. Laighean and Mhumhain are showing solidarity. No one really knows what is going to happen. War, probably. Looks like you might see a bit of action after all, young lad.'

'Looking forward to it,' Ferdia replied, happily.

'Ha! That's the spirit, lad!' He thought for a moment. 'You from Emain Mhaca, you say?'

'We did,' I said, intervening.

'One of the cadets there is missing, I read. And some old guy who works with the BP? The Shield, as it happens.'

'We heard. Mac Dara, wasn't it? The cadet's name?' I asked.

'Yeah, that's the one. Nephew of the assassin. They got him, you know. The DG have made an arrest. Mac Dara'll be standing trial.'

'Oh?'

'Guilty, of course. Firing squad for him!'

It hadn't taken long for the news to filter down to Ó'Móráin and his triad. Conall mac Dara had been charged with the attempted murder of his nation's leader. He had known it even before his meeting with mac an Bhreithiún. What is more, mac an Bhreithiún knew that he knew. More hypocrisy, he thought. For all the bureaucracy that lay strewn across the lawgiver's desk, the files, the scrolls, the authoritative ink stamps, the paperweights, the ridiculous, antiquated quills propped up in a holder, policies and procedures meant very little in reality. Information had leaked or had been allowed to leak. The evidence against mac Dara, mac an Bhreithiún had stated, was overwhelming. The outcome of the trial was a mere formality.

Ó'Móráin had pondered on what he would have done in mac Dara's place. Would he have sacrificed the life of a political leader in order to save that of another, or others, close to him? Without question. He had two grown up children himself. His dedication to duty over the years may have badly impaired his relationship with Eithne and Daire, but he would never willingly put his children's lives in danger. No, impossible. How could he live with himself afterwards?

Still, it didn't sit well with him. Although Ó'Móráin had only met mac Dara for the first time at Uisneach, he had known of him for years. He was sure that mac Dara was also aware of his Connachta adversary too. You do not fight a war of attrition, across a scarred landscape of trenches that rarely moved, a war of action and reaction, attack and counter-attack, without scrutinising your opponent on every level, militarily, emotionally, psychologically, in the hope of some insight, some acquired advantage that might lead to a breakthrough, accelerate a conclusion and allow everyone, everyone, the chance to return home to their wives and children. Mac

Dara would have taken all that into account, of course. Even the risk of reigniting a war was not enough of a deterrent when someone you love's life was at stake. Ó'Móráin could understand that too. What he couldn't comprehend was why the nephew had been seized? He knew that mac Dara had a daughter. Surely, she would have been a better target? He had heard she worked in Béal Feirste? She would have been unprotected. And what was mac Róich's role in the grand scheme?

There were other things as well that merited further analysis. The triad. That bond was unbreakable, its sum being greater than its parts. *Three orders into one*, the words of the druidic anthem went. It was also the unwritten, unsung oath sworn by the triad. Its emblem was a raven. Two wings that offered opinions, flights of fancy if you like, and a head that made the final decision. It was the same across all the triads. To be forced to sacrifice yourself was bad enough. But sacrifice another in your triad? To snap the wing that would bring the triad crashing down to earth was unthinkable, at least to Ó'Móráin. But then, there was the signed confession of Caoimhín Breathnach, the triad mac Dara had used to perpetrate his crime.

And now the truce was over. Acting President Ó Braonáin had not been able to win over the hawks in the senate and, as a result, all

Connachta forces would no doubt be recalled to the frontlines. In addition, both Laighean and Mhumhain had publicly stated their support for Connachta. The former had even gone so far to have closed their border with Ulidia. The reason for this was less to do with the moral indignation that the Laighean leader, also in attendance on the Hill, could have shared the same fate as his opposite number in Connachta, but more to do with the ongoing manhunt for the assassins if they tried to make their way back to Ulidia. To do so, they would need to traverse Laighean or Protectorate territory. The latter had already closed its borders. The Bardic Press had neglected to release any of these details, of course, or, according to mac an Bhreithiún, the assassins' embarrassing use of a Laighean and Mhumhain transport detail as cover for their infiltration of the Hill.

All in all, mac Dara did not have much of a chance. Breathnach's confession had sealed both their fates. The Laighean and Mhumhain transport were currently being interrogated by the DG. The two assassins would soon be found, or if they had escaped, two others would be implicated and that would be the end of the affair. Somebody had to pay. The war would recommence, and mac Dara would not be around to witness Ulidia's ultimate defeat.

'You wanted to see me? Ó'Móráin, isn't it?'

'*Commander* Ó'Móráin.'

'Of course, shall we take a stroll?'

They were in the tropical gardens located at the epicentre of the Roundhouse. Under the sweating roofs of glass panes, a huge basalt sundial looked up through a massive dome of cast-iron and glass. The current Arch Druid, and all those who had preceded him, had endeavoured to outdo each other by adding to the interior of the dome ever more rare and exotic botanic samples from all corners of the Federation and beyond. What had started as a simple garden, a tranquil respite from the daily pressures of the Houses of Bards, Brehon Law and Vates, had quickly developed into a hothouse for the horticulture of nectarines, figs, grapes and cut flowers. Afterwards, it had expanded into a full-scale greenhouse which accommodated ferns, palms, orchids and dozens of other imported plants. Mottled butterflies flitted amongst the foliage while frogs and lizards gaped lazily from pools and miniature waterfalls. Three tall doors, yawning open from the different Houses, led visitors into sunrooms which acclimatized them before their arrival, under a blanket of sky, into the gardens themselves and eventually, if they wished, the suffering heat of the conservatory.

'Impressive, isn't it, commander?'

'It's hot, senator. Too hot!' Ó'Móráin removed his peaked cap and unbuttoned his tunic. The heat was still stifling though, and, in a few seconds, he was persuaded to remove it entirely. He folded his tunic neatly and placed it on a bench. Mac Murchadhna watched him carefully.

'You take great pride in that uniform, commander.'

'Does that surprise you?' Ó'Móráin replied.

'No, of course not. You remind me of someone though. Come, we can pick your jacket up on the return journey.'

The young senator was immaculately dressed in a thin, white linen suit; a wide-brimmed hat and a pair of tinted eye-pieces shielded him from the sun. When he had asked to meet the senator, mac Murchadhna had suggested 'the gardens'. Of course, the Ulidian had failed to mention that he would be exposed to the equatorial heat of a *fulacht fiadh*, a roasting pit in which he, like a pig, felt like he had been casually dropped. Mac Murchadhna, on the other hand, had come prepared. He obviously was the kind of man who liked to have an advantage, needed to have the odds in his favour. Ó'Móráin would have to conduct himself with greater acuity than he had done with his prior meeting with the Arch Druid.

'I have to admit, commander. This is a bit unusual. Momentous even.'

'These are momentous times.'

'That's true,' the young senator agreed. 'You

know, for all intents and purposes, I could be committing treason merely by talking to you. The truce is over. Technically, our respective countries are already at war.'

'There's time yet.'

'Is there?'

'It'll take a while for full engagement to really begin. Troops will need to return to their posts in an tSionainn.'

'Might not be that simple.'

'Why not?'

Mac Murchadhna studied the Connachta commander more closely. His rough, dark beard was glistening with minuscule globules of perspiration. His shoulder-length hair, hanging like wings either side of his face, reminded of the limp, sodden feathers of a blackbird. Sodden and rather pathetic. Yes, that was it. It was Mac Dara. Ó'Móráin reminded him of mac Dara. The two commanders were so alike. Both were grunting, unsophisticated supporting actors in a theatre of ideas they could never possibly understand.

'Why not?' repeated Ó'Móráin.

'The citizens of an tSionainn have had a taste of peace over the last few months. You know, commander, even your own people in Loch Rí are restless. They are sick of war. They want a 'normalisation'. You can appreciate that, can't you?'

'Of course, senator, but I don't have any control over that.'

'I know. I know. But the population there, and I suppose my own people in the Iron Mountains, have enjoyed the stability the peace process has provided since Imbolc. Recent polls suggest both communities are supportive of the new Assembly. Laighean and Mhumhain are involved...as is the Federation as a whole.'

'I can't see any way out of it, senator. If our senate has made the decision to end the truce...'

'...Hmm...we'll see. Anyway, commander, perhaps we should talk about why you wanted to see me before we both take root.' The senator grinned: a disarming, false parting of the lips that revealed a flash of teeth as treacherous as that of the Venus flytrap they had just passed. If mac Murchadhna were the trap, what did that make him?

'It's about mac Dara. Have you seen him?'

'Why do you ask?' The jaws of the flytrap had suddenly snapped shut.

'Listen, senator, it's none of my business...'

'...Yes?'

'It doesn't feel right?'

'Of course, it doesn't, commander. Mac Dara is innocent.'

'You think so?'

'I'm his lawgiver, commander. What else do you want me to say?' Mac Murchadhna grinned again. Ó'Móráin stared at the man's beaming face and tried to refocus. 'But why are you so interested? Surely, mac Dara's no friend of yours?'

'Of course not, senator. I think it's a disgrace what has happened to our president.'

'Any news, commander, from your people over in the Vates?'

'He's stable. My triad is with him around the clock? Backup is on its way from home.'

'Surely, you don't think…?'

'If it isn't mac Dara, then who knows?' Ó'Móráin said. 'My president might still be in danger!'

'Yes, of course,' the senator replied, 'but I think you are worrying unnecessarily. The assassins are long gone.'

'But those who organised the assassination are still at large. They could try again.'

'True, commander. But, then again, if the objective of the plot were to end the truce, then they have succeeded regardless of whether your president survives.'

'Not if mac Dara is found innocent. That's why I wanted to see you. I was wondering if there was any hope for him?'

'You know I can't discuss the case with anyone outside my own legal team, never mind an enemy of Ulidia.' He smiled again. 'Sorry, no offence intended.'

'None taken. But it doesn't make sense.'

Ó'Móráin spent a minute expressing his concerns to mac Murchadhna. The young senator seemed surprised by the force of seasoned soldier's logic.

'I appreciate that, commander, especially your insights regarding the honour of the triad. I have thought the same myself.'

'So?'

'It always boils down to evidence, Ó'Móráin, written or verbal. Without Breathnach, they have nothing. All I can say is, they have multiple sources...two druidic guards and certain members of the Bardic Press. Both confirm Breathnach's statement. I can't say more.'

'One last thing, senator, which section of the BP were approached by Breathnach?'

That's the problem, commander. The Ulidian section. Specifically, the Béal Feirste Banner. It's our own people that are lighting the fires to mac Dara's pyre!'

23

Finn didn't know whether it was the sudden, unexpected apparition of his mother or the sight of her, kitted out for battle, which had shocked him the most. The two versions of her on offer failed to coalesce in his young mind. It had been months since he had last seen her, and he had never seen her like this. It wasn't just the uniform, the rifle or the blood and grime that besmirched her face. It was the fact that, in spite of all that, she was undeniably still his mother. The same warm sparkle of eyes, the same running touch of her fingers through his hair, the same soft cradle of arms. He had rushed into them, the discipline of the RBK Youth training manual happily discarded.

'Careful, Finn.' she chuckled. 'I have a couple of grenades around my waist.'

'Mother! How?! I don't understand!'

'I know, son. I'll explain everything. First of all, are you ok? Hurt?'

'No I... we are fine! Lorcan and me...we knew that *someone* would come. We just didn't think it'd be you, mother. Did we, Lorcan?'

'No, lad. We didn't... Hello Aoife.'

'Lorcan,' Aoife said, coldly.

'Mum, how did you get here? Why are you dressed like that? Did you kill Bren?'

'Who?'

'The Connachta. I heard him cry out.'

'No, they're both gone, son. You're fine now.'

'But how? I thought you were at the clearing stations. Mother, the war's started again. They think Conall killed the Connachta president! We have to help, mother! We have to...!'

'We will, son. We will. Listen, Finn, I need to speak to Lorcan for a few minutes. Can you do me a favour?'

'Yes, what?'

'I noticed a well on my way here. Can you go and get us all some water? It's just in the clearing to the left of the Connachta's shack. Be careful, mind. Stay away from the blaze. It shouldn't be long before the fire dies down.'

'But mother, I want to hear...' Finn protested

'...Please Finn! Do as you're told!'

'Yes, mother.' He lowered his head and left.

Lorcan looked at Aoife for a moment. 'Bit hard on the lad?' he said.

'What happened?' she asked, ignoring him.

'You need to ask? How did you get here, Aoife?'

'First of all, tell me. What happened? In your own words.'

Lorcan narrated the story of the last couple of days, his capture, Finn's abduction, the news from Uisneach about Conall. Aoife nodded her head occasionally. None of what Lorcan was relating seemed like news to her.

'Why do you think they took you?'

'The Connachta said something about concern about my influence with the BP but I don't believe it.'

'What do you think?'

'It has to be tied in with what's happening in Uisneach. To Conall. I don't know what.'

'You were supposed to take care of the boy!' Aoife exclaimed, at last. 'Maybe Conall was right. I should have left him with the mac Daras.'

Lorcan looked away. 'I'm sorry, Aoife. There, I said it! There was nothing I could do!' He turned his head and looked at her. 'I am sorry.'

Aoife looked at him, took a few steps towards him and then embraced him.

'Missed you, old man.'

'And you, Aoife. And you.'

She pulled away from him slightly, tilted her head and whispered in his ear. 'He's here, Lorcan.'

'Who?'

'Lewis. The aos sí told me. He's here. He came across. Your son's here, Lorcan!'

'I was twenty three years old when I fell in love for the first... and last time. 1948. A long time ago. Nearly thirty...aagh...years...!'

'Really?' the kind face replied. 'It's never too late, you know.'

'Ha!... Yes...Deirdre...'

'...Deirdre? Was that her name?

'...Cathbad...'

'Cathbad? After the druid? Is that *your* name?' the vate enquired, tearing off a strip of bandage.

'Lorcan.'

'Lorcan? Your name's Lorcan. Good. Now... I need you to stay awake. Keep talking, Lorcan. Ok?...Ok?'

'Yes,' Lorcan replied, weakly.

It was 1978 when Lorcan first met Aoife. He had been on assignment from the Ulidian Shield, reporting from the frontlines, partly trying to play the hero for his editor back in Emain Mhaca, but, if he were honest, mostly trying to extricate some vestige of heroism deep within the well of self-doubt within himself. He wanted a story, something real, something more than the usual patriotic platitudes and jingoistic junkets he had been hitherto forced to pen and pass off to an eager public who had no idea of what war really involved. He was a junior editor and he wanted to make a difference, he later told Aoife. And what had he got instead for his trouble? Two stray bullets from a Connachta sniper: one in the leg and one more serious in his lower abdomen. Was that enough reality for you, mac Róich? he could almost hear the gods enquire. The vate whose job it was to save his life was Aoife mac Dara. Looking back, it was the shot of morphine that had made him so loose-tongued, and her need for him to stay conscious.

Aoife heard a simple story at first. Normally, young soldiers, in similar situations, cried out for their mothers she had been amazed to discover. They spoke of wives, girlfriends, children. She had been trained by the VMC to stay calm, keep the patient alive at all costs and, above all, make them feel comfortable. Lorcan's account had drawn her in because it was one of lost love, old romance and, as the story continued, because of the family from which Deirdre hailed -one of the most powerful families in Ulidia: the mac Nessas.

Deirdre was only nineteen when she stormed the barricades of Lorcan's life, scaled the ramparts of his heart, hoisted her flag over his soul forever. Yes, he had said, it was just like that -an invasion into the very fibre of his very being. And when she had insinuated herself into his every working thought and absent-minded reverie, she pulled up the drawbridge and set the castle adrift. It was to be just the two of them, insular, quietly nurturing their love, safe behind the thick walls of their fortifications

They had first met at Lughnasa, at a private congregation of Ulidian elite in Béal Feirste, there to celebrate the opening of the newly erected Temple of Lugh. As daughter of the Senatorial Chair, Deirdre had been specially selected to light the first fires. Lorcan's father, who was a senator and a leading light in the House of Bards, had also received an invitation to attend. He had brought along his gifted, but unsettled, son in the hope that this gathering of the powerful and influential in society would somehow impress upon the young man a new steadfastness and determination to succeed in life. It didn't quite work out as his father had planned.

The mac Nessas had always been a noble and historical clan. However, in recent years, something had gone awry. This particular generation of the family tree, it was believed, had borne a branch the leaves of which were cruel, twisted and lifeless. Sometime in the previous century a toxin had entered into the mac Nessa arboreal network and had poisoned the roots. Deirdre was the exception.

Her mother, Étain, had died when she was eight years old. She had finally escaped from the brutish, vulgar arrogance of her husband, Deirdre's father, by taking her own life. The circumstances of her death, however, were not known outside of the family. Deirdre's brother Darragh, the future president, was anvil to his father's hammer and even then predestined to go further in his footsteps and become the first mac Nessa to acquire the presidency in over a hundred years.

The relationship with Lorcan, of course, had to be kept a secret. Furtive, clandestine trysts under cover of darkness, or a brushing of hands as they passed one another in the bright sunshine of a crowded marketplace, were all they had to sustain their passion. As it grew over the subsequent months, the couple took more risks. The stakes were high. Lorcan's father's career would have been jeopardised, possibly ended, if word of the son's relationship were to leak to the Bardic Press. But this was nothing compared with the loss to the mac Nessa name if a Connachta or Laighean news sheet had somehow managed to prise apart the scandal and splash it across their morning headlines. Local press could be controlled, but the damage to young Darragh's fledgling political career would have been irreparable if word of the liaison had reached abroad.

With the news that Deirdre had fallen pregnant, Lorcan knew that time was limited. He began to make provisions for their future. He had family in Alba where both he and his future wife could set home. They would need money, naturally, to elope, but Lorcan was confident that he had enough savings to survive until he found himself a bardic apprenticeship in Cille Mhàrtainn or in another such metropolitan hub there.

'What happened?' Aoife asked.

It was several days after the impact of Lorcan's initial injuries. The wind and rain outside was threatening to buckle the canvas canopy of Vatic Medical Corp Station 4, a long, rectangular tent which gave rest and recuperation to the injured and wounded in battle. Lorcan was propped up in bed, reclining on a straw pillow, attempting to do justice to a chunk of bread that had been made from the flour of dried, ground turnips.

'You know the deal?'

'You'll get me discharged! You know that?!'

'Someone as pretty as you? Never.'

Aoife slipped a small flask of whiskey from beneath her skirts and poured her favourite patient a small measure.

'There. That's your lot. Now, Alba?'

Lorcan took a long sip and smiled sadly.

'I don't think you will enjoy the rest.'

'Go on,' Aoife whispered.

'One night,' Lorcan continued, 'just before the summer solstice the following year, we decided to make our way by boat to Alba. I had bought passage for two on a ship from Béal Feirste. We caught a steamed transport from Emain Mhaca and arrived at the port for the overnight crossing. Deirdre was three months pregnant by then. Her face was not that well-known, mine definitely wasn't, but we...' he began to chuckle, '...she disguised herself with a wig and I had a false moustache. Anyway, it didn't matter. Mac Nessa's people were already in position at the docks. My father was there too.'

'How'd they find out?'

'Darragh mac Nessa. For some reason, Deirdre loved her older brother and he, for his part, might have had some genuine affection for her too. She did not trust him enough to let him into her confidence, of course, but that spring he had discovered he was being sent off to Avebury for a year, under the tutelage of some renown political figure or other, and he wanted to spend more time with his sister. Who knew when they would next see each other? Anyway, somebody had spotted us, some paid informant, and little Darragh had been appointed with the task to find out more...I suppose he was successful.'

'And then?'

'We were brought back to Emain Mhaca. That was the last time I saw her...alive.' Lorcan closed his eyes as if replaying the memory once more behind the closed shutters of his mind. He clutched his blanket and then began to cough suddenly. Apart from everything else, he had picked up a cold in the last twenty-four hours. Aoife swiftly reached for a jug and poured him a glass of water. 'I suppose another nip is out of the question?'

'Go on then. For medicinal reasons.'

Newly fortified, he began again. 'A week later, I heard Deirdre was removed from the family home. All I ever found out was that she was staying with an aunt on the north coast along with, I am sure, a whole gander of other women...midwife, nurse maids and so on. Of course, I begged my father to let me see her that first week but, if you can believe it, a triad of RBK had been employed to ensure that wouldn't be possible. For all intents and purposes, I couldn't leave the house except under armed guard. Deirdre's father had also stepped up security around the mac Nessa residence. I wasn't able to get near Deirdre and believe me I tried! The whole affair was being hushed up, I suppose, until arrangements were made to get Deirdre out of the city.'

'What happened after she left?'

'Nothing. Absolutely nothing. One night, soon afterwards, my father called me into his study and explained, in no uncertain terms, that I was never to speak of the 'episode' again. The mac Nessas were a powerful family and could make life very difficult for the mac Róichs.'

'You mean he was threatened?'

'Probably. I had never seen my father look the way he did that night. I remember his hand trembled slightly as he poured himself a glass of whiskey from an old sideboard he kept replenished for private senatorial meetings. He rarely drank, you see -his own father had issues in that regard. That was another sign.'

'Another?'

'My mother, Ethniu, hadn't been well even before the discovery of the affair. She had always had a nervous disposition. Anyway, when news of what had happened reached her, she had a relapse, at least that's what my father said, and took to her bed. That night, you see, I told my father I couldn't care less about the mac Nessa's, their past lineage and future, political ambitions. Nothing was going to get in my way. I was going to be hand-fasted to Deirdre one way or the other. And then... well, I was led to an understanding that my mother's health relied on my acquiescence, at least temporarily, until she recovered. He would arrange something with mac Nessa in the meantime.'

'It wasn't true.'

'No... maybe...partly. I don't know. My mother died eighteen months later of a brain haemorrhage. The vates said it could have happened at any time.'

'I'm sorry,' Aoife said. 'And had he arranged something? Your father?'

'Yes. He took...measures.' Lorcan lowered his head and placed a hand over his brow. 'Sorry, Aoife, do you mind if we stop for now.' He yawned. 'I've suddenly come across a bit tired.' He slid down into his bed while Aoife re-adjusted his pillow. 'Tomorrow. We can finish.'

'Told you about that whiskey!' Aoife joked as her patient turned over on his side. But there was no reply. Lorcan was already fast asleep.

As it transpired, there was no tomorrow. Aoife was reassigned to a different clearing station as a result of a new intake of injured on another section of the frontline. She never got a chance to say goodbye to Lorcan as by the time she returned he had already gone.

It wasn't until a few months later, in early 1979, that she met him again. It was at a conference in Emain Mhaca, a special symposium marking a decade of war held by the Ulidian branch of the Three Orders. Bards, lawgivers and vates were providing a series of retrospectives on the ongoing conflict to final year undergraduates at the university. At lunch, Aoife spotted Lorcan with a large beaker of cider, standing alone at the bar, reading a news sheet and looking thoroughly bored.

'At least it's not whiskey.'

He looked up from his reading and, with a raised eyebrow, gave the young woman a smile. 'No, just cider. Bit early for the other.'

'As long as you stay awake this time, Lorcan.' There was a pause. 'Aoife,' she prompted. 'We *met* at the clearing stations a few months back.'

'I remember,' he replied.

'How's your leg?'

'Fine. Fine,' he replied, instinctively patting his right thigh

He was different, of course. A passing acquaintance with death changes a man, of course. It can make him maudlin, self-reflective. This was the real, sober Lorcan mac Róich, realigned, one not inured to abrupt, revelatory outbursts about his private life or nostalgic, sentimental testimonials about his past. He seemed taller, and naturally more reserved. She could read it on his face; first his confusion, and then his uncertainty. 'I haven't told anyone, Lorcan. And I never will,' she said, reassuring him.

They shared a drink. And then another. And when the bodhrán was beaten to call attendees back to the theatre for the afternoon's speeches they remained on their stools and ordered another set of drinks.

'Aoife, have you met Cían?' Lorcan asked, indicating the young man, pouring them a fresh beaker of cider each.

'No. Nice to meet you, Cían.' The young man nodded, embarrassed by the unexpected attention of such a beautiful woman.

'He's a student. Studying Brehon Law,' Lorcan continued.

'Oh?

'And I am a bard. And you're a vate. 'Three Orders into One'. How about our own private seminar?'

Afterwards the two reconciled friends made a tour of the local taverns. While they may have come across as a strange pairing, a middle-aged man and his young pretty consort, cloistered in the nook of an afternoon alehouse, they realised that they had more in common than any passing waiter could ever have imagined. Aoife loved the stories of his travels in the Carthaginian Union; Lorcan adored the inauguration of what would soon be her life, as yet unlived, stretched out before her, her only encumbrance the impossibility of choice.

In the end, it wasn't the alcohol that made him trust her again. No, there were other forces at work, forces whose will he had to obey. And yet, if it had to be someone, why not her? After all, Aoife had already proven a reliable custodian of his secrets. The release of information regarding his affair with Deirdre mac Nessa would be damaging, even now, not only to Senator Darragh mac Nessa but also to his ambitions of becoming editor of the Ulidian Shield. And yet, she had said nothing. That on its own had to prove something.

But it wasn't just that. If truth be told, there was something about this young woman which reminded him of Deirdre. He couldn't help but think that his Deirdre would have liked Aoife mac Dara, would have encouraged the friendship between them -for that's all it was, friendship. Lorcan harboured no romantic intentions. Aoife was the daughter he had never had.

'You haven't asked?'

She looked away, found herself slowly exhaling. She picked up her beaker of cider, had second thoughts and placed it down again.

'It's not my place, Lorcan. You don't have to tell me anything...anymore.'

'She died in childbirth.'

'Yes. I thought as much. I am so sorry, Lorcan.' She grabbed his hand. 'What happened afterwards?'

'Her father wanted nothing to do with the child. It was a boy, by the way. His antipathy towards my family from that point on knew no bounds. Of course, in his opinion, it was my fault that his daughter had died. He carried that bitterness to his grave, but not before passing it on to his son, Darragh.'

'What happened to the boy?'

Aoife stared at Lorcan. The colour had drained from his face. He lowered his head, his shoulders suddenly shrunken. If he could have managed it, he would have sailed away at that moment and never been seen again. 'If it's too painful...'

'...Yes, it is. But...but...'

'Look I'm sorry, Lorcan. Let's change the subject.'

'It's not what you think, Aoife. Not even remotely what you think. My son is alive. At least, I think he is still alive. I haven't seen him since he was two summers old.'

'Was he fostered?'

'In a way, yes.'

'In a way?'

Lorcan paused and took another draught of cider. The other secret, the one he had carried with him for nearly thirty years, was more overwhelming, more universal than the first. The Druidic Council would have sentenced him to death for blasphemy if it had discovered it. He didn't even know if he still believed any of it himself. Perhaps, telling Aoife would release him from the awful burden of carrying its weight for so many years. Perhaps it was because he had wanted someone else to bear the brunt of it or, at least, confirm the rationale of his failing logic. In the end, he knew, he had no choice. Looking back, it was that day when the seeds were sown that changed both their lives irrevocably. He looked around the bar to make sure they could not be overheard.

'Tell me, Aoife, do you still attend the Seventh Day?'

'The Seventh Day? No, not often. I enjoy the festivals, of course. If I am honest, like most, probably less to do with Lugh than the holiday itself.'

'What about the aos sí?'

'You mean the sacred people of the mound? Never really think of them. They're from the Otherworld, aren't they?'

'Yes, and that is why we build our temples and stone circles on these mounds. They are gateways to this other world.'

'I suppose so.'

'Aoife, what if I were to tell you that these aos sí do not inhabit this world with other beings similar to them? What if their role is to provide passage from one world to the other, from this world to the other world...and from the other world to this one?'

She took a sip of cider. 'Interesting theory, but no stranger, I guess, than what passes for religion in the druidic schools. You yourself have told me stories from your travels beyond the Federation. From what you say, we have a minority stake in the overall forum of ideas.'

'Yes, we have based our religion on hearsay. Do you know in the CU they call us 'pagans'?'

'What's a pagan?'

'It doesn't matter. What if we have got it all wrong? Listen, I haven't worked it all out myself but what if the aos sí aren't supernatural beings in the sense that we understand the word? They are not related, or connected, to the Tuatha Dé Danann from which all our deities derive. Those gods were invented to explain activity at these mounds and circles, activity carried out by the aos sí.'

'Sorry, my head's beginning to spin, Lorcan,' Aoife laughed.

'No, listen. It's true, Aoife...I know it's true. I have seen it!

'Seen it?'

'There is another world, out there. But it's not the place where the gods live or where we go to die. It's a world, just like ours. Another Earth. These aos sí aren't human but they're not gods either. They just do what they do...did what they did.'

'What did they do Lorcan?

The mac Nessas wanted to...dispose of my son, Aoife. My father, however, threatened to go to the Bardic Press and expose the whole affair. So they reached an agreement.'

'An agreement?'

'Yes. My father would take care of the child, but only until it was old enough to be fostered, after which it was to be removed entirely from Éireann. Mac Nessa didn't want to run the risk of the child's identity being discovered and used against his family. He had high hopes for his son, Darragh, it seems. I was to have no contact with the child either. The boy was to be raised anonymously, probably in Alba.'

'That's terrible.'

'I hated my father for agreeing to those terms without my consent. I didn't speak to him for months afterwards. During that time, though, I came up with a plan to take the child as soon as it was old enough and disappear with it forever. You see, I had grown... attached to the young boy.'

'So you are saying these aos sí took your boy to another world?!'

'My father must have sensed that I was about to do something rash. I suppose he did not want me to ruin my life. You see, when I was a boy, I had a foster brother. He was a bit... different, not like other Ulidian boys. He was only with us for three years, but we were very close...the brother I never had, I suppose. Anyway, he was brought, and eventually taken away, by a couple called the Ó'Corcráins. It was that same couple that took my boy away too. After it happened, my father explained everything to me.'

'What was that?'

'That they were aos sí and that they communicated with certain individuals in both worlds, forming links, restoring balances and so on. My father was one of those individuals. He told me it was all part of some greater plan but that it was necessary for the future of Ulidia and the Federation. He didn't know the full details but that my son crossing to this other world was part of the plan.'

'What's your son's name?'

'Lugaid. My father told me, though, that would not be his name in the other world. The aos sí at least told him that.'

'What do people call him there?'

'Lewis.'

''Lewis'', Aoife repeated, whistling the peculiar sibilance of the word between her teeth

'This is going to sound crazy, but I was wondering if you would like to go there and meet him.'

24

The consumption of alcohol was banned in Uisneach. Pilgrims there were encouraged to observe a solemn but ostentatious piety, a consecrated display of religious fervour as they paraded slowly through the streets of the old part of town, making their votive offerings and burning incense sticks between the toes of their god of preference. It was an exercise in hypocrisy, of course. The surrounding towns compensated for Uisneach's abstinence. Thousands filled their inns and taverns every month, barely sobering up in time before making the short journey back to the sanctuary of the holy city.

The reputation of the Bardic Press for softening up unwilling witnesses with hard drinking was well-known. Their young reporters were notorious for their tenacious pursuit of a headline, and if that meant risking liver failure as they coaxed and cajoled with ale and stout, then it was a price worth paying.

Ó'Móráin knew that the BP covering the Beltane assassination would have to alleviate their boredom somehow as they took turns waiting for their testimonies to be heard. Loch Craobh was the first and closest town he tried. In the fourth tavern, he found the men he was looking for.

It was called 'The Giant Hag' named after the local legend of an over-sized and grotesque deity who, sometime in prehistory, had rather clumsily dropped stones down from the heavens onto Earth, thus creating a panoply of monuments around which the entire town had grown. The nearby tombs and hills, the *Sliabh na Caillí*, also gave its name to this supernatural being. On the wall behind the bar, pictures had been hung with artistic impressions of how the event might have happened. In the midst of these was affixed a larger portrait of the giant hag herself under which some wise-acre had scrawled: 'The Wife!'. The darkness of the tavern, lit up only sporadically by the odd ethanol lamp, its low roof, slanting, slate floor and tilted, wooden cross beams made any new arrival check the steadiness of their legs before even a drop of ale had been consumed. It was a couple of hours after lunch and only the die-hard, professional drinkers had stayed on, most of which preferred their own company: old scraggly men with flat caps, blackthorn canes and rosy faces that looked up with interest at Ó'Móráin as he entered, sized him up, made a mental note of his appearance before refocusing on the smooth, silken heads of their porter.

He had obviously not come in uniform. That was against the law. But Ó'Móráin knew that as soon as he opened his mouth, he would have been marked as a foreigner. Fortunately, he was spared the attention. There were other foreigners present. From a corner booth he could hear the familiar, guttural tones of Ulidia.

'Mind if I join you?'

'That depends, Ó'Móráin,' answered the first Béal Feirste man.

'Of course, you remember me.'

'Sure, you've a face, my friend, that's hard to forget,' added a second from Laighean.

'You're a long way from home?' This time, a more amiable, Mhumhain accent.

'As are you. As are we all.'

There were five of them. At least one employee from the Béal Feirste Banner and one from a Mhumhain news sheet, probably the Mhumhain Messenger. A copy of a Laighean news sheet was folded in front of the other who had spoken. Two further drinkers, who had yet to address Ó'Móráin, could have been from anywhere. They looked down into their drinks and tried to hide from Ó'Móráin's gaze.

Living on the same island created a very small genetic pool and the Bardic Press, like the Druidic Order as a whole, did not recognise borders. Even Connachta and Ulidian BP could sit together in the Protectorate, swap stories over a tincture of whiskey or two and not feel even the slightest iota of patriotic responsibility. The BP too was like a secret priesthood. The nationalistic ardour of its daily slogans and rhetoric was easily forgotten in the private sanctum of the public house.

'So, may I join you?' Ó'Móráin enquired again.

'As I said, my Connachta chum,' replied the same Béal Feirste journalist, holding up his empty beaker, 'that depends...?'

'Drinks all round then.'

There was a roar of celebration behind him as Ó'Móráin turned to make his order at the bar. By the time five ciders had been poured and he had returned to their table he noticed two of the company had already departed.

'Where are your friends?'

'Ach them? Sure didn't they have to go. Sláinte all the same!' replied the Mhumhain man, smiling.

Ó'Móráin quickly turned on his heels and left the tavern. On the street outside, he looked left and right, took a gamble and opted for left. Around another corner, he peered down the busy thoroughfare, trying to make out the heads of the two BP men whom he had just allowed to escape. They were nowhere to be seen.

'Here lad,' he said, kneeling down to match

the height of a young lad playing outside the tavern. The youngster was about five summers old and had a small, wooden shield in his left hand, his face smudged with apple sauce. 'There's a shilling in it for you, if you can help me. You can buy yourself a sword with that. You see two men leave here a minute ago? They were my height, no beard and were wearing dark suits.'

'You're not wearing a suit, mister.'

'I know that lad. You see the two men though?'

'They went that way,' said the boy, pointing right.

'Lugh, shine on me!' Ó'Móráin exclaimed. 'For I am a bloody fool!'

Back inside the tavern, he took a seat beside the BP.

'So, who are they?'

'Why do you want to know, Connachta?' said the Ulidian

'Look you northern idiot! I am trying to help!'

'Are you now? And how would that be then?'

Ó'Móráin sighed. He would never locate the others if he didn't 'let down his shield', an old saying that his wife often used against him. He would need to bring these men into his circle of trust.

'Only the biggest story you fellows will ever have the chance of hearing. That's if I am correct, of course. Imagine the headlines in the Banner and...' he looked at the other two reporters'...and all across Mhumhain and Laighean! Exclusive rights! Here and now! The makings of all your careers!'

'Your information first,' said the Mhumhain man, suddenly serious. 'And I will throw in a few drinks for free.'

They had been extraordinarily cooperative, Ó'Móráin thought, as he left the tavern. The enticing bait of a fat, juicy story wriggling on the end of fish-hook had been too difficult to resist. They would have to cast their lines together, simultaneously, at the appointed time, Ó'Móráin had said, and it was he, and he alone, who would decide when the moment was right. At least, not until after he had located the two reporters he was looking for. In exchange for their names and current addresses, Ó'Móráin had furnished them with his suspicions concerning the guilt or otherwise of Commander Conall mac Dara. There was very little to go on, he had admitted. In their place, it wouldn't have been enough. And yet they had listened, less to the words he had spoken and more to the passion in his voice. Most of all, it was the absurd improbability of a commander in the Connachta army launching into a fierce defence of his supposed opposite in Ulidia.

The two men were originally from Daire, a city on the north coast of Ulidia, commonly known throughout Éireann as the 'place of the oak-dwellers'. The oak was the tree under which the first druids had congregated to commune with the gods. As a result, the city was famous for the annual contribution of its youth into the druidic schools. The people of the oak were deemed by some to be more attuned, more sensitive to the spirits of their dead ancestors. Daire also had its fair share of charlatans, ungifted seers who peddled their wares at night to the recently bereaved, bivouacked in its sprawling woods; they dealt in the forgery of hope while accepting the currency of despair. Calgach and Adair were from two such families. It seemed they had turned their back on one business of deception only to join another in the form of the Bardic Press.

'You know what those people are like! An embarrassment to all Ulidia! The BP cannot civilise men like that!' the Béal Feirste man had declared. 'You can have their names gladly.'

Of course, he could have saved himself the trip. He could have simply gone to mac an Bhreithiún for details of the Daire journalists, but instinct told him not to do so. It was the same intuition that had hunched on his shoulder in the aftermath of his president's assassination. It had led him by the hand, ever forward, and yes, it had even persuaded him that he could trust the representatives of the Bardic Press!

Back in Uisneach, he walked the streets of the city, amazed by the vitality of colours he witnessed and the smells of local and Federation cuisine. It was always tourist season in Uisneach, but there was always something different about a spring or summer festival. He worked his way through the crowds, hearing a variation of Éireann accents and Federation languages: a mixture of Helvetian, Allobrogian and Teuton stewing in a cauldron with Conamara and Morne.

The two men had rented accommodation for themselves in a first floor apartment above a small bakery. The BP were footing the bill, and, like their colleagues, they had had to extend their tenancy until the result of the investigation into Ó'Flaithearta. A stairwell on the side of the building provided immediate access to the premises above.

He tried the bakery first. A large, rotund man with a jolly set of whiskers, informed him that the two Ulidians had left early in the morning and had yet to return. He had been busy all day, of course, putting icing on cakes for 'sweet-toothed foreigners' and could not guarantee that the men had not slipped past his shop window. Ó'Móráin thanked the proprietor and took his leave. He crossed the street and sat down on one half of an empty beach beside an exasperated Laighean mother who had straddled on her right hip the cross-sectioned legs of a mewling infant. No amount of cradling or coddling could appease the child. The mother smiled apologetically at Ó'Móráin who, for the sheer lack of anything better to do, began pulling faces at the baby. He thought of his own children at that age and so much of their childhood that he had missed out on. The baby suddenly stopped crying and began to gurgle in delight at the weird contortions Ó'Móráin's face was making.

After just under an hour of waiting, Ó'Móráin spotted the two Daire men, weaving a course through the confluence of shoppers and street traders, their eyes shifting warily at everyone around them. One of them was carrying a paper bag of provisions. Ó'Móráin guessed that the two of them had decided to hold up in their apartment for the night. He watched them negotiate the external stairs to their room and then decided to wait a further few minutes. In his pocket, he felt the warm smoothness of his Bel 33 revolver under the sticky wetness of his palm.

'What a bloody mess, Calgach!' Adair said, putting down his bundle, almost overburdening the small, rickety table of what passed for furniture in their shared rental property. 'Did you see the look on the man's face? He'll have our balls for his wife's earrings!'

'Don't worry, Adair. We'll get the first steam transport back tomorrow morning.'

'Are you insane? With the border closed? How do you think that would look? And then there's the bloody lawgiver!' Adair exclaimed.

'He'd get over it. Seems the toad has already his mind up anyway.' Calgach replied.

'Hmm... still...' Adair sat down and ran a hand through his hair. 'It's ok for you. I am the only photographer I see in this room.'

'Relax, Adair. All we have to say is what we were told to say.'

'What? That we were approached by Breathnach to allow some of the Laighean and Mhumhain transport to provide filler for the photographs, a bit of colour to brighten up everybody's day? You know that's not what happened.'

'Breathnach himself admitted it, didn't he?' replied Calgach.

'I know. I know. That's what I don't get. Why would he say that?'

'Who knows? Or cares!'

'I bloody knew you should have said no to him?' Adair said.

'Say no to *him*? Now I know you it's *you* who's insane!'

Adair sighed. 'What about Ó'Móráin?'

'What about him? We stay here. Or we leave. If we stay, we push forward our interview with mac an Bhreithiún. The lawgiver will shield us from Ó'Móráin.'

'And *him*?' Adair asked.

'We stay away from him! Look, they want mac Dara dead. That's obvious. I'd rather take on mac Dara, Ó'Móráin, mac an Bhreithiún and the whole Connachta army before I cross that man!'

'And what man's that, I wonder?'

They both looked around. There, in the doorway, a Bel 33 revolver was being aimed in their direction. It was gloved neatly in the hand of Commander Rian Ó'Móráin, 3rd Finnbhennach division of the Connachta army.

It was almost dark by the time Ó'Móráin arrived back at the Roundhouse. Unlike the members of the Bardic Press, he and his triad had been graced with congenial quarters there. It was the least that the Druidic Council could do, after all, and provided instant access to their recuperating Head of State. Ó'Móráin's room even had electric light and a connecting water closet. He had practiced flushing it, amazed by the way the swirl of rushing water siphoned itself around the smoothness of a bowl only to disappear somewhere he couldn't quite figure out. If only he could flush away the mess he had found himself in, he thought, as he provided his security pass to the two druidic guards who saluted him as he passed through the main vestibule of the House of Brehon Law. Two floors beneath him, in less salubrious rooms than his own, Conall mac Dara and his own triad were subject to druidic hospitality of a different kind.

'I want to see the brehon lawgiver?' he asked a bored-looking clerk, shuffling papers around a pristine glass-top desk whilst sucking on the nib of an ink pen.

'Which one? We have quite a few?' the clerk answered, flippantly.

'Which one? Which one? Hmm...let me see... Maybe, the one dealing with the Ó'Flaithearta case! Which one do you bloody think, you pen-pushing pinhead?!' Ó'Móráin roared, showing the terrified secretary his pass.

'Err...my apologies...commander...Lawgiver mac an Bhreithiún is no longer here. He left over an hour ago, sir!'

'Anything I can do, commander?' sounded a voice, behind him. Ó'Móráin recognised it immediately.

'I thought you were in Ulidia,' he replied, turning to face the man.

'I was. But now the president is secure. Given the events of the last twenty-four hours, he thought it best I return.'

Ó'Móráin looked at the twinkling, blue eyes and slender lips of Ulidian President mac Nessa's speech-writer, and most vociferous spokesman, Bradán mac Neill. He shook his head and let out a soft chuckle. Mac Neill touched his nose.

'What's so funny?'

'Bloody Ulidians! Everywhere I look!'

'Oh?'

'Bloody Ulidians!' Ó'Móráin repeated.

'So what is it?' the commander asked, raising a cow horn of chicory root to his lips. In the absence of a real drink, this was the best that Uisneach had to offer. It had taken them quite a while to find a chicory stand still open after 21.00. The cow horn was infamous in ancient times for its uneven base, rendering it impossible to put down, thus providing a merry excuse for continuing the celebration of a newborn calf, say. During festivals, they always seemed to reappear, part of the nostalgic nonsense that swept the island at that time. The temperature this evening though had dropped unexpectedly, however, and both Ó'Móráin and mac Neill were only too pleased to wrap their fingers around the snug warmth of their drinks.

Mac Neill gazed into the semi-darkness over Ó'Móráin's shoulder.

'Hard to believe, isn't it?'

'What?

'Look. The Hill in all its glory. It wasn't that long ago...'

The commander moved to survey the Hill;

the pinks, reds and dark blues of the sky around it shimmering in the gloaming.

'Well?'

'I know you have been conducting your own private 'investigations' into the assassination, commander.'

'Who says?'

'Now, commander, surely you know that the Protectorate, Laighean, Mhumhain, anywhere, in fact, in the Federation which *isn't* Ulidia or Connachta, *is* a hotbed of government sponsored spies and free-lance operatives from both our countries.'

'So?'

'So, we know about your little trip to Loch Craobh this afternoon. As do your own people, I am sure.'

'Why not stop me then if you are all so clever?'

'I suppose that would not have served our mutual interests.'

'What do you mean? *Mutual* interests? Ó'Móráin asked.

'According to the Bardic Press, we are already at war. But, you notice, neither side has fired a shot in anger yet.'

'Only a matter of time, mac Neill.'

'Of course. If public events follow their current course.'

'And privately?'

'The doves in your senate and mine want

peace. As do the citizens of the disputed territories. As do you. And as does commander mac Dara.'

'Is that why he was set up?'

'You really believe that, don't you, commander?' Mac Neill's eyes opened even wider in wonder. 'But now, of course, you know for sure.'

'I knew something wasn't right,' Ó'Móráin replied, after a pause. He looked at the Hill in the distance and shook his head.

'You're wondering if you can trust me, aren't you?'

'I don't trust anyone, mac Neill!'

'Not even Ó Gallachóir and Ó Floinn, your own triad?'

Ó'Móráin did not answer. A few days ago, he would have cut the throat of anyone who would have even insinuated otherwise. Now? Mac Neill was right. He didn't know.

'Fine, commander. I understand,' mac Neill continued. 'You can't trust anyone. Not even the lawgiver! That's who you wanted to see just then, wasn't it?'

'Mac an Bhreithiún. You think he's involved?'

'Maybe. Maybe not. He might simply be an unknowing accomplice. Or he might be just another strand in the web, following orders from the spider at the centre. But that's the point, commander. Until we know for sure, we need to tread carefully.'

'Who's *we*?'

'The people who really want peace, commander. When you are dealing with an enemy who operates principally in the shadows then that is the terrain on which you too must operate. But now, events of the last few days have taken us all by surprise. You think you can no longer trust your triad? Until the morning of the assassination, I didn't know I could trust Commander mac Dara. You know it was mac Murchadhna who gave mac Dara the assignment in the first place?'

This was news to Ó'Móráin. At the mention of the senator's name, he felt a cold wind pass through his body.

'Mac Nessa would have known about it though.'

'Of course, he did. Ó'Móráin, the president...and those closest around him, I mean, really close...have long suspected something slightly amiss has entered our political system in the last few years. Your president noticed it too. A foul corruption...'

'...Well, politics is...'

'...Yes, I know, politics is corrupt. Mac Murchadhna is proof of that. Probably the Senatorial Chair Úi Eochada as well. And Lugh knows who else. But this transcends local politics. This is something more. It's coming from something outside of ourselves, or above...'

'I have no idea what you are talking about.'

'Alright, imagine a long, cruel hand above this island, a twisted vine of fingers, their tapering tips reaching everywhere. It nudges one side this way and then nudges the other side another.'

'The Federation?'

'We don't know how far it goes. Only, some of us have felt its clammy touch on our shoulders.'

'And mac Murchadhna?'

'We know it was mac Murchadhna who approached the Daire reporters. Not himself personally, but one of his people. So, the assassins used the cover of the transport detail to get to the Protectorate and then the services of the BP to have an excuse to be there on the morning of Beltane.'

'So we have to find out the truth?'

'Not we, Ó'Móráin. You!'

'I might have guessed.'

'If I, or anyone in my government, or yours for that matter, are seen to be involved, it will let the enemy know that we are aware of what's going on.'

'But who's to gain from whatever it is that's going on?'

'Arms manufacturers, for one. That's how mac Murchadhna was co-opted, of course. You know his family business?'

'I know it.' Of course, Ó'Móráin did. That

was the first thing he had thought of when he had enticed, with menace, mac Murchadhna's name out of the two Daire men earlier.

'But think Ó'Móráin...mac Murchadhna is just one part of it. Don't just think about who is to gain from the continuation of war.' Mac Neill looked around, hesitant to go on. They were alone on the cobbled street. The moon had long since disappeared. Mac Neill took Ó'Móráin's arm and led him away from the light of a nearby ethanol street lamp. He whispered: 'Think also about who gained from the prospect of peace as well. Take this.'

'What is it?'

'My address in Uisneach.' Ó'Móráin took the tiny card, pocketed it and looked down at his drink. It had gone cold in his hand. He suddenly felt very tired. He looked up towards the Hill again. The colours around it had disappeared. In its place, a low, sinister cloud had descended, shrouding it in blackness.

'Cheer up Ó'Móráin! Mac Neill said, lifting the mood. 'You won't be completely alone. You'll have help.'

'Who?'

'Your old nemesis Commander mac Dara. Maybe, you should see about getting him out of jail, eh?'

25

'We have to get to Uisneach! And we have to get there now!'

'We can't do anything for Conall,' Maggo said. 'Our priority is finding Finn and Lorcan...and hopefully Aoife.'

'Maggo's right, Ferdia. According to this,' I passed him the farmer's copy of the Béal Feirste Banner, 'he's in the Arch Druid's Roundhouse. It will be fully protected, impregnable.'

'They're bloody well going to shoot him!' Ferdia exclaimed again.

'There has to be a trial first. We will have time to get to Connachta and then Uisneach. But, if he's innocent...'

'...*If*? What do you bloody mean *if*?'

'Just a figure of speech,' I added, hastily. 'Of course he's innocent.'

'What Mr Summer means,' Maggo explained, 'is there will be time for his legal representatives to accumulate the necessary evidence to prove his innocence.'

Ferdia looked at us both wide-eyed. 'Are you two visiting from the bloody moon? On holiday on Planet Earth maybe? Do you have any idea how the brehon law works?'

We both thought it wise not to reply.

'No, I didn't think so. Mhaca's...!

'...It will be fine, I am sure of it,' Maggo interrupted. 'You just need to have a little *faith*, Ferdia.'

'Huh?'

'Isn't that so, Mr Summer?''

'Yes, of course.' I opened the boot of the chariot and took out a canister of fuel. I winked at the young man. He beamed back, happily.

'Why the hell didn't I go with the other two?' Ferdia said to himself, shaking his head. 'We still have to cross the border into Laighean. How do you suggest we do that?'

I opened the front passenger door, raised the seat, located the fuel cap beneath and poured in a full bottle of ethanol. Thankfully, it had not taken me too long to work out that the fuel tank was underneath the carriage of the vehicle. I was not sure my ignorance of chariot mechanics was what Ferdia wanted to witness right now.

'With more of this,' I answered. 'We will need to get more fuel. And by using our...' I tapped the side of my head with my index finger twice.

It was Maggo's turn to look bewildered.

'Our...finger?'

'No, Maggo. Our intelligence.'

The young man looked across anxiously at

Ferdia. 'Ah! Of course, our...intelligence.'

It was strange how the mind worked, Aoife thought. As a vate, she had been trained to compartmentalise her emotions and create for them neat little rooms in her head. She had learned to shut away her memories in some and lock away her anxieties and fears in others. It helped her when dealing with the horrors of war. It also benefited her in the other world. Her time there had not gone according to plan, of course. She wasn't supposed to have fallen in love with Lewis. She certainly hadn't intended to become pregnant and bear his child. No, her task was to observe the new world, befriend Lorcan's son, get to know him and then, at the appropriate time, leave and provide her older friend with a detailed report of her findings. She knew better now, of course, that any control she thought she had had was merely an illusion. All of it had been preordained, a thin ribbon of timeline that the one called Cathbad could tie in a bow around his little finger.

Lorcan had entreated her to travel through a portal to another world. What he had neglected to say was that it was Cathbad who had asked him to ask her to do so. Aoife only discovered the truth of this upon her return to her own world and after presenting Lorcan with the news of his new baby grandson.

Their second meeting, at the conference in

Emain Mhaca, had not been by chance, Lorcan had had to admit. He had been given the time and place of Aoife's reappearance in his life by Cathbad. Lorcan had been told to reconnect with her, the caring vate who had catered to his every need on the frontlines. Cathbad, it transpired, had visited Lorcan not long after his return from an tSionainn.

And what manner of power did the sentinel really possess? Perhaps, he could simply see up and down the timeline, Aoife had wondered, turning his head one way and then another, past and future, the way one does when crossing the road. Was that why he needed the aos sí? Perhaps, his function was simply to open and close the portal. Perhaps, he couldn't directly impact upon events without the willing cooperation of others.

I keep thinking of those bullets,' Aoife remembered Lorcan saying to her, as he held his grandson in his lap for the first time. 'They were, after all, the reason how you and I first met. Could Cathbad have altered their path? Perhaps not. That might have been asking too much. I don't know. And yet he was aware that they were going to be fired from that Connachta sniper's rifle. I am sure of that. Could he have persuaded someone to unwittingly stand in their path at a given moment and thus save me from injury? Maybe. Could he somehow have manipulated it so you, Aoife, were the vate on duty that day? Probably, with the help of others. But you must believe me, Aoife, I never knew that the objective of your visit to this other world was to give birth to Finn. If Cathbad knew, he never told me!'

The months Lorcan spent convalescing from his injuries were long and, as usual, he spent most of that time alone. For the first few weeks, he said, he had been unable, or unwilling, to get out of bed. He couldn't tell whether it was laziness or fear that perpetuated his lengthy sojourn at home. He still hadn't penned the article for which he had been sent to the war zone to write. His editor, understanding Lorcan's situation, had not made an issue of requesting it. Of course, he needed time to recuperate. He had been missed. Everyone was thinking of him. He was the intrepid, brave, frontline reporter, risking everything for a story. For a while, that itself was the story.

As the weeks passed, however, his troublesome housekeeper began a campaign of chastisement against him. He ought to get some fresh air. He should stop feeling sorry for himself. Ulidian soldiers were still dying every day and someone needed to humanise their plight.

More weeks passed. A letter from the Ulidian Shield soon reached him, urgently demanding the article he had yet not written, had not even thought of writing. The war was still going on, the letter had said, and things, as he knew, were changing daily. Lorcan didn't know, nor cared to know. A creeping lethargy had somehow managed to overwhelm his vital functions like a languid, narcotic drift against which he had no defence. It might have been the medication he was on. Perhaps it was the traumatic experiences he had witnessed in the trenches.

And then, his housekeeper began grumbling about objects that had begun to go missing in his roundhouse.

'So it was the aos sí who led you here to us?' Lorcan asked.

'Yes, which means...'

'...which means Cathbad. Which also means his project, or whatever this is all about, is about to unfold. Finn was part of it and so now is Lewis. What's it all about, Aoife? Did they say anything?'

'Those two? You must be joking! They told me where you were...'

'...Outside Cruachan Aí?'

'Yes. That's where we are. I was in the Iron Mountains, just about to cross the border into Ulidia, when the two of them suddenly materialised. They gave me vague directions here and then revealed, quite casually of course, that Lewis had crossed.'

'How were they? Have they changed?'

'Same as your description of them. One red-haired, freckled beanpole and one purple ballet dancer in a tutu?'

'A tutu?'

'The dress you said Bridge likes to wear. That's what they call it...over there. I keep forgetting, Lorcan, you have never been.'

Lorcan sat down at the table and absentmindedly started to check the inside of his jacket pocket.

'Bloody pipe! I left...it got left behind.'

'You still smoke that disgusting thing?'

'Not anymore, apparently!'

She smiled and sat down beside him.

'So Lugaid is here, Aoife?'

'Yes. The aos sí were just with him in Emain Mhaca. He, Maggo...

'...Maggo? Him too?'

'Seems that way,' Aoife replied. 'Lewis, Maggo and some loud-mouthed RBK cadet, they said, are making their way here to find us. Our light-footed friends are winging their way back to Ulidia to let them now. All being well, we'll meet them at the clearing stations. Back where it all started for us, Lorcan.'

'I still can't believe it. My son, Lugaid!' Aoife breathed heavily and looked away. 'You worried?'

'About meeting Lewis? Of course, I bloody am. It was just one night, Lorcan, a lifetime ago, a world away.'

'You must have meant something to him,

Aoife? For him to come across!'

'His son...my son... means a lot to him. Probably. As for the rest, I don't know.'

'You can't mean that Aoife! For one thing, Cathbad wouldn't be doing all this, whatever this is, if you *and* Lewis weren't important.'

'Important? Maybe. But as a couple, in a relationship? Together? Now? With all this going on?'

'Cathbad...'

'...And that's another thing. You said so, yourself! You don't say no to Cathbad. You know how he operates. He puts a brain-ball in your head, and you can't move for fear of it cracking apart, that is until you agree to do what he says!'

'So now you think Lugaid doesn't even want to be here. He's been coerced!' Lorcan exclaimed, shaking his head.

'Weren't you?!' she shouted suddenly.

'Yes' Lorcan replied, sadly. 'When I arranged for you to cross. And before that, when my father arranged for Lugaid...' It was Lorcan's turn to exhale deeply. He slammed his fist hard down on the table. 'Lugh knows, I miss my bloody pipe!'

They looked at each other for a moment and then both broke out into joint fits of hysterical laughter.

'You know I have my own reunion to look forward to, Aoife,' Lorcan said, finally, regaining his composure. 'My own son. Don't you think that doesn't scare me half to death?'

'I know. You and Lewis. Lewis and Finn. Me and Lewis.'

'Not forgetting, Finn and me...You know the problem with us, Aoife?'

'What?'

'We're too bloody alike?'

'True,' she replied. 'But it's not just us, Lorcan,' she continued, after a pause. 'I have to put my own feelings to the side. We both do. It's about the rest of it. Conall. Finn. My son's just been kidnapped. He's part of some grand design that Cathbad's been working on since you and your friend Pritchard last saw each other! And now, just for good measure, I have to tell him he has a father who is still alive!'

'My father's still alive?!' There, in the space where the door had once been, stood Finn, consternation etched all across his face. From a hole in his bucket, a tiny trickle of water had begun, just then, to leak out.

I had only had a few hours in Lorcan's library to come to terms with my new world. I knew I had needed to flesh out the particulars of Pritchard's brief synopsis of where I was. I didn't mind, however. Being back in a library again, amidst the tannic aroma of leather-bound volumes that perched side by side on the mildewed stuffiness of shelves -

that was an atmosphere I could breathe in any world. I thought of Eva, back in my world, cherry-picking knowledge from the shelves of Belfast's Central Library, making sense of television and popular music, the prospect of the nuclear family huddled in the rubble of a nuclear war. She might have had more time than I to readjust, but her new world was infinitely less complicated than the one she had just left.

And so, it wasn't just Lorcan's compilation of history and politics that had made their initial appeal to my desperate acquisition of information. I had also come across a large, modern atlas of 'Éireann' which not only outlined county and national borders, but also provided aggregated population densities of most cities, towns and villages on the island and, naturally, the major and minor routes between them. A topographical and meteorological section of the book I could afford to leave behind.

I tore out the pages I thought I might need and stuffed them into my pocket.

'So the Kingdom of Breifne,' Maggo said, poring over the crumpled map that he had smoothed out on his knees in the seat beside me, 'is where we are now heading, Mr Summer.'

'Yes, we cross Breifne and that will take us into the Iron Mountains.'

'I thought only Mhumhain had a king. I have never heard of this King of Breifne?'

'There is no bloody king in Breifne!' Ferdia exclaimed, newly exasperated in the back seat. 'It's just what it's called: 'Kingdom of Breifne'! There used to be a king, but not anymore!'

'Aw, did he lose his head?' Maggo teased.

'You'll lose your bloody head in a minute, Mags!' replied Ferdia, gripping the hilt of his sword.

'It'll not take us long. A couple of hours at the most.'

'I still don't understand why you have chosen this route,' Ferdia said. 'Your friends said to head towards Uisneach and then cut across into Connachta.'

'Laighean's border's closed, Ferdia,' I replied. If we get to the Iron Mountains...'

'Ah, here they are. 'Iron Mountains', Maggo read aloud. On the map, Ferdia. See?'

'The only place we can go from there is into the war zone!' Ferdia replied, ignoring Maggo. 'Need I remind you the war is about to kick off again?'

'We'll work something out. The Ulidians will give us safe passage. If we can get to an tSionainn from the mountains, maybe get a boat, sail into Loch Rí, that'll take us to Connachta.'

'Very clever, Mr Summer,' supported Maggo, tracing the route with his finger on the map.

'Madness! Complete madness!' exclaimed

Ferdia. 'And what are going to do in Connachta? Ask random passers-by: 'Oh, excuse me, we are looking for a boy, kidnapped by your state? Any idea where you think he may be? No? That's a shame! And by the way, he's the nephew of the man who tried to kill your president?''

'You have any better plans, cadet? I asked. 'All I know is that it's best we keep moving.'

My use of the word 'cadet' seemed to have made an impact on the boy. For the next quarter of an hour he didn't say a word. I could see him in my mirror, staring thoughtfully at the cross-guard of his sword. I couldn't tell whether he was sulking or feeling remorseful at his constant negativity. We trundled onwards and very soon entered the ancient kingdom of Breifne. Ferdia was right. In this world, it existed in semantics only. Its old borders now straddled a number of Ulidian counties and even one that used to belong to Connachta. It was an old Pale, long since vanished, like the Norman one which had existed back home centuries ago. It was now no different to every border on a map that had changed over time, like a piece of string caught in a light breeze. The Ulidia-Connachta border would be thought of in the same way a hundred years from now. Maybe even less.

'Tell me, sir. Are you excited about meeting Finn?'

'More nervous than excited, Maggo,' I replied, checking my mirror again. The rocking of the chariot had put the brave warrior back there to sleep.

'And what will you do when you find him?'

'Look for his mother, I suppose.'

'No, I mean, what will you do as soon as you find him? Will you rush towards him, lift him up into your arms?'

'You've been watching too many movies, Maggo!' I said.

'Movies?'

'Err...I mean the motion pictures...you know, that narrate a story on a large screen.'

'At the playhouse, you mean?' He thought for a moment. 'I have never been to the Bardic Mhaca since I have been here. All the stories in Ulidia are about war. But I saw one in Valletta once.' He smiled at the memory.

'Oh?'

'A funny picture with a clown. And a girl.' He blushed.

'Well, there you are, Maggo. The pictures in the WCA are exactly the same. Love... and everything that goes along with it.'

'You still love Aoife, Finn's mother?'

He had the directness of a child, this Maggo, I thought. He had a way of cornering you, cutting through your defences, and all with the soothing undertones of a voice that was a hypnotist's dream. And he didn't need a sword for any of it.

'It's complicated.'

'But with Finn, it's simpler.' He disarmed me with his smile and faced the road ahead. It had begun to rain, for the first time since I had arrived in this world. I opened the window to feel its wet embrace, warm and cool at the same time.

'Finn! Listen!'

'Is my father still alive, mother?'

The moment had finally arrived. Aoife had always known it. And yet the wonders she had seen in the otherworld, the sentinel, and the disconcerting presentiment that had overwhelmed her when she had first met Lewis in that strange hotel on New Year's Eve, had prepared her very little for it.

It wasn't just that she had fallen in love with him that night. It wasn't simply that she had stepped off a cliff and thrown herself head first into a void. All she had had to do, after all, was to become acquainted, then befriend Lewis, ascertain his dreams and learn the essence of who he was. But she wasn't a spy. She hadn't been trained in espionage. She couldn't impersonate those undercover Ulidian agents that skulked the counties of Connachta, gleaning information from loquacious locals who should know better.

No. It wasn't any of that. It was that she

knew that her actions that evening, helpless though they had been, were meant to have happened and had taken place according to the masterplan Cathbad had shaped, like a mathematical design chalked onto a Victorian schoolteacher's board. Was that why he chose to dress like that? He, the stern tutor, and we, the obedient pupils? And his cane? Was that the reparation that awaited if you did not obey his will?

All along, Aoife knew that Finn was a reminder, not just of Lewis, but that Cathbad's game was not over. Now, Finn had been put in danger and she wanted the danger to stop. Not that she regretted any of it. She loved Finn too much. But why had she listened to a madman like Lorcan? He had to be mad, of course. Another world? It wasn't possible! But it was. He had shown her proof. She had let it get that far. It would be an adventure of a lifetime...of two lifetimes. And she loved adventure, didn't she?

'Finn! Please! Sit down. I can explain.'

He dropped the bucket of water heavily to the floor. It fell onto its side, spewing its contents overboard.

'Is he alive?! Yes or no?!'

'Yes.'

'Finn. It's complicated,' Lorcan intervened.

'Shut up! It's nothing to do with you?!'

'Finn, how dare you speak to Lorcan like that!'

'Where is he? Éireann? The Federation? CU?' Finn insisted.

'He's in Éireann, son.'

'Where? Not Ulidia, surely? Connachta? Is he in the RBK?'

'Finn, your father has just returned. I thought he was dead. But he's back. That's why I am here.'

'It's true, boy,' Lorcan said.

'Have you seen him, mother?' Finn asked

'No.'

'Who told you then?'

'Some friends'

'What friends?'

'Their names are Angus and Brigid. He's on his way to see you.'

'He needn't bother!' Finn exclaimed. 'Anyway, it's too late! Why is he showing up now? Is it because he found out I was kidnapped?'

'In a way, yes.'

'Well, I don't care, mother! It's too late!' Finn kicked the bucket at his feet. 'It's too late!' He turned to leave.

'He didn't know about you, Finn.'

Finn turned back and looked straight at Aoife.

'What do you mean?'

'He wasn't told about you.'

'You mean *you*, don't you?! *You* didn't tell him about me!!'

'I couldn't, son,' Aoife said, collapsing back

onto her chair. For a moment there was silence. Finn looked at Lorcan and then back at his mother.

'Why the hell not, mother?!'

'Because...'

'Because what...?' Finn demanded.

'Because your father...he's not from this world, Finn.'

The Iron Mountains were Ulidia's last stand against a Connachta invasion. They were not a natural defence, of course, like the Alps or Pindus Range of ancient Rome and Greece. They were instead a psychological barrier, a point of no return, beyond which all of Ulidia unfurled like a prize waiting to be unlocked. The actual defensive line was on the other side of the quiet, mountain range. The disputed territories of an tSionainn lay further on.

No doubt it was the discovery of their precious, metallic deposits in the 1600s that had impressed upon the military strategists of the time the need to corral the mountains into the Ulidian fold. Traces of a canal still existed at the foot of its main peak, Sliabh an Iarainn, where ore was conveyed three miles to smelting works, before being loaded onto boats, moored at the nearby Loch Aillionn.

However, the mountain had also made a significant contribution to druidic lore. 'The Book of Invasions', a book I had read as an undergraduate, spoke of the arrival of the Tuatha Dé Danann, landing their floating ships on its highest summit, before doing battle with the Firbolg, another race of supernatural entities, at the Battle of Moytura.

So far we had been lucky. We had encountered a few Ulidian patrols on route, but no one had paid our geriatric jalopy much attention. Nothing had changed in the last hour or so of our journey except for the landscape: grassy slopes stretching out thinly over the limestone beneath, whitethorn and gorse sprouting on drumlins that sat like eggs in a basket beneath the vastness of a threatening sky.

We reached our first checkpoint just as the rain began to ease. Two Ulidian soldiers were manning a roadblock, made up of one of their chariots parked unceremoniously across the road, the surface of which was sloppy with shale, beech husks and water-filled divots. Ferdia had warned that there would be Cernach Reivers, this time, named after the legendary Conall Cernach who, it was claimed, used to sleep with the head of a Connachta warrior under his knee. I could see why the name had been chosen.

'If we can get through this first patrol, our chariot will be 'marked',' Ferdia had explained, by which he meant that the patrols afterward would feel less inclined to be thorough with their questions.

'Where are you folk heading?' the first reiver demanded, as I unwound my window.

'Bardic Press. We are heading to the clearing stations,' I said, as nonchalantly as I could. He was strongly built, unshaven and had a front tooth missing. His subordinate looked on icily, chewing on something in his mouth, some gristle of meat, I supposed. The grinding effect gave his face a predatory, coiled look, ready to snap into action, as did his rifle, aimed as it was directly at the middle of my forehead. Both looked as though they were in their early or mid-thirties but were probably a lot younger. War had that effect on you.

'Who are these two?' he asked, noticing the bardic credentials of the chariot.

'This gentleman is a reporter with the Ulidian Shield. He is here to cover the evacuation of the clearing stations for his news sheet.'

'He can speak for himself, I suppose,' grunted the reiver. 'This true?' he asked, staring at Maggo.

'Yes sir,' answered Maggo politely. These are my papers.' Maggo handed a fistful of documentation across to the soldier. The soldier squinted as he read.

'Says here, you are from the CU?'

'Yes, sir. Resident in your great country for six months now.' The soldier glared at Maggo. He was used to having his boots licked, I thought. In the distance, I suddenly made out the sound of another engine, clattering closer towards us. The reiver glanced briefly in its direction. It looked like another military chariot.

'And you lad?'

'My name is Cadet Ferdia Ó Ceallaigh, RBK Youth, Emain Mhaca,' Ferdia stated, fiercely.

'Are you now?' The soldier glanced back at his colleague. 'RBK Youth, eh?'

'Yes, sir!' Ferdia replied.

'Well, well. We are honoured, aren't we, Reiver Chremthainn?!'

'Yes, sir.' the other said, without smiling.

The second chariot had ground to a halt. I could hear a door open and close, but its occupant was shielded by the first chariot that bisected the road in front.

'RBK Youth!' the reiver whistled, sarcastically. 'Impressive! If only our parents had had the shillings, reiver, for the RBK Youth!'

'Yes, sir.'

'Well now, Cadet Ó Ceallaigh, what's your part in all of this?'

'Me? I'm doing an assignment.'

'An assignment?

'It's for my father,' Ferdia added

'Your father? And what does your father do, may I ask?'

'He's a vate,' Ferdia replied, confused.

'Ah, a vate. Of course. Shillings to be made there. And where does he practise his medicine? Back in Dún na nGall, I suppose?'

'Here, in the war zone,' answered Ferdia, nonplussed. 'He works at the clearing stations. These two are giving me a lift. I've got identity papers, sir!'

I, for my part, could have hugged the boy there and then. The reiver grimaced. His colleague spat out whatever was in his mouth. It was black, unguent and befitting his superior's mood

'And what are you? Some sort of cultural liaison? Where's that accent from?

'The WCA.'

'The WCA?!' the reiver repeated, incredulously. 'What is this, some sort of joke? WCA, CU and a RBK cadet traipsing around the country in a BP rattletrap? Papers! All of you! Now!' The other reiver raised his rifle at the sound of his officer's voice, then slowly relaxed it again. 'Papers!!' the officer shouted again.

'I think you'll find they are all in order.'

The reiver turned around. In front of him stood a tall, thin, gangling soldier; the number of spirals on his sleeve denoted that he outranked everyone present. Under his peaked, military cap, I picked out a random curl of red.

26

Mac an Bhreithiún had refused to believe Ó'Móráin at first. The Connachta commander had been waiting for him in his office the next morning, seated insolently in the brehon lawgiver's own chair, stroking playfully the feathers of a quill. In his possession, he had two signed confessions, one from Calgach and one from Adair, the reporters from the Béal Feirste Banner that had implicated his main suspect for the assassination on Ó'Flaithearta, Conall mac Dara.

'This doesn't prove a thing, Ó'Móráin,' the lawgiver said, after reading both statements. 'Confessions obtained under duress will not stand up in a Brehon law court...and by the way, please get out of my chair.'

'There was no duress, lawgiver,' Ó'Móráin said, standing up. 'They were only too happy to set the record straight.'

'But mac Murchadhna? It's unbelievable,' he replied, sitting down. 'A young, promising senator, a lawgiver...'

'...He had an obvious motive. We all know his family's connections to the manufacturing of, and trade in, weapons of war.'

'The first, of course, is true. But the second is merely hearsay, unsubstantiated. Like these confessions, they too are worthless.'

'Mac Murchadhna asked mac Dara to lead the security detail on the Hill, correct? The lawgiver nodded. 'And then, there's the fact that it is he, of all people, who steps into the fray...what...to defend mac Dara? Keep an eye on the case, more like.'

'And none of that is evidence, Ó'Móráin!'

'It raises doubt, mac an Bhreithiún. And that's a start. I want permission to have those guards re-interviewed, the ones who apparently passed on this note to mac Dara. They claim Breathnach bribed them, was that it?'

'They can't be touched, Ó'Móráin. You know that. The Druidic Order looks after its own. They will mete out their own punishment in that regard.'

'Convenient.' the commander sighed. 'Well, Breathnach then. He holds the key to your whole case!'

'Exactly, Ó'Móráin. *My* case. Why the hell would I help you to undermine my own case?'

'Because you are clever and ambitious enough not to take on such a case, mac an Bhreithiún. And then there's your conscience.'

'My conscience is fine, Ó'Móráin.'

'Really? Look, lawgiver, just interview Breathnach again. You know pressure's being applied. Or let me talk to him?'

'No! You've meddled enough, Ó'Móráin.'

They had reached an impasse. Ó'Móráin had feared it might come to this. Breathnach's stranglehold over the facts, such as they were, had to be broken. To do so, he would have to trust mac an Bhreithiún. Mac Neill had warned him to exercise caution, but the commander was enough of a soldier to understand when sacrifices had to be made for the greater good.

'I spoke to mac Neill.'

'Bradán mac Neill, mac Nessa's spokesman?'

'Yes, and he has the backing of the Ulidian president.'

'Backing? For what?'

'He didn't give me all the details but...'

'...but?'

'He implied mac Murchadhna is simply a fraction of the whole. He talked about those who stood to benefit from the war.'

'Yes, we all know that Ó'Móráin.'

'He also mentioned others who had gained from the peace.'

'He said what?'

'That's what he said. 'Think about those who gained from the prospect of peace', I think those were his exact words. What did he mean by that, I wonder?'

Mac an Bhreithiún stared at Ó'Móráin. The seconds passed. The commander began to feel uncomfortable. He had the feeling the lawgiver was staring straight through him.

'Guard!' he exclaimed, finally. A druidic guard entered the room. He had a CT rifle, slung over his shoulder

'Yes, lawgiver?'

'A minor matter, officer. I think it's time we have another word with Caoimhín Breathnach.'

'Yes, sir.'

'And guard?'

'Yes.'

'Bring mac Dara as well.'

Arch Druid mac Nuadat was kneeling in front of a statue of Bel when he was interrupted by a knock at the door of his private chamber. He frowned, gathered in the long wings of his gown and stood up.

'Come!' he bellowed, imperiously.

'It's the senator, your divinity,' announced the obsequious tones of one of his footmen.'

'Very well. The usual entrance.'

The Arch Druid approached his chair, picked up a jar of cold cream on transit, and applied some to his hands. Moments later, he heard another knock.

'Enter,' he said softly.

It didn't matter how many times mac Murchadhna had been to speak with mac Nuadat, the young senator couldn't help but marvel each time he entered the Arch Druid's private chamber. The burnished veneer of the oak furniture, softened with plush, soothing, velvet upholstery; the gleaming, white stuccoed ceiling above, embossed with arcane symbols and motifs; and the gilt-edged statues of the gods that mac Nuadat rotated monthly according to the druidic calendar. It was envy, the Arch Druid soon realised. envy of his power that captivated the young senator. That was why, after all, he had selected the Tír Eoghain man.

'You know, senator, in some parts of the Federation,' he nodded towards the statue, 'Bel is considered more important than even Lugh.'

'Surely not, your divinity.'

The Arch Druid grimaced. The fool knows that, the Arch Druid thought. Why pretend otherwise? 'Yes, Lugh, as you should know, is merely an Éireann god. Bel is worshipped throughout our Federation. He's a sign of the times, senator.'

'Yes, Arch Druid.'

'He is also the god of war. As is Lugh. So many gods of war,' he mused, settling into his chair. 'So shall we begin?'

'Your divinity...'

'...My people inform me that Ó'Móráin has been conducting his own investigation on Protectorate soil...'

'...Arch Druid...'

'I would caution you, senator, not to interrupt me!' the Arch Druid snapped. 'The commander has spoken to the Bardic Press?'

'Yes.'

'Tell me, senator, why was the issue of the reporters not...expedited?'

'I thought, Arch Druid, that it would raise too much suspicion, especially given that the druidic guards also had to be...disappeared.'

'That wasn't your decision to make, senator. Now, Ó'Móráin is making waves.'

'That could not have been predicted.'

'Perhaps not, but he has discovered your part in the affair, no doubt.'

'Idle gossip, Arch Druid. Nothing to worry about. They will be encouraged to retract their statements. I am already preparing a libel case against them.'

'What? And bring more attention to us? No, senator. Our northern friends will never see Ulidia again. It's already been taken care of.'

'That might look...'

'...You don't have to worry about that. A reassignment to the war zone has already been arranged by our associates in the Bardic Press. They will meet with an accident there. Not just them, a few others will die in the... explosion. That will look better, no?' Mac Murchadhna swallowed. 'In the meantime, their deaths will be counterbalanced with the reappearance of our two druidic guards.'

'But aren't they...?'

'...Must I do all your thinking for you?! I will

443

have two more of my guards replace the originals. Does it really matter? None of it actually happened, mac Murchadhna. Breathnach never bribed anyone to pass on a note...are you fully understanding this, senator?

'Yes, your divinity.'

'The testimony of two of my guards and a senior RBK will be enough to outweigh the ravings of two dryads from Daire. The trial will take place immediately. You will play your role.'

'And the lawgiver?'

'He will play his. Leave him to me.'

'Yes, your divinity.'

'As you leave, senator, can you ask the guard at the door to come in?'

'Your divinity?'

'What are the latest reports?'

'Chaotic, as you expected.'

'The Bardic Press.'

'Equivocating. The population, as a whole, does not know if war will commence or not.'

'Mhumhain and Laighean?'

'Local Bardic Press there are already hinting at the 'Ulidian menace', the need to preserve the peace, uniformity of action and so on.'

Mac Nuadat looked at his senior druidic guard, Fiachna. He had been in service to the previous occupant of his chair and it had therefore taken years for the Arch Druid to trust the old veteran. Now, he knew, like most of his internal cadre, the man's loyalty was unflinching.

'The situation in the war zone?'

'Our occupation of an tSionnain and the peace process, in general, has the complete support of the population there.'

'Weapons?'

'Fully militarised. Mac Murchadhna has come through on his end. As have our corporate interests in Laighean. Federation Druidic Council has also given us the go-ahead.'

'Good. Good. Ulidian forces?'

'As expected. Moving back to the war zone.'

'Ó Braonáin?'

'You were right about him too, your divinity. Feeble. He has refused to give the order for Connachta troops to return to the war zone. Their senate is outraged!'

'Oh, we mustn't be too hard on him, Fiachna. He's only doing what he is being told,' the Arch Druid smiled. 'Ó'Flaithearta?'

'No change. He'll live, though.'

'It doesn't matter either way...now. The assassins?'

'Back in Laighean and Mhumhain, respectively. You have leverage there as well now.'

'It's not them I am worried about. How about mac Nessa?

'Outraged. What else could you expect?'

'He's not to be underestimated. Of all of

them, he's the only one who actually knows the truth. The real truth.' He paused. 'Speaking of which, Fiachna. The boy, Finn. I hope the news of that affair is just as good...'

Ó'Móráin had not seen mac Dara and his sub-commander Breathnach since that night on the Hill. So much had happened since that he had problems keeping track of it all. Both men looked as though they hadn't slept. Mac Dara, at least, appeared revived, stimulated by the curiosity of seeing his war-time nemesis again. Breathnach, on the other hand, looked defeated, a beaten man.

'We don't have long,' mac an Bhreithiún said. 'The Druidic Guard were less than enthusiastic to release you both.'

'What's going on? What's this Connachta doing here? Here to gloat, maybe?'

'Saving your sorry arse, Ulidian!' Conall stepped towards Ó'Móráin. 'Any time you are ready, mac Dara!'

'Gentlemen, please. We are all here to help.'

'Where's my lawgiver, mac Murchadhna?!' Conall asked, his fists clenched.

'Mac Murchadhna? Hear that, Breathnach? He wants to speak to your old pal, mac Murchadhna?' Ó'Móráin laughed.

'What's he getting at, Caoimhín? Caoimhín?!'

Breathnach kept his head lowered, his face

hidden by the length of his unwashed hair.

'Mac Dara! Please! Let me explain,' the law-giver began. 'Commander Ó'Móráin here has been trying to help you over the last day or so.'

'I don't know why I bothered!' Ó'Móráin added.

'Commander, perhaps I should explain how we all managed to arrive at this point.'

Ó'Móráin shrugged, holding his hands up in resignation.

It took only a few minutes for the lawgiver to update Conall and his triad on the events of the last forty-eight hours. When he had finished, Conall sat down, stunned by the sheer volume of information he didn't have time to process. After a moment, he looked up.

'Caoimhín,' he whispered, 'it's true then? Your statement? What did they do? They threatened your family, didn't they?' Breathnach looked away. 'Caoimhín!'

'It's no use, Conall. It's not just mac Mur-chadhna!' the sub-commander blurted out, abruptly. 'They're everywhere!' Tears glistened in his eyes; his face flushed with rage.

'Who are they?' Ó'Móráin asked.

'Your people too. Connachta, Laighean, Al-bion, Allobroges...they are all involved!!'

'Involved in what, Caoimhín?!'

'And what did we ever get, Conall?! You fight an enemy for years! That's fine! I'm a soldier! That's what I am trained to do! And then, you find out, Connachta is not the enemy. Part of it is and part of it isn't. This bit of Laighean, that bit of Mhumhain. Neither the raven nor the dove, Conall! Neither the raven nor the dove! But you were never meant to be sentenced to death. Mac Murchadhna was supposed to defend you!'

'What are you talking about?'

'Mac Murchadhna! He's working for them!'

'Who, Caoimhín?! Who? For the love of Lugh!'

'The Druidic Order! The bloody Druidic Order!'

And then it all came out, a catharsis of all the poison that he had had to keep down, maintain in the pit of his stomach for so long. He only knew what Mac Murchadhna had told him. Yes, there had been bribes. His role was to implicate his commanding officer, in writing, to the brehon lawgiver. He would sacrifice himself for the benefit of his family, their financial security, but Conall was to be found innocent. Mac Murchadna had promised that.

'I swear, Conall!' the sub commander continued. 'You were not to be found guilty! They just wanted to get rid of Ó'Flaithearta!'

'But the Druidic Order? Why?' Conall asked.

'Mac Murchadha and half our senate are involved. Half of yours too, Ó'Móráin. Mac Murchadhna told me that what I was doing would bring peace to our island forever. Unite all our nations.'

'The dead are at peace too, Caoimhín,' Ó'Móráin replied, quietly.

'No, wait, I think I understand some of it, commander,' mac an Bhreithiún said. 'Mac Neill...'

'...Bloody hell, not mac Neill and all!' Conall exclaimed.

'I think he's one of the good guys, this time around, mac Dara. Mac Neill knows more of what's going on. He spoke of benefiting from the peace. The Druidic Order. They have benefited, haven't they? The Druidic Guard are armed. Soon, they will be patrolling the disputed territories.'

'That doesn't make sense, lawgiver. The war has just been reignited and it was they who lit the match,' Conall asked, wearily. 'Those territories will be bombed back into oblivion soon.'

'I know, but think, mac Dara! Laighean has closed its borders. Even Mhumhain has expressed discontent. Both nations were dragged into the peace process, weren't they? They are involved in the new Assembly in an tSionainn.'

'So?' Conall asked.

'So, they have been given an international perspective, all of a sudden, thinking beyond their borders. This has been planned out with great precision, for years probably.'

'I still don't get it!' Conall exclaimed.

'Look, the war will start again, but not in the disputed territories. That issue has been resolved. In this interim of peace, since the festival of Imbolc, the DO has been planning for war.'

'Who with? The rest of the bloody island?!' Conall cried out. 'They don't have the military capability!'

'No, mac Dara. Not with the rest of Éireann. With Ulidia.'

'Ulidia?' Conall exclaimed.

'That's where the war will be fought. Gentlemen,' he announced carefully, 'I think Mhumhain, Laighean, Connachta, under the auspices of the Druidic Order, are considering an invasion of Ulidia.' His words reverberated around the room, echoing in the air like a chorus of shells erupting overhead.

'But why Ulidia?' Conall asked.

'The most intransigent and bellicose of our four nations. Obvious target. Maybe the Arch Druid simply doesn't like mac Nessa, I don't know. Or he suspects that mac Nessa might be aware of what is going on.'

'But why would mac Nessa allow Ulidia to enter the peace process?' Conall asked.

'Biding his time, perhaps. No doubt, to put the pieces together. Finding out just who he could trust. But if Breathnach is correct, and the ultimate goal is to unite our island, create one political entity, then Ulidia, I would say, would be the main stumbling block.

'Err...I think Connachta would have something to say about it too!' Ó'Móráin interjected.

'Oh, they would get around to Connachta eventually,' the lawgiver replied.

'And I suppose the Arch Druid would lead this new Éireann?' Conall asked again.

'Probably,' the lawgiver answered. Only mac Neill knows for sure. If he's still in the Protectorate, I suggest you get to him as soon as you can. He'll know what to do next.'

'You are letting us go?' Ó'Móráin asked in disbelief.

'By this window. Lucky for you, we're on the first floor!'

'But why?' Conall asked. 'What about you?'

The lawgiver pointed at his chin. 'You overpowered me.'

'They'll never believe...'

'...If the DO are involved, then they have the support of the Federation Druidic Order as well. And let's not forget the Bardic Press. It's more about just one lawgiver now, ambitious or otherwise!' He smiled at Conall. Conall nodded. 'You will need weapons. I left rifles for the three of you in the grounds below...just in case.'

'Thanks, lawgiver. Listen, I...' Conall began to say.

'It's fine, mac Dara...don't mention it.'

'No, that's not what I meant. I appreciate

this. I really do. But before I can commit to anything else, I need to find my sister and my nephew. They're still missing, aren't they?'

'You have no idea where they are, mac Dara,' the lawgiver replied. 'As I said before, the RBK and Ulidian army are looking for them now. They are not a priority at this moment in time!'

'Not for you, maybe...'

'...You need to locate mac Neill and get word to mac Nessa,' insisted mac an Bhreithiún.

'I have to try!' Conall exclaimed.

'Mac Dara,' Ó'Móráin said, 'if they are not in Ulidia, they are probably in Connachta. Probably a couple of our less than salubrious citizens have taken them, looking for a bounty. I will have the lawgiver send my triad to find them. They know the terrain. If they are there, you have my word, they will be found. The lawgiver can also fill them in on what's going on...maybe they can bend the ear of some of our allies in our senate.

Both mac Dara and mac an Bhreithiún nodded in agreement.

'Right,' Conall said, finally. 'So, where are those guns again?'

27

Finn could not believe what he had just heard. Beneath his feet lay the overturned bucket; its water had long since seeped through the cracks of the floor. For as long as he could remember, Finn had felt just like that bucket. Like it, there had been a hole somewhere deep inside him. His mother had done her best. She had tried to patch up the gaps in his life, but then she had begun to spend ever increasingly longer periods of time away from home. He had yearned for common ground with someone. Lorcan was kind, but too old. Conall was young enough, but too distant. He had sought and needed a father in his life and now he had discovered he had one...in another world.

'In another world?' Finn looked at Lorcan for help. 'What does she mean, Lorcan?'

'It's true, lad,' Lorcan answered.

'You mean the moon, or...or... other planets?'

'No, son. Not other planets in this cosmos. In a different one,' Aoife replied. 'A different cosmos.'

Finn looked away and noticed the bucket again. It was too much. Too much water. The hole was being filled, but he was drowning inside.

'How is that possible?' he asked.

'Think of it as another world that isn't far away like the moon. It's close by, within range, but you simply can't see it. Like a dog whistle, Finn. The dog can hear it, but we humans can't. But the sound still exists.'

'I don't...understand,' Finn stammered.

'Listen, Finn, it will take a while to explain everything to you. We can talk on the way to the stations.'

'And my father is there?'

'He's looking for you. He wants to meet you, son.'

'But this world?' Finn asked again. 'Where is it?

'It's another world like ours, just a little bit different.'

'What? You've been there?'

'That's where I met your father.'

Finn thought for a moment. 'What's his name, mother?'

'His birth name was Lugaid. But he calls himself Lewis now,' Lorcan interjected.

'You knew about this too, I suppose!' Finn exclaimed.

'Yes, lad. I did. You see, Finn, Lugaid is my son. I'm your grandfather!'

Aoife had been provided with a Connachta hospital chariot by the aos sí. Where and how they had managed to acquire it, she hadn't bothered to ask. Her journey through the disputed territories, Loch Rí and Connachta itself had been uneventful. Strangely, she had noticed, most Connachta troops were heading in the opposite direction to the frontlines. But hadn't the truce just ended? In any case, the sight of a uniformed vate at the wheel of a hospital chariot did not raise any suspicion as she made her way to Cruachan Aí. The change of uniform, rifle and ammunition had been also kindly supplied by her winged emissaries.

Now she was on the return journey to the Iron Mountains with Lorcan and Finn. That might prove to be a little bit more problematic.

Finn had asked her so many questions, of course, and she had done her best to answer them truthfully. He wasn't, she knew, allowing himself time to process her words. He was still insecure. No doubt it was because he didn't know how long she, his mother, would be around. He wanted to maximise his time with her by gleaning all he could before she inevitably left his life again. It made her sad to think of him like this, vulnerable and alone.

But it was understandable. She hadn't been there enough for him. The war had consumed her. Her need to contribute. Her boundless passion to aid the sick and wounded. And yet, had that been an excuse? Had she just run off for yet another adventure? Had she been avoiding her role as Finn's mother, the comparative humdrum of domesticity in Emain Mhaca, *because* of everything she had been through in the other world? And wasn't it this enthusiasm for an alternative to the normality of daily existence which had compelled Cathbad to select her, of all people, to risk everything by journeying through a veil to another Earth? Maybe. But the war was now over, and she was determined to make up for lost time. Perhaps it might even work out with Lewis and the three of them could set up home together?

'Can we talk?' Lorcan asked from behind. He and Finn, as before, were at the back of a hospital chariot, keeping out of sight, in case they were suddenly stopped by a Connachta patrol.

'I don't think I can, Lorcan. I am not sure I have any words left.'

'I know. He's asleep now. The poor lad's exhausted.'

Aoife glanced behind her quickly and noticed Finn sitting huddled in a corner, his head lowered into his raised knees.

'Well?'

A few things? One of immediate concern and another that's been troubling me for a while.'

'Go on.'

'You have realised, of course, that the Connachta are on the move in the opposite direction to where they should be going.'

'Perhaps folk have seen sense. Maybe the war is over.'

'Hmm, I don't think so. Both sides had left a few garrisons behind after the truce, but this looks like a complete withdrawal. I don't understand it.'

'What's the other thing?'

'The boy and me. Why were we taken? You sure the aos sí didn't say anything?'

'No.'

'It's just that with your news of Lugaid's return, I can't help but think it's all connected somehow.'

'How could it be?' Lorcan looked away. 'Lorcan, how could it be?'

'I don't know. Just a feeling. You, me and Finn. Cathbad and the aos sí. Lugaid, Ferdia and Maggo. Triads. So many triads.'

We had disposed of Lorcan's old chariot as Angus had very generously donated his confiscated Ulidian military transport to the overall cause. He was now driving us, through one checkpoint after another, with all the credentials necessary to forge our course, deep into the Iron Mountains and onto the clearing stations on the Ulidian side of the war zone. I sat beside him, watching as he steered and changed gears, absorbed in the momentary import of the task at hand. I struggled to believe that this was the same person, or being, that had eavesdropped on my evening with Surridge one night in a Belfast bar, had served me in an Armagh coffee house. I wondered how long, and why, he and his colleague, had tracked my movements. Ferdia and Maggo sat together in the back seat, the jolting impact of potholes in the road ahead causing them to jostle shoulders for space.

When he had passed the final security outpost, Angus found a suitable spot to pull over. We all got out to stretch our legs. Not too far in the distance, I could make out the misty waters of the River Shannon, innocently running its course southwards. It was control over that river that had first incited the war.

'Not too far away now,' Angus said.

'From the clearing stations?' I asked.

'From Aoife,' he replied.

'You found her?' I asked in a faltering voice.

'Wonderful news, sir! Wonderful!' sounded the delighted voice of Maggo who was filling a canteen from a nearby stream.

'What about Finn?' Ferdia asked.

'Aoife has found them, both Finn *and* Lorcan!' Angus confirmed.

'Praise the heavens!' Maggo declared.

'Will you bloody well shut up?!' Ferdia exclaimed. 'Where are they?' he asked Angus.

'They are coming to meet us.'

'What then?' I asked.

'A happy reunion, Lewis.'

'And then afterwards? Uisneach? To rescue Conall?'

'Things have moved on there, Lewis. Bridge is helping our friend Conall as we speak.'

'Wait! Who's this Bridge character?' Ferdia asked.

'So, we are not going to Uisneach?' I enquired.

'No, we're still going to Uisneach. It's just that our motives have changed, that's all.'

'What do you mean?'

'Our real motives. Your motive. The real reason why you are here.'

'I thought I was here to rescue the boy?' I asked.

'Hello?! Sorry?! Hello?!' Ferdia interjected again. 'Can someone tell me what's going on?!'

'Now Lewis, surely you must know your role here is a lot bigger than that,' replied Angus.

'Someone?! Anyone?!' exclaimed Ferdia.

'Bloody Cathbad! I knew I shouldn't have trusted him!' I said, anger rising in my voice.

'Cathbad? You mean *the* Cathbad?' Ferdia asked.

'Who's Cathbad?' Maggo asked sweetly.

'Cathbad only wants the best for you, your family and this island,' Angus said. 'This world, for that matter. Be honest, Lewis. What did you have before? In your world. What was your life there? Bitterness. Self-reproach. Solitude.' Angus smiled. 'A crazy man living upstairs from you. Soon, you will have Aoife back, a son and...'

'...and what?' Angus looked away. 'What?' I asked.

'A father.'

'A father?'

'Yes, that's right, Lewis. Lorcan is your father.'

'My goodness!' Maggo exclaimed. 'My goodness!'

'My father?' I felt my legs weaken and the insides of my stomach suddenly hollow. I steadied myself against the bonnet of the truck.

'Yes.'

'But how? How?'

'That is his story to tell, Lewis. It's only right for a father to tell it to his son?'

'Unbelievable! Bloody unbelievable!' Ferdia shouted. 'Lugh, if they don't speak to me...!

''Right?' What do you know about 'right'?' I shouted.

'It would have been too much for you. Like the things in your house, Lewis. Remember? How would you have felt if I had made your whole house disappear? That would have been too much, wouldn't it?'

'Still...'

'...It was necessary, Lewis. When you understand the whole, you will accept that part of it?'

'So, tell me. Tell me it all.'

Angus stared into the distance. 'I can tell you the truth, only as it is related to you alone and which will help us in our mission here.'

'What does that mean exactly?'

'What I have just said. Your family -your real family, together again is important for you... as a whole. For us, it is one part of the whole. I can't put it any simpler than that.'

'So, tell me!' I shouted again, beside myself. 'Just tell me what you can!'

Angus sighed. 'This could have waited until we met the others.'

'Sorry for the inconvenience,' I responded sarcastically.

'At bloody last!' Ferdia roared.

'The Arch Druid...' Angus began

'...This mac Nuadat...?'

'...Yes, the top dog in the old druid ladder,' Angus explained. 'On the one hand,' the aos sí held out a hand, as if sampling the weight of one side of a set of scales, 'there's the war, the political future of Éireann and maybe even the fate of the Federation. To be honest, though, Cathbad doesn't care that much about any of that. They are worldly affairs and, though he may prefer a certain outcome, the policy is normally...err...non-interventionist.'

'OK.'

'What he, and therefore Bridge and I, have an investment in is the other side,' he extended his other hand and moved it as if it were weighing air.

'There's another?' I asked, in disbelief.

'Yes. Of course. The *other-worldly* side. Now, this Arch Druid mac Nuadat, like all the Arch Druids before him, along with the inner core of the Druidic Council, have always been aware of the existence of our portals. The very basis of their religion relies on this knowledge.'

'Yes, I can see that.'

Angus took me to the side.

'Ultimately, their religion is false, Lewis,' Angus whispered. 'You know that, of course. But the nature of their faith, their belief in sacred sites and so on, has allowed them to stumble upon one truth, at least. A scientific truth.'

'The inter-dimensional portals?' I said.

'That's right. The portals. They have interrogated and killed almost everyone they know who has crossed to the other side and returned to theirs.'

'So, there are people in my world who are actually from this world.'

'Of course, these people do not upset the balance. The sentinels choose them and we, the aos sí, facilitate...if we are asked.'

'You weren't asked to facilitate for Aoife, were you?'

'No, her mission was different.'

'How so?'

'She didn't know her mission.'

'What do you mean?'

'Better if she explains that to you. Ok?'

'I suppose.'

'Now this mac Nuadat. He's different from the usual overseer that their Council selects. He wasn't born on the mainland...'

'...Sorry?'

'Never mind. Mac Nuadat, and a few of his coterie, want complete power. He wants the whole island for his dominion, but he also wants to close the portals.'

'Close the portals? Why?'

'Think about it, Lewis. They are a threat not only to him but their whole pagan system of control. Don't you think the Druidic Council knows that their religion, on your side of the portal, is nothing more than an ancient relic, an anachronism, overrun by the monotheistic religions that followed it? How do you think they reacted to the knowledge that your Emain Mhaca and your Uisneach are merely historical carbuncles, blemishes on the landscape, gaped at by tourists in the same way as apes are in a zoo?'

I thought about this and could appreciate the sincerity of what Angus was saying. Looking across, Ferdia was pacing up and down angrily, wielding his sword like a scythe at the verge of long grass that lined the road ahead while Maggo risked limbs in an attempt to pacify him.

'So, what am I to do with any of this? What about Finn, Lorcan and Aoife? What's their role?'

'We are where we are supposed to be.'

'What does that mean?'

'Cathbad has foreseen this moment. Only you, Finn and Lorcan can close the portals. The Arch Druid knows that too.'

It was late afternoon when they reached the shores of Loch Rí. Just beyond, lay the Connachta side of the disputed territories and the Iron Mountains further on still. According to legend, Queen Mebd had met an untimely end nearby, struck, of all things, by a hard lump of cheese hurled by an Ulidian warrior. Before the invention of cheese, it would have sticks and stones, Aoife thought. And before that?

Finn had not spoken to either of them since awakening. He sat sullenly in the back of the chariot, staring into the middle distance, occasionally turning his head to look out through the window at the range of islands that populated the famous lake. Aoife could not say for certain that he was actually seeing them at all. Perhaps, with the revelation of another world, his own world had begun to lack substance, she thought. The serene surface of the lake, in any case, would only have added to his confusion; it mirrored the clouds above in a bewildering figment of water and sky, perfectly sutured by a pale horizon.

The dramatic change in the landscape as they entered the war zone was not something, however, that eyes could avoid. There could be no day-dreaming it away; no pursuance of an idle, random thought down a rabbit hole of forgetfulness, no tenacity of focused introspection could ever prohibit you from coming to terms with the devastation that had been wrought upon the terrain there. Aoife had seen it all before. Lorcan too. But for Finn, this was the first time he had borne witness to the smouldering stump of wasteland that now masqueraded as nature. Trees split asunder by shells; black, malignant craters that seemed to drain the remnants of moisture from the surrounding earth; the facades of soot-stained farmhouses, with spaces for doors and windows that led nowhere but into a mock interior of rubble and junk. A blister of trenches zigzagged what once were pastures, their abandoned parapets raised above like discoloured scabs. Colour seemed absent. An entire environment had eloped elsewhere. Dirt, slime and fetid water sludged and oozed into rivers, splashing the tyres of our chariot as we passed by.

Finn looked on, unable to tear himself away

from what his eyes were telling him. There was a reason why it was called 'no man's land'. No man or woman could ever live in such a hell again.

And yet, in a while, it had passed behind them. Up ahead, Finn could detect a mountain range. In comparison to what he had just seen, the mountains might have been rainbows, no more or less real than what had gone before.

I understood everything now. I was happier that I understood but not about what I had been asked to understand. I had been given more pieces of the jigsaw, but the picture I had to put together was not the picture I thought it would be. I needed the final pieces of the puzzle and, for them, I had to rely on others: my son and my father. From everyone else, I needed to gain the strength to carry on.

'So, your name's not Aidan, I suppose,' Ferdia was saying.

'No, it's Angus.'

'And Brenda is a bridge,' Maggo said.

'No, you damn Punic fool! Her name's Bridge! That's right, Angus, isn't it?'

'Yeah.'

'So...err...why's she called Bridge?' Ferdia enquired, hesitantly.

'It's Brigid, really,' Angus winked.

'You're not *the* Angus and Brigid...?'

'Ach, come on now, Ferd. Do I look like *the*

Angus?'

'No, no,' Ferdia stammered, embarrassed.

'Angels!' Maggo uttered, suddenly. 'You're an angel!'

'Definitely not...way above our pay grade!'

'Sorry?'

'Never mind,' the aos sí replied.

'What are those?' I asked, looking at the road ahead.

'Those, Mr Summer, are the Ulidian clearing stations.'

It was strange being back at the clearing stations. It was there, after all, that the direction of Aoife's life had changed irrevocably. She shared a look with Lorcan and realised that he too was thinking the same. It was the first time he had been back to the stations in over a decade. She watched him struggle to hold back the tears. This place had that effect on you, she thought.

They had considered it best to abandon their Connachta chariot a few miles back. Lorcan was finding it difficult to carry on, his old wounds seizing the opportunity, it seemed, to flare up again, in recognition, almost, of the place where they had first been inflicted. Several times, they had had to pause for him to rest, but he had refused to lean on them for support. He had always been stubborn, Aoife knew, but if this was the last leg of the journey, he wanted to make it unaided. She owed him that at least.

It had only been a few days since she had been there last, but already the stations were once again a hive of activity. Tents, marquees and canvassed pavilions were being hastily re-erected on top of the same oblong patches of dried grass that had marked their previous foundation. Stretcher bearer relay posts, walking wounded collecting stations, sick collecting and rest stations were all being constructed by orderlies under the shrill, barking command of vatic medical officers. Lines of wagons, their horses in front grazing lazily from troughs, lay primed and ready to convey the dead to collective funeral pyres or, for the luckier ones, to nearby field hospitals for long-term convalescence. There were soldiers everywhere; some unloading food and water from supply chariots; some, newer recruits, being drilled in perfect, symmetrical formations before the clamorous imperative of superior officers; some patrolling the stations' perimeter; some being charioted off to their trenches; some eating, drinking and smoking from trestle tables laid out in the summer sun.

'This is madness,' Lorcan said. 'Don't they know there is no one out there for them to fight?'

'I know,' Aoife replied. 'Look, I'll try to find out what's going on. We will need another chariot to get across the mountains.'

They walked on. Finn, lingering behind the others, was completely dumb struck by everything around him. The sheer abundance of life here, in stark contrast with the grim desolation of the war zone he had just left, was almost too much for him to bear. He stopped at a field tent where water was being ladled into cups for lines of thirsty soldiers. He was still in his RBK cadet's uniform and hoped that would be good enough to earn him a little refreshment. Up ahead in the long queue, some sort of commotion was taking place.

'What the hell do you mean he can't get a drink? Give me two cups and I'll give him mine!' Finn heard a familiar voice exclaim.

'Soldiers only! He's not even bloody Ulidian!' came the abrupt retort.

'Balls!' Finn heard his best friend reply,

Maggo and Ferdia had wandered off to look for food, water and other supplies, leaving me with Angus. We wove our way through the multitude of medics and soldiers, almost all of whom, upon seeing the aos sí in uniform, froze, saluted and dashed off to their next task. Angus laughed.

'You having fun?' I asked.

'You have to admit, Lewis, you do have to have a wee laugh at them.'

'What? Being sent off to war to get slaughtered!'

'That's none of my business,' he answered.

'Just as the wars in my world are none of your business, too.'

'Sometimes, we lend a hand if certain events need to align with our own objectives. But wars? Things of that scale? I couldn't prevent them even if I wanted to.'

'Do you want to?' I asked. He didn't reply. Perhaps, it didn't matter either way. I thought of the line from Shakespeare: '*As flies to wanton boys are we to the gods; they kill us for their sport.*' They weren't gods, Cathbad, Angus and Bridge. That was the point they were trying to make, and you couldn't, I suppose, have it both ways. 'How are we going to get across the war zone?' I asked, changing the subject.

'You won't have to?'

'Why not?'

'There's not going to be a war, at least not there.'

'What do you mean?' I asked.

'Besides, your search,' he said, looking away, 'is at an end. Don't you see?'

With the usual vibration of air, out of the corner of my eye, he had gone. But I, for once, did not care. There, coming out of the crowd, running towards me, I saw her. Eva Beaufort. In this world, Aoife mac Dara. The mother of my son.

28

Mac an Bhreithiún had been true to his word. Three CT rifles were, as promised, concealed beneath the foliage of a large yew tree directly below the window. The three men hunkered a moment for cover. Ó'Móráin examined his rifle.

'Bloody Ulidian insignia!' he whispered.

'Mine's Connachta,' replied Conall. 'Seems we are all on the same side now. The DG were given our guns, remember? Good to have a few back. That's right, Caoimhín, isn't it?'

'Yes, sir,' the sub-commander replied, quietly.

'Shame we can't get Oisín involved in this particular suicide mission.'

'How many, mac Dara?' Ó'Móráin asked.

'Too many.'

They were at the arc of the Roundhouse that was the House of Brehon Law. Like the two other Houses, it was guarded by at least a dozen or so Druidic Guard. Conall reckoned half of those were stationed on the external perimeter and the other half's remit was to see off those lucky enough to make it to the steps of the building itself.

'This is madness, mac Dara,' Ó'Móráin said. 'I should be in the Vates, looking after my president.'

'He's safe enough, Ó'Móráin. His part in the business is at an end. They'll not touch him.'

'Maybe,' Ó'Móráin said.

'Where's mac Neill then?' asked Conall

'He's nearby, in the city.'

'He's a slippery one. He knew better than to shack up here. But, three rifles, Ó'Móráin, aren't going to cut it. How the hell are you going to get out of here?'

'You boys need help?' It was a female's voice. All three of them looked up. Standing before them was a purple-haired woman of average height, wearing a short, stiff dress that projected from her waist. A pair of stockinged legs and a high-buttoned, military tunic added to her crude, outlandish ensemble. She had appeared, it seemed, out of absolutely nowhere, but in her arms, she was holding the largest weapon they had ever seen.

The Arch Druid was enjoying breakfast in his chamber when he first became aware of the steady staccato of gunfire coming from another part of the Roundhouse. He jumped to his feet as two of his guards rushed in.

'What in the name of all the gods is going on?'

'It's mac Dara, your Divinity. He's escaped. Breathnach and Ó'Móráin are with him!'

'How? How was this allowed to happen?'

'It seems they overwhelmed the lawgiver, your Divinity.'

'Bring mac an Bhreithiún to me! Mac Murchadhna too!'

'The Ulidian left last night.'

'Did he now?' the Arch Druid mused. 'Bring the lawgiver, at least. And send reinforcements to the House of Brehon Law!'

'We already did, your Divinity. The security guards...they are all dead!'

It would have been a lie to say that she had not changed, but the years since had not been unduly harsh. Her eyes and hair had lost none of their original lustre. Aside from a few extra wrinkles around her eyes when she smiled, and a more ample fullness of shoulders as I held her closely in my arms, it was the same Eva I had known all those years ago.

Seeing her again was akin to falling, once more, into the natural rhythms of an unnatural passion. I think Aoife felt it too. She clung to me like one does to the fringe of a cliff; I clung to her as if to a half-forgotten wisp of melody, desperately attempting to resurrect the words of a song that could serve to communicate the intensity of how I felt.

I had not prepared myself for this, however.

I had been too afraid of the raw conviction of that side of myself, too embarrassed, too wary of rejection. I had interred, in deep wells, both the memory of my past with Eva and any aspiration I held for my future with Aoife. My body shuddered then as I held her, all my fears of rejection joyously absolved. I was finally at peace, comforted by the acknowledgement that whatever it was that we had shared had been shared in equal measure by both of us.

'You can let me go now,' she said, finally.

'Sorry. I am so sorry, Aoife... If I had known about Finn...'

'It wasn't your fault, or mine either. Meeting you like that, it wasn't planned. It was Cathbad.'

I nodded and held her again. Releasing her, I found myself smiling.

'What are you smiling at?'

'I can understand you so much better than before.'

'Yes,' she laughed, 'you're the one who is speaking my language now.'

'Lugaid!' I turned to see an old man, hobbling with great difficulty towards me. His face was a wash of tears. 'Lugaid!' he said again.

'Father?' I exclaimed, my voice cracking.

'You know?' Aoife asked.

'The aos sí...'

'...Go to him,' she said.

And so we embraced. Father and son. We

wept. We offered mitigations and justifications, exonerations and vindications, but in the end, none of it mattered any longer. For the next hour or so, Lorcan, my father, sat with me, held my hand, and imparted, between staggered breaths, the brief biography of his life as it related to me, Deirdre, my mother and Aoife. I listened without interrupting, reacting to every twist and turn, every high and low, as if I myself had undergone them.

As a child, I had yearned for this moment. I knew there had to have been a reason for my abandonment. I also knew it had to have been a story like the one I heard that day, not so much different from the narratives I invented for myself as a child.

And I completely understood. None of it had been his fault. He had done all he could. And me? I had a father again.

'Father,' I said, finally, 'we don't have a lot of time. The aos sí...'

'...Oh, I am so tired, so sick of them, Lewis,' Aoife said. 'Can't we just forget Cathbad and the aos sí?'

'No, we can't. The Arch Druid...'

'...Arch Druid mac Nuadat? What's he got to do with any of this?' she asked.

I took a breath. 'The portals. He wants to use me, Lorcan and Finn to close the portals.'

'What? But why you? Can't Cathbad stop him?'

'Yes, but he needs us.'

'I don't understand, Lewis.'

'All I know is that I was brought over to this world as bait.'

'Bait?!'

'Yes, he would have killed Lorcan and Finn otherwise, but he needs all three of us alive. Cathbad couldn't protect them but he could use me.'

'But how? Why?'

'It has something to do with our shared DNA.'

'Our what?'

'It's like our blood, Aoife. Something happens to our blood, our DNA, when we travel to and from my world to yours. An interaction between the portal and the person using it. It changes their genetic make-up forever. Do you understand?'

'I think so.'

I tried desperately to remember what Angus had revealed to me. 'The Druidic Council has access to lots of portals throughout Éireann, but they can neither open them nor close them. Only a sentinel can do that. The Order know, or have guessed from their study of the myths and legends around the Trinity Knot...'

'...You mean the Trinity Knot on the Cat Stone at Uisneach?'

'Yes, they know, or think they know, that three people, with similar DNA to begin with and who have previously used the portal, can be brought together in a triad, or trinity, to close them forever.'

'But why Lewis? Why is the Arch Druid so afraid of the portals?'

'Lots of reasons. according to Angus.'

'Wait, if the Arch Druid wants to use you to close the portals, shouldn't we get as far away as possible from Uisneach?'

'I thought so too. But Cathbad has seen the timeline. Somehow our going to Uisneach will stop the Arch Druid and the Council.'

'Hold on, wait a minute. It won't work! Lorcan has never used the portal! He's never been to your world. Tell him, Lorcan... Lorcan?'

But the old man was already shaking his head.

'You crossed over, didn't you?' Aoife asked.

'I had to make sure Lugaid was safe, Aoife. Settled. Just for a little while. To make sure he was with good...parents. You see, Aoife, once you use the portal to and from the worlds, you can't use it again. I didn't know that until later. That's why I needed you to find out about Lugaid. How he was. Cathbad, naturally, had his own reasons...I couldn't do it myself. You would have done the same for Finn.'

'Done what for me?'

We turned around together. It was Finn, my son.

'Hello Finn,' I said, holding out my hands.

'Who are you?' he replied.

'Who the hell are you?' Conall asked.

They were on the way to the city of Uisneach, a short trip by chariot, even shorter by a stolen chariot driven by a maniacal psychopath with a predilection for speed and a penchant for machine guns.

'Name's Brigid, but you can call me Bridge.'

'You can slow down,' Ó'Móráin said, from behind. 'We're not being followed No one bloody left to follow us!'

'I have never seen anything like it,' said Caoimhín, sitting beside Ó'Móráin. 'Those guards. You just mowed them down. They never had a chance! Your gun...what is it?'

'Err...I think you mean my...well, it's not strictly mine, I sort of...borrowed it...it's a M249 Squad Assault Weapon. And no, you wouldn't have seen anything like it, Caoimhín. Not yet. Not in this world anyway.'

'What do you mean 'this world?' Conall asked.

'And how do you know my name?' Caoimhín added.

Bridge chuckled. 'What about you, Ó'Móráin? Don't you have any questions?'

'Yeah, what's the stupid, bloody thing you're wearing around your waist?'

The assault on the Druidic Guard at the Roundhouse had been swift and merciless, as swift and merciless as anything Conall had ever witnessed in war. A weapon like that, and a hundred more like it, could bring the twenty-five-year war between Ulidia and Connachta to a rapid conclusion, Ó'Móráin was probably thinking the same thing, he thought. Neither he, Caoimhín or the Connachta had had to fire off a single shot back at the Roundhouse. It was over too quick for that.

'Ok, boys, here's the deal,' Bridge said, 'I will give you all I think you need to know in order to undertake the missions at hand.'

'What do you mean? Missions?' Conall asked.

'The only mission we have is finding mac Neill,' Ó'Móráin said.

'So, you can get a message via him back to mac Nessa,' Bridge replied. 'Is that it?'

'How did you know that?' Ó'Móráin asked, suspiciously.

'All in good time, commander. But there's more at stake than just the political future of this little island?'

'Oh, and what would that be?' Conall asked.

Bridge pulled over and turned off the chariot's engine. They were in the suburbs of Uisneach, not too far from the centre of the city. She closed her eyes and smiled. 'A little matter of saving your sister, your nephew, your nephew's father and grandfather!'

'You better start talking!' Conall replied,

grabbing the woman by the shoulder. 'Or so help me...!'

The aos sí smiled. 'Tell me, gentlemen, do you believe in fairies?' she asked.

'Hello Finn' I repeated. He looked at me, not knowing what to say.

I tried to think of how I had felt at his age. Our lives before could not have been more different, of course. Warrior schools and grammar schools had very little in common. The sharpest object I had ever come close to at his age was the nib of a fountain pen, never mind a titanium sword. He had been on dawn patrols while I had been on Sunday strolls; while I had slouched, he had stood to attention; while he had wanted to serve, I had served my own wants. And yet, here we were, Finn and I, a son from this world and a father from another. And here also were we: Lorcan and me, a son from another world and a father from this. Two ships had set sail a long time ago and none of us had been able to control the winds that had guided us. I knew what Finn was going through as I too had gone through it. That was where our ships could find common ground. I had made the final journey across through the portal and it was I, and only I, who could provide the anchor to our lives. But as I began to speak again, it was Lorcan who plundered the words straight out of my mouth. It was his first and greatest act of charity.

'Finn,' he said, 'there was a reason why your mother asked me to be your guardian. You know we met, actually not too far away from here. I had just been shot...'

'Yes, Lorcan, I know. You have told me all that before. My mother nursed you back to health.'

Was it my imagination or had I just noticed my father wince at Finn's use of the word 'Lorcan'?'

'Yes, lad. I know you have been through a lot, have had to listen to even more. This is your father. That, of course, is true. And there is so much to say about how he came to be your father. His name...my name for him, is Lugaid. Lugaid, after Lugh. But you see, Finn, there's more. Just a little more. Lugaid is my son. I am your grandfather.'

Later on, we ate together, around a trestle table full of all the food we could muster around the stations, canopied against the night sky in an empty tent. There were further revelations, all-too-brief synopses, lives savoured like the beaker of cider on a hot day when you know there is only time for one drink. Ferdia and Maggo sat and listened too, their mouths wide open between mouthfuls of food. There were no more secrets. We were no longer in triads.

I thought, as I sipped my cold drink, of

where we had come from up to that point and also where we were heading. I thought of the Trinity Knot. We had just disentangled the strands of lies that had governed our lives up until then, that had wrapped us up in bonds; and now, we would have to unravel a different type of ligature, one vastly more significant than the trivial machinations of our mere mortal lives. But I was confident. And why shouldn't I have been? A grandfather, father and son from the noble houses of Mac Róich, mac Nessa and mac Dara? They could do anything, couldn't they?

'You know, Sencha,' a voice said, coming from the entrance to our tent, 'there's nothing I like better than a family get-together. How about you brother?' The voice caught us all off-guard.

'Couldn't agree more, Bren,' Sencha replied, a pistol pointed in our direction. 'Couldn't agree more.'

Words were a prized commodity for Bradán mac Neill. He enjoyed their subtle inflections and delicate modulations. He prided himself in his ability to manipulate them into phrases and sentences, the cold mechanics of a process by which he induced a sort of coma on his listening public, a trance under which his voice became a thought in their heads, the source of which they identified as their own. Even President mac Nessa was not immune from Mac Neill's hypnotic charms.

And yet, with the arrival of mac Dara, Ó'Móráin and Breathnach at his small, rented house in the heart of the tourist district of Uisneach, the skilled orator found himself, for once, lost for words.

'So, let me get this straight,' mac Neill said, 'you're telling me that mac an Bhreithiún believes an invasion of Ulidia is imminent?'

'Based on what Caoimhín here has told us,' Conall said, 'it was the only conclusion left available to the lawgiver. I, for one, believe it.'

'Me as well,' Ó'Móráin added, in support.

'If this is true,' mac Neill said, looking through the window at the street below, 'the situation is far worse that even mac Nessa expected. I mean, we suspected that mac Nuadat wished to extend druidic power beyond the Protectorate, perhaps as a ploy to raise his profile in the Federation with a view to becoming Federation Arch Druid. But this...? And you think Connachta will go along with this, Ó'Móráin?'

'Ó Braonáin is weak. He will do anything the Arch Druid says. By the time the other half of our senate has had time to react, it will already be too late.'

'It's incredible,' mac Neill mused, 'Mhumhain and Laighean manipulated as well..."

'The Druidic Order and the Bardic Press,'

Caoimhín said, 'what are they? They are the only two institutions that operate within and without Éireann.'

'Which tells us that whatever mac Nuadat has planned has the full support of the Federation. But why? Why is one Arch Druid so important to them?'

'I think we know,' Conall said.

'Know? Know what?'

Conall briefly went through the circumstances surrounding their escape from the Roundhouse.

'So, this 'Bridge'...she had some sort of futuristic weapon?'

'That's not even the half of it! Look, mac Neill, I don't know who... or what she is,' Conall said.

''What' she is?'

'She vanished, mac Neill!' Caoimhín exclaimed, abruptly.

'Vanished? Where? How?'

'She said something about keeping an urgent appointment in Emain Mhaca...Look, we all saw it, mac Neill, or thought we saw it. That's right, commander, isn't it? Ó'Móráin? One moment she was there...tell him! You both saw it!'

'Gentleman, gentleman. I am sorry. I simply cannot believe...'

'...Listen, mac Neill. You didn't see what she did! I don't understand it myself but what she told us fits,' Conall said.

'Fits? How?'

'There's more to all of this than we know. It seems the Arch Druid wishes to close some gateways...to...err.... another world...'

'...Gateways? Oh, come now, mac Dara.' Mac Neill replied, with a chuckle.

'Just listen, mac Neill! For once in your bloody life, just listen!'

Mac Neill sat down and with his hands bade Conall to begin.

'These gateways lead to another world. The Arch Druid wants them closed. It seems, according to this Bridge, that life in this other world is a bit like our own but a bit different too. She didn't go into details. Suffice to say, this world scares mac Nuadat and, presumably, the Federation too.'

'Why?' Mac Neill asked.

'The Druidic Order and the Federation don't exist in that other world.'

Mac Neill raised an eyebrow. 'Go on.'

'The gateway at the Cat Stone...the Trinity Knot...that's where mac Nuadat can prevent the gateways from ever opening again...Apparently...' Conall looked around, seemingly for encouragement. Ó'Móráin nodded. Caoimhin did likewise. '...Apparently, only my nephew, his father and ...grandfather, Lorcan mac Róich can achieve this.'

'Your nephew? The one that's missing? His grandfather is Lorcan mac Róich?'

'Yes, mac Neill. And his father, we are told, is from this other world.'

Mac Neill looked at mac Dara and then at the other two soldiers standing in front of him. If anyone else, a senator, lawgiver or druid, say, had just told him such an absurd, comical anecdote, he would not have believed them for a moment. And yet, there was something in the earnestness of the three men's faces looking at him now. They were the faces of men that could attest to life's true horrors, authenticate its brutality and affirm its consequences. No. Conall was telling the truth, or at the very least, was convinced he was telling the truth.

'Where are they now?' mac Neill asked.

'They are on their way here,' Conall replied. 'My sister is with them as well. Bridge said she's with two others. An RBK Youth cadet and a Carthaginian. A friend of mine called Maggo.'

'A Carthaginian?' Mac Neill shook his head. 'What the hell is going on here, mac Dara?' Conall smiled. 'So, mac Nuadat will go to them? To the Cat Stone?'

'Probably,' said Ó'Móráin. 'We don't know. Look, mac Neill, it doesn't matter whether you, or we, believe any of this. It's enough that mac Nuadat does believe it. If we can remove the Arch Druid from the state of play, the rest of the Council might follow. And who knows the impact on everything and everyone else.'

Mac Neill thought for a moment. 'Ok. Here's

what we will do. I will get word to mac Nessa and the RBK. We need to bring our troops back from the warzone and have them prepare the borders for invasion. Ó'Móráin, you need to inform your senate…'

'…My triad already have their orders to do so.'

'Good, hopefully, the hawks in Connachta will see sense. In the meantime, I will have mac Nessa deliver a speech outlining our suspicions. Hopefully, that will be enough to confuse and delay any action Mhumhain or Laighean are thinking of taking.'

'What about the Druidic Guard? They still have a lot of our weaponry,' Conall asked.

'And ours!' Ó'Móráin added.

'We can't do anything about them until Ulidia is secure. Look, gentlemen, if this is all true, and the Federation wants a unified Éireann under mac Nuadat, we could all be heading for war.'

'We need to help the boy, mac Róich and this other…stranger!' Conall exclaimed.

'You say they are on their way to Uisneach?' Mac Neill asked.

'Yes.'

'And mac Murchadhna?

'No idea.'

'Well then, my dear friends, there's nothing for it. Conall is right. You must all do what you can to stop mac Nuadat. And I am sorry, but until the situation becomes clearer, you are on your own.'

29

The thing about a conspiracy, mac Nuadat thought, is that there comes a point when it has to reveal itself, breach the surface of events like the tip of an iceberg concealing the threat beneath. There was always going to be this precarious period of interim when even the most locked mind questioned the prison bars that enclosed it. He had, without doubt, underestimated Ó'Móráin. He had relied too heavily on the ambitious zeal of the lawgiver, mac an Bhreithiún. Even mac Murchadhna had proved untrustworthy. The young senator had still not been seen since before the attack on the Roundhouse.

So, they had escaped, Ó'Móráin, mac Dara and Breathnach. But what of it? What could they do? What advantage had they really gained? War against Ulidia was inevitable. Its momentum could no longer be halted. He would ensure those Connachta forces loyal to the Order could reclaim their weapons for the imminent invasion. And then? After Ulidia? The remaining rebels in Connachta would have to submit. Then, a new peace process could begin. Federation troops would enforce it. The nations would unite, and he would be their de facto leader.

He considered mac Nessa. He had been a worthy adversary, but it was only a matter of time before even he would have to succumb. Then, he would learn more of the president's knowledge, if any, of the existence of the portal technology. His sister's son, he knew, had travelled there. He had learned of her affair with the journalist mac Róich. But did mac Nessa know where his nephew had been taken? If so, his information would be vital in comprehending the real dangers of this other world, the world beyond the gates of the portals.

And then there were the sentinels and the aos sí.

'Your Divinity?'

'Yes, Fiachna. You may approach. What news?'

The old guard crept slowly into his master's chamber. He hesitated. He was labouring with something heavy in a hessian bag.

'Well, what is it?'

'You were correct, your Divinity. It was one of them. A woman.'

Mac Nuadat made an arch of his fingers and inhaled deeply.

'What's in the bag, Fiachna?'

'It's her...weapon, your divinity. The one she

used to...well...'

'Let me see it.'

It took all of the old man's remaining strength to transport the heavy weapon onto the table before the Arch Druid.

'The Druidic Guard says...well, that's the trigger...'

'Yes, I think I know how it works!' he snapped. The Arch Druid marvelled at the weapon. He picked it up and felt its weight. Such power it would give to the hands that wielded it! He frowned, suddenly. It was a threat, he realised. A calling card. The aos sí had obviously an infinite number of these weapons at their disposal and they had simply wanted him to be aware of that fact. It was a warning to desist, to abstain from further action. And yet, all it had achieved was to make mac Nuadat more convinced. A world where such weapons existed would, in time, mean the end of his.

'Your triad...'

'...Yes?' mac Nuadat said, looking at the old man with renewed interest.

'They have recaptured the boy and his grandfather and...' the old man smiled. '...and, your Divinity, they have the other-worlder too!'

'Wonderful! Wonderful!' the Arch Druid exclaimed, jumping to his feet. 'Where are they?'

'On their way to Uisneach.'

'Good. Very good, Fiachna. Tell me, did the Guard say if this...' he indicated the rifle, '...thing was still armed.'

'It is, your Divinity. You simply...'

'...And mac an Bhreithiún?' interrupted the Arch Druid.

'He's outside.'

'Hmm, a change of plan, Fiachna. Have him questioned and then, when we learn everything he knows, have one of the Guard execute him with this. Poetic justice, no?'

'Yes, your Divinity.' The old man turned to leave.

'But Fiachna.'

'Yes, your Divinity?'

'Let me know when the execution takes place. I want to witness this in action!'

'It's just like old times, Lorcan,' Bren said.

'If you harm my son, or grandson, I'll...!'

'...Oh? Son? Grandson? I see you have all become acquainted. So much the better.'

Several hours had passed and their military transport had already reached the suburbs of the city. This time there had been no need for blindfolds, no need for pretence. Bren and his older brother had misplaced their Connachta accents, had mislaid their flat caps. They had shaved, changed clothes and were barely recognisable from the men they were before. Only Bren's left arm, now in a sling, could ever have identified him in the role he had played in the events of before. It had been a good act, but the performance, it seemed, was no longer required.

'Tell me,' Lorcan asked. 'Why all the Connachta nonsense? Why take us to Cruachan Aí?'

'Just a ruse, old man. The Arch Druid needed to keep you and the boy out of the way until this other one turned up. Besides, there was a lot going on at the Roundhouse!' He laughed.

'How's your arm? I hope it's not troubling you too much,' Aoife asked him, smirking.

'It will improve. You, on the other hand, Aoife,' he smiled, 'the Arch Druid has plans for you. He'll want to know all about your little vacation to the other side. You too, mac Róich. But especially you.' He looked at me. 'What do they call you? Lewis, is it?'

I would have struck him there and then, but my hands had been tied behind my back. Our feet had also been bound. Bren kept his pistol trained on us while Sencha, his partner, drove upfront. Lorcan, Finn and I sat on one side of the military vehicle; Aoife, Ferdia and Maggo on the other.

'His name's Lugaid?' Lorcan said.

'Lugaid? You called him that?' exclaimed Bren. 'Did you hear that, Sencha? The man who wants to destroy our gods and this old fool calls him after Lugh!'

'I heard,' Sencha replied.

'Is that true? You want to destroy our gods?' Finn asked, looking at me in despair.

'No, son. It's not like that.'

'Sure, it is.' Bren insisted. 'Probably in league with that one there,' he said, indicating Maggo. 'That's right. You! Pune! You would love our Federation to come toppling down, wouldn't you?!' Maggo shook his head and looked away.

'Father!' Finn cried out.

'He's lying, Finn. Please believe me.'

'What your father says is true, son,' Aoife said.

'It's these two, their Order and their Arch Druid,' I added. 'That's who the enemy is.'

'Our people are not going to see it that way,' Bren replied. 'Who are they going to believe? You? You think you can bring down an entire system of belief overnight? After the gateways are closed, other-worlder, our vates will have a closer look at you. They'll take you apart piece by piece and see what makes you tick.'

'Try that, birdbrain, and I will stick that good arm of yours where Lugh doesn't shine!'

It was Ferdia, of course. Who else could bring the discussion to a close, in such intemperate a fashion? I closed my eyes and smiled to myself. We sat in silence for the rest of the way, each of us with our own thoughts, until we arrived at the base of the Hill of Uisneach.

'What shall we do with the rest of them?' Bren asked Sencha when the latter had brought the vehicle to a halt.

'The cadet, the Carthaginian and the boy's mother can be brought directly to the Roundhouse. I'll lead the others to the Stone. Our Guard will want to question the woman. The other two can be disposed of, I suppose.'

'Ferdia! Maggo!' Finn cried out. 'Bastards! Leave them alone! Mother!!'

'Do not worry, young Finn,' Maggo said, smiling. 'Have faith. All of you. All will be well.'

'That's right, Pune!' snarled Bren. You keep telling yourself that!'

'So, mac Dara, any suggestions?'

They were crouching some distance off from the foot of the Hill, using a copse of young ash trees for cover. They had all observed the arrival of the chariot in the valley below but, unfortunately, the group inside had disembarked the wrong side of the vehicle making a long distance shot impossible. The chariot had driven off in the direction of Uisneach, leaving one man alone with what looked like Finn, Lorcan and the stranger from the other world. They were now making their way along the path that led to the Cat Stone.

'Too risky,' he replied, 'I would need to get closer. We're losing light as well.'

'Well, whatever we have to do, we have to do it now,' Ó'Móráin replied. 'Mac Nuadat will be here as soon as word reaches the Roundhouse. He'll not be alone either.'

'Our people here are safe until then. At least we can be guaranteed of that. I wish we had that bloody gun from before.' Conall said.

'So...?' Ó'Móráin asked, looking at the Ulidian commander.

'Aoife and the others. They don't need them for whatever their plans are at the Cat Stone. One of us will have to tail back to the Roundhouse and perform some heroics.'

'I'll do it, sir,' Caoimhín said. Conall looked at his sub commander. Caoimhín had dishonoured himself and his triad. But too much emotional attachment clouded one's judgement and, inevitably, led to mistakes. And mistakes, in his experience, more often than not got you killed. As if guessing his thoughts, Ó'Móráin intervened.

'I'll go, mac Dara. I had the run of the place while you were twiddling your thumbs under lock and key. They're only bloody druids, after all. Not proper soldiers, eh? Besides, I wouldn't want to split up your triad!'

'Thanks, Ó'Móráin.' Conall said. 'But you both will go.'

'You are sure, mac Dara?'

'Yes,' Conall replied. 'I'll be fine, here. There's only one of them, after all.'

'But sir...!' Caoimhín protested.

'That's an order, sub-commander!'

Caoimhín lowered his head. 'Yes, sir,' he mumbled. Conall could see the disappointment in his triad's eyes.

'Oh, Caoimhín?'

'Yes?'

'If you see Oisín...?

'I know, sir. I know. We'll get him out of there. Don't worry, sir.' The sub commander saluted.

Conall hesitated, then returned the salute.

I looked across at the horizon. The city of Uisneach, a city that perhaps I would never visit, was beginning to switch on its lights in anticipation of dusk. Just another evening and to follow, for everyone else, another morning. It was truly remarkable, I thought, what this civilisation had accomplished. Uisneach had paid homage to a pantheon of lost gods, institutionalised those gods into a religion and codified that religion into a theocracy which, no doubt, had begun with the best of the intentions. However, the Druidic Order, upon discovery of certain antagonistic truths, through fear, had inserted itself between the people and these gods. Their only objective now, it seemed, was self-preservation.

I thought of my own quiet Uisneach at home, Armagh and the sleepy mound that overlooked its ecclesiastical capital. Why should their tranquillity be disturbed by any of this? One day, in my world, some high-browed quantum physicist or dreadlocked new-ager would stumble across the truth of the portals and, if so, how would our own authorities respond?

Perhaps, mac Nuadat was right. Perhaps, the gateways needed to be closed. Should some interdimensional being like Cathbad have free rein to interfere with either of our worlds? If the Druidic Order had created a religion, had that not been because of Cathbad and the aos sí? But then again, I reasoned, wasn't the sentinel merely accomplishing the task laid out for it, performing its primary function to open and close gateways?

Such was my thinking as we made our way to the Cat Stone. I shook my head. Here I was, sleepwalking towards death, like the man in Surridge's story, and yet, forever the professor, trying to calibrate and evaluate everything before me, when the only thing that mattered, the only thing, was the safety of my father and my son. For now, the enemy was the Arch Druid, I decided. Everything else could wait.

'You know, lad,' Sencha said, when we reached the Stone, 'back in the day, children, not much older than you, were handfasted at a stone like this. A trial marriage, of a year and a day.' Sencha untied Finn's hands. 'If you run, lad, have no fear, I will shoot.'

Next Sencha ordered Finn to untie me and

Lorcan, all the time maintaining his pistol on all of us. After this, I was made to tie Finn's wrist with the same binds to Lorcan's. Sencha then tied Lorcan's other wrist to mine and checked that the fastenings were secure. He took out a knife.

'A sacrifice? Is that what this is?' Lorcan shouted, suddenly.

'No idea, old man. Who knows? This is all just an experiment, after all.'

'You don't know what you are doing, do you?' I exclaimed. 'None of you!'

'We know enough! And that's all that matters!'

'Do you? Do you really?'

The voice was not my own.

'Knife and pistol. Slowly. On the ground.'

'Uncle!' Finn cried out.

'Hello, lad,' Conall replied. He caught Lorcan's eye. 'Mac Róich.'

'Took your time, mac Dara,' said Lorcan, a smile playing on his lips.

'And you must be...?'

'Lugaid,' I said.

He looked at me a moment, before turning back to Sencha. 'Your weapons.'

'Ah, commander mac Dara. I thought you would never get here,' Sencha said, nonchalantly.

'I hate to disappoint. Now, once again. Your knife and pistol!'

Sencha grinned and threw both weapons to the ground. 'You know, Ulidian, you haven't got a chance, don't you?'

'Pig-headed where I come from. Now move back, just a few steps.'

'No, you really don't have a chance,' he repeated.

'Hello, mac Dara. I'm afraid the druid is correct. Throw down *your* weapon if you don't mind.'

It was mac Murchadhna. The young senator was armed with a CT rifle Conall did not recognise. Over his shoulder, he was carrying a canvas bag. Even Sencha seemed surprised to see him.

'Apologies to all concerned but I had to see how things played out. You both understand, don't you?' Sencha nodded. 'And all the megalithic tombs around here. Such wonderful hiding places,' he added, flashing a smile.

'Interesting weapon you have there, mac Murchadhna,' Sencha said, bending to pick up his pistol.

'Tut tut!' mac Murchadhna warned, shaking his head. Sencha looked up. 'It's an automatic. Latest design.'

'What are you playing at? Are you taking their side now?' Sencha said, straightening up.

'Let's say, I am open for renegotiation,' mac Murchadhna replied.

'What are you talking about? You double-crossing us, senator? Why? Your family is getting what it wants. War. And with that, power and unlimited wealth. That was the agreement.

'Hmm...that was before.'

'Before what?'

'You know how long my family has been involved in armaments? Centuries. Now, take this rifle. As I said, it's the latest model. As good as anything in the WCA. The Federation could invade the Union if they wanted to with it.'

'So?'

'But then, you see, I heard the wondrous, dulcet tones of another weapon. Clickety-click! Clickety-click! Took out the entire DG at the Roundhouse. Am I right, mac Dara?'

Conall did not answer.

'I know nothing about that, mac Murchadhna.'

'In the wrong hands, that weapon...the development of that weapon, could tip the balance in favour of the nation, or nations, that possessed it. And the company that manufactured the weapon for the nation? Well, that would be unlimited power.'

'As I said, I don't know anything about it.'

'No? Really? It wouldn't have something to do with the reason why we are all standing here like idiots in front of this bloody rock, would it? And mac Róich? The boy? And this... who the hell is this anyway?!' he shouted, looking at me.

No one spoke. I looked back at the horizon and noticed a beet-red half-sun poised to dip its head beneath the surface of the world. The ensuing silence was broken by the sound of a chariot engine. It was instantly recognisable as belonging to the Arch Druid.

'Me?' I said, my eyes on the chariot, 'I'm Lugaid mac Róich.'

They had commandeered a passing chariot and abandoned it just beyond the walls of the Roundhouse. Its occupant, an elderly vate making his way back into the city, had no doubt been taken aback by the sudden appearance of two soldiers, in foreign uniforms, on his route home from the House of Vates. Ó'Móráin and Caoimhín had left him, bound, gagged but unharmed, in the back seat of the transport. He would be fine until morning. They had less hope for themselves.

'I suppose you're in charge of this little suicide mission, commander? You are the ranking officer,' Caoimhín said.

'Thanks for reminding me!' Ó'Móráin replied. The commander scanned the grounds of the Roundhouse. 'Different personnel than before. Obviously. Probably from the local Uisneach DG. They'll be unfamiliar with their roles.'

'Shitting themselves, you mean!'

The commander smiled. 'Hmm, let's hope so. Knives only, Breathnach. Up close. And best wait for nightfall.'

'Quick and easy!' Caoimhin concurred. 'So, they do train you for this type of operation in Connachta?' he joked.

The commander smiled again. 'Just a bit.'

'And once inside?'

'The cadet, the one Bridge called Ferdia, the Carthaginian...if they are still alive, then Aoife, and hopefully your other triad, Oisín. But sub-commander...?'

'Yeah?'

'No unnecessary risks. Like mac Dara said. Understood?'

'You're the boss,' Caoimhín replied.

'I suggest you put that weapon down, senator.' Bren said.

'Really?' mac Murchadhna replied. Instead, he redirected his rifle towards Finn, standing next to me. 'And what would happen if I simply pulled the trigger?'

'You do and I will kill you!' I exclaimed.

'Interesting accent you have there, stranger. Where might you be from?'

'Senator!' The Arch Druid intervened. 'My triad is correct. Lower your weapon and I will explain everything. This can all be resolved to our mutual satisfaction. You have my personal guarantee.'

Mac Nuadat was dressed in a black robe and cowl, not unlike a medieval monk, I thought, ironically. Unlike the last time he had stood on the sacred Hill nearby, he had wished for no fanfare, no crowds, no entourage except Bren and two druidic guards, one of which was carrying a large assault weapon. The last thing the Arch Druid wanted to do was to draw attention to it, himself or anything that was about to happen.

'You have been keeping me in the dark,' mac Murchadhna said.

'This...' he waved a hand towards the Stone, 'never involved you.'

'Oh? Perhaps, if I might be so bold, your... Divinity,' the senator performed a mock bow, 'I might be the judge of that. After all, I am a lawgiver!'

'Oh? Suddenly you are a lawgiver! Conall said, sarcastically.

'Very well,' the Arch Druid replied. 'Proceed, ask what you may.'

'First, the weapon your guard is having such difficulty carrying. Who built it?'

'I really don't know, senator. That's the truth.'

'I see. Where did it come from?' the senator asked.

'Again, I am not absolutely sure, senator.'

The senator turned his rifle onto the Arch Druid and sighed. 'These answers are not very promising, are they, Arch Druid?'

'Why not ask the stranger? I have a feeling that he is in a better position to give you everything you need to know.'

'Fine.' He turned towards me. 'Lugaid, you said your name was? That weapon. What do you know about it?'

'Looks American,' I said.

'Amer-...what? What did you say?'

'American,' I repeated. 'The USA. Your WCA, or part of it.'

'American? Is this some sort of a joke?' The senator looked around and laughed. Noticing that no one was joining in on his amusement he stopped. 'What's he talking about?' he asked mac Nuadat. The Arch Druid did not reply.

'He doesn't know.' I said. 'None of you do, except perhaps the bits and pieces, the scraps of information, he...' I pointed at the Arch Druid, 'has tortured out of people.'

'What's he talking about?' mac Murchadhna insisted.

'He doesn't know about America because, senator, America doesn't know about this world, about places like this: dolmens, stones, sacred bloody hills! You want to know why we are all here? We are here because, as your religion accidentally discovered aeons ago, this rock is not just a rock. It's an energetic marker on a global grid of ley lines that feeds on electro-magnetism. They are also gateways, portals, corridors...whatever you want to call them...to another world. Not to the world of bloody fairies, but to my world! My Uisneach, my Éireann and my bloody version of the WCA!'

'Go on,' said the Arch Druid. 'You have piqued my curiosity.'

'So,' I continued, 'we are here this evening to shut down these portals...'

'...Shut them down?' Mac Murchadhna interrupted.

'But, of course, senator. Finn, Lorcan and I are here to use our genetic imprints to close down these portals forever. Unless that weapon has changed your mind, mac Nuadat?'

'No, it hasn't,' the Arch Druid replied, solemnly.

'Hold on! Hold on! You are saying that you are from this world and you travelled through this portal? Your world...'

'...is not too much different from your own, except our technology...'

'...is far superior to ours...'

'...about seventy or eighty years ahead.'

'Mac Nuadat!' implored the young senator, turning towards mac Nuadat.

'It's too dangerous, mac Murchadhna. The Council...the Federation Council have already decided that the portals must be closed!'

'Are you mad? Consider the benefits...' He turned to face Conall. 'Mac Dara?

You are a soldier! Think of the advantage Ulidia would have over the rest of the island!' Conall remained silent, leaving Mac Murchadhna's voice to tailor off, swept away by the stillness of the darkness that had quickly descended upon us.

'That's right, senator. He's not interested. None of them are. There's more at stake than just petty economies and trivial war games. Isn't that right, mac Nuadat?'

'How much do you know?' mac Nuadat asked me.

'Not how it works. Or even if it will work. But I think I understand why?'

'Care to explain? You've been doing so well up to now.'

'Your Druidic Order is about power and control,' I began. 'You perform ceremonies and rituals at these ancient sites, perhaps you have even found a way to harness their energies. But you can't control them. There are too many of them. They open and close all over your Federation during your feasts and festivals and you are powerless to prevent people coming and going as they please. You cannot stop the sentinels and the aos sí and you have to work in the shadows against them. The reason being...'

'...The reason being...?'

'...the revelation, to every citizen on this island, that you are working in secret against the very gods, or manifestation of the gods, you claim to worship!' The Arch Druid looked around the circle. Bren and Sencha looked away. They shuffled their feet, uncomfortably. 'So, if you cannot control, you must destroy. It's as simple as that.'

'No one is destroying anything!' mac Murchadha exclaimed. 'You!' He shouted at the guard holding the weapon. 'Pass that to me, slowly.' The guard looked at the Arch Druid. Mac Nuadat nodded. The guard moved carefully towards mac Murchadhna. The senator placed his own rifle in his left hand, still aiming it in our direction, and stretched out his right for the larger firearm.

Whether it was the surprising weight of the weapon, or the fumbling nature of the exchange, mac Murchadhna would never know. A shot once more rang out across the saturnine gloom of Uisneach, similar to the one that had downed a president. Mac Murchadhna remained upright a moment, like a dummy in a shop window; a last, beaming smile frozen momentarily in time. A little red dot had appeared like a chakra bead on the senator's young, unwrinkled forehead...and then, a faint trickle of blood.

30

He had been trained well, Ó'Móráin thought, as they made their way into the House of Vates: the flat of a knife was all it had taken the Ulidian to lever loose a ground floor window frame. Already, four guards had been dispatched, silently and methodically; two on the perimeter and two in the centre of the grounds. He had been correct. The replacement guards were not really qualified for the task in hand. A combination of inexperience, nerves and the element of surprise had worked in their favour. So far.

They had assumed it best to enter the Roundhouse via the House of Vates. The DG had probably doubled their contingent in the area around the House of Brehon Law where the cells were located, he thought, and although it would mean covering more ground and a greater chance of discovery, Ó'Móráin calculated that the odds still worked out in their favour. As luck would have it, the vate, whose chariot they had borrowed, had been kind enough to volunteer some useful information regarding the House's interior and the quickest route through to the Brehon Law arc of the Roundhouse and the cells beneath.

'You've been there before?' Caoimhín whispered, as they moved quietly through the dark hallways of the Vates, on their way to the hothouse and its gardens that lay at the centre of the Roundhouse.

'Yes, we can use the gardens to gain access to the House of Brehon Law. I visited them when I met that bastard mac Murchadhna!'

'Mac Murchadhna?'

'Long story!'

As they moved further inwards, the two men began to encounter more guards patrolling, in clockwise and anti-clockwise circuits, the wide-open corridors of the House of Vates. There weren't enough of them, however, to extend their lines adequately to prevent Caoimhín and Ó'Móráin from simple incursions through and beyond to the botanic heart of the Roundhouse. Quite a few must still be at the bedside of the Connachta president several floors above, Ó'Móráin thought. Two more dead guards later, they found themselves under the glass roofs of the central conservatory.

'We go through quietly. Don't touch anything.' Ó'Móráin said in a low voice. The door to the other House will have guards as well.' Caoimhin looked up. A full moon was peering down at him through the glass above. He looked across at the commander, taken aback by the intensity in the soldier's eyes. No wonder, he thought, war with Connachta had lasted so long.

The light, however, facilitated their progress, creating eerie, unnerving shadows on the trellised walls as they passed. Finally, they reached the interior entrance to the House of Brehon Law.

'Guards?' Caoimhín asked.

'Just the two. Looking our way. There goes our advantage.'

'Shit!' Caoimhín exclaimed. 'Where's that light coming from?'

'Torches, just above their heads.'

'Let me have a look.' They swapped positions and the Ulidian sub commander peeked around the corner of the wall that shielded them from view of the guards.

'They're lazy, commander,' Caoimhín whispered. 'Their fingers aren't even on their triggers.'

'And?'

'A few yards between us and them. I reckon we can rush them.'

'No, Breathnach.'

'There's no other way, commander. How good are you with a knife?'

'Sub commander, I said no! That's an order!'

'You're forgetting, commander. I'm not under your command! Ready? On the count of three...'

'...Breathnach...!'

'...Two...'

'...Bloody Ulidian fool...!'

'...One!'

'Was that strictly necessary?' Conall shouted.

The impact of the bullet from Bren's pistol had propelled Mac Murchadha backwards onto the foot of the Cat Stone, his head slumped onto his chest, his and Bridge's weapon lying either side of his sprawled legs. The druidic guards had rushed to grab them before returning them safely into the hands of the Arch Druid's own personal triad.

'Necessary?' the Arch Druid replied, 'Yes. But a pity too. He would have proved useful, moving forward. Just as you, mac Dara, have proved useful. Still, we will make use of the weapon, perhaps integrate its technology slowly, bit by bit, into our own. As it is, it is far too dangerous. If it ever got into the wrong hands, it could be used against the Federation.'

'You really are a mad man!' Conall exclaimed. 'All those lives that we have lost in war in Éireann. All that we will lose when it starts again!'

'You still don't understand, do you, mac Dara? I am Federation before I am Éireann. Éireann is simply a stepping stone to where the real power lies. And with this, the closure of the gates, I will be well-rewarded. Soon, with another three like these, we can use the power of the Trinity Knot to shut down all the gateways throughout the Federation.'

He looked up to see a full moon hanging in the sky overhead. 'You two will need to light the torches,' mac Nuadat ordered his guards, 'but first of all, dispense with the senator. Bren give me that pistol. I will keep an eye on mac Dara.'

The two druidic guides did as they were asked and stood now, forming a bridge of light either side of the Cat Stone.

'Bren, bring the three of them forward. Sencha, you have the knife?'

'Yes, your Divinity.'

Lorcan, Finn and I were nudged at gunpoint to the Cat Stone.

'Tell me, Lugaid. Do you have the Stone of Divisions in your Uisneach?'

'Yes,' I replied.

'Interesting. And the Trinity Knot?'

'No.'

'A shame...for your world. According to our scriptures, it appeared overnight, carved onto the rock, a symbol of our determination, our will.'

'Will?'

'To resist...the new religion. The vile creed coming out of Carthage. It was a sign from the gods, a divine invitation to renew our faith in them.'

'You think that's what it means?'

'I know it does, Lugaid. And if you listened to the stirrings of your heart, you would know that too. After all, was it not intuition, instinct, your own heart that led you into this world? Your father, son and the woman Aoife, your love for them all has guided you across the Great Divide. That's what the Trinity Knot means...your own son and father know the truth of it. The coming together of three into one. That's the purpose of every triad, after all. And that's your purpose. You see the moon? All of you, look up! Tonight, we honour its cycle, our triple-goddess of maiden, mother and crone! Sencha, their hands, place them over the Knot.' Conall lurched forward but the Arch Druid fired off a shot that whistled just over his head. 'Stay back, mac Dara! The next one won't miss!'

We strained, Finn, Lorcan and me, to break free from each other. Suddenly, I felt the heavy blow of a rifle butt on my right shoulder. The pain surged like a bolt of lightning through my body and brought me to my knees. I looked up at the Arch Druid.

'You have it all wrong, mac Nuadat!' I laughed. 'The Trinity Knot! In my world, it's not a triple goddess. It is three aspects of one God. You know what the Carthaginians believe. And the WCA! It's believed in my world too and that, that is what you are most afraid of! You are surrounded in this world! And in mine? You're nothing but a myth!'

'Silence! Blasphemy! Sencha, the knife! Make the incisions now!' Sencha, from behind, prised open the fingers of Lorcan's hand and made a diagonal cut onto the old man's flesh. He did the same with Finn's hand. The boy screamed out in pain. 'Bren, the same for the other-worlder!' the Arch Druid ordered, noticing Sencha struggle to maintain his hold on the others. I received another blow on the shoulder for good measure and almost blacked out. Then, I felt my right arm being twisted in front of me and the searing pain of a knife slash a deep slice into my hand. A blow from behind struck Lorcan and I saw his head loll forwards.

'Bastards! Leave him alone!' I roared.

Lorcan's limp hand was thrust down over the markings of the Stone. I received another punch to the back of the head.

'Father!' Finn cried out.

Finn's hand too was pressed down upon the rock.

'You bloody idiots! You have no idea...!

I felt a steel grip close around my wrist like a vice. I lashed out with my free arm. It made a swooping sound as it carved a line through thin air. My other arm was now no longer under my control. It was being moved, almost robotically, by both Sencha and Bren towards the Stone.

And then I felt the skin of my palm wince as it made contact with the roughly hewn boulder.

It was not the type of manoeuvre they taught you in the RBK Youth, but it was the only thing Caoimhín could think of at that time. If it didn't work, then so be it, he thought. What had they to lose? The sound of gunfire, as a prelude to entering the House of Brehon Law, would have rendered the whole enterprise redundant in any case.

Killing a man with a knife is always personal. One hand over the mouth, and the other one with a knife, from behind, adroitly separating two ends of the carotid artery. That was the procedure followed in training. It's different, however, when you can see the lights of your victim's eyes glaze over into death.

Caoimhín blinked the memory of it away as he followed on the shoulder of the Connachta to the top of a stone stairwell.

'This time, Breathnach, you do what I say! Understood?!' Ó'Móráin warned.

'It worked, didn't it?' Caoimhin replied.

The commander, ignoring this, leaned over the banister and looked down. 'The cells are just below. Grenades?'

'Only two.'

There was minimal light at the top of the staircase but down below they could make out the warm glow of torch light. Ó'Móráin stared in disbelief at the explosives Caoimhín was holding out in front of him.

'Two?!'

'That's all Bridge had,' Caoimhin whispered. Ó'Móráin shook his head. 'And guards?'

'Who knows? Most of their reinforcements, probably.'

'Great!'

They were amateurs though, Ó'Móráin thought to himself, as he led the Ulidian to the bottom of the steps and snatched a quick look down the first passage. There must have been over a dozen cells in total, if Caoimhín was to be believed, running perpendicularly along two corridors. They hadn't even bothered to set fire to the braziers along the first, so they had all had to have been neatly packed along the second: Oisín, the cadet, Maggo and perhaps even Aoife. Very convenient of them. Perhaps this might even work. He smiled to himself.

'Who are you? Where do you think you are going?'

The voice came from behind them. It belonged to an older man, dressed in a black livery. In his hand, a pistol jerked nervously.

It was as if my hand had been suspended

briefly into a grainy, molten solution; a powdery, hot mixture of grit and liquid warmth. I felt my fingers merge with the surface of the rock, then sink slightly beneath, like a handprint in hot sand. An image flashed into my head of fire, unleashed from the interior of the rock. But it was not just this rock, I knew. It was the elemental forces of nature: earth, water, fire and air trapped and compressed into all solid matter like a diamond at the heart of a lump of coal buried hundreds of feet underground. An overlong exposure would have seared my flesh, but the electrical feedback from the stone prevented this from happening. I snapped my hand back and noticed the Trinity Knot had become inflamed, a circuit of fire was travelling through its intersecting grooves. I recoiled backwards, just in time to witness the knot crack open like an egg and an invisible pulse of energy from within cause the stone to shudder. A second later, it sent out a tremendous wave of generated power, a sonic boom that rippled outwards in all directions.

It felt like a landmine had detonated beneath our feet, reeling us backwards in mid-air, before a tumbling of head and shoulders acknowledged our return to hard ground.

And then silence.

The impact of the explosion had cleft the Cat Stone into three neat fragments, a vertical severance which stopped just a metre from its base, but which transformed the rock into a three-leafed plant, its leaves like clover projecting at equal angles from a central pod. I managed to get to my feet, astonished to learn that not only was I still alive but I was no longer tied to Finn or Lorcan.

'Finn! Lorcan!' I cried out.

'I'm fine,' shouted Finn.'

'Lorcan!' I yelled again.

'I'm afraid, Lugaid, your father is still unconscious,' I heard Sencha say. 'I think he might have missed the entire performance.'

'It appears that we have succeeded!' the Arch Druid called out. 'The gateway has been closed. And you. You are still alive, Lugaid. I am delighted.'

'Oh?'

'It means that I will have the pleasure of eradicating you myself!'

I saw Bren pick up the dark shadow of something from the grass. It was Bridge's weapon. He stepped closer towards me.

'Father! No!' I heard Finn cry. Finn made to run towards me, but Sencha grabbed him and pinned him with an arm around his throat.

'It's ok, son.'

'Yes,' the Arch Druid said, 'it will be ok. You know, Lugaid, I have changed my mind. I no longer need to know about the other world. I have no reason to keep you alive. Not now, we can close the portal. You? You are simply...evidence. Bren, I think it's time to send our friend here to...the next world.'

Bren held the rifle aloft, shouldered it and took aim.

''I don't think so.' It was Conall. I had forgotten all about the Ulidian commander. 'Let the boy go!' he roared. 'Or mac Nuadat here will be in the next world before the stranger!'

And then there was light.

'You don't want to do that, old man,' Ó'Móráin said.

'Put the gun down and you won't get hurt,' Caoimhín added.

Fiachna was holding the pistol as though its metal were incandescent, as heavy as the anvil upon which it had been newly forged.

'No... no... the Arch Druid...I must tell...!' The old man's face was ashen pale, transfixed, caught between a flailing sense of duty and a morbid fear of death. Both veterans had seen that look before in the faces of much younger comrades in the trenches of an tSionainn.

'Just put the gun down,' Ó'Móráin said, softly. 'Turn around and go back to bed. No harm will come to you.'

Fiachna hesitated. Ó'Móráin could see the indecision in his eyes; he was role-playing the scene, observing himself from the corner of his room, safely coddled away under the blankets of his bed. But then, his face hardened. The old servant opened his mouth to scream.

The Ulidian dashed forward with his knife as Fiachna's gun went off in his hands.

'Caoimhín!!' Ó'Móráin screamed.

For a moment, I thought night had turned into day. The sky had come alive, a series of blinding strobe flares in which, for a few seconds, everything trembled. It was more a quaking of air than of earth. I caught glimpses of Finn and the Arch Druid, flitting in and out of existence. They were there, and then not there, then there again. The Cat Stone, too, phased in and out of dimensional space. It was destroyed, then whole again, and once more destroyed. The city of Uisneach in the valley below vanished, only to reappear immediately. Inside I felt my body in a state of flux. It buzzed as if filled with tiny electric moths, all flapping their wings to the dazzling brilliance of the light.

And then the moon and the stars filled the heavens once more as the blackness of space unfolded like a curtain once more across the sky.

We must have all lost consciousness as it was dawn by the time I came around. I stood up and looked around. Finn, Lorcan and the others were still recumbent on the ground before me. The Arch Druid, his triad and guards were also still passed out; Sencha and Bren, even in sleep, either side of their master. I had to see if Finn, Lorcan and Conall were ok.

'They are fine, Lugaid. Don't worry. Let them sleep.'

I looked around to see Bridge, standing there, balancing her assault weapon on the pivot of one shoulder.

Ó'Móráin had just about enough time to dispatch the old man with his knife before turning on his heels and making off quickly for the end of the corridor. If he could, he would go back for Caoimhín, but he already knew that it was too late for the Ulidian sub commander. The reverberation of Fiachna's shot had already alerted the druidic guards and, for a few brief moments, it was a simple race to the intersection where both passages met. Ó'Móráin's first grenade was already primed by the time he reached it. He didn't need to look up but rolled it along the floor underneath the stampede of feet that were rushing towards him. He took cover and heard an almost instantaneous explosion ring out, bringing with it a shockwave of smoke hurtling in his direction.

He didn't know how many guards there had been, but there were bodies and limbs now scattered everywhere. In the prevailing plume of dust, he could hear the wailing moans of survivors, writhing in agony in the smoke beneath his feet. He threaded carefully, using the aftermath of the mortar blast as cover. He quickly shot two more guards who had appeared suddenly from behind a collapsed wall. A couple of cell doors had been blown inwards, but a cursory glance revealed no occupants inside.

'Over here!' he heard a voice cry out. The accent was Ulidian.

'Oisín?' Ó'Móráin yelled.

'Yeah!' said the sub commander from within.

Ó'Móráin looked around for a set of keys. He spotted them, dangling from the waist of a dying guard. As he bent over to grasp them, he noticed the man's left leg was now a bloody mess, his eyes, two bulging balls of shocked whiteness. He was doing well not to scream out like the others, Ó'Móráin thought.

'You know where the others are?' he asked as soon as he had opened the cell door.

'No,' Oisín replied. 'But I definitely heard new prisoners being led to the cells earlier! Wait, you're Ó'Móráin, aren't you?'

'Sssh!' the commander said. 'You hear that?'

They both listened intently. They could make out the dull thud of a door being kicked repeatedly; it was coming from the far end of the passageway.

'Quick, sub commander! We don't have a lot of time!'

The clumping sound got louder as they approached.

'Is that you, cadet?' Ó'Móráin yelled.

The sound of kicking increased again. The Connachta unlocked the door to reveal Ferdia and Maggo inside, their mouths had been gagged with cloth.

'It was because of this one,' Maggo declared, as soon as he was free to speak, 'always shouting at the guards!'

'Never mind that!' Ó'Móráin shouted. 'Any sign of Aoife?'

'The bastards separated us! I think they took her away for questioning!' Ferdia exclaimed.

At that moment, they could make out the sound of boots stamping overhead.

'The rest of the DG will be here any minute. Oisín, take this!' Ó'Móráin handed the sub commander his rifle. 'The rest of you, stand back! This,' he said, taking out his second grenade from his pocket, 'will have to take out as many of them as it can!' Suddenly, the commotion above came to a halt. 'Unless of course...'

They all listened. The silence lasted a second or so. And then it began. They all listened, their gaze fixed upwards, as if willing their eyes to burn holes through the ceiling above and testify to the havoc being wrought there. They heard about half a minute of sustained gunfire, interspersed with the sounds of glass and broken furniture.

'What the…?' exclaimed Ferdia.

'…Quiet!' warned Ó'Móráin.

Another few seconds later, they heard the sound of further steps, descending a stairwell in their direction. Ó'Móráin readied his grenade and directed the others to take cover.

The steps increased in volume. And then they stopped. They were now just behind the corner of the adjacent passageway.

'You can put that down, commander! You think I was going to let Bridge have all the fun!'

It was Angus. 'And look who I found in the master's chamber!'

'You must be Aoife,' Ó'Móráin said.

'What…what just happened?' I asked Bridge.

'What was meant to happen, happened!'

'What the hell does that mean?!' I shouted, indignantly. I was sick to death with it all. The self-indulgent innuendoes and the half-baked truths, the care-free manipulations and the sleight of hand manoeuvres. Yes, the aos sí had helped, but it had always been on their own terms. They had an inhumane disregard for human life while claiming to hold humanity in high regard. And then it struck me. Cathbad, Angus and Bridge; they were less interested in saving our worlds and its inhabitants than they were in preserving their control over the connection between those worlds. They had seen civilisations come and go, after all. Brigid had made it clear from the beginning. That was why she preferred to call herself Bridge. It was just the connection that mattered to them.

'Cathbad had a sentinel send back a pulse from Uisneach, your Uisneach. It overrode the energy output coming from the Cat Stone in this world.'

'I don't understand.'

Bridge gave me a puzzled look. 'Mac Nuadat had little to no understanding of any of it, of course,' Bridge sighed.

'That makes two of us,' I said. 'How…?'

'…It's quite simple, Lewis. Your DNA is a double helix, right? You are aware of that?'

'Yes, of course.'

'The helix is long, like an antenna, say. But what is it made from? It's composed of a crystalline solution. And what do crystals do? They transmit and receive energetic information throughout the electro-magnetic grid on the surface of the earth…what you call ley lines. When, you, Lorcan and Finn came through the portal, your DNA changed…ever so slightly. It received new information, a new electro-magnetic imprint from the other world. That's why you have a double helix, Lewis. It's made for travel between both worlds, like a kind of passport, encoded deep into your DNA.'

'You mean we are supposed to travel between worlds.'

'Aeons ago, that was what happened. But then humanity, in both worlds, through the passing of many millennia, forgot the simple fact that they have more than one home. Some remembered and built stone circles and so on, but the ruling hierarchies of the day rejected these for their own selfish interests. And the knowledge was allowed to fade once more.'

'So, you and Cathbad exist to bring some travellers across. Why not all?'

'Only certain people, or families, possess enough remnants of previous excursions between the worlds, carried down their genetic lineage, to render us able to...activate them.'

'So, you just pop into people's lives and turn them upside down.'

'You don't understand, Lewis. That's what humanity is supposed to do. The universe, like code, is binary. Most solar systems in this universe possess two suns. Your own star is an exception to the rule. You have heard of string theory? It's not a theory. Multiple dimensions exist, but even they do so in pairs.

'And the Arch Druid...?'

'...He, in his overwhelming ignorance, wished to use the ancient symbol of the Trinity Knot along with your DNA, to release a shutdown sequence between one portal on this island with another portal on yours. If successful, he would have done the same throughout the whole of Éireann, his Federation and then...? Who knows? If all the portals are closed, the effects on both worlds would be catastrophic!'

'But you allowed us to be used. You let him get so close!'

'Only the accumulated, seismic force of the negative wave...'

'...Negative wave...? I interrupted.

'Yes, have you not considered what the Trinity Knot is? It's a symbol of their mass deception. Triads, multiples of three...they're everywhere in this world...a sacred number, they say. It's not, Lewis. The universal number is two! Someone, in their past, must have realised that and used the number three to mask the truth.'

I thought about this a moment. 'Go on,' I said, finally.

'So, only the force of the negative wave, energised by your altered DNA and collided with Cathbad's opposing, positive wave, could ever have been enough to counteract the former and redress the balance.'

'Redress the balance? So, all of this was just an effort to maintain the status quo? What's to stop mac Nuadat, or anybody else for that matter, trying again, with another three travellers on another bloody Trinity Knot somewhere else?'

Bridge looked at me and smiled. 'He can't.'

'Why not?'

'We needed you, Lewis, to stop the Arch Druid, yes. But you also helped us. Greatly.'

'What do you mean?'

'Up until now, the portals could only be opened, by sentinels, on those dates in the annual cycle when the earth's grid is at its most...pliable. Solstices, equinoxes and so on.'

'Yes, I know that.'

'Now, a sentinel can open the portals between the two Uisneachs at any time. The inter-dimensional barrier which the sentinels normally open and close has been altered there. There's no need to wait for particular times in the annual calendar when the energy is sufficiently built up. It's a major breakthrough, a return to how things used to be, how they soon will be again, I hope.'

It was too much for me to take in. I suddenly felt overcome with fatigue, as if another barrier within myself had also been torn down. I looked at the bodies lying in the grass beneath my feet and envied them their rest.

'What now?'

'I will wake up your friends. Angus is with the others.' Bridge closed her eyes momentarily. 'Yes, they are fine. You can join them. Now, if you wish.'

'What about the Druidic Order?'

'One battle at a time, Lewis.'

'And the Arch Druid?'

'He will discover that he has become suddenly unemployed. He will be sent back to his homeland, along with his triad!'

'His homeland?'

Bridge smiled. 'Tell me, Lewis, do you still have your map?'

I felt inside for the folded piece of paper I had torn out from the atlas in Lorcan's library. 'Yes,' I replied.

'Mac Nuadat is from Hy Brasil...a perfect exile, as it turns out.'

I stared at the map of Éireann. I hadn't noticed it before but there, a hundred miles or so off its west Atlantic coast, was marked the small, mythical, phantom island of Hy Brasil which, according to legend, appeared and disappeared one day every seven years. 'Hy Brasil! It exists!'

'Of course. In this world,' Bridge confirmed, moving slightly to my left. 'Things are not over, you know, Mr Summer. Keep your eyes open. Stay alert. They appear and disappear. Just like the island. Just like your furniture.'

And then, I felt the customary vibration in the air. When I looked to the side, I knew the aos sí would be gone.

The days that followed were like the moments when you first awake, or fall asleep, like the mystical, intermediary, groggy shift from one level of consciousness to another. We were caught somewhere between; all of us, delighted to be together and alive, and yet fearful that any time an aos sí would materialise and whisk us off to a dark, monolithic slab somewhere where our hands would once more be applied on some ancient carving, or rune, etched in coloured dye.

It was a memorable time and we shared it together, knowing that it could not last.

As soon as Bridge had left, the others, my new family, woke up as if the spell that had cast them under had magically ascended. The Arch Druid and his two guards, his triad Sencha and Bren, slept on, however, motionless; their breathing was so shallow, it was as if it too were trapped, subtly balancing feathers on a scale, between points of inhalation and exhalation.

As we made our way back to Uisneach, on foot, we could make out thin lines of grey smoke in the distance, rising and swelling in the early morning sky above the Roundhouse. Trudging onwards, we came across Aoife, Ferdia, Maggo and the others. We had met somewhere in the middle, it seemed; with joyous faces, they told us their story and we told them ours, an equitable exchange of remarkable fortune, the wheel of which had been spun by different aos sí. Conall had wanted to go back for Caoimhín's body but Ó'Móráin held him back; the two of them wrestling each other into the dirt until they could wrestle no more.

I have no memory of our journey back to Emain Mhaca, except to say that I held Aoife's hand the whole way. Mac Neill was true to his word. News of the Arch Druid's Federation-backed conspiracy had reached the news sheets and, as a result, the border with Laighean was once more reopened. And so, it was that we spent two wonderful days at Lorcan's home, eating, drinking, sleeping or simply staring vacantly into space, comfortable in each other's silences.

Ó'Móráin was the first to leave. While the invasion of Ulidia had been stalled, forces in Éireann had rapidly bifurcated across different lines: pro and anti-Federation

clans, those in favour and those against mac Nuadat, were now newly poised to strike one another, Connachta versus Connachta; Ulidian versus Ulidian. Finn, Ferdia and Conall had had to return to their billets. Even Maggo, whose papers had expired, had made the decision to return to his home, in the event of war breaking out all across the island. We shared an emotional farewell with him at Béal Feirste docks; Lorcan and Finn fighting back the tears while the young man smiled, waving from the ship as it disembarked.

'I will see you soon, my pagan friends!' he cried out, as the white-water churned its wake; we followed its path until his ship was a small speck of shadow on the horizon.

One evening, several days after Maggo's departure, Aoife and I were sitting together after dinner. We had just left Lorcan's. My father had, the day before, announced his retirement from the Ulidian Shield, offering as his only reason the decision to spend more time with his family. He had wanted us to be the first to know.

'He's changed,' Aoife said, suddenly. 'I have never seen him so content.' I smiled. 'And you,' she nudged me playfully, 'are you content?'

'Yes, of course.' I held her close for a moment and then released her. 'It's just…'

'You miss your world?'

'I miss my parents. I wish I had had a chance to say goodbye.'

'Maybe the aos sí can get word to them. Tell them you are safe.'

'Maybe,' I said, thoughtfully.

'Anything else?'

'I was just thinking…'

'Thinking?'

'This war,' I said, 'you will have to go soon, more clearing stations…'

'We've been through that…'

'…No, that's not it. I was just thinking of home. It's just…it's just that the minute my people there find peace, I have to go and find myself another bloody war!'

'Well, you are named after Lugh, the god of war!'

I laughed. 'True,' I said.

But it wasn't true. I was a man who just wanted peace. Most of all, I wanted peace of mind. I looked at Aoife and thought of Rose. I thought of two diametrically opposed women, one alive and one dead, who had only me in common. I thought of Pritchard and Surridge. I thought of Ulidia and Connachta. I thought of Catholics and Protestants. I thought of Conall and Ó'Móráin. I thought of Maggo and Ferdia. I thought of my son Finn and the son in the other world I had never had. I thought of night here and day there. And I thought of myself, as always, the equator between two poles. Perhaps there was more to me that met the eye, enough of me to reconcile others; enough, I hoped, to reconcile the different parts of myself.

I looked at Aoife and smiled.

'Would you like to tie the knot? I asked

She looked at me, not understanding the question.

TALES OF ULIDIA:

SWORD AND STONE

BOOK 2

1

My Carthaginian host, Maggo, grinned widely as he posed for a photograph by one of the megalithic pillars that comprised the Xaghra Stone Circle. We were at a funerary complex of caves on the island of Gaulos, part of the archipelago of Melita, known in my world as Malta.

I had missed his smile in the eighteen months since I had last seen him, the same smile now as before, as buoyant as the ship that had disembarked Béal Feirste docks then; his hand, I remember, waving farewell, amidst the gloom, in a wide, merry arc.

His uncle, Gisco, with whom I had been staying for the last few days, shared the same familial trait as his nephew; a preference for hope over despair, the optimism of the half full glass over the pessimistic brewery of empty bottles that littered the streets of Ulidia which Maggo had left behind.

'You see, Mr Summer,' Gisco had explained at dinner the previous evening, pinching a slippery, violet olive between his fingers, 'this little Bidni is tiny...a defective fruit really, but it produces the most delicious oil in all of the Union and has done so for thousands of years. You wouldn't believe it, would you? It is small, but brave; unassuming but resilient.' He had smiled then, nodding at his nephew across the dinner table who, in return, flashed a perfect set of teeth.

I knew this already, of course. Gisco was proud of his nephew and, in a way, so was I. For such a young man, Maggo had already demonstrated a capacity for enduring more that most during his six-month sojourn in Éireann the previous year. He had, along with so many others, risked everything to help me. For that, I would always be grateful.

'Your turn, Mr Summer,' Maggo said, still smiling. 'Pass me the...what did you call it before?'

'Box camera,' I replied, handing the device to my young friend.

'Yes, 'box camera',' he repeated slowly. He took it from my hands and, with a flourish of his fingers, encouraged me to adopt a suitable, professorial pose in front of the entrance to one of the caves which, many millennia ago, had been a last resting place for so many dead.

'Tell me, where did you get this apparatus, Mr Summer?'

'Alexandria,' I replied. 'Last week.'

'Wonderful,' Maggo said.

I stood, a leather satchel over my left shoulder, one hand on my hip and the other in my pocket, trying to look as casual as possible, but feeling quite ridiculous. It was still early, but already far too warm for my linen jacket which had spent the last hour folded neatly in my arm. A gentle trickle of perspiration was percolating a path down my spine. The lens of the camera momentarily blinded me as it reflected the sun into my face. I shielded my eyes, saluting the sky for its lack of clouds and thought about buying a hat in Mosta later.

'Remain still for just one more second Mr Summer...that's it...almost...yes...thank you.' I heard a shutter click and immediately re-laxed. 'There you are professor. Immortalised. Just like one of your statues, frozen forever in time.'

It was my first time in the Carthaginian Union, the regional bloc of nation states that had coalesced gradually over the centuries out of the ashes of the Holy Carthaginian Empire. In my world none of it existed, of course. There, Hannibal's elephant armies had never stomped their way across the Rubicon and laid to waste the burgeoning city of Rome. Here, in contrast, the Roman Empire had never existed, and the Punic general had reigned victorious. The outcome of one military campaign had been enough to change this world forever, had spliced history and left it to spiral down a different path. Perhaps, as an archaeologist, this was why I had come to this hypogeum in the sand; its underground tombs belonged to a time before the temporal schism, when our mutual histories were still aligned. Since I could never return to my world, this was the next best thing to being home.

'Shall we return to the main island, Mr Summer?' Maggo asked.

'You know, Maggo,' I replied, relieving him of the camera, 'you *can* call me, Lewis. We know each other well enough.'

'But I do like your name. 'Summer'. So unusual. Reminds me of home.'

'You are home,' I reminded him.

We caught the midday ferry to Cirkewwa and, from there, made our way in Maggo's uncle's touring car to the latter's home in Mosta in the centre of the island. Since his return to Melita, Maggo had chosen to live with Gisco, a widower, as opposed to the more obvious choice of Valletta where he studied. In six months, he would finally graduate as a fully qualified journalist. It was his university that had arranged for his work placement at the *Ulidian Shield*, the newspaper in Emain Mhaca which had been under the editorship of my father, Lorcan mac Róich.

In Mosta, we found a restaurant overlooking the famous basilica of Saint Paul and ate *lampuki* soaked up with the crust of the local bread. Over coffee, Maggo began the conversation which I had been dreading since my arrival on the island.

'So, are you going to tell me why you are here?'

'Wasn't my letter clear?' I began, defensively. 'The university kindly gave me some time off and I thought I would get out of the Federation for a while, undertake some archaeological surveys elsewhere. Where better than Alexandria and perhaps even Carthage? So, I caught the boat from Massalia...'

'...But why are you *here*?' he persisted.

'To see you, old friend. Why else?'

'Hmm.' Maggo frowned, tilted his head slightly and observed me closely. 'I have been thinking of you a lot, Mr Summer, how it must be for you. Dealing with the past...'

'...That is my job, Maggo. The past.'

'I do not mean that,' he said, politely, taking a final sip of coffee, before wiping his lips with a napkin. 'Yes, you work with antiquities, artifacts and so on, but from your point of view, that box camera,' he pointed at my satchel, 'and my vintage vehicle are as much relics to you as anything you will see in the museums of Alexandria. And then there is your past in your world, the people you left behind.'

'I have no regrets, Maggo. You know that. I have a wife now, a son and a father.'

'Then, why are you not with them?'

'As I said...'

'...You have become very good at it, Mr Summer,' he interrupted.

'What?' I asked.

'Lying.'

It wasn't just his positivity then that hadn't altered since our last meeting. It was his unique directness as well. Maggo could have tamed a lion with the pureness of his heart but he could also lead a bovine expedition into your room full of precious china and not care what cracked apart if he thought it was for your benefit. I located an invisible spot in the air over his shoulder and stared at it with feigned interest. But I knew it pointless. In Ulidia, he had stood out as the only Christian in a land full of pagans. And yet there was more to it than that. Talking to Maggo was like being in a confessional, regardless of the location. Everyone in the world, in both worlds, was an open book to him and he had learned, very early in life, to read between the lines. I wrung my hands together in defeat and realised why penitents liked to accessorise with rosary beads.

'Am I lying?' I said, after a short pause.

'Of course, I know being in this world means it is necessary to lie every day,' he replied, ignoring my question. 'I suppose your colleagues at the university believe you are from the WCA?' I nodded. 'So?' he persevered.

'Aoife...' I began.

'Yes?'

'After our wedding, or 'handfasting', Aoife went back to the clearing stations. You know what it was like. War was imminent and she, as always, wanted to help. Finn returned to base and I felt...well...exposed.'

'Exposed?'

'The adventure, if that's what you want to call it, had come to an end. Everyone had gone their separate ways: Conall, Ó Móráin... you... and I was left in a world where people had to do their laundry and work for a living. It was like the aos sí had never appeared in my life. I read every scroll in Lorcan's library, travelled to every part of the Federation but...you are right, Maggo...it was more a step back in time than a step *through* a portal into another world. It's 1995 to you but for me it's the roaring twenties...without the roar.'

'The roaring twenties?'

'Never mind, my friend,' I laughed. 'Ignore me. I just miss Aoife, I suppose. When war didn't break out after all, she received her orders to stay on at the stations. The RBK and Ulidian command did not wish to make the same mistake as before.'

'There's something else, too, Mr Summer.'

'Yes?

'Yes. You have studied and researched the Celts your whole life. Their archaeology, their mythology. And now? You are here. The statues have come alive and the temples are full. And what do you find? People. Simply people, flawed, less than heroic. Cú Chulainn is doing the dishes and Lugh is just a ball of fire in the sky,' he winked, 'but do not tell *them* that!'

'I won't if you won't,' I replied, playfully.

'So, Mr Summer, I suggest you spend some time here with me in Melita. Try to relax. To-night, I will make you a traditional meal -an old recipe of my mother's. I do not have to be back in Valletta until the beginning of next week. I can show you the city and then, after that, return to Éireann, go to the clearing sta-tions and be reunited with your Bride of Mosta once more.'

'Bride of Mosta?'

'Just an old story I learned as a child. I will tell you it on our way.'

'On our way where?'

'To the Cumbo Tower, of course. It's more modern than what you are used to, five hun-dred years old or so, but you remind me of the hero in it. After all, Mr Summer, you came through time and space to find the one you love. You are not going to give up on her just because you have to do the dishes now and again.'

Gisco Abejer's face reminded me of old shoe leather. He polished it each morning, I im-agined, just after shaving, and before setting off for his olive groves where he had laboured, each day for the last thirty years. All this, he reminded us proudly, to dress the salads of the Carthaginian Union and beyond with an oil that had no equal on either side of the Mediterranean. His wife, Elissa, had died in her early twenties, struck down with a cancer that had mercilessly cut through her young body with the same calculation as the knife she had used to slice her wedding cake the year before. That was the only image Maggo had of her, a radiant angel in white smiling shyly through her wedding veil; Gisco's carefully placed hand upon that of his new wife's while his own mother, Elissa's older sister, Tamyra, looked on with tears in her eyes. Maggo had not spoken of it yet but his mother had died in the eighteen months since I had last seen him. He had loved her dearly and I had not yet had the courage to bring up the subject other than a long letter of condolence I had written to him at the time of her death.

Tamyra and her husband had been fond of Gisco, Maggo said. He had never remarried, and even if he had, Maggo suspected that Gisco and a second wife would still have been made welcome into the Calleja household. Gisco and Maggo's father, Hanno, had both worked the Bidni groves together. Afterwards, Gisco took over the management of the family business with the blessing of his sister-in-law who received an equal share of the profits. Since Hanno had died, Gisco had, with great deference, slowly and surreptitiously occupied the space in Maggo's life vacated by his father. The manoeuvre had been subtle but Gisco need not have worried. Maggo had adored his uncle as a father even though Gisco had sided with his mother and objected to his work placement in Ulidia.

'Lewis,' Gisco said, carrying a steaming platter of rabbit pie from the stove and nestling it carefully on the kitchen table, 'my nephew is a wonderful cook. Just like a woman. Both the Calleja girls could cook. The best cooks in the entire village.'

'Lorcan would love this,' I said, watching the old man divide the pie into equal thirds. I say 'old' although Gisco was probably in his early fifties. I was only five years younger but Gisco's hair, unlike mine, was a shock of white feathery strands parted at the side. His arms however, straining through his cotton shirt, still maintained ample reserves of sinewy strength, I thought, unlike his back which gave him no end of problems.

'How is he? Does he miss my couscous?' Maggo enquired.

'Never stops talking about it,' I joked.

'And Finn? He must be in the full RBK by now?'

'RBK?' Gisco enquired, passing me a plate of

pie.

'Red Branch Knights, uncle. I have told you about them.'

'Nonsense,' his uncle replied. 'Are they red? No! Do they live in a tree? Travel by horse? No! The Federation is the devil's own kingdom, Lewis. You are best to take your wife and family with you to the WCA. Least there, they are Christian!'

'Now uncle, we must respect everyone's right to determine their own lives. Citizens in the Federation are not all the same. There are good and bad, just like here in the Union.'

'But they are heathens, Maggo!' Gisco said. 'They worship false gods!'

'As did we, uncle, until the Word was shipwrecked on our shores.'

'Hmm...well, I for one, am glad you are back home...with your own people.'

Maggo sighed. He remained silent until it was time for the blessing. Gisco uttered it, as he had done the evenings before, while Maggo and I bowed our heads in reverence. As soon as we lifted them to eat, there was a loud knock on the door. Gisco frowned and rose from the table.

'Who could that be, I wonder?' Maggo asked. It was late and receiving unexpected guests was apparently not the custom in the sleepy town of Mosta.

'Well, we shall soon see, nephew. Stay here

with our guest, Maggo. Probably, just Giannis...
my neighbour,' he explained to me. 'Always
looking to borrow something or other.'

He left and made his way down the narrow
hallway that led to the main door. I heard a
lock slide open and then my host begin an in-
distinct exchange with someone, the formality of which made me think the visitor was a
stranger to the house. I looked at Maggo who
had raised a finger to his lip and tilted his ear in
the direction of the door in a vain attempt to
hear what was going on.

Whatever the nature of the conversation it
was long enough for me to begin to feel a
draught creep a slow path to where I was sitting. Outside, the temperature had dropped
dramatically. It had been dark now for several hours. We were in what they called in the
Union the last remaining days of the 'month of
waiting', only a few weeks before the festival
of Christ, or November as I had always known
it.

Suddenly, all was quiet. The stillness was
closely followed by the closing of the main
door and the sound of footsteps coming towards us.

'Mr Summer,' Gisco said, proudly, entering
the kitchen, 'this gentleman has come all the
way from Athens to see you.'

'I do apologise, Professor Summer. I know it
is late, but I have just arrived on the island. It is

a matter of the utmost urgency.'

I stood up and offered the new arrival my hand. He was a young man, in his early thirties, I conjectured, and dressed in an ill-fitting pin-stripe suit, hat and tie. The collar button of his shirt was loose which gave me the impression the man was not accustomed to such formality of attire. He smiled apologetically, took my hand and glanced nervously at the free chair. He looked weary; his fatigue made worse by the heaviness of the briefcase he held in his right hand.

'Please, have a seat, Mr...?

'Professor Alexandros Bakirtzis, University of Anatolia,' he replied, sitting down. He stood up almost immediately, however, placed an apologetic hand on his chest and made a slight bow to Maggo and Gisco before being seated once more.

'So, how can I be of help, professor?'

'Professor, what am I about to reveal is of extreme secrecy,' the young man replied, opening his briefcase and removing a top layer of thin papers. 'This', he said, 'has been signed by Bishop Andrew of Hellas and has the seal of Patriarch John the Tenth himself.'

'My goodness! My goodness!' exclaimed Maggo.

'And this,' he continued nervously, 'has been signed by the Directorate of Science of the Hellenistic government.' He handed the documents to me as if it they were precious scrolls of touch-paper, released from the vacuumed vaults of the Library of Alexandria and which might at any stage set themselves alight and disintegrate into ash. 'And this one is from the Chancellor of the University of Anatolia, approving my visit to you. And this one is from...'

'...Yes, yes, professor,' I interrupted softly, glancing at the young man's credentials. 'You can be assured that all here accept the authority on whose behalf you are about to speak.'

'Speak?'

'Well, yes, professor...the reason for your visit?'

'You do not know?'

'Know? No.'

'Oh!'

There was a long pause during which I thought the whole affair was going to descend into slapstick. Perhaps the papers were not genuine, after all, I thought. Perhaps, the young visitor would next produce a *pungi* and charm a snake out of his case while we watched on, catching flies with wide-open mouths.

'So?' I added, maintaining the rhyme.

'I thought...I thought you knew, Professor Summer...at least about the excavations. When I said I was from Anatolia...?'

'Excavations?'

'Yes, the discovery, or shall I say, rediscovery of a new temple complex in Anatolia. Just outside Édessa.'

'Édessa?' I repeated, shaking my head. 'And when was this?'

'Last year.'

'Ah, well, I was slightly...err...pre-occupied last year. But tell me, what is the nature of the excavations? Are they significant?'

'Significant? Professor Summer! Édessa changes everything! The discoveries there pre-date Sumer by over half a millennium!'

'10000 BC? But that's incredible.'

'Yes, professor. That is six thousand years before the great henge of Avebury. It is truly remarkable. A pristine series of sites, professor, almost perfectly preserved. Evidence of civilisation five thousand years before civilisation is supposed to have started.'

'Truly remarkable,' I replied, scanning the professor's documentation again. 'But Professor Bakirtzis, I am afraid I still don't understand. What has any of this to do with me?'

'Professor Summer,' he whispered, 'may I speak to you in private?'

I glanced at Maggo who in turn glanced at Gisco.

'Uncle,' Maggo said, 'why not allow these gentlemen the opportunity to converse privately? How about paying our neighbour a visit? I have not spoken with our old friend Giannis for many months?'

'Well, why not?' Gisco replied, 'I will just place everyone's plate on the stove.'

As soon as they were alone, Professor Bakirtzis delved into his briefcase once more and produced a series of grainy photographs.

'Professor Summer, we in the Carthaginian Union are not unaware of your heroic exploits last year.'

'Oh?'

'The portal at Uisneach. Your part in its opening...and closure.'

'I see.' I inhaled deeply. 'But how...?'

'...We have our spies in the CU too, you know.'

The man speaking to me now was not the man from before. There was a trained efficiency at work in his voice and gestures; the affected, bumbling professor routine had obviously been for the birds.

'Who are you?' I asked.

'Who I am is of no consequence, professor.'

'And the papers?'

'No. They, at least, are genuine...an indication of the importance of the task at hand.'

'Task?'

'Professor, we are aware of your...provenance. We know, or should I say, 'hope' we know, that you pose no threat to the Union. You are a Christian?'

'Well, let us say I am not a pagan.'

'But you are from a more 'civilised' world,

more like our Union, less like their Federation.'

"Civilised' is not a word that immediately comes to mind when describing Belfast...'

'...Belfast?'

'...Never mind...but yes, we have democracy, elections, economies adequate to feed population densities in most of the world.'

'Believe me, professor, our clerics in the Union would love to learn more of this world but time is against us. Unfortunately.'

'You know about the portals then?'

'Yes.'

'The Druidic Order's attempts to control them?'

'Yes...and the dangers that would cause us.'

'Wait. This Édessa you mentioned. You've found a portal there, haven't you?!'

'We think so?'

'Think?'

'We have found something. An artifact.'

'Yes?'

'We were hoping if you could help us identify it.' The young man passed me the first of a series of photographs. The poor quality of the picture was to be expected from a technology dating from almost 70 years ago. The outline of the object, however, had enough definition to leave me in no doubt to what it was.

'May I see the others?' I asked.

The artifact was the same in every photograph, snapped at different angles. I shuffled through them quickly. If I had flipped their edges, the artifact would have sprung to life, rotating as if on a carousel.

'You know what it is?'

'Of course,' I replied. 'May I ask your name, not your real name, of course, just something to call you by. I'd rather not call you 'professor'.'

'How about Bostar?' he suggested.

'Well, Bostar,' I said. 'What time is the next boat to Anatolia?

Printed in Great Britain
by Amazon